Sue

Your p

constantly

beautiful story.

each one.

IN PIECES

GIA RILEY

Gia Riley

In Pieces

ISBN-13 978-1518687747
ISBN-10 1518687741

Cover Designer:
Perfect Pear Creative Covers

Interior Design and Formatting:
Christine Borgford, Perfectly Publishable

dedication

To first loves.
Even when it feels like the world is against you, keep going.
Your pieces are constantly forming a beautiful story.

playlist

Enjoy the playlist while you read:

In Case – Demi Lovato
Young Love – Kip Moore
18 – One Direction
Sledgehammer – Fifth Harmony
Show You Off – Dan & Shay
Pieces – Ella Henderson
Come With Me – Echosmith
Stay – Florida Georgia Line
Disappear – Christina Li
Love You Like That – Canaan Smith
Believe – Justin Bieber
Of These Chains – Red
Cry – Alexx Calise
I'm Not Perfect – Lori Martini
Who's To Say – Vanessa Carlton
Love Me Like You Mean It – Kelsea Ballerini
Flashlight – Jessie J
Missed – Ella Henderson
They Don't Know About Us – One Direction
Down – Jason Walker
Unbeautiful – Lesley Roy
Skinny Love – Birdy
Better In Time – Leona Lewis

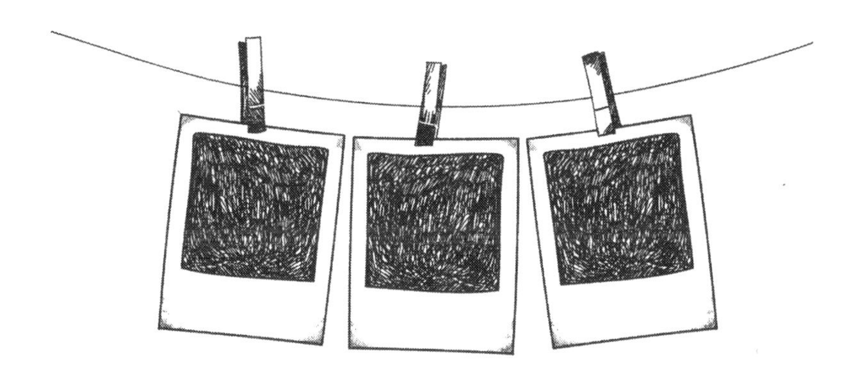

CHAPTER ONE

kinsley

THE APARTMENT'S QUIET when I get up for my first day of school. I've spent four years of high school waiting to be a senior. Now that the day has come, I don't feel much different than when I was a junior, but at least I'm one step closer to graduation.

Still, being a senior doesn't make waking up at six in the morning any easier. In fact, I groaned as soon as my feet hit the floor half an hour ago. My entire body feels the after effects of working a double shift at the diner last night. Being the last night of summer vacation, I wanted to get in as many hours as possible before I had to start worrying about homework and school.

After a hot shower, followed by a cold dousing of water to wake up, I'm dressed and ready for my day. At least I think I am.

I even curled my hair, and put on more make-up than I normally do. I don't know who I'm trying to impress, nobody cares. When they're not spreading new rumors about me, they're usually oblivious to my mere existence.

"Mornin' Kinsley," Carson says, as he walks out of his room the same time I do, half naked.

I've known Carson for as long as I can remember—he's pretty much a second brother to me even though we aren't actually related. Which is a good thing considering I had a wicked crush on him for a long time.

He started out as my brother Wyatt's friend, and slowly morphed into a part of our family. Now that Wyatt's away at college, he's moved into the protector roll without even having to be asked. He ended up here when my older sister, Kate, needed help paying the bills. He willingly took Wyatt's old room, with the stipulation that Wyatt could crash in it whenever he wanted to come home.

"All set for school?"

"Yeah, leaving in a couple minutes," I mumble, as a yawn escapes my tired body.

Carson's in school too, only he commutes instead of living on campus. He's focused on finishing his criminal justice degree as quickly as possible, so he can enroll in the police academy. It scares me when I imagine him on the streets late at night, protecting the world from hate, but there's nothing he's ever wanted to do more. Even when we were kids, and would play cops and robbers, he'd always be the cop.

He follows me to the kitchen where he watches me pour coffee into my travel mug. I'm useless without it after working so late. His eyes bore into the back of my head as I stir way too much sugar into my coffee.

It's weird having him here. I thought it would be fun, interesting even, but I've caught him checking me out more times than I can count. Problem is, I've always noticed him—especially when he's walking around without a shirt, like he is right now. All the hours he spends in the gym are showing, and it makes it even harder to see him as my friend, and not the attractive nineteen-year-old, college freshman that he is.

Though it doesn't matter how hot I think Carson is. Wyatt would never allow us to pursue one another. Then again, Wyatt wouldn't want me with any guy, no matter who it was. It's part of the reason why I've never had a boyfriend let alone dated. It's always been easier to pretend I wasn't interested, just to keep my brother happy. The past few years we've had enough going on without him having to worry about who I was swapping spit with.

"Your hair looks different."

I pick up the end of my freshly cut hair and lay it back down on my shoulder. "It's the same."

"Must be the make-up. It makes you look older."

I shake my head. "My make-up's the same as it always is." I'm hardly wearing any other than a little lip gloss, mascara, and some powder.

"Hmm," he says. "Well, you look really nice."

I turn around and smile, shyly. "Thank you." I wasn't planning to leave for ten more minutes, but after that last comment, it's time to go. "Have a good day."

I'm out the front door and walking toward the wooden staircase that leads to the driveway when Carson props himself against the open apartment door, watching me walk away. "Be careful, Kinsley. And don't let any of those dipshits screw with you. I mean it."

I laugh because he's so much like my brother when it comes to who I spend time with. "Don't worry Carson, I'll wait until the third day before I screw anyone."

I expect him to laugh at me, to even toss a smart ass remark back, but he doesn't. His arms are crossed over his chest, and he looks like he wants to hurt someone. "Kins, you better be kidding."

"I am, jeez. You act like I'm a slut. Have I ever brought a guy around?"

He thinks about it for a second, and then his face softens. "I know you're not a slut. Hell, I wouldn't let you be a slut."

Isn't that the truth. "So, we're good here?" I can't walk away if he's mad at me. His opinion matters too much.

He nods his head. "We're good. See ya later."

"See ya." Once he turns and walks back into the apartment, I descend down the rest of the stairs. I can't say I was expecting a reaction like that one, but then again, Carson's changed since he moved in. This new version suddenly cares how I dress, how much make-up I wear, and who I'm with. It's nothing like when Wyatt was still here—back when he treated me like I was one of the guys.

Though it wouldn't surprise me if Wyatt put him up to it. He probably cares because he was told to. Lord knows he has enough on his plate without having to worry about what I'm doing.

But I have bigger problems to deal with, like my car starting. It's sounded like a ninety-year-old man with emphysema for far too long. The added clanking sound is only getting worse, and I have no choice but to get it checked out. That means more money I don't have down the drain.

Missing school isn't an option, so I have to pay for it even if I don't have the money. My days at school are never easy, but it's where I get to do my favorite things—see my best friend, Becca, and work on my collection. If I plan on getting into Parsons School of Design, I need to work harder than I ever have. My interview in New York City is only a few short months away. There is no Plan B.

With luck, I make it to school, pulling into my assigned spot. The parking lot's already starting to fill up—much faster than usual. Today's the one day of the year people are actually early for class. Tomorrow, the mad dash before the bell will begin.

"You coming, woman?" Becca's knocking on my window, smiling like a loon. She loves the first day of school almost as much as the last. It's the part in the middle that's a drag.

"I'm coming."

"Whatcha got first, Kin?"

"Advanced photography."

My schedule is loaded with art and design electives, and I'm hoping they'll help set me apart during my interview. The more I can add to my portfolio, the better my chances are of being accepted into the design program at Parsons. Though, no matter how impressive I can make my portfolio, it's still going to be a stretch for a small town girl from Pennsylvania to make it in the Big Apple. But if anyone's up for the challenge, it's me.

"What do you have?"

"Chem Lab."

"Sounds like a snooze fest. Good luck with that." I always give her a hard time about her demanding schedule, but Becca's dream is to be a doctor—a pediatrician. In fact, she's had her sights set on The University of Pennsylvania's Perelman School of Medicine, one of the top five medical programs in the country, for as long as I can remember. And Becca's fierce enough to make it happen. Go big or go home, right?

"I can't believe it's senior year already. I feel like we were just like those kids." She points to a group of nervous freshmen who look like they're about to throw up in the grass.

"Nah, we were so much cooler than that," I toss back, knowing for a fact we were because three years ago, I was completely, blissfully, happy. I still had a family—a real family with a mother and a father.

"Sorry," she says, as she kicks a rock across the sidewalk. "I wasn't thinking when I said that."

"Stop, it's fine, really. Now, please tell me you have first lunch so I don't have to wait all day to see your face again."

She scans our schedules, holding them side by side. She starts waving them in the air when we finally match up. "I do! We have gym together, too."

"I hate gym. I suck at sports and you know it. I'm much better at watching them."

"I can't disagree with that. I've seen you in action," she says, laughing. "Your brother hogged all the coordination genes."

Wyatt was a standout wide receiver on the football team. They even played him as a freshman he was that good. Now, he's at Penn State University, on a full athletic scholarship.

"You're probably right. He's good at everything."

"Except math. Poor guy can't add for shit."

I snort because she's so clueless. "He sucked on purpose, so you'd tutor him after school." My brother had a crush on Becca all year long, but Becca never gave him a shot because he was going away to school this year. And with plans of her own the following year, they'd never be in the same place at the same time. It's a shame, really, they'd be great together. She's what he needs to calm his ass down, maybe even tame him a little, and he's what she needs to have some fun—without her nose being stuck in a book.

Becca doesn't say another word about Wyatt, and I don't bring him up again. I can tell she misses him though. She may have complained about the tutoring sessions at first, saying what a lost cause it was, but secretly, she looked forward to them as much as he did.

We get to my first class before hers, and although I'm a little early, I go inside anyway. I hate walking into a classroom full of eyes—especially when I know most of them only see me as Wyatt's little sister—the sad, little, orphan girl.

"Good morning, Kinsley," Mr. Jasper says, as he lays a copy of the class syllabus on each desk.

"Morning, Mr. Jasper."

"Sit wherever you'd like, doesn't matter. You won't spend

much time at your table anyway once we get rolling."

"Okay." That's what I love about photography. You can't learn without doing, which means I stay busy. As long as I'm creating, I'm not thinking, and that's a very good thing. I toss my bag onto the table in the back corner, closest to the darkroom. I can't wait to get back inside.

I glance over the syllabus while the classroom fills up, little by little. The senior class is just shy of three hundred students, so all the faces walking through the door are familiar, but there's one that stands out the most—Rhett Taylor.

Rhett and I don't travel in the same social circles. I've known him since kindergarten, but other than being aware of whom the other one is, we don't know much about each other besides what we see at school.

Ever since freshman year, I've crushed on his green eyes more than I haven't, but I've never had the guts to do anything about it. He's popular and the star athlete on the football team now that my brother has moved on. But what separates him from the other guys in our class, is his personality. He's never once belittled someone beneath him in the food chain, where those less popular easily fall prey to the sharks. The sharks all take great pride in going out of their way to make life miserable for others, yet Rhett's never been one of them. I've never understood why he hasn't used the power of popularity to his advantage, but he wouldn't be Rhett if he acted any other way.

Combine his personality with his athletic build, killer smile, and tan skin, and you have six feet of male perfection. What girl wouldn't want to date the hottest guy on the football team? The nerds want to know him, the cheerleaders want to date him, and his friends want to be him. But in my eyes, it's always gone beyond the physical. Call it a hunch, but I know there's more to Rhett than he lets the rest of the school see. Problem is, I'm not sure anyone else has even bothered to notice—except for me.

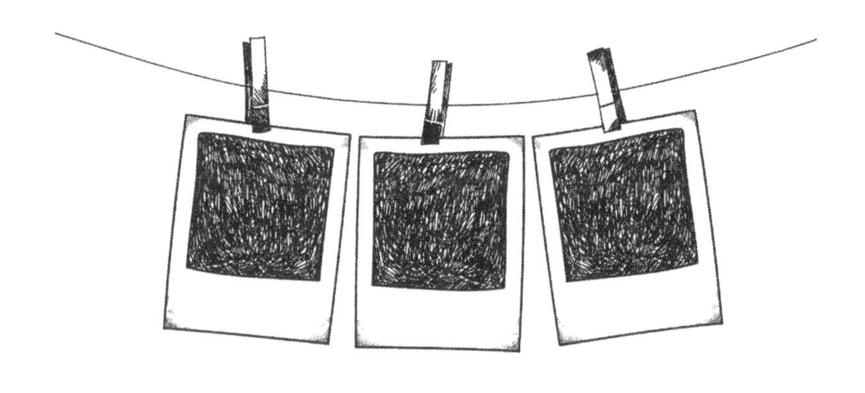

CHAPTER TWO

kinsley

MR. JASPER ONLY spoke for fifteen minutes. It seemed more like an hour with Rhett practically sitting next to me. He smells as good as he looks.

After Mr. Jasper finished going over the course syllabus, like every other teacher will do at the start of class today, he set us free to work on our first assignment. It's taken me straight to the art lab where I'm most comfortable. I use a mannequin to drape one of my favorite fabrics into the beginning stages of a dress. After mixing just the right textures of fabric together, it photographs flawlessly.

Photography, much like any form of art, can be a risk. That's always been the appeal for me, but truth be told, I didn't really care for photography at first. In fact, I kind of hated it—only because I put a lot of pressure on myself to come up with the perfect image. After spending an entire semester last year messing around with the camera, I realized the best images aren't perfect at all. Sometimes, they're a little rough around the edges, even perceived in different ways depending on who's looking at them. Most importantly, they're special *because* they're unique.

If only the world viewed life the same way.

Hurrying back to class, I'm so anxious to get inside the darkroom, I didn't even realize it only took me fifteen minutes, but when I walk into an empty classroom, it's clear I'm the first to finish.

"That was fast, Kinsley."

I nod my head at Mr. Jasper. "I knew what I wanted to take a picture of before I left the room."

After I put my camera back in its case, I stand inside the column that spins me around into the darkroom. I love taking pictures, but developing them, watching as they come to life, is what had me falling in love with the medium last year.

"Hey, Kinsley."

I thought I was the first one back, but as I step into the darkroom and hear my name, there's no mistaking Rhett—even if my eyes are still adjusting. "Hey."

I walk over to where he's standing, grabbing an apron off the hook on the wall. It's next to the list of darkroom rules, but right now, my only concern is remembering how to breathe.

He looks up and smiles at me. It's not the reaction I was expecting considering I figured he'd ignore me like he usually does. Rhett even makes room for me at the end of the table, right next to him.

We work in silence for the first few minutes, making the small room seem even more awkward than it already is. But what do I say to him? It's not like we're friends or anything.

"I feel like I could hear an ant sneeze right now," Rhett says, out of the blue.

"You probably could."

"Did you have a good summer?"

Again, he surprises me when he asks me questions like he actually cares. "I worked a lot and I spent a week at the beach with Becca's family. Wyatt took me to a Luke Bryan concert. That was pretty cool. How was yours?"

He shrugs his shoulders like it was just, eh. There's no way his life is ever mediocre, so I know he had to have done at least a couple of interesting things. His family usually goes on pretty expensive vacations every summer. "Decent. Did the beach thing and worked my summer job before football started. The usual."

I nod my head, surprised again when he doesn't brag or boast. "Sounds nice."

There's another lull in the conversation, but it's not as uncomfortable as when I first walked in. In fact, if I was meeting Rhett for the first time today, I'd think he was reserved—slightly quiet even. And that's not the kind of word anyone would typically use to describe him.

"How's Wyatt? He's at PSU right?"

"Yeah, I haven't heard from him in a couple days. I'm sure he's living it up though. Usually does."

"Can't argue with that," Rhett says, with a knowing smile.

Being teammates for a couple years, he knows all too well how much my brother enjoys partying and female attention. "He can be a jackass, I know."

Rhett laughs, "Can't argue there, either."

"Most guys in this school are though–especially the ones on the team."

"Ouch," he says, covering his heart.

"I didn't mean you. You're different."

He looks up at me, a confused expression on his face. "Thank you, I think."

"Sorry, that came out wrong."

"What *did* you mean?"

I tuck my hair behind my ear, thankful it's dark enough in here to hide the fact that I'm turning red. "I don't know what I was trying to say. They definitely wouldn't be talking to me right now if they were in your shoes though, that's for sure. That already makes you a non-asshole—at least for today."

His shoulders shake, as he laughs at me. I regret ever opening my mouth. "Forget it, sorry."

"Na, I get what you're saying—even if you did have a shitty delivery."

"Thanks, I wasn't trying to call you an asshole. You aren't."

"I'm glad you think so."

Why am I so bad at this? "My opinion doesn't really matter anyway."

I wait for him to laugh at me, again, but he doesn't. This time, he looks at me with a straight face when he says, "Your opinion matters, Kinsley."

I shrug my shoulders. "Probably not."

"Well, it matters to me."

I stop what I'm doing to look at him. The way he said it matters to him, was kind, caring even. It makes no sense why he of all people would care. "It does?"

He nods his head, turning to face me. "Of course it does. You're real. You don't bullshit. I respect that from a chick."

"I'm a girl, not a chick. Chicks are usually bitchy—at least from my experiences. Wyatt's had enough of them at the house over the years for me to know the difference."

"Sounds like you met some winners."

"I have, but I have a lot of time to think, too. People watching is my thing. You can figure out a lot about a person just by watching them."

"Okay, then tell me what else you think—about *me*."

If I answer him, I'm pretty much admitting I watch him. Though he did ask for my opinion, it doesn't seem like a good idea to give it. I swallow, chewing on my lip, as I try to come up with something to say that won't result in any embarrassing confessions or hurt feelings. "Um, well. I don't know, Rhett."

"Sure you do. You have lots of opinions, you just don't say them out loud very often."

He couldn't be more right. I'm usually too afraid to speak up, so I don't. "True."

"Why don't you?"

"Because everyone has too much dirt on me as it is, and nobody really cares what I have to say anyway. I'd rather stay invisible than stand out." I don't need anyone slinging trash at me about my past. It's not worth being heard if I'm only going to be mocked. Plus, until this year, my brother did enough talking for the both of us.

"Kinsley, we've known each other a really long time. Just because we don't hang out, doesn't mean I don't observe things, too. You don't think people *see* you, but they do. I see you. Every single day."

"I like to blend in."

"Why?"

"Because I'm not some spray tanned, cheerleader Barbie with long legs, hair extensions, fake nails, and a push-up bra. Those girls are living one big lie. Their appearance is as fake as their personality. And I can't be fake." I have too many skeletons to pretend to be anything other than what I am.

"And *that's* why I notice you, Kinsley."

"You notice me? You want me to believe *the* Rhett Taylor notices *me*."

"Yes."

"Why? You're you, and I'm me. We're opposites." I don't ask him because I'm fishing for compliments. I ask because I'm intrigued—genuinely curious as to why Rhett would ever be trying to figure me out.

"Maybe I like you," he says, without a hint of mockery in

his tone. "And opposites attract."

"Okay, Paula Abdul." I try to play off what he said, but all I can do is swallow around the lump in my throat. I wasn't expecting an answer like that one. "What's the deal?"

"There is no deal, Kinsley. Can I borrow that?" He gestures toward the bottle of developer in my hand.

I stand, staring at him, wondering what the catch is. There's no way Rhett likes me for me. There has to be more to it.

"The bottle," he says, again.

I hand it to him. "Sure, I'm finished."

As he takes it from me, our fingers touch ever so slightly. I pull my hand away from his like he electrocuted me, again earning a chuckle from him.

"You okay?" he questions.

I clear my throat. "I'm fine." I want to ask him what he means when he says he likes me, but I don't. The dreamer in me wants it to mean exactly what it sounds like, but that's only setting myself up for disappointment. High school isn't a *Disney* movie.

He lets me concentrate on my assignment for a few minutes, and I'm thankful. We had a half hour to take a picture of something inspiring. I knew right away I'd find my greatest source of inspiration in the art lab. Considering Rhett took less time than I did to complete his assignment, he must have shot the football field or the weight room, where all the magic happens, before hurrying back.

I swirl my picture around and around in the tray, waiting for it to finish. Out of the corner of my eye, I chance another impatient peek at Rhett's tray. His picture is farther along than mine, and I have to blink my eyes a couple times to make sure I'm actually seeing what I think I'm seeing. It's like looking into a mirror with my own face staring back at me.

"Why did you take that?" I ask him. He's going to fail today's assignment if he doesn't go take another picture. He doesn't have time to mess around, or Mr. Jasper will kick him out of the darkroom.

His face remains serious, not giving away a single clue. Maybe it's a cruel joke, and I'm today's shark prey, but he only shrugs his shoulders like it's perfectly normal for him to have a picture of me in his possession. "I'm creating art. What's it look like?"

"It looks like me, that's what." He can't be serious right now. I'm not art. Kinsley West is a lot of things, but art isn't one of them.

"I'm glad we got that straightened out."

"But, Rhett, you didn't do the assignment. You won't get any credit."

He raises his head, searching for my deep brown eyes in the already darkened room. Sometimes they're so dark, I can't even find my own pupils in the mirror. "Who says I didn't do the assignment?"

With the tongs in my hand, I point at his tray. "Rhett, that's a picture of me."

"I know it is. Maybe *you* inspire me. Did you ever consider that?"

Absolutely not.

All I can do is I stare into the red plastic tray as my face floats around inside it. Nobody's ever told me I inspire them before, but I can't let him know how much his words mean to me. Not when I'm still trying to figure out if I believe him or not. "Good luck explaining that to Mr. Jasper."

"I don't have to explain anything, the picture speaks for itself."

This is the only chance I may ever have to hear what Rhett thinks of me. Not what everyone else thinks, but his own personal opinion of a girl who has been in his life without every really being in his life. So, I whisper, "What does the picture say?"

He sets the solution back on the table, pulls the photograph out of the tray, and hangs it behind us to dry—where the rest of the class will be able to see it, too. He points to it as it hangs. "That I captured the prettiest girl in the school."

Is he for real right now?

There is no way Rhett Taylor just told me I was the prettiest girl in the whole school. It makes no sense considering he can have any girl he wants, and most of his choices are more beautiful at eighteen than I will *ever* be.

Plus, I'm not his type. I'm not one of the bubbly cheerleaders who scream his name from the sidelines every Friday night, and I'm not one of the groupies following him from school to practice, watching as he sips his Gatorade. I'm just me—the girl who gets good grades, has a passion to design, and works part time at the diner to afford my car payments and art supplies.

"Breathe, Kinsley. We all have secrets, even you, but now you know my truth."

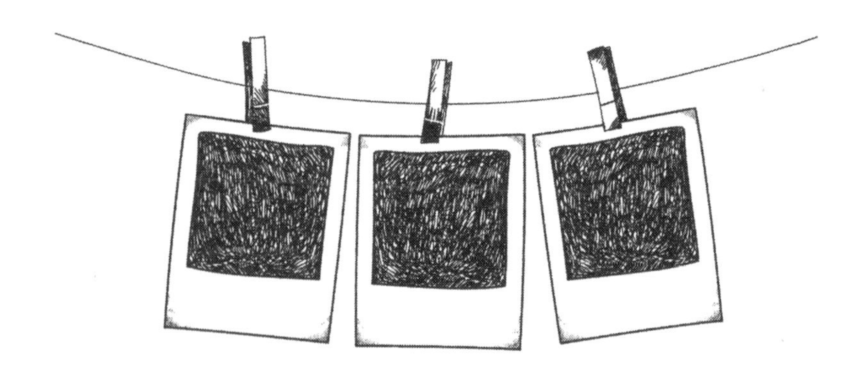

CHAPTER THREE

kinsley

"ARE YOU GOING to tell me why Rhett Taylor can't seem to take his eyes off you for five seconds?" Becca asks, as she takes a bite of her double cheeseburger, so full of ketchup, it oozes out from under the bun. I don't know how she can eat complete and total junk without ever gaining a pound.

"What?"

She rolls her eyes like I'm out of my mind. "I'm serious, Kin, he hasn't stopped checking you out."

"Maybe you're the one he's checking out. Ever think of that?"

I haven't had a chance to tell her about photography class yet, so her comment catches me off guard. I'm still debating if I want to keep what happened between Rhett and me a secret, or not. Part of me wants to tell her, just to make it seem more real—like I wasn't imagining him telling me I'm pretty or calling me an inspiration.

"Don't play dumb, Kinsley. I heard all about his confession from Mandi. Once she found out, it was spread around the school in less than an hour. That's got to be some kind of record, you know."

This isn't good. I don't want to be the talk of the school. That's how vicious rumors begin, and they never end well, either. "How did Mandi find out?" I ask, as I push the lettuce from my salad from one side of the plate to the other. I was hungry until this conversation started, but now my stomach is in too many knots to eat.

"Apparently, she was in the darkroom, and witnessed it."

Mandi isn't even in advanced photography, but she is taking the beginners class in the adjoining room. My guess, she was hoping to steal some time with Rhett and snuck in the darkroom. She's had a thing for him for as long as I can remember. They even dated off and on, but each time, it didn't last long—none of his relationships ever do. "I didn't see her. I thought it was just the two of us in there."

"Because you were too busy drooling over Rhett. I don't know, Kinsley, I never thought I'd see the day you'd go jock on me."

I smack Becca on the arm. "It wasn't like that at all, Becca. We were just talking, not that there's anything wrong with athletes, by the way." I don't mention I called them all assholes this morning before I knew one liked me.

She shakes her head in disagreement. "You're so full of shit."

"Come on, Becca. I have too many brain cells for him to be seriously interested. It would throw off the school ditz to muscle ratio or something. I can't screw that up." Then, just in case she doesn't buy what I'm trying to sell her, I toss in some extra reassurance by adding rumor to the mix. "And last I heard,

Mandi's the one who's crushing on Rhett again—not me."

Becca waves her hand in the air, dismissing my claim entirely. "You're talking nonsense. Rhett doesn't care about Mandi or any of the other senior girl drama. He avoids it like the plague."

"What makes you say that? Do *you* like him?"

"Pfft. No, not since we were ten."

Why am I only finding out about this now when I've known Becca since middle school? I didn't even know she knew Rhett that well. "Seriously?"

"Yeah, we used to be neighbors—before my parents split up and I moved across town. I had a crush on him, and he knew it. I wanted to be in his club so bad, I even let him make me eat dirt to get in."

"You ate dirt for a boy's attention?"

"Yeah, I'm not proud of it, but I did call him names for making me do it. His mom was hanging wash on the line and heard every single word I said to her darling little boy."

"What happened?"

"She sent me home. I wasn't allowed to play at their house anymore because I was a bad influence with a potty mouth. Her words, not mine."

I laugh into my napkin. "Why doesn't that surprise me?"

She takes a sip of her iced tea before continuing. "Trust me, Kinsley, he would never make *you* eat dirt. Not with the way he's looking at you today. He might want to get you dirty though."

"I'm not getting dirty with anyone, Becca."

How she can draw these conclusions from a meaningless rumor she heard floating around school, is beyond me. Considering Mandi was the only witness, people should know better than to believe a word she says—even if there was truth to it this time.

Though I don't have to worry about what she said one way or another, because when I glance in his direction and find him looking at me exactly the way Becca described, the suspicions are confirmed. If everyone didn't already know, he's proving every word Mandi said to be the truth. That fact alone makes my heart rate speed up—my palms even start to sweat. I try to look away, but not before I catch him winking at me.

What is going on?

To anyone sitting around him, he appears engaged in the conversation at his table—not the least bit distracted. But each time I look his way, he senses it. It's like he's in two places at once—he's with his friends, and with me. It's the strangest feeling in the world sharing moments only the two of us know exist.

"You see it now, don't you?" Becca asks. "You can't keep your eyes off him, either."

"Maybe, but it doesn't mean anything. We've known each other all our lives, and now the first day of senior year, I'm supposed to believe he suddenly had an epiphany? I don't buy it."

"Don't do that," she scolds like a protective mother hen. "You don't give yourself enough credit. Any guy in this school would be lucky to have *you* as his girl."

"No guy in this school has ever *had* me. Have you thought about that? I'm a senior and I've never had a boyfriend." That sounds even more pathetic as I say the words aloud. It's also the reason I lack any kind of confidence when it comes to the opposite sex. I have nothing to compare to—no first kiss, no first time. Nothing.

"So what?" Becca says with a dismissive shrug of her shoulders. "There's a first time for everything. That's why it's called your first." She's not going to let me give up on the idea of more with Rhett, I can already tell.

"Becca, he has all kinds of experience. Why would he even look my way knowing I'm not easy? I don't want a random hookup with him or any other guy. I don't operate that way."

That's probably why I've never had a boyfriend in the first

place. They know I won't give it to them without a real relationship, so they don't even bother trying. Because why would an eighteen-year-old guy want to take a chance when he could have a sure thing?

"Then what do you want?"

"I want a guy to want me. And I want him to treat me like I matter. I mean, I know this is high school, and none of us are going to get married after we graduate, but I don't think wanting a relationship is too much to ask for. Is it?"

"Not if that's what you want."

"I'm probably crazy for imagining I could have anything real with Rhett, but all day long, I watch these girls throw themselves at guys like him. They look pathetic, and none of them are respected. Ten years from now, when I look back on high school, I don't want to remember it with regrets."

Becca nods her head, understanding what I'm saying, but I can tell she has an opinion. "What if you regret *not* hooking up with people?"

"Then that's something I'll have to live with, because right now, I think I'd regret it more if I just threw myself at a guy to say I did it."

"I wish I had your self-control, Kin. There are a couple guys in this school I'd jump on, no questions asked."

"That's where we differ. You were born an animal," I joke. She's a romantic, but she has a wild side, too. My brother couldn't resist the appeal along with a lot of other guys. Problem is, Becca is willing, but she's not easy. She has standards, high ones, and expects as much as she demands.

Becca smacks the lunch table with her palm. "That's it, Kinsley!"

"What? I'm not following."

"You're not an animal, and maybe that's exactly what Rhett *needs*. There are guys a lot worse than him when it comes to hooking up, but he can't change until he finds someone worth changing for, you know."

"I'll believe it when I see it, Becca. Come on, we have to get going or we'll be late for class."

Becca gathers her trash and stands up next to me. Rhett stands up from his spot at the other end of the cafeteria at the exact same time. Our eyes lock once more before I turn toward the trash cans to throw away my barely eaten lunch.

My stomach can't handle all these butterflies.

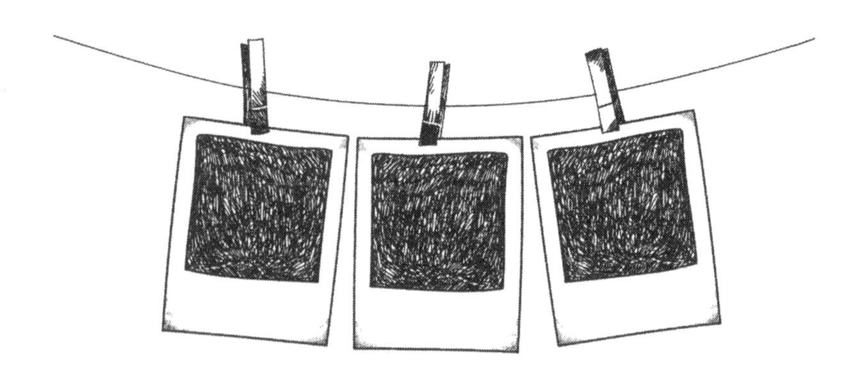

CHAPTER FOUR

kinsley

THE FINAL BELL rings, ending the first day of classes. Not wanting to be late for my shift, I scramble to pack up my bag and get to my locker as fast as I can.

"Jeez, slow down, woman," Becca says, as she hurries to catch me. "What's the rush?"

"I can't be late for work." I can think of a million other things I'd rather do on a Thursday night, but at least I have Friday night off for once. Tomorrow I can hang out with Becca and do whatever I want before the long Labor Day weekend.

"I thought you cut back your hours since school started? Is Kate giving you a hard time about money again?"

"No, she's been fine since Carson moved in and took some of the financial burden off our shoulders. This is my choice."

"I still can't believe Carson Hill lives with you. How do you function with that man-meat walking around all day long?"

"Did you forget who my brother is? I put blinders on and keep moving. Plus, Kate's there."

"And Kate was cool with it? No questions asked?"

"She had questions, but she needs the money. We were in a bad spot, and Carson was the answer."

Kate works full-time as a nurse's aide, on top of taking online classes to finish her nursing degree. Her plans for college took a detour after mom died and dad left. She makes good money doing what she does, but it's not fair for her to have to work her life away with nothing to show for it. At least with Carson and me contributing as much as we can, she can start saving for a better place of her own once I leave for Parsons.

Dad left us a little money before he took off, but it wasn't enough to last very long. Most of it was spent on bills, and the little bit that was left, went toward counseling for all the damage he caused. He thought he was helping, doing the right thing even, but in the end, he hurt us more than he ever thought possible.

He tried his best to be a good parent after mom died, and he was for a while, but as the days passed, we all knew it wasn't enough. Kate, Wyatt, and I watched as grief consumed our father to the point of self-destruction. In order to survive, he had to escape the only town he's ever lived in. We knew it was coming, he knew it was the only way, but it didn't make it hurt any less.

"I can't do it anymore, Kinny," he says, with a voice hoarse from crying.

Before today, I never saw a grown man fall to pieces the way my father was, right before my eyes. The man who has always been the heart and soul of our family was crumbling—so grief-stricken, he stopped living the life he used to love.

"Without your mother, I have nothing. I am nothing."

"You have me, Dad. I love you."

"I know you do, Kinny girl, but you remind me of her so much. Everywhere I look, everything I see, reminds me of your mother. It's like living in hell."

"What about your job? Your friends?"

"I was let go yesterday. I can't even concentrate—my work has been slipping, and then I got so behind, I stopped trying to catch up."

"But you were working twelve-hour days after the funeral."

"There's no excuse, Kinny. I wasn't holding up my end of the bargain, just like I'm not here. I can't blame them for firing me. I would have fired me, too. I can't fault my kids for hating me either."

"So, that's it? You're going to leave me? I lost mom, and now I'm losing you, too." It's not a question, but rather verbal confirmation that when this conversation is over, he'll be walking out of my life.

"I need to get my head on straight. I can't do it anymore."

I don't want to live this way, with a distant parent who would rather be anywhere than where he is, but I could never up and leave my family—my responsibility. "When will you be back? Do Kate and Wyatt know?"

He nods his head. "Couple months. There's a program in Florida Dr. Murphy is sending me to."

"And I'm supposed to stay with Kate until then? Wyatt, too?"

He nods his head. "Kate will be waiting for the both of you. She moved upstairs to a bigger apartment. There's enough room for the three of you, so take everything you need, clear your room out."

"We're losing the house?" I ask, in complete shock. This is the only home I've ever lived in. My bedroom has been painted the same pale pink color since I was born.

"I can't afford the rent without a job. When I get back, we'll move into a new house."

"Okay," I whisper. He's coming back. Maybe he hasn't given up on this life. It's the only thing that keeps me moving forward. I'll stay with my big sister for a little while and then we'll move into a new house and make new memories. It won't be so bad.

Though losing the memories in this house is the last piece of mom.

Once we leave, it will be like she's gone forever—for good. When I was low, I would picture her in the kitchen, making her famous brownies, or the time she had to patch a hole in the wall because we were playing baseball in the house on a rainy day, like she told us not to.

It brings tears to my eyes, and I don't want to cry. I'm tired—just plain tired of my world being ripped away from me.

"Don't be sad, Kinsley, please. I need you to be strong."

"I don't want to move, but I want you to get better. I love you."

He closes his eyes, absorbing my words like he doesn't deserve them. But he does—even if I've been the parent of the house since mom passed—filling her role the best I can. I don't think less of him for wanting to get help. He's made sure I've been seeing a counselor all while he's sat silently, wishing he was anywhere but here—his kids a constant reminder of what he lost.

I walk to his chair, leaning down to hug the man I've looked up to all my life. His strength has vanished, his soul's depleted, and his heart's been left in pieces. But he's alive—even if he's not really living anymore. "I love you, Dad."

"I love you, Kinny. So much."

Dad left that morning, and I haven't heard from him since. I lie, he called once from a pay phone in Chicago. I've never heard of a flight from Pennsylvania to Florida via Chicago. I didn't even know why he was there, but I could tell he was crying, nonetheless.

The moment he told me to clean out my room, and to take everything with me, should have been my first clue that he wasn't coming back. But I bought his lies about not being able to afford the house, and his plans to go to Florida for counseling. I never once questioned why he had to go nearly a thousand miles away to get his head on straight because if that was what it took to get my father back then I wanted him in the best place possible. I wanted him to have a chance to be happy—even if I had to be sad.

For a long time, I excused the lack of phone calls and letters, chalking it up to the restrictions in therapy. He should be focused on himself, not me. When days turned into weeks, weeks into months, and there was still no word, I knew I'd never get my promises. He ran away from his responsibilities, and he has no intention of ever coming back.

Being known around town as the abandoned teenager hasn't done my reputation any favors. Most people look at me with pity, Mandi even questioning how I can stand to look at myself in the mirror. I won't lie and say I've never considered ending it—I had some very dark days after my mom passed away, and even more after dad left. Turns out being abandoned hurts just as much as death.

Even Wyatt's gotten into fights defending me. He's heard the rumors, threatening anyone who said another word. He can't win every battle with his fists, and he knows that, but for a long time, it was our only defense—beat them down with fists before they can beat us down with their words.

Now that I've lost my personal body guard, my sister and Carson are all I have. It may not be a perfect living arrangement, but at only twenty-three, Kate's usually fair. All she asks is that I go to school when I'm supposed to, and to work as much as I can when I'm not.

"Hey, earth to Kinsley," Becca says, as she taps my arm to get my attention.

"Sorry. What'd you say?"

"You were really spaced out there for a few minutes. You're sure everything's okay at home?"

"I'm sure."

"I wish you would come live with me. My parents wouldn't care, they even said so."

She yanks on her locker door a few times before banging on the top corner of the metal door. "This stupid thing sticks like the one I had last year. I can't catch a break." She gives it one more swift kick with her shoe before it pops opens.

"I can't stay with you, Becca. You're all I have. If I'm living with you, it'll put a strain on our friendship, and we'd end up hating each other. Plus, Kate needs me. She was forced into that bigger apartment because of me, I can't stick her with the bills and take off, too." Only my dad gets to do that, apparently.

I stick my head in my own locker, reaching for the stack of books I have piled up on the shelf.

Becca huffs out a frustrated sigh. "You're a good sister, but I could never hate my best friend. You're only saying we'd fight because you think you're a burden."

"Becca, it is what it is." We continue talking though the metal, unloading the books we don't need to take home with us, and swapping them for the ones we need for our homework.

"Fine, but are you at least going to talk to Rhett before you go home?"

"I wasn't planning on it." It's not like we're suddenly a thing simply because he took a picture of me—and the entire school heard about it.

"I think you should go find him," she encourages.

"He's probably already at practice, and I wouldn't even know what to say if I did find him. You know I suck at this stuff." I hold the books I need to take home with me in my arms as I grab my bag off the floor. I slam my locker door shut with my foot and gasp.

Rhett's leaning against the lockers next to mine with his arms crossed and a smirk on his face. There's no telling how long he's been standing there, or how much of our conversation he overheard. Judging from his expression, he's heard enough.

"You don't want to talk to me?" he questions with a knowing wink.

I cover my face with my free hand, wishing the floor would suck me up and put me out of my misery. But Rhett wraps his hand around my wrist, pulling my hand away from my face.

"Don't cover this up."

"Why not? I'm a little humiliated if you haven't noticed."

"Because I like to look at you, Kinsley."

I duck my head, trying my best to hide the smile on my face. "I saw you looking at lunch," I admit.

The smile on his face grows. "I know it's not nice to stare, but I can't help it."

"Oh, shit," Becca mumbles from behind me. She's still standing in front of her locker watching our entire exchange. I'm going to get an earful after it ends, that's for sure.

"Are you heading home?"

"I have practice," he says.

Of course he does. I knew that, but I'm not thinking clearly. It only gets worse when he slides my backpack off my shoulder, unzipping the zipper, and one by one, tucking the books I'm holding inside the bag. Once the last one is inside, he zips it up and places it back on my shoulder. I don't think I blinked the entire time. "Thank you. You didn't have to do that."

"You're welcome. What about you? Where are you headed?"

"I have to work."

"Are you still working at the diner?"

I nod my head. "Yeah, I'm still there. I didn't realize you knew that."

"I know more than you think, Kinsley. Especially about you."

I bite my lip, but I can't hide my smile this time—and I'm not sure I even want to. "I should probably get going before I'm late."

I'd much rather stay in this hallway the rest of the night, getting to know Rhett better. He says he knows a lot about me, but there's so much I want to find out about him.

"Okay. I'll see you tomorrow morning in class—with my killer picture presentation." Slowly, he walks backwards, away from me, leaving me with another one of his signature winks that does all kinds of crazy things to my insides.

"See ya tomorrow, Rhett."

As casually as he left, I try to do the same with Becca, but she yanks on my backpack, stopping me before I'm even three steps away from my locker. "Hold up, killer."

"Becca, I have to get to work."

"Not until you finally admit he has a thing for you. I saw it with my own two eyes, Kinsley. He likes you, and I think it's safe to say, you like him, too."

I can't help but laugh at her. She's so serious, like she's telling me something I don't already know, but after talking to him there's no denying it. What's even crazier is, I'm crushing on him, too. When I woke up this morning, never in a million years did I imagine I'd end the first day of school with the possibility of Rhett lingering in my future.

"Come on, Kins, admit it before I'm late for practice. I don't want to run extra laps because I was standing in the hallway waiting for you to admit you want to jump his bones."

"I'm not agreeing to any jumping, but I like him. Happy now?"

"Ecstatic. Now go home and cover your binder in hearts with his initials in the middle."

"You're crazy. This isn't middle school, you know. Plus, if I go and do that, it would scare him away. Who knows, the way guys go through girls around here, by tomorrow morning, he could be into someone else. My luck he'll be with Mandi again by the end of the week."

"Kinsley West, don't make me smack you."

"I'm just being realistic, Becca. How about we drop it for now." In all honesty, I'm more used to people leaving my life than coming into it. It's more natural to me to have to let go than to allow someone in.

It's hard to open up—to give someone the benefit of the doubt, but for Rhett, I might be willing to try.

"We'll see," I tell her with a shrug of my shoulders.

"Don't blow it off as just another day, Kinsley. This is a big deal, and I'm happy for you. That," she points in the direction we just came from, "is not the same Rhett that made me eat dirt."

I laugh at the reminder of what he made her do all those years ago. Back when girls still had cooties, and we were more worried about who was "it" in a game of tag, than who was interested in dating each other.

Life was so easy then. I had both my parents, a house I called home, and I didn't care how popular I was. In fact, I'd rather play a game of Red Rover than try to figure out why Rhett suddenly finds me interesting. I was perfectly happy being a wallflower—even good at it. Now, he's gone and stirred up feelings. Feelings I've never experienced before, and that will most likely lead to trouble.

"Did you hear a word I said, Kinsley?"

"Yes, I'm listening. I'm glad Rhett's not a little punk anymore."

"That makes two of us. So, if he asks you out tomorrow ,tell him yes."

"Did he tell you he's going to ask me out? Don't lie, as your best friend your loyalty is with me."

"Calm down. He didn't tell me anything, but I can tell from how he's acting. I'm really good at reading people. If he's anything like he was when we were kids, he won't quit until he gets you either. He can be a stubborn fool—just like you."

"Okay."

"Okay?" she questions. "I just told you he's going to ask you out, and that's all you have to say?"

"No, I want him to, but I'm scared." I admit as I wrap my arms around my middle. Even saying the words makes me feel more exposed than I've ever been before. Only I trust Becca with my confession because she would never use it against me.

"Just be you, Kin. Let him see what's he's been missing all these years."

I can do that—I think. "Thank you for not laughing at me."

"Never. You're practically my sister. Plus, he has an older brother in pre-med."

"It all makes sense now. You want to use me to get to his brother."

"I'm not using anyone. Not that it would be so terrible to have to date Rhett to help me out. I mean, his brother is hot and he has a brain."

"Rhett has a brain. Even my brother has a brain, Becca."

"You know what I mean."

"I do, but I'm still holding out hope you'll be my sister someday. I gotta run though, so I'll see you in the morning. Oh, can you pick me up? My car's going in the shop for a few days. It's making that obnoxious clanking sound again. Brian, from the diner, said he'd take a look at it for me. Hopefully he'll save me some of the outrageous labor costs."

"That sounds so technical, but yes I'll pick you up."

"Thanks, Becca. You're a lifesaver."

I hurry to my car while Becca goes in the opposite direction to the locker room. Turning the key in the ignition, I pray it even starts. It does, but as expected, the noise returns as soon as I hear the engine. It only gets worse when I put the car in drive. Each time I have to hit the brake, I worry the car's going to stall. Which is why I panic a little bit when the crossing guard stops traffic just as I'm pulling up to the intersection.

"Come on, hurry." I whisper to myself.

I'm tapping my fingers on the steering wheel when a knock on my passenger side window scares the ever loving shit out of me. Rhett's standing on the other side of the glass, signaling for me to roll my window down. I fumble with the button, hitting my side before his.

"Didn't mean to scare you," he says with a stupid cute grin

on his face.

Dressed in his football gear, he's holding his helmet in one hand, and his shoulder pads in the other. All that's covering his chest is a thin cut-off T-shirt. I thought he was hot in his regular clothes, but he's even better in his uniform.

He clears his throat, and right away I realize he caught me checking him out. I look away as fast as I can, but he just laughs. "Like what you see?"

"Eh, it's okay."

"Wait, I want you to have the full experience. Maybe that'll change your mind."

Before I can tell him I was only kidding, he spins in a circle on his toes like the most ungraceful ballerina I've ever seen. He looks absolutely ridiculous, and I can't stop laughing at him. "Rhett, you're going to hurt yourself."

"There, that's better," he says, as he bends down to rest his arms on the edge of the opened window. "You're even prettier when you smile. But your car doesn't sound so good."

"It's going in the shop tonight." My Ford Focus isn't a total piece of shit, but it's been anything but reliable lately. I guess that's what happens when you have friends fix it for you who don't really know what they're doing. They fix one problem and create a new one.

"Do you need a ride to school tomorrow?"

"Becca's picking me up."

"What about a ride home from school? I can take you. Tomorrow's game day, so I usually go home for an hour or two after school. Clear my head before the game."

Becca would take me home if I needed her to, especially since we only live a couple minutes apart, but she told me to give him a chance. This seems like the perfect opportunity. "Sure, I'd appreciate it."

"Yeah?" he questions with a smile on his face. The truck behind me honks its horn, and I realize the crossing guard isn't holding traffic anymore. Rhett pulls his head out of my car and yells, "Go around! I'm trying to have a conversation."

I glance in the rearview mirror and notice it's one of Rhett's friends giving him a hard time. He listens to what Rhett says, as most usually do when he speaks, but not before yelling a few obscenities out the window. Rhett flips him off, but is laughing when he sticks his head back in the car. "Sorry about that. Jake's an idiot."

"It's my fault, I'm in the way."

"No, he doesn't really care. He's just pissed about running at practice that's why he's moving his truck closer to the locker room. Lazy ass. "

"Makes sense, I think."

"I guess. I'll see you tomorrow then, Kinsley."

I nod my head. "Thanks again. Bye, Rhett."

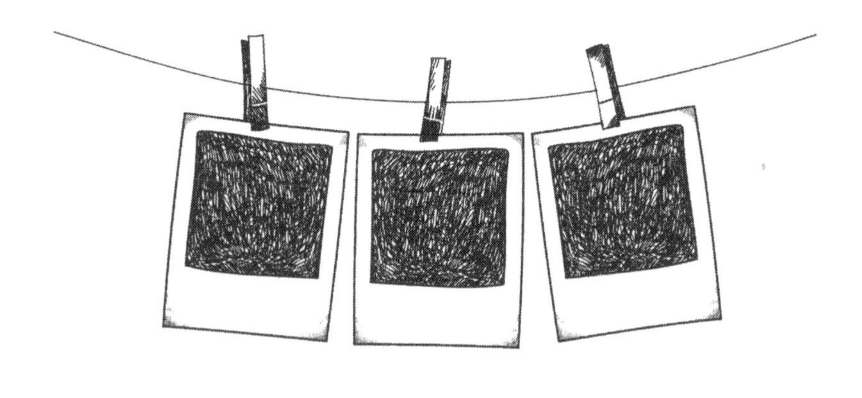

CHAPTER FIVE

kinsley

THE DINNER RUSH is just settling down when a group of punks from the freshman class stroll into my section and plop down in the corner booth. Of course my biggest table is given to bad tippers. Still, I saunter over to them like I'm thrilled to see my new customers. "My name's Kinsley, and I'll be taking care of you tonight. What can I get you boys to drink?"

"She's taking care of us tonight guys, you hear that?" The kid closest to me says, as he jabs his friend in the ribs. They all high five each other like they're about to get laid for the first time.

"What's your specialty?" Another asks, bringing on a second round of childish cackles.

There's so much I could say—so much I want to say, but I remain ever the professional while they ogle me like I'm on the menu. I've dealt with kids like them more times than I can count. It used to bother me, but now, I've learned to either ignore it or dish it back. It's not like they're going to spare any of their allowance for my tip, anyway.

"Do you know what you want to drink?" I ask, one more time, but still, there's no sense of urgency from them.

"What's your rush, little lady? You have all night to take care of us. This place is open twenty-four hours."

I point to the name tag pinned to my shirt. "My name is Kinsley. Please use it. And nobody has that kind of time. Besides, I wouldn't want your mothers coming in here after you. Now last chance for drinks. I have other customers."

After a collective round of, "I'll take a coke," I walk away, satisfied that I won that round.

I take my time filling their glasses, wishing I could dump a little something extra in them, but that's not how I operate. I may get treated poorly, but I never seek revenge.

After I set their glasses in front of them, they reach for their straws, shooting the wrappers in my face. "Do you know what you want to eat?"

"I'll take a side of you," the one in the corner says, not learning from the first time I put them in their place.

"Sorry, I don't hook up with little boys."

"None of us are little," he retorts with a smug grin on his face. They're the type to sit around measuring their manhood, too. It's how I know they definitely *are* little. You don't need to measure something that speaks for itself.

"You're freshmen, so cut the crap and order."

"Does your boss know you talk to customers like that? We can tell on you, ya know."

"Does your *mother* know you talk to older girls like that?"

They all roll their eyes, and before long they finally tell me what they actually want to eat. I'm typing the order into the computer for the kitchen staff when Betty, the owner who is more like a grandma than boss, reaches in the basket next to me for another handful of rolled silverware. "I sat another one in your section, honey. You're full, but the handsome devil requested you, so I couldn't very well put him in another section."

"That's okay. I need the money. My car's in the shop again. Brian took it home with him when his shift ended."

"You work so hard for a girl your age. I hate that you got dealt a bad hand, Kinsley. Most kids in this town don't care about jobs or money, and here you are, working your hind end off for me without having to be told twice."

"Betty, we've been over this. I have no other choice. I need to save as much money as I can, which hasn't been easy because my car won't stop breaking down."

Next thing I know, she's opening the register, pulling money out and shoving it in my pocket. "What are you doing?"

"What I should have done long ago. Take it, and don't say another word about it. You've never missed a shift in the two years you've worked here. You take on extra ones when I ask, even when I don't. And you skip your free meal more times than you eat it. I owe *you*, Kinsley. Let me do this for you."

"But, Betty." I've never accepted a handout in my life. I've always paid my own way no matter how tight I had to pinch my pennies.

"Not another word. My daughter didn't stick around after graduation, and you remind me so much of her. She had big dreams, too. Just like you. Now she lives clear across the world with a family of her own. We don't get to see each other more than once a year, so my staff is my family now. *You're* my family, Kinsley."

"I don't know how to thank you," I whisper, as I finger the wad of bills inside my pocket. It feels wrong to accept such a generous gift which is why I've already decided to pay her back once I have the money. I'm in such a tight spot, I have to accept her generosity.

She pats the top of my hand with her wrinkled one. With rings on every finger, and enough costume jewelry wrapped around her wrists and neck to open a boutique, she's the closest thing to a grandmother I have. "Breathe, honey. You'll get through this. You always do."

"Thank you, Betty. I mean it. Thank you."

She smiles and hands me a basket of bread for my new table. "Not another word about it. Now, go wait on that handsome devil."

He must be good looking to get *her* excited. She usually can't stand most of the teenagers that come in here, but those she does like, she treats well.

I grab a plate of butter for the bread, and walk to my table. I almost toss the entire basket on the floor when I realize my next customer is none other than Rhett.

He looks up from his menu, just as I stop next to his table. "Hi." I skip the rest of my normal introduction, setting the bread down before I drop it. "What would you like to drink?"

"Kinsley," he says with a shy smile. "You don't have to wait on me. I feel bad making you work."

Even though I'm curious as to why he came here, tonight of all nights, I tell him, "I'm here to work. I don't mind."

He stares at his menu, but hands it back to me. "I'm so lame. I already ate dinner at home." He ducks his head as he laughs, rubbing the back of his neck with his hand. And then he pierces me with his gorgeous green eyes. "I was looking for an excuse to see you tonight."

"You were?"

"Yeah, pathetic. Huh?"

I shake my head, but before I can tell him I've been thinking about him too, a spitball sails from a straw, pelting me on the side of my face. "Seriously?" I grumble. "Those little punks are on my last nerve."

Rhett pushes his chair back, but before he can stand up, I

hold out my arm to stop him. "I'll handle it."

"You sure?"

"Yes."

He scoots his chair back under the table, but gives the freshmen a look so menacing, they cower in the corner of the booth.

"They're mad at me. I guess spitballs are the only form of revenge their pea-sized brains can come up with."

"Why are they mad?"

"For not swooning when they tried to hit on me with their pimply charm."

He laughs and reaches into the basket for a roll. "So, I shouldn't take any notes from them?"

"None, but I'll stop rambling about them. Are you sure you don't want anything? A drink, at least?"

"I'm in no rush. How about a root beer."

"You got it."

"Oh wait, apple pie, too. Betty's is the best."

"It's my favorite."

I'm almost certain he stares at my butt the entire way to the kitchen where I hand his order to the cook. I load my tray with the hooligans' food along with Rhett's drink and pie, and as I was expecting, they're all laughing when I get back to their table. They think they're clever changing seats to try to mess me up. Thankfully, unlike them, I have a brain between my ears. "Do you boys need anything else?"

"I'm still waiting for my side of you," one mumbles. "You're smokin'." He takes a quick sip of his drink before setting the glass back down over the ring of condensation left on the placemat. He sucks on a piece of ice, but as he tries to do some ridiculous trick with his tongue to impress me, it shoots back his throat.

He claws at his neck, almost throwing up on the table right in front of me. His face is bright red from coughing so violently. "Jesus, don't hurt yourself." I wait a few seconds to make sure he's not going to die on my watch, and when I see his color return to normal, and he's able to catch his breath, I walk away.

Rhett watches the entire exchange, and he doesn't look happy about it. He motions for me to come over, and I do. "Do you always get treated like shit?"

"Not every day, but most. We get a lot of traffic from the high school."

"That's bullshit. Does your manager know what goes on in her restaurant?"

"Rhett, really. I'm used to it. If she kicked out every kid who gave me a hard time, she'd be out of business in a week." I look down at my hand, not even realizing it's on Rhett's arm, as I'm pleading with him to let their behavior slide. "Sorry."

Before I can snatch it away from him, he stops me. His warm skin against my cold hand takes the chill away, instantly. "Don't be, sorry." He lets me have my hand back, but not before his eyes roam across my face, settle on my lips for the briefest of seconds, and then find their way back to my eyes.

"Your car wasn't in the parking lot. I wasn't sure you were even here."

"Brian took my car." My voice cracks, and my mouth is suddenly so dry, it hurts to swallow. Rhett hands his cup to me, offering me a sip. "I'll get in trouble. I'm okay."

"Kinsley, take a drink."

I hold his cup up to my lips, and swallow a little bit of his root beer. I drink it all the time, but sharing it with him, it tastes better than it usually does. "Thank you."

"Who's Brian?"

"He's a new cook here, but he's also a mechanic, so he offered to help with my car." Rhett nods his head, and I can tell he has more questions. "What is it?"

"I didn't think you had a boyfriend."

"I don't. Brian's thirty-five and very married." The relief in his eyes can't be mistaken, and it gives me a little boost of confidence.

"How are you getting home tonight without your car?"

"I'll catch a ride with someone."

Rhett stares at the placemat in front of him, picking at the soggy corner from the dripping condensation on his glass. "I hate it, Kinsley."

"What do you hate?" I wait for him to look at me, and it takes a few seconds, but he does.

His eyes are intense yet sincere as he says, "That you're all alone. Your brother was a pain in the ass when it came to you, warning us all to stay away, but at least I knew you were in good hands when he was around."

Now it all makes sense. I'm a pity date. "Is that why you're here? You feel sorry for me? Because if it is, I manage just fine." I turn to walk away, but he grabs onto my apron string, pulling me back to his table.

"That's not why I'm here. I've wanted to ask you out for two years."

"Two years?" He's not making any sense. If he's wanted to, why hasn't he?

"Yes, for two long ass years I waited for your brother to go to college. Like I said, he warned us you were off limits. I knew I couldn't fight him on it—he would have kicked my ass and ruined any chance for us. So, I've been biding my time, waiting until the right moment before I approached you."

"Yet you've gone out with other girls, Rhett. You've been to dances, on dates, to parties. I may not have been there, but I hear all the gossip at school."

"I know, and I shouldn't have done that. I was too worried what everyone else thought of me. If I could go back and do it all over again, I would have taken a chance and stood up to your brother. I wouldn't have gone out with the other girls."

I shake my head. "You went out with a couple of them more than once. How do you explain that?"

He takes a sip of his drink before continuing. I watch his lips the entire time they're wrapped around the rim of the glass. "None of my relationships ever worked out, Kinsley. There was a reason for that."

"This is high school, Rhett. They're not supposed to last forever."

"Says who?"

"Me, I guess. We're eighteen, and forever is a lifetime away. How could I possibly know what I'll want when I'm fifty? Sometimes, I struggle with deciding what I want for lunch."

He listens, but with confidence he says, "They didn't work out because they weren't you, Kinsley. Every time I was with one of them, I thought about what it would be like to be with you instead. Before long, I realized it was better being with you in my head, as a dream, than it was being with any of them in reality."

I never realized Rhett was so poetic or that he was a romantic. Then again, I wouldn't have known considering we've spoken more today than the last eleven years of our lives combined. "That's intense." I reach in front of him to take his empty plate, but he stops me with his hand on mine.

"Don't."

"Aren't you finished?"

"I am. I mean don't pretend like it's weird for me to care about you."

"But it is. Rhett, I've gone to school with you all my life, and now we're almost finished. Isn't it a little late for all this?"

"I don't think so—that's not what I'm saying."

Before Rhett can say anything else, Betty interrupts. "Kinsley, you're needed in the kitchen."

"Coming." I take his plate, and grab his empty glass. "I'll get your check. Actually, it's on me. I'll see you tomorrow." I'd rather he just leave. I'm overwhelmed.

Betty's waiting for me at the register, just outside the

kitchen door. "Brian called, he figured out what's wrong with the car, but he's not going to be able to come for you."

"He did, that's a relief."

"Honey, you know I'd take you home if I still drove, but these old eyes aren't good at night."

I'm about to tell her I'll call Carson when Rhett chimes in. "I'll take her home. She did buy my pie. It's the least I can do."

Betty claps her hands with delight, oblivious to the conversation I just had with Rhett a few minutes ago. "That would be wonderful. I knew this young man was a good one as soon as I saw him. Thank you, dear."

I appreciate his offer, but I don't want to become a charity care, either. "He's already taking me home from school tomorrow. I don't want to inconvenience him."

"Kinsley, I'm offering. Let me take you home. I want to," he adds.

I don't want to argue with him. In fact, fighting with him is the last thing I want to do. I want to get to know him better—even if I still think he might be living in a dream world. "Okay. Thanks. My sister's at work, I'll let her know it's covered."

Rhett waits while I type out a text, and then says, "Let me see your phone."

I hand it to him and he glances at the message I sent Kate.

"Just a friend?" he says, with an unexpected hint of disappointment.

I try to grab the phone out of his hand, but he holds it higher than I can reach. "Rhett!"

"Hold on." He punches his number into my contacts. "There. Now you have no excuse. If you need me, you call me. And if you don't, text me anyway."

I laugh as he hands my phone back to me. "Clever." When I glance at the screen, I snort. Instead of listing his name in my contact list, like a normal person would, he listed himself as "NOT a friend."

"You know that's going to come up on the screen—if you ever call me."

"*When* I call you," he stresses. "That was the point."

"Okay, *when* you call."

Rhett leans closer to my screen, checking to see if Kate responded. "She okay with it?"

I tap out one more message to my sister. "Yeah, she's fine with it."

"Are you going to tell her my name if she asks? Or are you going to make something up?"

I'm not sure I'm ready to tell Kate about Rhett. Not that there's much to tell. "I might tell her. I have to see what kind of mood she's in. She's weird about guys, sometimes."

"Good. She should be."

I laugh at how firm his response is. "Are you warning me of your asshole ways?"

"Kinsley, I'm one of the good ones, I promise you that. Your sister is, too, if she's looking out for you."

"She's a great sister." I shouldn't, but I get a little defensive for the simple fact that Kate's the closest thing to a parent I have. She's judged by everyone in town for getting stuck with her little sister and brother—even if she's never once complained about it.

Rhett tugs on my apron again, pulling me close enough that he can slide his arm around my waist. "That's why I want her to know about me. If she means so much to you, then I want to know her. In fact, I'm not taking you home until you agree to tell her who I am."

"Why didn't that approach work with my brother?"

Rhett winces when I call him out. "Kinsley, that's different, and you know it. Plus, I have a bad feeling Wyatt will still try to kick my ass if he finds out."

"That doesn't concern you? Doesn't make you want to hide like you did before?"

He's completely serious when he says, "No, I'm done staying away. I told you I waited long enough."

His words hit me hard, make me nervous even, but I'm still trying to process the fact that my brother challenged the entire school, warning all the guys what would happen to them if they so much as asked me to a dance. "I can't believe Wyatt scared all the guys away. It makes a lot of sense now."

"You didn't know?"

"I didn't know, but I had my suspicions. Either way, he didn't make life any easier for me. It sucked never being asked to a dance, or on a date. I figured I was just that repulsive."

Rhett rests his arms on my shoulders, placing his finger beneath my chin. I have no choice but to look him right in the eye. "You're beautiful, Kinsley West. Absolutely beautiful. I'm sorry I waited so long."

I want to duck my head and hide, but he doesn't let me. "I don't know what to say to that."

"You don't have to say anything—just tell your sister my name. We'll take it from there."

"And if she doesn't want me getting into a car with some guy she doesn't know, then you're crazy quest to drive me places won't happen, and I'll be out a ride. You still think it's a good idea?"

"I'm not just *any* guy, Kinsley."

I laugh, because he's completely serious—and a little bit right. "No, you definitely aren't just any guy, Rhett. I mean, you're *the* Rhett Taylor. She might pass out once I tell her."

He taps the tip of my nose with his finger. "See, that's why I like you. You could give two shits about who I am."

"It's a great name, and you're well respected in this town for your accomplishments on the field, but there's more to you than that. I can tell."

He sighs in relief. "Yeah? So, you're going to stick around to find out the rest?"

I shrug my shoulders. "Depends."

"On?"

I pull away from him, even though I loved being so close, practically wrapped up in his arms. I need a little space before I say this next part. "It depends on you."

"Then I have no worries. You're mine."

"Are you going to show me the *real* you, or the one you think I want to see? I want to get to know the guy who has been waiting two years for me. He's the one I'm interested in."

With a look serious enough to pierce through me, yet gentle enough to feel cherished, he says, "I want you to see *all* of me, Kinsley."

Whether it's littered with underlying sexual innuendos or not, I take his comment in stride. Because like it or not, I want to get to know Rhett, and the only way to do that, is to give him a shot. Even if I'm scared I won't be what he was looking for. Two years is a lot of expectation to live up to. "Okay."

"Okay? You want to see me?"

"If that means hanging out, then sure."

He smiles so wide it's contagious. "I knew coming here was a good idea."

I bump into him with my body, playfully nudging him. "Oh yeah? So you could get a free meal?"

He shakes his head. "No, I'm paying you for the food now that I know you're not going to run."

"You were going to make me pay if you didn't get what you wanted?"

He shakes his head, looking slightly exasperated. "It sounds terrible when you say it like that, Kinsley. I was just going to use it as leverage."

"That's not playing fair, Rhett."

"I never said I played fair," he says with a crooked brow.

I shake my head. He's exhausting. "I want the real you, not the asshole. Remember that."

"You got it, gorgeous."

By the time we finish our conversation, two of my tables already left, including the table of freshmen. I pick up my tips from the first two tables, and clear the dirty dishes. Rhett follows behind me, helping me carry a few things into the kitchen without even being asked. "I'm not sharing my tips with you," I joke.

"I don't want your money. Plus, I'm the one who owes you."

The third table is where the punks were sitting. They've left the exact change on the plastic tray, yet there's a ten dollar bill on top. I turn to Rhett, handing him the ten dollars. "That was sweet, but I already knew they weren't going to leave me a tip."

He shoves his hands in his pockets, not accepting the money. "I don't know what you're talking about."

"Rhett, don't lie. This is your money." Since he's making no effort to take it, I reach around his back, and stuff it in his back pocket.

"Kinsley," he calls out, as I walk away. "You can't grope my ass and then leave."

Laughing, but ignoring him, I stuff the crumpled bills the boys left into the slots of the cash register. Rhett comes up beside me and asks, "How'd you know?"

"Their money's all scrunched up. That bill isn't. Plus, they wouldn't have counted out pennies if they were bothering to leave me a tip."

"So, let me get this straight. You're out money for serving me, since you picked up my bill, and now they stiffed you. You're lucky to break even tonight at this rate."

I don't tell him Betty loaned me money for my car, and that I have a wad of cash in my pocket. Though he finds it for himself when he takes the ten out of his back pocket and shoves it in the front of my apron. "What's that?"

"Money."

He removes his hand, peeking inside at the wad of bills. "Do you always carry around that kind of cash?"

"No." I have too much pride to tell him I'm broke, and that it's not mine. I don't even blame him when he stares at me, trying to figure out what I'm not saying.

"Is it yours?"

"No."

"Did you take it?"

And this is where our differences are apparent. He doesn't trust me, but I don't trust him either. Maybe we're even.

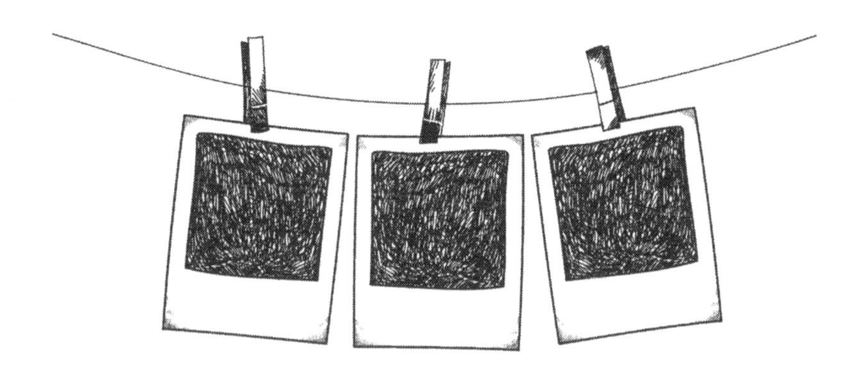

CHAPTER SIX

kinsley

INSTEAD OF EXPLAINING where the money came from, I ran into the kitchen to hide. It probably only makes me look even guiltier than I already do, but how was I supposed to explain to Rhett that I accepted money after turning his away? I looked like a hypocrite—and I knew it.

Rhett didn't bother to chase me, either, not that he was allowed in the kitchen. Though after the long speech he made not even a half hour ago, I'm disappointed he didn't. For a guy who wants a chance so badly, who had to bide his time, waiting for the perfect moment to come for me, he gave up pretty easily.

Betty drops a stack of dirty plates onto the sink counter next to me, groaning from the strain on her arms. "Did the boy leave?"

"I don't know. He thought I ripped you off. He's probably home by now."

With her hands on her hips, she narrows her eyes. "I have half a mind to go set him straight. You are my best employee," she says, shaking her head in disbelief. "You go on home. You're done here for the night."

"You're sure you don't want me to stay and finish these dishes for you?"

"Positive."

I dry my hands on my apron and lean down to give Betty a hug. I'll never forget what she did for me tonight. How she's made my life a little bit easier without even thinking twice about it. I've been let down so many times, it makes moments like these that much more meaningful.

Punching my time card in the machine that dates back to the stone age, I stare at my reflection in the mirror that's been hanging in the hallway just as long. The florescent lighting gives my normally dark hair an auburn glow. A few strands escaped my ponytail, and I have a noticeable stain on the front of my polo from some ketchup. Who knows what Rhett ever saw in me in the first place—I'm a mess.

Even I know it's too late and way too dark to be walking the entire way home all alone, so I do the only thing I can think of—I find Carson's name in my list of contacts. The pang of disappointment that hits me, is surprising. I didn't realize how much I was looking forward to spending a little extra time with Rhett.

"What are you doing?"

My body jerks from the unexpected voice, and my phone falls to the dirty floor of the vestibule, spinning in a circle until it stops next to Rhett's foot. He leans down to pick it up and hand it back to me, but not before taking a look at the screen. "Why are you calling Carson?"

"I thought you left."

His cocks his head to the side, appearing genuinely confused. "Why would I leave? I'm taking you home."

"I figured after you accused me of being a thief, you took off."

"Kinsley, I'm sorry. It was a dick thing to say. If I could take it back, I would."

"You can't, but thank you for apologizing."

He moves closer to where I'm standing, bending to look me in the eye. "Fair warning, there's a chance I'm going to do a lot of other stupid shit—even if I don't intend to."

"I can't wait," I joke. But this time my smile peers though my earlier anger. He may have jumped to conclusions that weren't fair, but I can see he's sorry and that he knows he messed up.

"Now that we got that out of the way, can I take you home?"

"Yes, I'm tired. This day's had more drama than I'm used to."

"Come on." We walk side by side down the stairs and into the almost deserted parking lot. His hand brushes mine, but instead of adding some distance between us, he clasps my hand in his, lacing our fingers together. I stare at our joined hands because even something as simple as holding hands is a first for me.

"Is this okay?" he questions, obviously worried he overstepped a boundary.

I nod my head, afraid of what I'll see when I look at him—so I don't. "Yes," I whisper.

He points to his truck with his free hand. "I'm over there."

Rumor has it, the brand new Ford F-150 was a gift from his grandparents. Some kids get graduation gifts, while Rhett gets one for simply starting a new school year.

"You can ask. Everyone else has."

I scrunch my nose up, confused about what I'm supposed to be asking. "About?"

"The truck. It's been the topic of conversation at practice the entire week."

"It's really nice."

"I know, but I didn't ask for it," he insists. I'm not sure why it's so important for me to know that, but clearly he wants to discuss it before we get inside.

"Rhett, it doesn't matter to me what you drive. Things don't matter to me—probably because I don't have many. So, I don't care if your truck came from Peyton Manning or your family. It's yours and it's awesome. That's all that matters."

A smile breaks out over his previously worried face. "You know who Peyton Manning is?"

I chuckle, "That's all you heard me say?"

"No, I heard every word you said, but it's hot when you start tossing quarterbacks into the conversation."

"Then you'll be happy to know, I like sports. I know who Peyton is—you'd have to live in oblivion not to. He's a fourteen time pro-bowler. That's huge."

Rhett's eyes widen when I break out the statistics. He forgets I have an older brother who is also obsessed with football. With only one TV in the apartment, I had no choice but to watch a lot of football games. "Shit, Kinsley. I'm think I'm in love. I mean, I already knew I liked you, but damn. You just rocked my world."

"You're crazy."

"What's crazy about that?"

"All of it." I take the key fob out of his hands to unlock the doors. When I reach for the handle, he finally snaps out of the daze I put him in.

"I got it. Let me help you get in, shorty."

Before I can climb in without his help, his hands are around my waist, lifting me effortlessly into the passenger seat. "I could have handled it."

"You could have."

"But?"

"But, I'm not about to pass up a reason to touch you," he says, as he shuts my door, and walks around the front of the truck with a satisfied smirk on his face.

It's adorable—he's adorable. No, who am I kidding? He's hot, and for reasons I'll never understand, he's interested in me.

"You can put whatever you want on the radio."

"I'm okay with this. I like country music." Plus, I have no idea how to work all the buttons on the radio. I drive an older car that doesn't have satellite radio or a built in navigation system.

"Country music *and* sports. You're two for two."

"Does that mean I'm a keeper?"

"Definitely," he says, in complete seriousness—all the playfulness from before now gone from his voice.

I pull my hair out of the ponytail I wear it in for work, and Rhett glances at me out of the corner of his eye, as I'm massaging my scalp.

"Headache?"

"A little. I think I'm mostly tired. I worked a double last night."

"I give you credit. I worked over the summer, before football started. I don't know how you go to school all day and then work all night."

"I don't have a choice."

"And that's why driving this truck sucks."

"What do you mean?"

"My parents want me to have it, and my grandparents have this insane desire to spoil me." He shrugs his shoulders. "I sound so ungrateful, but I don't need this thing. I'd rather someone have it that needs it, but they don't see it that way. They want me to have everything, which I appreciate, but it makes it harder to blend in when they're waving their money around."

"I get what you're saying, but they're your family."

"I'm sorry. Here I am pissed off at my family."

I cut him off before he can say anything else. "And I don't have one."

He nods his head. "Yeah, dick move number two. I told you there'd be many."

"It's fine, really. I've had a lot of time to try to make sense of it. I hate to tell you though, you couldn't blend in if you tried. Three quarters of this town comes out to see you play every Friday night. You're even on the news."

"That I can't help."

"Just like I can't help my situation, either. We are who we are whether we like it or not."

"You're saying I'm supposed to look the part? Be who everyone else expects me to be, or thinks I already am?"

"That's not what I'm saying. Can I ask why it even matters to you? Any other guy on the team would kill to be in your position—to have all that attention. All those girls begging to be his."

"First off, only one girl matters to me." He glances at me. "Secondly, it matters because I want a real shot with you, and I don't want rumors or expectations to screw up your opinion of me before you have a chance to get to know me. I guess I want you to see *me*, and not a position on the football field like everyone else."

He's right, I've had an opinion of him for years. Now that I think about it, I could be totally wrong about the guy I always assumed he was. I don't think I am though. I see beyond the bullshit.

"Rhett, people judge me every single day of my life because of decisions my father made. I know the rumors floating around, I've heard them all. Yet here you are, talking to me despite that. If anyone gets it, I do."

I remember the first day back to school after dad left. Word around town traveled quickly, and I lashed out at Kate because I was equally ashamed and angry. All that did was secure me a trip to a counselor before she lost me entirely. At the time, I hated her for it, especially when everyone in school called me crazy for seeing a shrink, but looking back on it, it was a blessing in disguise. Had my sister not read the warning signs as well as she did, I could very well be a high school dropout doing god knows what with god knows who.

"I don't care what other people think about us, Kinsley. I only care what you think of me—and how you make me feel."

My voice wavers the slightest bit when I ask, "How do I make you feel?"

"Alive," he says, simply.

"Well that's better than dead."

His shoulders shake and he reaches over to squeeze my leg just above the knee. "I like when you're a smartass, too. What I mean is, you don't have expectations. You don't assume anything—it's refreshing."

"Well, I do have one expectation."

He smiles, "I knew it was too good to be true. Lay it on me."

"I can't yet."

"When can you?" he asks, curiously.

"Soon—maybe."

"Adding a little mystery to the mix, I like it. I actually have one for you, too."

I fidget in my seat, not sure if I'm ready to hear what Rhett expects of me or from me. This is another area where we're worlds apart.

"Don't look so nervous."

"I am," I whisper.

"Kinsley, it's not like that. Look at me."

I turn my head, expecting to be laughed at, but he's not even smiling. "What?"

"For starters, that's not what we're about. I'm not looking

for a random hook up. Secondly, I was trying to ask you to Fall Fest."

"The music festival? That's your expectation?"

"The one and only."

The eighteen-year-old inside of me wants to jump up and down, but I've had to grow up a lot faster than most kids my age. Automatically, my mind focuses on the cost. With having to pay Betty back, I don't know when I'll be able to save enough money to go to Fall Fest. I do know it won't be in time for this year's festival. That's for sure.

At the next red light, Rhett looks puzzled when I don't immediately respond one way or the other. "You said you like country music, right?"

"I do, but I don't think I'll be able to go."

"Why not?"

I feel like such a loser. Moments like these make the anger I've tried so hard to get rid of bubble to the surface. I shouldn't have to worry about money or making it on my own. I should be living it up this last year of high school. "I just can't. I'm sorry, Rhett."

"Kinsley, please tell me why. If it's me, if you're not interested, I can handle it."

As soon as he says something as ridiculous as that, I realize I have to tell him the truth. I can't let him think I don't like him, or that I don't want to spend time with him—because I want that more than anything. So, I swallow my pride before I hurt his feelings any more than I already have.

"I can't afford the ticket." There, I said it. Now that I have, I'm ashamed. If I could, I'd open my truck door, and walk the rest of the way home, just to spare myself the humiliation.

Sensing my discomfort, Rhett reaches over and grabs my hand. His thumb rubs tiny circles back and forth over my skin. I can hardly breathe with him touching me, but I don't want him to stop, either.

"I'm taking you this year, Kinsley. We stay in tents on the festival grounds, so other than the ticket and food, there's really no other costs. It's a little on the hick side if you aren't into camping, and it's a little miserable if it rains, but still crazy fun."

"Rhett."

"I'm not above begging, Kinsley. The guys always take their girls. I'll be the odd man out without you."

His hand leaves mine as he turns to pull into my driveway, but he grabs it again as soon as the truck is in park. "Which one's yours?"

"Top right," I tell him. "Number 422."

"It's nice."

"Pfft, no it's not."

"Don't make it less than it is. You think people talk about you, and maybe they do, but not everyone disrespects you. I respect how hard you work. I'd never survive all you've been though. You're brave."

"You think I'm brave? Rhett, I'm scared shitless every morning I wake up. I worry how I'm going to keep my car running. How I'm going to manage school and work again—if it's all for nothing because I won't be able to afford New York once I get there anyway. That's if they even accept me. But then I remember, it could always be worse. Some kids at school have it so much worse than I do, and that's what keeps me going."

"Like I said, you're brave, Kinsley."

"I get jealous." I look down at our joined hands, wishing I felt as strong as he thinks I am. "Sometimes, I just want to live in our old house, and I want my life to be the way it used to be—when my mom was alive."

"I want that for you, too. I couldn't even imagine what it would be like to go home and be on my own. Do you get along with your sister at least?"

I nod my head. Kate's been my one constant. "We fight like sisters do, but we get along for the most part. It's been different though, since she started working nights to make some extra money."

"You're alone? I had no idea."

"No, I'm not alone. Carson's home most nights. He was Kate's doing, mostly. She has her sights set on a house after I graduate—one closer to Philadelphia. She's been taking as many shifts at night as she can so she has more time to do school stuff during the day. I can't fault her for going after her own dreams. Not when I plan on doing the same."

"What's in Philly?"

"Opportunity, basically. Plus, that's where her boyfriend is originally from. They were in the process of moving in together when Dad left. She stayed for me and Wyatt, but I know she's itching to get out of here. She sacrificed a lot for me which is why I tolerate her boyfriend."

"Tolerate? He's a dick?"

"Not usually, but he's pissed she's stuck with me. I can tell."

"Kate's your guardian?"

I nod my head. "Wyatt's too—well before he turned eighteen."

Rhett runs his hands through his hair, processing my reality. I dumped a lot on him tonight—more than he probably thought he'd ever have to hear. Even if it makes him uncomfortable, I'll never lie about my situation. It's not ideal, it's even pretty terrible, but it's mine.

"Please come with me to the festival, Kinsley. At least for those two nights, you'll be with me—and I'll know you're safe. It'll make me feel better about having to leave you here tonight."

I open Rhett's palm and without even realizing I'm doing it, I trace the pattern of a heart, over and over. "I'll go," I whisper. Finally, I get the courage to look him in the eye. "Thank you. It's hard for me to accept handouts."

"It's not a handout. It's a guy asking a girl on a date. That's all."

"A date, huh? An overnight date."

"Yes, but if you're not comfortable staying with me, I can bring a separate tent for you to sleep in. There's no pressure. All I want is for you to have fun."

I shake my head. "I don't need my own tent." If I'm going, I'm staying with Rhett.

"You'll really go with me? You're saying, yes?"

"We're jumping right in, aren't we? They don't even do overnight dates on *The Bachelor* until the end of the season."

"Don't worry, by the time we go to the festival, my status will be changed in your contact list."

I laugh, remembering how he's listed right now. "To what?"

"Boyfriend," he says with confidence. "We can change it right now if you want. I don't intend on backing off."

I sit starring at Rhett, slightly in shock. Okay, a whole lot in shock. This entire day has been unreal. When I woke up this morning, I was just Kinsley. Now, I'm sitting in Rhett's truck, and he just asked me on a date. I'm pretty sure he asked me to be his girlfriend, too.

"Rhett, I don't know what to say."

He shifts in his seat, picking up on my uneasiness. "I'm not trying to scare you, Kinsley, but I can't tell if you're taking me seriously or not. This isn't a joke to me."

I hear what he's asking of me—what he wants, but I've never had a boyfriend before. Rhett could end up breaking my heart. On the flip side, he could be worth the risk. There's only one way to find out. Considering I never do anything halfway, now's as good a time as any to go for it. For once, I decide to live in the moment, to take his word for face value—I hand him my phone without second guessing it. I want this. I want Rhett.

"Yeah? Seriously?" he asks, as he takes my phone. "You keep surprising me tonight."

"I believe you. It's really fast, and I had no idea my day

would turn out like this, but if you want me."

"You'll be my girl?"

I nod my head. "Yes, I'll be your girl." There's no use drawing it out. Before long, we'll both be going our separate ways. I want to make the most of the time we have left. Whether we last a week or a couple months, at least we can say we tried. We'll always have our memories.

"Hold that thought." He types frantically at my phone, screwing up a few times before he gets it right. Once his contact information is the way he wants it, he hands my phone back to me.

I glance at the screen. "*Your boyfriend.*" Has replaced "Not just a Friend".

"Clever," I tell him, as my stomach does summersaults. Those are two words I never thought I'd see. He brings our joined hands to his mouth, and gives the back of my hand a kiss.

Holy shit, Rhett Taylor is my boyfriend.

"This is my favorite day of school."

I smile. "It's the first day of school, Rhett. It rarely sucks."

"I got a flat tire last year. I also broke up with Mandi that morning."

"Coincidence?"

"Pfft. Not a chance. She flattened it at lunch time."

We laugh for a few more minutes, talking about nothing and everything at the same time. "It's getting late. I don't want you to get in trouble." I may not have anyone keeping tabs on me when I come and go, but surely Rhett's parents won't like him staying out late with a girl. I reach down to grab my bag off the floor of the car, and Rhett shifts, suddenly looking nervous that I have to go.

"You said you had Becca picking you up in the morning, but can I come get you? I'll call her if you want me to."

"You can pick me up, but I'll tell her. She'll kill me if I don't tell her you showed up at the diner. Then, she's going to freak out when I tell her the rest. You don't care if she knows, do you?"

He shakes his head. "We're not a secret. Everyone will know tomorrow."

I hadn't even considered the reactions I'll get at school. "They're going to think you lost your mind." It almost makes me want to reconsider—almost being the key word. I couldn't take it back if I tried.

"If anyone gives you a hard time, you send them to me, okay? It's me and you now."

"Okay."

"By the way, where do I stand with Becca? Is she still pissed about the dirt?"

"Yes, she is," I tell him, as I laugh at the thought of her licking dirt off the ground. She's such a germaphobe and now I know how it all started. "She also talks really highly of you. You left quite the impression on her."

He stares through the windshield with a smile on his face. "I'll be sure to thank her in the morning. I was such a little punk back then. I'm surprised she didn't kick me in the balls—I deserved it."

"Don't tempt her. She would still cash in if she could."

He cringes. "Good to know."

We sit in comfortable silence for a few more seconds before I call it a night for a second time. "See you in the morning." With my bag in hand, I reach for the door handle.

"Kinsley, wait." Rhett leans over, and before I realize what's happening, his lips are pressed against mine.

I'm having my first kiss, in a truck, with Rhett Taylor. His lips melt into mine, and he pulls away before kissing me a second time. It's an innocent kiss, that doesn't last more than a few seconds, but as wonderful as it was, I'm sure I did it all wrong. I might even smell like an onion.

I do the only logical thing I can think of, I slip out of his arms, open my door the rest of the way, and stumble out of his truck. I'm already halfway up the wooden staircase to my apartment by the time Rhett's out of the truck, calling after me.

I have to be the biggest fool on the planet for running, but I don't stop. I can't stop. Not until I'm safely inside the apartment. I hit the light switch and yelp when I find Carson sitting in the living room, in the dark. "What are you doing? You scared me."

"I was waiting for you to get home before I went to bed."

"Oh, you didn't have to wait up. I'm always home late on work nights." I hurry by him, in desperate need of a shower, and a chill pill.

"What did you do," I whisper to myself, over and over.

"I'm wondering the same thing."

I spin around with my shirt in my hands, startled. "Jesus, Carson. Stop doing that." I'm not used to him being here. There was a two week period after Wyatt left for school where I was all alone. I'm not used to having company after so many nights by myself.

Carson's eyes travel the length of me, and when he does nothing, other than take me in, I realize I'm standing in front of him in my bra and work pants. Once my mind catches up with my hormones, I reach for the door, shutting it in his face.

Within the span of ten minutes, I had my first kiss with my first boyfriend before running like a bat out of hell away from him. Shortly after, a guy saw me in my bra for the first time—who wasn't my boyfriend. This day needs to be over before it gets any crazier.

I let the warm water cascade over my tired body, praying at any point I'll stop feeling like the biggest fool on the planet. But the water runs cold before that happens, so I get out, and dry off. After pulling on a pair of boxers and a tank top, I slide under my covers. I reach for the plug to charge my phone, and see I have a waiting text—from Rhett.

Rhett: Why did you run?

How do I explain to him that I've never kissed a guy before, and that I'm pretty sure I was terrible at it? Before I start typing an answer to his first question, a second follows. There's no time to read it, when Carson knocks on my door. "Come in."

The knob turns, and he stands in the doorway doing his best to look me in the eye instead of at my chest. "I'm sorry about before. I didn't mean to make you uncomfortable."

I wave my hand in the air, dismissively, like it was no big deal. Right now, compared to my Rhett drama, it's not so bad. "I have to be more careful. I'm the one who's sorry."

Carson walks closer, stopping next to my bed.

"Can I sit for a second?"

I scoot over, giving him a little space on the edge of my bed. "What is it?"

He exhales, running his hand over his face. "I saw you with that kid in the truck."

"What did you see, exactly?"

"I saw him with his tongue down your throat."

I sit up, pulling my blankets up to cover my chest. "You were spying on me?"

He shakes his head. "I was waiting for you to get home. I saw the head lights pull in, and when they didn't turn off right away, I got up and looked. I saw him kiss you."

"You *were* spying."

"Who is he?"

"My boyfriend."

Carson recoils like I smacked him. "You were busy today."

"What's that supposed to mean?"

"Nothing. I'm just surprised."

"Why? Please don't tell Wyatt. You have to promise me, Carson. He'll start shit. Do you know he told all the guys not to touch me? I'm the one that should get to yell at him."

The way Carson stares at me, he almost looks disappointed. It was two tiny kisses. It's not a big deal.

"Just be careful, Kinsley."

"I've been taking care of myself for a long time. I know what I'm doing."

Carson stands up. "I won't tell Wyatt if you promise to tell him yourself the next time you talk to him. I don't want to be put in the middle."

"Thank you. I'll tell Wyatt soon. Things with Rhett are brand new. I don't want to mess them up before we even get started."

"I understand. Goodnight, Kinsley." He turns and walks out of my room, but I can't shake the strange feeling that comes over me. Like something isn't right. Like I made a mistake even when I don't think I did. In fact, I know I didn't.

I swipe the lock button on my screen and read my next text.

Rhett: Am I still picking you up in the morning?

I answer that question easily. Even if I am an idiot, I still want him to take me to school.

Kinsley: Yes, please.

He responds right away, just like I thought he would.

Rhett: Was it that bad?

Kinsley: ???

Rhett: The kiss. Was it that awful for you?

Kinsley: No!

Rhett: Are you sure?

Kinsley: Positive. I was nervous.

Rhett: I'm glad I wasn't the only one.

I never would have thought a guy like him would get nervous. He's the one who knows what he's doing.

Kinsley: I'm not good at this stuff. I'm sorry.

Rhett: Stop worrying. It's not like you've never kissed a dude before.

I'm too embarrassed to admit that I haven't, so I don't. I'll keep my secret to myself.

Kinsley: G'nite.

Rhett: Nite babe.

CHAPTER SEVEN

kinsley

IF I WASN'T so tired, I'm sure I would have been up half the night rereading the texts from Rhett, and remembering the way his lips felt when they touched mine. Both definitely make getting out of bed a lot easier this morning. Not only do I have a day with Rhett, but I have his football game tonight to look forward to.

Football's a big deal in this town. It's a way of life that begins as soon as kids are strong enough to keep the helmet on their head without falling over. It may seem like an exaggeration, but it's not. Wyatt started playing on a team when he was only six. Before that, it was flag football. It's why year after year, our high school is one of the top in the state—if not the best.

"Kinsley, are you eating breakfast this morning?" Kate yells from the kitchen. On mornings she works third shift, she tries to eat with me before going to sleep. It's nice to see her for a few minutes, even if it isn't much.

"I'm coming." I take one last look in the mirror. It's nothing fancy, jeans and a school pride T-shirt, the customary attire on game days, but today, it feels a little different. Today, I'm supporting Rhett.

"Hurry up," Kate yells a little louder this time.

"Sorry, I took another shower when I got up, but I used body wash instead of shampoo by mistake. Now my hair feels weird. Then, the wire in my favorite bra broke when I was putting it on."

"Um, Kins."

I look up from my bag, the one I'm mindlessly digging through as I spew my problems to my sister. Only she's not the only one listening. "Rhett?" I glance at my watch wondering if I'm running late, but I wouldn't normally leave for at least fifteen more minutes. "What are you doing here?"

Kate winks at me, giving me a knowing look. I haven't even told her about him yet. "I found this hottie sitting in the driveway when I got home. I couldn't very well let him sit out there by himself," she says with a smile.

"I bet you did," I mumble.

"What was that?"

"I said thank you."

Rhett's grinning when I sit on my usual stool at the island which happens to be next to him. He reaches over and rests his hand on my thigh like he did in the car on the way home last night. I didn't realize how much I liked it until he did it again, just now.

"Sleep well?" he asks, as he pops a piece of banana into his mouth.

"I did once I finally fell asleep." I leave out the part about Carson walking in on me half naked. I don't think he'd appreciate that too much—neither would Kate.

Kate slides a bowl of oatmeal in front of me and sets a plate of scrambled eggs in front of Rhett. She doesn't normally make me breakfast let alone cook much at all. She's pulling out all the stops this morning, and I'm thankful for her—for making us seem like we have a normal routine like every other family in America.

Rhett digs into his food, moaning around a mouthful. "These don't taste like my mom's rubbery eggs."

"That good, huh?" Kate asks, smiling.

My stomach growls as I take another big bite of my oatmeal. Rhett looks at my stomach, laughing. "Sorry, I'm starving."

"Don't apologize. I'm stoked you eat. I swear chicks think it's a turn off to consume food." He takes another bite of his eggs, and then continues. "You didn't eat much yesterday though—probably why you're so hungry today."

I stop with my spoon halfway to my mouth. "I ate. I had a salad."

"You didn't eat much of it."

Kate looks up from the sink where she's washing dishes, doing her best not to pry her way into our conversation, but I know she's listening to every single word. At least he didn't start talking about kissing me in the car. I don't think I'd be able to handle explaining that to her this early in the morning.

"We should get going." I stand up and hand my empty bowl to Kate. She takes it and kisses me on the cheek. As she does, she whispers in my ear, "He's hot, and he's into you."

"I know," I whisper back. "We're sort of together."

She covers her mouth with the back of her soapy hand. "Really?"

I nod my head. "Really."

"I want details later. All of them."

"Okay. We'll catch up this weekend. Get some sleep."

Rhett hands his empty plate to my sister with a huge smile on his face that matches hers. "Thanks for breakfast, Kate."

"You're welcome, anytime, Rhett. Just take care of my little sister. She's pretty important to me."

Rhett grabs his keys off the counter, and then slings my backpack over his shoulder. "I intend to," he says, adorably.

We walk hand in hand out the front door, and as I turn to walk down the stairs, I notice Carson at the bottom with two grocery bags in his hands, waiting to come up. His head is tilted to the side, like he's pretty sure this might be the same guy from last night. "Who's your friend, Kinsley?"

It's awkward, for a number of reasons, but I have no choice other than introducing the two. "Rhett, this is my other roommate, Carson. He's one of Wyatt's friends." I wouldn't need introductions if Carson had gone to school with us, but his parents were strict growing up, placing him in the lone Catholic school in the area instead of public. "Carson, this is Rhett. A friend of mine."

The two size each other up, why I don't know considering there's no competition between them. "Can I talk to you a second, Kinsley?" Carson asks.

"Sure, but I don't have long. We have to get to school."

"It'll just take a second."

I turn to Rhett. "I'll be right over."

Rhett nods his head, and walks to his truck, glancing over his shoulder a few times before he gets there.

"What's up?"

Carson sets the bags on the stairs, and turns toward me. "I didn't realize you were seeing Rhett."

"I told you last night."

"We didn't get into specifics, you were a little under dressed for that, but I'm not sure it's a good idea—especially now that I know it's him."

"Why not? What does it matter who it is?"

He exhales before continuing. "Because even I know your brother isn't a Rhett fan. He's been with a lot of girls. I don't want you to end up a number in a long line of has beens. Plus, Wyatt would kill me if I knew what was going on and didn't try to stop it."

"Carson, you promised. You told me you'd let me tell him when the time was right. Rhett's a good person, and Wyatt won't like anyone I date anyway. It doesn't matter if he knows him or not."

He cocks an eyebrow. "I don't know about that. He wouldn't have a problem with you dating me."

I roll my eyes. "You're his best friend, so you don't count."

"Gee, thanks, Kins."

I pinch the bridge of my nose, wishing we weren't even having this conversation. Why can't he just be happy for me? Everyone always has to challenge my decisions. "You know what I mean."

"I'm not sure I do."

"Carson, come on. You can't go back on your word now. If you care about me at all, you'll let me live a little. This is senior year. I'll never get another one."

He stares at Rhett's truck, and finally, I can tell I have him on my side. At least for a little while. "Fine, but I still don't like it."

"You don't have to like it, but I want you to respect it."

Carson picks up the bags on the step. Before he walks away, he says, "When he breaks your heart, I'll be here for you. Just remember that."

I stare at his back as he walks up the rest of the stairs and into the apartment. I'm pretty sure I can trust him, but he's right. My brother will kill him if he finds out he didn't tell him about Rhett as soon as he knew, but it's a risk I'm willing to take. For now, anyway. Wyatt can't always control me the way he thinks he can.

Rhett walks around his truck to help me inside when he sees our conversation is over. "Everything okay?"

"Yeah, we're cool." I spare him the details. He doesn't need to know what Carson thinks of him. It's mostly a stereotype anyway considering they've never spoken two words to one another. He's going on what he thinks he knows, not what he actually does.

Rhett doesn't say much for most of the drive, and he doesn't reach for my hand like he usually does whenever he's next to me. "What's wrong?"

"Carson wasn't what I was expecting," he says, truthfully.

"What were you expecting?"

"I don't know. The way you talked yesterday, I assumed he was Kate's boyfriend for some reason."

There's a five year age difference between the two, which isn't crazy or anything, but Kate and Carson definitely don't have a romantic spark. I never said they were together, but Rhett must have assumed. "No, he's just a friend."

Rhett nods his head, still not saying much. It only eats away at me more. I can't seem to please anyone this morning. "What's bugging you? Just say it."

"You introduced me as your *friend*."

"You can't be serious right now."

He says nothing in response.

"I wasn't even thinking when I introduced you. It just came out that way. I told Kate we're together—she knows. Her opinion matters way more than Carson's."

"It felt like you were trying to spare his feelings, or something, and I guess I didn't realize he was our age—or that he had a thing for you."

"Rhett, please. You're making a big deal out of nothing. I promise."

"Kin, I saw the way he looked at you. I'd know that look anywhere because I've felt it, too."

"How did he look at me?"

Without skipping a single beat, he says, "Like he wants you to be his."

There's nothing I can possibly say to that. If I deny it, I'm blowing off his feelings. And if I tell him he's right, he'll never stop worrying about Carson. I wish he understood I don't want Carson, even if there's a chance he does want me. "You make me nervous when you get quiet."

"Can I ask you something?"

"Is it about Carson? Because I promise you're the only guy I want."

"No, it's not about him. I believe you when you tell me you don't like him. I think it's just harder because you live with a guy who's not your brother. If he did want to date you, the possibility is always there for it to happen."

"It won't. I wouldn't lie to you, Rhett."

"I know you wouldn't. It's different this time."

"How so?"

"I've never worried about losing someone before, especially when I just got her. It's usually them trying to hold on to me—and that makes me sound like the biggest dick ever. But it's always been true. I'm not used to being the jealous one."

I thought I was the only one experiencing a relationship for the first time, but as it turns out, this isn't how it typically works for him either. I didn't even know Rhett knew the meaning of the word jealous.

"Please don't let the idea of Carson mess us up."

"I'll try. Can I ask you one more thing before we put this whole conversation behind us?"

"Sure."

Rhett reaches out and grabs my hand. It's how I know we're in a better place and that he's accepting Carson for the time being.

"Why did you run away last night? You're gonna give me a complex if you take off every time I kiss you."

Again, I'm blindsided. I was hoping he forgot about last night. It's been awhile since I had a panic attack, but as this morning goes on, I'm inching closer and closer. Between Rhett's unexpected breakfast date, the run in with Carson, and trying to explain myself in a way he'll understand, I'm overwhelmed again. This wouldn't be so hard for any other girl—any other girl with experience and a normal family. "I'm sorry I ran away. It was nothing you did wrong."

"But you're not going to tell me why, are you?"

I shake my head. "You'd laugh if I told you. It's my insecurities. That's all."

"I won't laugh, Kinsley. I promise."

I lean my head against the back of my seat, and while this is all new to me I know it won't get any easier until we get on the same page. Right now, Rhett thinks I'm like everyone else—and I like that. But we're doing the honesty thing this morning, which means I have to fess up, too.

There will never be an easy way to lead into this conversation, but as we pull into the parking lot at school, I need more time. I don't want to rush through it. "I'll tell you everything, but can we do it after school instead?"

"Sure, I'm still taking you home. You're coming to my game, right?"

"Yeah, I usually go to all the games with Becca if I'm not working."

"It'll be cool having you in the stands," he says, with a proud smile on his face. "What about the party after the game at Jake's farm?"

"I've never been to a football party before."

"Then this is the perfect opportunity to have some fun."

If that wasn't enough, he reaches behind his seat, and pulls out one of his game jerseys. "Will you wear this today?"

I was sure someone else was already wearing it, which is why I stare at the fabric in his hands, dumbfounded that it's mine for the taking. He wants me to wear his number all day long—for the entire school to see. Showing up in his truck is a statement, but this, this is a declaration.

He takes my hesitation as not wanting to, stumbling over his words as he says, "You don't have to if you don't want to, but I'd like my girlfriend to wear it."

"I wasn't expecting you to ask me. In fact, I was pretty sure someone else already had it. I thought I was going to have to watch Mandi walking around with your number on her back all day."

He shakes his head. "That's not how this works. You're my girl, so it's automatically yours."

"Then I'd be honored to wear it."

He hands it to me with a smile on his face, and I slide it over my head. As he helps me pull my arms through the holes, I realize how much I like having something of his wrapped around me. It even smells like his cologne.

There's no chance I'm blending in today. Today, the whole school will see I'm taken.

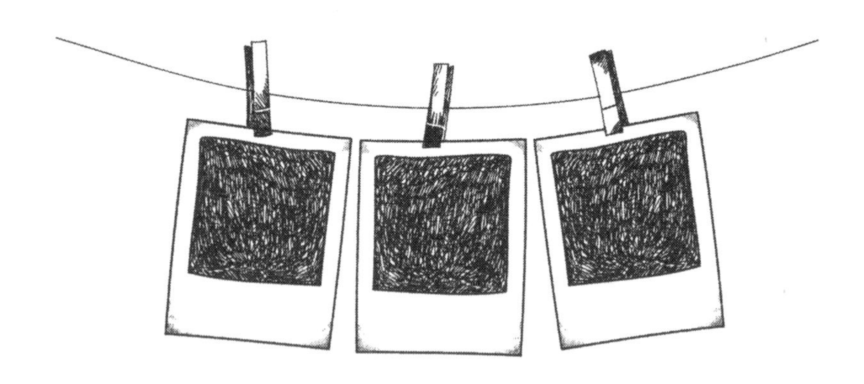

CHAPTER EIGHT

kinsley

"WHAT ARE YOU wearing?"

I shove the last book I'll need for the morning into my bag, and close my locker. Mandi's standing next to me, looking as disgusted as ever. She was blessed with resting bitch face, making her even more intimidating than she already is. "What does it look like?"

I turn away from her, not caring what she has to say. It's never nice anyway. She doesn't let me get far before she's by my side again, spewing more shit.

"That jersey was supposed to be *mine* this week. How'd you get it?"

"For someone who knows it all, you missed the memo. Rhett gave it to me this morning—in his car."

"Why were *you* in *his* car?"

"Because he brought me to school."

She laughs at me like I'm delusional. I try to walk around her, but she pulls on my arm, spinning me around. Poking me in the chest, she says, "Don't get too comfortable, Kinsley. I'll get it back next week, so don't suddenly think you're special. Rhett still loves me."

"Keep telling yourself that," I mumble.

"What did you say?"

"I said, Rhett is my boyfriend."

This time, she jumps back like I set her on fire. "You have lost your mind, little girl."

"Don't you ever get tired, Mandi? Move on, let it go. Rhett has." This time, I don't give her a chance to respond. Instead, I leave her with her jaw hanging open, and hurry to my first period class before the bell rings. Today was the first time I ever stood up to her—and it feels amazing.

In fact, I'm still riding my high when my phone buzzes in my pocket. I pull it out, hoping it's Becca letting me know where she is. Of all the days for her to be late.

Of course, I'm not that lucky. Somehow, word has even reached my brother.

Wyatt: Rhett Taylor, really?

Kinsley: What?

Wyatt: Rhett took you to school today? What's his deal?

Kinsley: No deal. My car is in the shop.

Wyatt: Is Becca's car in the shop, too?

Kinsley: No, smartass.

Wyatt: That's what I thought. I don't like it, Kin. You need to end whatever you started.

Kinsley: I'm not happy with you, either. I can't believe you told every guy in this school to stay away from me, Wyatt. I'm so embarrassed. I'm not giving up Rhett.

As I walk into my photography class, twenty pairs of eyes are on me, inspecting me from head to toe. I can thank Mandi and Wyatt for making me late.

"Phone away, Kinsley," Mr. Jasper says, when the bell rings.

I shove my phone in my pocket, effectively shutting my brother up. For the time being, anyway. Carson promised me he wouldn't tell, which only leaves two people—Kate or Mandi.

I'm deep in thought about it when Rhett tugs on my jersey as I sit down. "I like this on you."

"I'm glad someone does."

"What do you mean?"

"It's nothing I can't handle."

Rhett picks up his bag and hops over his stool to sit in the empty one next to me. "Who was it?"

The last thing I want to do is complain. I'm happy—I really am. Even if Mandi made me feel it was only a matter of time before Rhett came to his senses and ran back to her. "It's nothing, really. I'm okay."

"I see it in your eyes, something's wrong. Tell me what it is."

"It was Mandi. She told me you're still in love with her."

Rhett squeezes the pencil in his hand so hard, it snaps in half. "I was never in love with Mandi."

I believe him because the way he acts around her, definitely isn't anything that can be confused with love. "Do you still have any feelings for her?"

He shakes his head while playing with the pieces of his broken pencil. "None. I'll tell her to back off."

"That will only make it worse."

"She'll get used to it," he says, confidently.

I can't help but think it's only wishful thinking. She's not the kind of girl to give up easily. Before I can say anything else, Mr. Jasper begins class.

"Rhett, you're up first. Let's see what inspires you," Mr. Jasper announces to the room.

He winks at me before he pushes his stool under the table, walking confidently to the front of the room. He doesn't stand nervously like I would. Instead, he hops on top of the work table with his perfectly framed picture in his hand. I haven't seen the final version yet.

"My choice was Kinsley West," he starts. "At first when we were asked to take a picture of something inspiring, I thought of the football field with my helmet sitting on the fifty yard line, but I'm sure that's been done. It would have been a great shot, but the more I thought about it, I wanted something only I had—something special to me. And that would be Kinsley."

There's a collective round of sighs from the girls in the class, wishing it was them he was talking about. Some of them turn around to stare at me, no doubt wondering what it is he finds so appealing. Others actually look like they want to be me—and that's never happened before either. I have no choice but to duck my head and stare at the doodles I have scribbled on the front of my folder. Anything to make myself less visible.

"I followed Kinsley while she took her picture for her own presentation. She didn't know I was near her, and without her permission, I took this shot."

"It's a beautiful picture, Rhett. Can you tell us about one of the properties you focused on? Either lighting, composition, or scale."

Rhett nods his head. "Honestly, I got lucky. Kinsley was standing in the perfect spot. The lighting is just the sun shining through the window behind her. It's drawn to her the same way

I am." He pauses for a moment before shrugging his shoulders. "I can't really explain it, but it makes perfect sense to me. She's my sunny-girl—she makes me happy."

Mr. Jasper nods his head. "I think we're all following. I just have one more question." He turns to face the entire class before continuing. "I'll be asking each one of you why you picked your source of inspiration, so start thinking of your answers." And then he faces Rhett again, and I know what's coming. It's a question I'm both scared and excited to hear the answer to. "Rhett, why did you choose Kinsley as your inspiration?"

"Look at her," he says. The sweet timbre of his voice forces me to raise my eyes to find his. As soon as our gazes meet, he says, "She's everything."

Mr. Jasper clears his throat, not so subtly ending our moment. "Is there anything else you'd like to add before you take your seat?"

"Yeah, just one more thing. Will you go to homecoming with me, Sunny?"

I cover my face with my hands, shocked stupid for the second time today. He can't keep doing this to me. My heart is thumping so wildly, I can't focus. All I can do is watch as he hops off the table, hands his picture to Mr. Jasper, and takes his seat next to me—still waiting for an answer.

I blink slowly, my expression blank. "Is that a yes?" he questions.

"You are absolutely crazy, Rhett."

"That's a yes, isn't it?"

I want to smack him, but I can't. His presentation was intense, and I'm quickly learning that's how he rolls with most everything he does. Rhett doesn't do anything halfway—he's all in, all the time.

"I'll go with you."

"You hear that guys? She said yes!"

I drop my head to the table. "Ohmigod," I whisper.

Luckily, Mr. Jasper continues class, ending my embarrassment when everyone turns around to face the front of the room again. Rhett leans in, pulling my stool toward him so I'm sitting sideways in between his legs. His hand reaches for mine, and he links our fingers together before resting them on my thigh.

"You're cute when you're nervous," he whispers, only loud enough for me to hear.

I raise my head to watch the rest of the presentations, not once chancing a glance in Rhett's direction. I'm afraid what'd I find if I looked at him. Even my own presentation is a blur, as I stumble through every one of my explanations. All I feel is Rhett's energy—his eyes holding me when his body can't.

It stays that way for the rest of the class as Rhett's fingers rub light trails up and down my back. We're in the back, and nobody else can see, which only makes it that much better. He's not doing this for attention. He's doing it because he wants to touch me, and so I know I'm his.

The only thing that makes him stop touching me, is the sound of the bell, ending first period. "I'm glad you said yes to the dance. It would have really sucked if you didn't."

"I almost threw up," I admit with a laugh. "I had no idea what you were going to say today."

"I meant every word I said."

"I feel like I'm dreaming, Rhett. Like this is one big joke and tomorrow I'll wake up and go back to being the nobody I was."

He tips my chin up. "This is real, I promise."

"My brother knows."

"Really? How bad does he want to beat my face in?"

I smile. "Pretty bad, I think. That's part of the reason I was late. He sent me a text. I have no idea who told him, but there must be a snitch around here somewhere."

"We'll figure it out. I hate that he's mad at you because of me though." Rhett looks a little angry, but I get where he's coming from. It would be so much easier if people would mind their own business and leave us alone.

"It doesn't matter. I was planning on telling Wyatt myself. I love him, but he doesn't get to decide who I go out with."

"You mean that?"

I nod my head. "It might take a while, but he'll have to get used to it. I'm not giving you up."

He leans in and kisses my forehead. "You have no idea how happy that makes me, Sunny. Now, get your cute butt to class before you're late. I'll see you at lunch."

"I like when you call me that."

He smirks. "Good, because I wasn't planning on stopping anytime soon."

The sunshine brought us together—a simple picture with a bright halo surrounding me. I'll never forget how one frame changed my entire world. The day Rhett saw me for me and captured it forever.

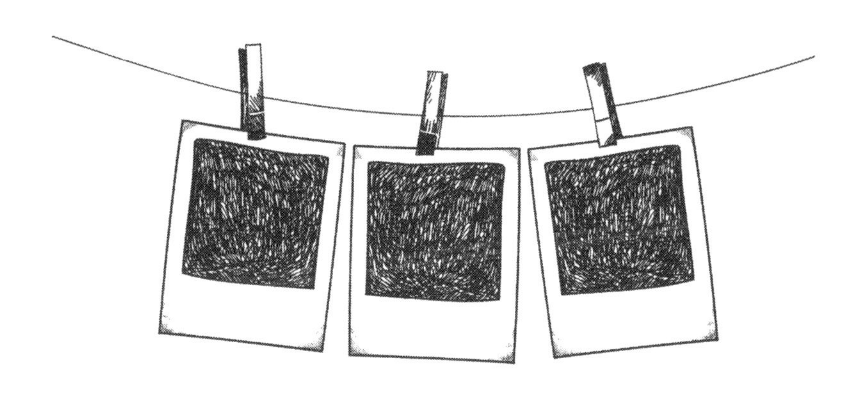

CHAPTER NINE

rhett

"DUDE, KINSLEY'S FRIEND is smokin' hot. Think she has a date for the dance yet?"

I already know who he's talking about before I even look toward the entrance where my Sunny- girl is walking into the cafeteria with Becca. They're deep in conversation, and after the morning I put Kinsley through, it wouldn't surprise me if they were talking about me.

"Becca's a cool girl. You interested?"

"I might be. I need a date and I sure as hell don't want to get stuck with Mandi. It's bad enough I had to give her my jersey this morning when she was crying on my shoulder about not having yours."

My best friend can be a complete and total pain in the ass, but he's also had my back for as long as I can remember. It the reason why I can overlook most of the stupid stuff he does on a daily basis—including giving his jersey to Mandi. "You didn't have to give it to her, you know.

"I know, I was going to give it to Becca the same time I asked her to the dance, but then Mandi came along and she scares me, man. She jacked up my plans."

I can't help but laugh at him, mostly because he's right. Saying no to Mandi is like risking getting your balls permanently shoved down your throat for the rest of senior year. "You still have time to ask her, and you better. I already asked Kinsley."

"It's not weird? Best friends with best friends?"

"Na, fair warning though. Wyatt had a thing for Becca. Rumor has it he almost failed his math class just so she'd keep tutoring him."

Jake looks impressed, if not slightly annoyed. "Got to give him credit, I was never his biggest fan on the field, but it takes guts to jeopardize your GPA and your football career for a girl. Doesn't change what I'm about to do though."

If there's someone who could compete with Wyatt for the jackass of the year award, it would be Jake. "Didn't think it would."

"I'm just sayin', if you can get the girl, I can get the girl. I don't even need you to wish me luck, that's how confident I am. I'll be back."

I laugh at him mostly because Becca's going to say, yes. It's not like he even has to worry, but I still like putting the fear of Wyatt in him. He doesn't seem worried as he runs across the cafeteria, cocky as he accused Wyatt of being, and slides on his knees until he comes to a screeching halt right in front of Becca. He stays on bended knee, taking her hand in his until she's nodding her head that she'll go to the dance with him. He stands up, swings her around in a circle, and then jogs back to the table leaving her completely dazed. It's typical Jake behavior.

"Talk about a grand gesture," I tell him when he gets back

to the table.

"Nailed it didn't I? Wyatt can suck it."

"It was pretty badass."

Kinsley scans the room, searching for me, but doesn't spot me right away. I wave my hand in the air, whistling for her attention. She ducks her head and shuffles over to me, not wanting the spotlight that's currently shining on her. I'm trying to work on a softer approach, but sometimes I forget. The girls I've dated in the past never cared. They're usually louder than I am. Then again, they aren't Kinsley. That's why I like her so much—because she isn't like them at all.

"Guys move your asses in a little. Let my girl through."

"Thank you," she says, when she finally gets to the seat I saved her. Once she's settled, she barely looks at me, instead pushing her lettuce around on her plate the same way she did yesterday. Something's bothering her.

Trying to take my own advice, I lean close to her, so nobody else hears me talking. "What happened?"

"I snagged your jersey on my locker. It's not a big tear, and I can fix it up to look like new. I'm really sorry."

She's so nervous about jacking up my jersey, but I couldn't care less. There's a chance I'll do worse to it before she wears it again, anyway. Her rambling's cute though. She treats it like her prized possession. "I'd still like you if you ripped it to shreds, don't worry about it."

That earns me a glare from Mandi. She got her red lipstick on one of my jerseys last year. I remember yelling at her for it.

"Is she going to sit here every day?" Mandi asks. "I didn't realize this table was accepting the needy." She then glances at Becca and adds, "Or the desperate." For added effect, she makes sure to fiddle with Jake's jersey, rubbing it under Becca's nose.

Becca's mouth drops open in shock. It's bad enough Mandi's flaunting Jake's jersey in front of her, and now she's insulting the both of them, publically. I almost jump in, but when Becca's fired up, there's no stopping her. She's the same firecracker she was back when we were ten.

She slams her fork down on her tray. "I don't know who you think you are, but I'd rather be known as anything other than the bitch you are. And for the record, Jake gave you that jersey today because he felt sorry for you."

Mandi scoffs. "Why would he feel sorry for me? He practically begged me to wear it. It happens all the time though."

"You're so full of it. He wanted me to wear it, but you were too busy acting like a two-year-old over Rhett giving his to Kinsley. So, if there are any charity cases or desperate people at this table, it would be you." Becca stands up with her half eaten lunch still on her tray, her mouth set in a firm line, and storms out of the cafeteria.

Jake stays in his seat, but gives a big, "hoorah," to Becca's work. He even points at her as she walks away and says, "That chick is badass."

I can't argue with him there. Although my girl doesn't look as amused as Jake and I do. I can tell she's worried for her friend on top of her own disappointment. Mandi knows how to ruin a lunch period.

"I should go make sure she's okay," Kinsley says, not even waiting for me to respond before she gets up and leaves.

I'm pissed Mandi ruined the little bit of time we have together, but confronting her again won't do any good. It will only piss her off more and the last thing I want to do is make Kinsley's life any harder than it already is.

Neither Becca or Kinsley are in the hallway outside the cafeteria, so I peek my head around the corner of the girls' bathroom, and I can hear them talking.

"I don't know how you deal with this stuff every day of your life, Kinsley. It sucks and it hurts."

"After a while you start to get used to it. Eventually, it hurts less and you become numb."

"I don't want Jake to know I was crying."

"I won't tell anyone. Go find him. You'll feel better after you talk to him."

"He's really hot and he might even like me, but Kin, I don't want you to think I'm disrespecting Wyatt's feelings for me by talking to Jake. I know Wyatt likes me, and I don't want to put you in a bad place with your brother."

"I get it. Wyatt's long distance. It would make being together hard. You don't have to explain it to me."

"Thanks. Oh, and Kin. I'm happy for you. If anyone deserves Rhett, it's you."

Becca almost runs into me on her way out, the glassiness of her eyes still noticeable from her tears. Jake will know she was crying even if she doesn't want him to. I stop her before she leaves, hoping to ease some of her worries. "Your comeback was killer, Becca. Don't sweat it."

She gives me a warm smile—the first one I've gotten since we were ten. "Thanks. Kinsley's inside. It's empty."

I never doubted her support, but I'm glad I have it. Unfortunately, Kinsley isn't as nonchalant about me being where I'm not supposed to, gasping the farther I walk inside the girls' bathroom. "What are you doing? You can't be in in here."

I point to the wall, shaking my head in disgust. "This says to call me for a good time. That's not even my number. It's false advertising."

She rewards me with her gorgeous smile, forgetting about the added stress I'm giving her. "I'm glad it's the wrong number."

"You mean that?"

"Yes. I don't want other girls finding out how good a time you are, or even calling you."

I take her heavy bag off her shoulder, holding it for her while we talk. "I'm a really good time, ya know."

She rolls her eyes at my cheesy flirtation, but she's not really mad. Not at all. She even looks a little curious when she says, "I can only imagine."

"God, I'd love to show you." I move closer, wrapping my arms around her waist. My lips are only a few centimeters from her neck, and I know she can feel my breath on her skin when I inhale the sweet smell of her hair. "You smell like coconuts. It makes me want to go to the beach instead of algebra."

"You and me both."

I would be content holding her in my arms for the rest of the afternoon, but the bell ending our lunch period ruins our cozy moment. This has been the closest I've been to her since we shared our first kiss. I want nothing more than to kiss her again, but I get the impression she's not quite ready for that yet. I'm hoping she tells me why after school when I have her all to myself.

"You okay?"

"She cried. Becca doesn't cry much—she's usually tough as nails."

"Mandi's jealous—that's why she's acting the way she is."

Kinsley turns around in my arms, giving me a sad smile. "It's not easy being replaced. I get it, but I don't want to fight with her every day. It's not worth it."

"I'll talk to her again. I don't want to lose you, Sunny."

"It's been a crazy couple of days, but I don't want to lose you either."

"No matter what, that's your spot next to me. Becca, too. Okay? And if you ever need anything and I'm not around, you can trust Jake. He's loud and a little bit over the top, but he's a good person."

"I like him—he's good for Becca."

"Even though Wyatt could be, too?"

She shrugs her shoulders. "I can't get involved in that saga. Whether they end up together or not, it's their call. I just want them both to be happy."

I tap the tip of her nose with my finger. "And I just want you to be happy. I'll see you in a bit, my Sunny-girl."

"See ya."

I turn around one last time, tossing the black marker I still have in my pocket from art class at her. I point to my name and number on the wall. "Scratch that out before you go. This good time is reserved for you."

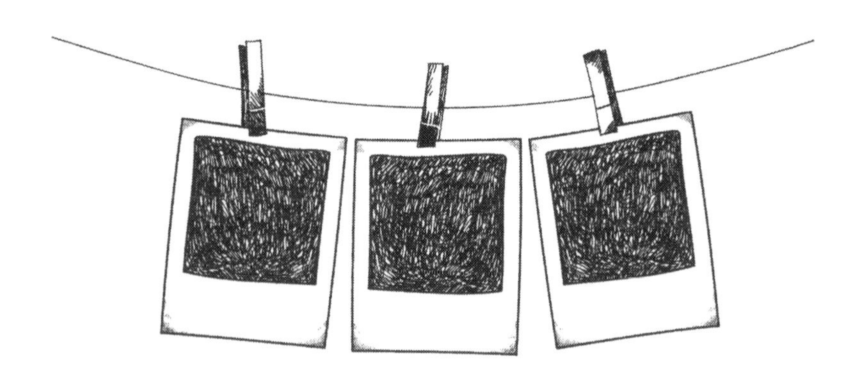

CHAPTER TEN

rhett

THE LAST HALF hour before the bell rings, every Friday afternoon, the pep band walks every inch of the hallways, pounding out their school spirit in the form of music. The starters from the team join the band as they run through a medley of upbeat songs sure to put the entire student body in the mood for a big win.

Most of the time, I block out all the noise when I'm on the field, focusing solely on the play calls and nothing else. But this is what gets me in the right mindset to kick some ass on the field. I could go out there right now and run a mile without getting winded—that's how amped up I already am. There's always something a little extra special about the home opener—especially considering this is the last one I'll have at Central.

Led by the cheerleaders, students from every classroom

clog the doorways, cheering as we walk by. I spot Kinsley in her study hall, waving to me. I'm able to cut around a few of the guys to grab her hand, and pull her out of her room toward the center of the pack.

"Rhett!" She yells over the sound of the drums pounding wildly in front of us. "I have to go back. I'll get in trouble."

I don't let go of her. I simply smile, and spin her around in a circle while we dance to the beat of the music. "Don't worry so much, Sunny. Just live it up. You feel that?"

She shakes her head. "Feel what?"

"We're going to kill them tonight, and my girl's going to see every second of it. Doesn't get much better than that."

"You're crazy!" she says, with wild eyes, but she feels it too. I know she does.

These are the moments I never want to forget. When we're in our fifties, working the daily grind, day in and day out, I want to look back on high school with a smile knowing these years were as good as it gets. That I didn't waste a single second of the best years of my life.

Hoisting Kinsley on my shoulders, she yelps in surprise, but squeezes her thighs around my neck. I can feel her laughter as she bounces on top of me, enjoying being on top of the world.

It's only after the final song ends that I lower her to the ground. "What'd you think?"

"That was incredible!"

My smile stretches wild from her excitement. "I gotta get you back to class before your teacher figures out you're missing. Come on."

"I'm going to get a detention, aren't I?"

"No, I'll make sure it's cool. Mr. Thomas is a huge sports fan. He'll understand." We have to fight against the flow of traffic the entire way back to her study hall, but I don't even have to bargain with the teacher considering Mr. Thomas is so busy explaining the answer to a problem, he doesn't even see Kinsley slip back into the room. I can thank Shannon for being one of the few students to care about calculus on a Friday afternoon.

Since I don't have to get back to my own study hall, I sit on the floor next to Kinsley's locker. I'm flicking through my texts when Becca nudges me with her foot. "You again," she says with a smile on her face. "You're really doing this, aren't you?"

"Why does everyone keep doubting me? She's an awesome girl. I can't be the only one to notice."

"Honestly, I'm glad it's you, Rhett. I trust you. We haven't been friends for a really long time, but you'll take care of her. That much I'm sure of."

I pull Becca into a hug, making sure to mess up her hair, and piss her off. "I knew you didn't still hate me. I promise I'll never make you eat another stitch of dirt as long as I live."

Becca gives me the stink eye, pulling away from me as she fixes her messed up curls.

Kinsley pauses before sliding in between the two of us to get to her locker. "What was that all about?" she asks, curiously.

Becca gives me an evil grin. "Rhett was just telling me how hard he cried while watching *The Notebook* last night."

I give her credit, she's quick on her feet. Between her come-back at lunch, and this one, I realize how much I'm going to en-joy getting to know Becca again. In only two days I've managed to repair a friendship and gain the girl I've always wanted. I'd say week one was a success.

Becca's finished at her locker, but Kinsley's still struggling to get into hers. "Let me help, what's the combination?"

She looks up at me with her big brown eyes, thankful for the help, though a little embarrassed she couldn't get it open on her own. "Um, it's four, twenty-two, nine, eleven."

I twist the lock back and forth as she rattles off each num-ber, popping it open on the first try. "There you go, Sunny."

"Thanks."

"Sunny?" Becca asks. "Where'd that one come from?"

"Rhett's picture of me."

I wrap her in another hug. "And she smells like coconut and sunshine".

Becca snickers. "You two have it so much worse than I thought."

Kinsley finishes with her locker, and shrugs her shoulders. "I don't mind the nickname. I spent a year of my life being called much worse."

"What did they call you?"

Kinsley glares at Becca before she has a chance to open her mouth. "Don't you even tell him, Becca," she warns with a stern look. She's pissed and it's kinda cute.

"Now I have to know," I tell them. "Who do I have to beat up for picking on you."

My girl remains silent, so I look to Becca for an answer. "They called her flash," she tells me, as she breaks out into a fit of hysterics.

"Why?"

Kinsley storms off. "Thanks a lot, Becca," she murmurs.

Becca throws her hands in the air. "Oh, come on, Kinsley. It's been like four years. Nobody even remembers anymore."

"What does flash even mean?"

"She's going to kill me anyway, so I might as well just tell you. On second thought, I'll let her decide how much she tells you. To make a long story short, she forgot her underwear this one time and flashed a bunch of people."

I tip my head back, laughing. "That's not so bad, but I'm definitely getting her to give me the details. That's for the info, Becca." I hurry to catch up to Kinsley, wrapping my arm around her shoulder and pulling her close. "Don't worry, Sunny. I go commando sometimes, too. It's very refreshing."

She gasps, her hand covering her mouth before she instinctively pushes me away from her. "I can't believe she told you! I'm going to kill her."

Becca finally catches up, but she doesn't stop to listen to the earful Kinsley has for her. "Text me about the game. I'll pick you up."

Aggravated with the both of us, Kinsley stomps off toward my truck. Only she's going in the wrong direction. "Other way, killer," I tell her. I make sure I stay a few steps behind her, hoping she cools down by the time I get her all to myself. We have a lot to talk about, and I don't waste any time on stuff that doesn't really matter.

Just as she climbs into the passenger seat, I stand next to her, helping her click her seatbelt into place. With my best puppy dog face, I reach for her hand. "Don't be mad, Sunny."

She tries hard not to laugh at me, but I can see a crack of a smile forming on her lips. "Will you please get in the car," she pleads, but even I know she's not actually mad anymore.

She's still quiet when I pull out of the parking place. This isn't how I wanted today to go. "Are we good? Or do I need to tease you some more to get you to talk to me?"

All at once, it comes pouring out of her. "So I forgot to wear my cover up. Big deal!" As animated as she's ever been, her hands fly into the air as she explains the situation that earned her the title of flash. "I was a cheerleader in middle school for a hot minute. Basically until I met Mandi. Anyway, we wore maroon granny panties over our regular underwear to cover us up. It's a safeguard so when we did jumps, and our skirts flew up, there wasn't a show. Only I forgot to put mine on one day, and it just so happened to be the very same day I wore my first thong. I bared my naked ass cheeks to the entire gymnasium. All while they chanted, "flash, over and over again. I even chanted along with them at first because I thought they were talking about one of the guys on the court."

It's actually a lot worse than I thought it would be. I can only imagine how mortified she must have been once she realized what was happening. "I'm a little bit sorry I missed it.

Does that make me a creep?"

She covers her face with her hands, sliding down in the seat like she'd rather melt into the floor boards than sit next to me. "I'm really glad you weren't there. It's bad enough half the student body *was.*"

I reach over and squeeze the spot on her thigh, right above her knee, that makes her squirm. "You're feisty when you're mad, you know."

"My brother and sister would agree. I should probably apologize for yelling at Becca."

"It's actually cute. And I wouldn't say that about most chicks. Usually, it's enough to drive me nuts, but not you, Sunny. You make me hot."

"Ohmigod. You did not just say that." She sits back up, holding onto the dash she's laughing so hard. "Wait, you were supposed to turn down Sycamore Street to get to my house."

I glance at her out of the corner of his eye. She's going back to my house. We need to talk and there's something I want to show her. "I thought we could hang at my house."

"Oh, I don't know why I assumed we were going to mine," she says, quietly.

I pull into my driveway, and help her out of the truck. She hops down, hesitantly. "Don't worry, it's fine. I want you here."

Holding her hand, I take her through the front door, even though we never use it, but she's a guest and should be treated like one. First, her eyes take in the staircase that wraps around the foyer and then they end up on the crystal chandelier hanging from the ceiling above our heads. It's always reminded me of something that belongs in a Las Vegas hotel instead of inside a house.

"This is really nice, Rhett."

"Thanks. My mom's an interior designer. She redecorates constantly. Sometimes the walls change colors while I'm at school. Once I thought I walked into the neighbor's house by mistake."

She follows me into the kitchen where mom has a plate of chocolate chip cookies waiting along with a note. "Want a Coke?"

"Sure."

I set a can in front of her, and when she picks it up, I notice the slight tremble to her hand. "Why are you nervous, Sunny?" My parents are at the club until the game starts. It's just us."

"Sorry, I've never done this before. Other than Becca's house, I don't really go many places."

I nod my head toward the living room. "Come on, then, I want to show you something in my room."

"Your room?" she questions. "Am I allowed up there?"

I chuckle, she's adorable sometimes. "Yes, you're allowed in my room."

She follows me up the rest of the stairs, and I lead her to the last door on the left. "This is me."

With my hand still on the knob, I wait for her to go in first. She shuffles in and stares at my bed in the center of the room. "That's where you sleep?"

My bed is round and looks more like a giant bird nest than an actual bed. That's why it's not shoved up against one of the walls. "Yup." The only pictures I bothered to hang on the wall are black and white photographs I took myself. There's a desk in front of the window with a built in bookshelf next to it and that's about it. It's minimalistic to say the least.

She looks over her shoulder after she takes it all in. "This is really cool. Did you design it?"

I kick my shoes off and flop down on my bed. Patting the spot next to me, I invite her to sit down next to me. "My mom likes to decorate. She gave me a catalog to look though for the tenth time in a year, insisting I needed to fix up my boring room. I was happy with the way it was, but if she wanted a challenge, I'd give her one. I thought I was pushing my luck when I picked out some expensive, outrageous shit she would never go for. Turns out, she actually liked it. So, now I have this palace. It's growing on me, but I'm not sure it would have been my first choice. The bed even spins."

"I would kill to have that kind of design freedom. I could think of a million things to do to every room in the apartment, especially to Carson's room. He's a nice guy, but his tastes are so boring."

I'm not sure I like the fact that she's been inside Carson's room to know what his belongings look like. But I squash that fun fact and concentrate of the two of us. "I bet you're really good at design. I saw how content you were when I took your picture."

"I love it," she says.

It's really quiet, so I grab the remote lying next to my pillow and press a button. To anyone, the picture on the wall looks like a black and white piece of art. But once the button's pressed, it changes from art to a flat screen TV. Jeopardy lights up the screen, my favorite game show of all time. If only Turd Ferguson was on today.

"You watch Jeopardy?"

I pretend to be offended. "I'm not just a pretty face, Kinsley."

This time, we're both laughing. "Okay, sorry," she says.

"I'm just messing with you, but how about a friendly wager."

"What kind of wager?"

I come up with a ridiculous game on the fly, but I get the impression my girl needs an ice breaker—something to help her relax while she's with me. "For each question I get right, I get to kiss you."

"And what about the ones *I* get right? Do I have to kiss you?"

"You don't have to, but I hope you want to."

She thinks about it for a second, even tilting her head to the side the slightest bit like she's trying to figure out if there's a catch. Eventually, she says, "So either way, we're kissing."

"Yeah, unless we both get the question wrong—then we suffer. But it's Teen Jeopardy week, so we should get some right at least. I mean, I'm pretty smart, but you'll have to try hard to keep up with me," I joke, playfully.

"Okay, you're on, Rhett."

I tug on her arm a little bit. "Come over here."

She kicks her shoes off and climbs across the mattress until she's resting in the crook of my arm. She fits next to me like she's always belonged there, and I realize this game isn't going to be as easy as I thought it was. Now that she's close, all I want to do is scoop her up and hold her, forgetting about the game entirely.

But as soon as the first question flashes on the screen, it's game on. "What famous document begins: "When in the course of human events. .?"

I yell out, "The Declaration of Independence!"

"Wrong!" She yells, even though it's the right answer.

"Why is it wrong?"

"You forgot to say, "what is" before your answer. No kiss for you."

"Okay, fine, but give me a chance to redeem myself. I'm not a quitter."

The next question is up. "What Alabama city saw state troopers attack Civil Rights marchers on Edmund Pettis Bridge?"

"What is Selma!" I yell with excitement. I got it right and remembered her rule. "I owe you a kiss, Kinsley West."

She pushes up on her elbow so she's looking down at me, and for a minute, I think she's about to cash in without waiting for me to kiss her first. "Now?"

"Now's good." I cup her cheek in my hand, not even caring we're missing questions. I have what I want already. "You're the prettiest girl I've ever kissed, Sunny." My lips inch closer to hers, but right before I have her, she turns her head, giving me her cheek instead.

"I'm sorry," she says, hopping off my bed, and reaching for her sneakers. "I should go."

"What's wrong? I wasn't trying to pressure you. You know that, right?"

She concentrates on her shoe laces, not even looking at me when she speaks. "I'm sorry. It's not you. I just can't do this."

Before I know what's even happening, she's running out of my bedroom toward the stairs. I'm hot on her heels for the simple fact that she can't keep running away from me like this. Not until she explains why it keeps happening. "Talk to me, Sunny. What's going on?"

She runs her fingers through my hair, both frustrated and angry, but I can't figure out why. What did I do to make her so upset when we were fine a minute before? She doesn't look like she wants me to touch her, but I do anyway, resting my hands on her shoulders. "Tell me, Sunny. I want to make this better."

"I don't want to run away from you, Rhett. I really don't."

I rub her back the way I did in class this morning. "Then don't. Stay with me."

"Can we sit down on the couch for a minute? I'm sorry."

"We can go anywhere you want. I don't want you to leave, but I don't want you to be upset, either."

"The couch is fine."

I lead her over to the sectional, sitting her on my lap. "Start at the beginning and don't say it's nothing—because it's definitely something."

She nods her head, and I sigh in relief. I'm not sure I could take another rejection from her when I'm trying to show her how much I care about her.

"Yesterday in your car, that was my first time." She pauses, her voice quivering as she says the words to me. "You were my first kiss, Rhett."

I lean my head back against the couch, closing my eyes as I whisper to myself. "Shit." Kinsley shifts on my lap, and I realize I need to say something to her. Something that isn't a swear word. "You mean you've never done anything—like ever?"

My sweet girl shakes her head and I can see the moment she panics, the moment she assumes I'm not going to want a thing to do with her now that I know how inexperienced she is. She stands up, immediately pulling my jersey over her head and handing it back to me. "I'll call Carson for a ride."

Is she crazy? "Whoa, wait a minute. You're not leaving." I didn't want Carson near her before, but now that she's told me she's as pure as they come, I don't even want his name to fall from her lips.

She wrings her hands together, nervously. "You don't want me to leave?"

"No, not at all. Sit down, please." I hand my jersey back to her. "And put this back on. I still want you to wear it to the game."

"Really?"

I wait for her to pull her head through the hole, and once it's back where it belongs, I continue. "I had no idea, Kinsley. I assumed you were experienced. I mean, I was hoping you weren't, but if I had known last night was your first kiss, it wouldn't have happened in my truck."

"Does everyone assume I'm a slut because I don't have parents telling me what not to do?"

Laughing, I shake my head. She took what I said the wrong way. "No, Sunny. Nobody thinks that. I assumed it because I'm attracted to you, and I know a lot of guys in school are, too. I never thought I'd be the first one to kiss your lips."

"Now you're talking nonsense, Rhett."

"You don't see yourself the way I do, but trust me, I wouldn't make it up, and I really wouldn't want to be with you if you were a slut. I mean, flash was kind of a slut, but -." She smacks me in the chest before I can continue. As hard as I try not to laugh, I can't hold it in.

"She was slutty, wasn't she. I still can't believe I did that."

"Shit happens, but let's talk about this kiss."

She groans like it's a painful topic. Nothing about kissing Sunny will ever be painful. It only hurts when I can't kiss her. "Do we have to?"

"We have to, Kinsley. I should have done so much better. Your first kiss should be so awesome you run home and write about it in your little, pink diary. The one with the tiny metal key you keep under your pillow." Again, she laughs at me. I assumed all chicks had a diary. At least they always seem to in the movies.

"I don't have a diary, Rhett. At least not since I was ten."

"Well, even if you don't, you should want to gossip about it—like girls do. Did you tell Becca we kissed?"

She looks down at her hands again, biting on her bottom lip. "Not really."

"Because it wasn't memorable. See, I gotta do better."

"It was memorable, Rhett. I was just terrible at it, and didn't want anyone to know I messed it up. That's why I ran away. You caught me off guard, and then I panicked."

She's gone an entire day thinking she's a terrible kisser. "You're really serious right now? Kissing you was awesome, Sunny. Really fuckin' awesome."

"You don't want to hurt my feelings, so you're being nice."

"Holding a door for you is nice. Carrying your backpack is nice, too. Nothing about kissing you is *nice*. It's the best thing ever." I inch my way toward her. She gets one warning this time. "I'm going to kiss you again, right now."

I reach out for her porcelain skin, holding her face like it could shatter if I'm not careful. This kiss is already more intimate than our first. I'm not holding her so she can't run away. I'm holding her because she deserves to be cherished.

Never taking her eyes off me, she leans into my arms, slowly licking her lips with her tongue. My eyes fixate on that bottom lip of hers as her teeth rake over it ever so slightly. I watch her until I'm too close to see and can only feel.

We start out slow, and like I told her before, nothing about kissing her is nice. As her lips tangle with mine, she gains more and more confidence. Little by little she stops worrying and starts feeling it the way I am. Already it's ten times better than the kiss we shared in my truck—this is the one that matters. This kiss is our game changer.

I show her with each swipe of my tongue exactly how much I want her—that she's mine. Laying her down on the cushions, I'm careful not to put my weight on her as I move over top of her, but she's latched onto my shirt so tightly, she doesn't give me a choice to go anywhere other than where I'm at.

My arms are shaking from holding myself up for so long, but I don't want to stop kissing her. I pull away for a second, my eyes darting back and forth between her lips and her gorgeous brown eyes. A slow, easy smile breaks out on my face. "You're sure you've never done that before, Sunny?"

She runs her hands up and down my arms, nodding her head. "You're my first, Rhett."

I blink slowly, absorbing her words. "God, I love the way that sounds." I'm so drunk on Kinsley, I can't even wrap my head around the fact that she's all mine.

"You do?"

"Sunny, I want to be *all* your firsts."

"I DON'T WANT to take you home," I whisper against the smooth skin of her neck. "I wish we could stay like this until morning." My Sunny's lying on top of me. We've been cuddling on the living room couch for almost an hour, alternating between kissing and talking.

All of this may be new to her, but the way she's looking at me right now isn't the way she was looking at me when we left school today. For the first time, I feel like she truly trusts me—that's she not holding back, or keeping any secrets from me.

We're finally on the same page.

I kiss the top of her head and she holds onto me a little tighter like she doesn't want to let go either. "I wish we could stay here, too. I like when you hold me."

"You'll see me after the game, and be right back in my arms. I promise."

She lifts her head from my chest, staring at me. Twice she blinks before she says a word. "Have you guys watched a lot of film on this team? They're going to play dirty like they always do, and I don't want you to get hurt."

"I love it when you talk sports, Sunny."

She laughs and nips at my lips, "Wyatt taught me a lot over the years."

"We probably shouldn't talk about him while you're lying on top of me."

"We probably shouldn't talk at all." She leans forward, finding my lips again, sucking on the bottom one to the point I can barely stand it. More than anything, I want to show her how much I want her, but there's no way we can do anything other than kiss.

"Sunny, I want you so bad."

She nods her head, but jumps away from me when her phone buzzes in her front pocket. "I should see who that is."

I give her one last kiss before she pushes off of me, and sits up, straddling my hips. After swiping her finger across the screen, she reads the message and types one back. "Everything okay?"

"Yeah. It's Carson."

I sit up as soon as his name leaves her lips. "What does he

want?"

She shows me the screen on her phone.

Carson: Where are you? I ordered pizza.

Kinsley: At Rhett's. I'll be home in fifteen minutes.

"Not going to lie, Sunny. I don't like you going home to him. It seems like a date."

"I promise you have nothing to worry about. He's just looking out for me. That's all."

I want to believe her. In fact, I do. It's him I don't trust. I saw the way he was looking at her when I was taking her to school this morning. He wants her. "If you say so."

"I want you, Rhett. Nobody else."

I press a kiss to her forehead, holding onto the fact that we're new. We have a long way to go, and neither of us plan on going anywhere anytime soon. "Come on, I'll take you home on my way back to school."

"But you didn't eat any dinner."

He chuckles at the mention of food. "You're all I was worried about."

"I'm sorry. We can stop and pick something up, or you can have some pizza at my house."

"You're cute when you ramble, Sunny, but don't worry about it. I don't think Carson wants me intruding on his dinner plans. I'll grab something on my way to school. Plus, there's always food in the locker room."

"You wouldn't be intruding because I invited you, but it's your call." She has a wicked gleam in her eyes again. One that's going to get her in a lot of trouble if she doesn't cut it out.

"I'm positive, but we're going to end up back on the couch if you don't stop looking at me like that, Sunny-girl."

She giggles, letting me pull her out the front door, and into my truck. The ride to her house isn't long enough, and before I know it, we're in her driveway.

She turns toward me, "Good luck tonight, Rhett. Watch out for number ninety. He likes to take cheap shots."

"I won't need any luck with you wearing my jersey. Meet me outside the locker room after the game."

She runs up the stairs to her apartment door, and just as she's putting her hand on the knob, the door opens. Carson's standing in front of her, without a shirt on. It takes all I have not to put my truck in park to tell him what I really think of him. He needs to learn to respect my girl and what we have.

But there's no use causing trouble for no reason. Until I have something to worry about, I'll let it slide. Tonight, all I'm worried about is impressing Kinsley on the field. I'm already confident in what we have off of it.

CHAPTER ELEVEN

kinsley

THE STANDS ARE practically shaking as the student section goes crazy. Rhett just scored his fourth touchdown of the night. Each time he crosses the line into the end zone, where a good portion of the entire student body is sitting, my classmates high five me, like I'm responsible.

"Kinsley, he's never played this good! This is all you, I know it," Becca gushes from her spot on the hard, metal bleachers. If my ass wasn't already numb, I'd think it fell off.

"He's having a good night, that's all."

"Pfft. Whatever. They're all playing well, but this is something special."

It's been awesome watching Rhett play, even if I've cringed every time he's taken a hit. When dirty number ninety gets near him, I can't even look at the field. But after three more plays, our defense intercepts the ball, ending the game with a bang.

My eyes are glued to Rhett as I watch him celebrate the 42–7 blowout win. He hoists his helmet in the air, thanking the crowd for their support, but what he does next, surprises me. He faces the end zone where I'm sitting and points directly toward me, publically acknowledging that I'm his and he's mine.

Becca sighs next to me with a wistful gleam in her eyes. "What I wouldn't give for someone like him."

"Um, hello? You have Jake."

"No, you're right. I do have him, but Jake doesn't do *that*. Look at him."

I snort, realizing the night and day differences between our guys. Jake's running around half naked like the Incredible Hulk, his shoulder pads and helmet lying on the ground near the forty yard line, in a heap. "He's excited, that's all."

"If we weren't at a football game, everyone would think he was on drugs, Kins."

"Then why are you into him if you don't like the way he acts?"

She shies away from the question which isn't like her at all. "What is it?" Staring at the bleachers in front of her, she's hesitant. It makes no sense considering we've never kept anything from the other—especially where guys were concerned. She's known my crushes for as long as I can remember. Even if none of them ever amounted to anything.

"Because he's here. He likes me. And he's really hot."

"There are so many things wrong with that statement, Becca."

"Oh, who really cares. Come on, Kins. Lets go see the guys!" Becca grabs my hand and tugs me toward the fifty yard line. Most of the student section is already crowded around the team like they're a bunch of celebrities—and they are. That's how big football is in this town.

Swallowed up in a sea of maroon and gray bodies, the

stench of sweat mixes with the mild September air. It's not my favorite combination, that's for sure. It's like being stuck in the locker room surrounded by smelly socks.

Becca finds Jake first, and he hugs her, sweat and all. Germaphobe Becca suddenly couldn't care less about all the dirt on Jake's body. That's how I know she's crushing on him—hard.

"Great game, Jake." I stand on my tip toes to give him a hug, too. Just as I'm letting go, strong arms are around my middle, pulling me away from him.

"Get your own, Jake. This one's mine," Rhett says, playfully.

I turn around in his arms, and take him in. His shaggy brown hair is drenched with sweat. His jersey's covered in grass stains with paint from the end zone covering his shoulders. The helmet he's holding is dinged up, reminding me of all the painful shots he took tonight. Still, he's six feet of athletic perfection.

"What'd ya think, Sunny?"

"You were awesome, Rhett! Seriously awesome."

"You're definitely my good luck charm. That was fuckin' insane!"

He picks me up and spins me around—my laughter the only sound I hear despite being surrounded by hundreds of people. Being in his arms is my favorite place to be. "You're huge with all this equipment on."

Rhett leans down to peck my lips just as his parents make their way through the crowd. Rhett's dad smiles warmly at the two of us, but his mom is giving me a once over, thoroughly.

"Mom, Dad, this is Kinsley West—my girlfriend."

I reach out to shake their hands, his mom accepting with a half-smile on her face. But his dad bypasses my hand entirely, hugging me instead. "So, this is the girl that's been making my son so happy."

"This is the one," Rhett adds.

His mom kisses Rhett's cheek, doting on him like a proud mother hen. She checks each one of his scratches, making sure he's not injured. "I'm good Mom, don't worry so much."

Rhett wraps his arm around me again and I look up at him, into the glare of the lights. "Ready Sunny? We have some celebrating to do."

"Yes, but go shower. You stink!"

"I smell like victory, baby," he replies, with the cocky tone he earned tonight. "Meet me at the locker room."

Before I have a chance to respond, he's jogging toward the school, already pulling his shoulder pads up and over his head.

"Focus Kinsley," Becca whispers in my ear, after she catches me ogling my boyfriend.

Finally, I blink away the image of a naked Rhett, turning my attention to my best friend. "I thought I lost you."

"Sorry. Jake wants me to go to the football party with him. Do you care?"

"Why would I care?"

She looks down at the sidewalk, kicking at the weeds popping up between the cracks. "Because he's not your brother. And I don't want you to tell him about Jake."

Something is definitely bothering her. This isn't the first time she's brought up Wyatt today. "Have you talked to my brother since he's been at college?"

Becca nods her head, still not looking me in the eye. "I have."

"More than once?"

Again, a simple nod of her head. "We've talked a couple times. He's called me and I called him once."

"Really?" Wyatt calling to check on her doesn't surprise me, especially after they spent so much time together when she was tutoring him, but her calling him is unexpected. "I don't get it, Becca. If you care about him, why don't you give it a try? Why bother with Jake?"

Finally, she gives me an honest answer. "Because it's too hard being in different places. I want to trust Wyatt, but I'm not sure I could. Even if he promised he wouldn't touch a single girl on campus, I'd always wonder if he was being faithful to me."

"So, you're going to call each other and torture yourselves instead of having a little faith?"

"It's not torture. It's like talking to a friend—that's all. No different than when I call you."

I laugh at the way she's trying to convince both of us at the same time. She doesn't believe her own words, I can tell. "It's totally different and you know it. Just be careful with Jake. Don't be with him because he's the fall back guy. Be with him because you care about him. If you don't, then you know you're supposed to be with my brother."

Becca nods her head. "I do have one confession."

Now that she's told me she's been talking to my brother, I already know what she's going to say. "You told my brother about me and Rhett, didn't you?"

"I did. I'm sorry, Kins. I didn't mean to cause trouble, but I couldn't lie to him when he asked about you. Being in the middle isn't very fun."

I'm not mad at her. I can't be. I would never lie to my brother either if he straight up asked me. It wouldn't be easy to talk to him about Rhett, but I couldn't keep it from him. "Until tonight I thought it had to be Carson."

"Pffft. He wants you too much to break your trust. I still can't believe you two share a wall and you manage to control yourself every night."

"He's not making it easy, that's for sure. When Rhett dropped me off earlier, Carson was at the door half naked, with a pizza box in his hand. I'm almost positive Rhett saw him."

Becca's eyes nearly pop out of her head. "What I wouldn't give for a welcome home like that. It's not fair you have Wyatt for a brother, you're dating Rhett, and you live with Carson. How do you concentrate on anything?"

"You can remove my brother from that equation, Becca. That's gross."

"Sorry, anyway, did Carson say anything?"

"Oh he said plenty."

Plenty. . . .

I slide by Carson, wondering why he's opening the door for me half naked, with a pizza in his hand. "Sorry I'm a few minutes late."

I reach into the fridge for a drink, wishing Kate was home to act as a buffer. Carson hasn't come right out and told me how he feels, but he's making himself known with little effort. His moves are subtle, like the missing shirt, and they're noticed—mostly because he's making it hard for me to look anywhere else.

"Want some pizza?"

"Sure, Becca's picking me up in a little bit. We're going to the game."

"Really?" he asks, with a sad smile. "I got a movie to watch. The new one you wanted to see with the guy who rides the bulls. What time will you be home?"

I shrug my shoulders, hating how guilty I suddenly feel for having plans. Why isn't he going out with his friends like everyone else? "Not sure. There's a party afterward, Rhett's taking me to it."

Grabbling a slice of pizza from the box, I set it on my plate, and sit on the couch in the living room.

"Sounds cool."

"I've never been to one, so I'm not sure what to expect."

"Just be careful, Kinsley. And don't take drinks from anyone—even Rhett."

"Rhett wouldn't make me drink, or try to drug me, Carson. He's not a bad guy."

He pauses for a minute, mulling over his next move before tossing his plate of pizza on the coffee table. "Of all people, why him?"

His sudden mood change catches me off guard. "Why not? It's not like I've ever had any other offers."

"That doesn't mean you have to take the first offer you get, Kins."

"He's interested. I'm interested. It makes sense."

"What if I'm interested, too?"

I swallow the bite of pizza in my mouth, taken aback by his sudden confession. For so long, I've watched him, wanting a guy like him to sweep me off my feet—one with manners, a conscious, and values. And now here he is, telling me he wants me. Only his timing couldn't be worse. I already have all the things I was searching for—with Rhett.

Carson moves from the recliner toward the sofa. I scoot back on the couch, needing the distance between us. I'm not prepared for this conversation. Not now. He can't mess up what I have because he's suddenly jealous.

"Kinsley," he begins.

But I stop him before he can get a word out. "Don't, Carson. Please. We have to live together. Don't make it awkward."

"I'm not trying to make you uncomfortable, but I can't sit here and pretend I don't have feelings for you. I do—constantly. You're all I can think about most nights. Do you know how hard it is to go to sleep when you're only a room away?"

"Yes," I whisper. Our headboards are back-to-back with only a thin piece of drywall separating the two of us. Sometimes, I can hear him talking on his phone, or signing along to music while I'm trying to fall asleep. He's been a distraction since the day he moved in.

"We grew up together, Kinsley. Maybe we don't know everything about each other yet, but you know me. You know we'd be good together."

I don't know what we would be. I don't. There's no way to tell who I'd be a better match with. I have no experience when it comes to dating. All I have is what's in my heart. And right now, my heart is telling me I need Rhett. Still, there's one thing I need to know before this conversation goes any farther. "Am I the reason you agreed to move in here when Wyatt had to leave?"

"Shit, Kins."

"Just tell me. I need to know."

"Will it change your mind about me?"

"You haven't told me yet."

Carson reaches for my hand, and I let him have it. He pulls the bright yellow twisty tie, that was once wrapped around a loaf of bread, from his pocket. "Do you remember this?"

I try to cover my face with both hands, but he doesn't let me. "Look at me, Kinsley."

When I do, he slides the tie on my ring finger. The same way I did to him when I was nine-years-old—a lovesick little puppy with eyes for Carson.

"Do you remember what you said to me when you gave me this?"

I smile, still embarrassed. "Most of it." There's no way I'd ever forget that day. I was positive giving him a meaningless piece of wire meant something. It had to.

"Well, I remember every word you said. It was the summer before I was starting middle school. You were nervous because you were still stuck in the elementary school with the little kids. But even at nine, you were already more mature than I was at eleven."

"I thought I had it all figured out," I whisper.

"Maybe you did, Kins. You slid this ring on my finger, the same way I'm doing now, and told me not to forget you. That even though we'd start riding different buses, and go to different schools, that we wouldn't always be in two different places. That someday, we'd be in the same place—together."

"I remember."

He pulls me closer, until I'm sitting next to him. With both of my hands in his, and the twisty tie wrapped around my finger, he says, "Here I am, Kinsley. I'm here."

I bite the inside of my lip, praying I can get through this without crying. Becca knows better than anyone how much I crushed on him. He was always the slightly older boy who came and went with Wyatt. The one who treated me like a little sister until we were both old enough to understand what it was we were capable of feeling. I figured it out a lot sooner than Carson did. Only I gave it up when Rhett came along. I had to.

It kills me to tell him no. He's Carson—but he's not my Carson anymore.

He figures out my answer before I even get around to telling him. And it hurts even more than I thought it would. "I missed my shot, didn't I?"

I nod my head, still unable to tell him, no. It's slowly become my least favorite word in the dictionary.

He runs his hands through his hair, completely defeated. He's a good guy—one that deserves a girl who will fall for him the way I've fallen for Rhett. "I knew you liked me and I missed it."

"I'm sorry, Carson."

"I saw it in your eyes every time I was with Wyatt. I saw the way you looked at me, Kinsley. And I loved it."

He loved it? But he never once gave me a clue he did. "Why are you telling me now? What took you so long?" I gave him that silly ring eight years ago. Only it wasn't silly to me then, and it's still not silly to me now.

"I waited because I didn't think you were ready. I always thought once you were finished high school we'd find our way back to each other. I swore I'd let you have a normal high school experience without worrying about me, but so much changed once your mom died, and then your dad left. I had this insane desire to protect you, and that's why I'm here, Kins. To keep you safe. But you went and found a replacement, and once I knew about it, I realized waiting wasn't the right thing to do—I never imagined I'd lose my opportunity entirely."

"I'm sorry," I whisper again, over and over. "I didn't know what you wanted."

"And now that you know, it still doesn't change anything, does it?"

I shake my head. "I can't give up on Rhett. I care about you, Carson, I always have. But when I decided to try this with Rhett, I gave him my heart."

"I was with you when your mom passed, Kinsley. I was with you during the most awful times of your life—every single time you needed someone. I wiped the tears off your face, Kin. Doesn't that count for

something?"

"Of course it does. I needed you. You were there for me when my sister was depressed and Wyatt shut us out completley."

"Then what's wrong? Why are you choosing him?"

Carson's right, he was here during most of the bad times, all of the good ones, too. Still, he's not the one I promised my heart to. Had he told me this a couple weeks ago, there's no doubt in my mind I would have melted into his arms and never looked back. It would have been a no-brainer.

I trust Carson with my heart.

I care about him with every ounce of my soul.

But I can't pick him.

It's like losing someone I love all over again from the simple fact that I'm hurting him. "I'm sorry. I can't." I stand up in a rush, desperate to get away from him before I break down completely.

I don't get far. He reaches out for me, his hands settling on my hips like they belong there. "Carson, please," I beg.

"Kinsley Grace," he whispers, his own throat clogged with emotion. "Don't walk away."

"I have to, Carson."

I see the moment he accepts my decision. The moment the warmth disappears from his yes. He puts his mask back on, pretending like none of this ever happened. He drops his hands from my body, and allows me to pass by him.

Only now that he's allowing me to walk away, I can't. I simply stand next to him for a couple more seconds, watching as he lies down on the couch, covering his face with his arm. He's gotten me through so much pain, and now I'm the cause of it.

Finally, I turn to walk away.

"I'll kill him if he doesn't treat you right."

I don't doubt his threat for a single second.

"Holy mother of all things holy," Becca says in shock. "I didn't realize Carson was so intense. I really underestimated him."

"It was crazy. I still feel terrible."

"What'd you do with the ring?"

"I put it in my jewelry box next to my mom's diamond ring."

Becca starts to speak, but stops. She tries again and nothing comes out. My best friend has never been at a loss for words, yet she's choosing her next ones wisely. "You're sure you made the right choice?"

"No. I have no idea what I'm supposed to do. All I can do is go with my gut, and I guess if it's a mistake, then it's my mistake to make. Even if I did want to be with Carson, I would never be able to break up with Rhett. I can't hurt him like that—not when he makes me so happy."

"You also can't stay with him because you're worried about hurting his feelings."

"No, Becca. That's what I said, but it's not like that. When I was with Rhett this afternoon, I wasn't thinking about Carson or wondering what it would be like to be kissing him instead. It was all Rhett. The entire time."

"You also didn't know Carson wanted you, either."

"You're not helping, Becca."

"I'm sorry, but just think it over. You'll be with Rhett tonight. Worry about the rest tomorrow. You'll figure it out."

I smile at her, wanting her to desperately take her own advice. She's in her own mess with Jake and my brother. She catches on to what I'm thinking, holding her hands up in surrender. "Point made, Kins."

Rhett and Jake walk out of the locker room, side by side, saving us from the rest of this conversation. I'm ready to have some fun.

"You ready, Sunny?"

"Yep."

Jake takes Becca's hand, leading her to his car. She glances at me over her shoulder, smiling when she sees Rhett with his arm around me. *This is right. I know it is.* If Carson was meant for me, we would have known sooner. Right?

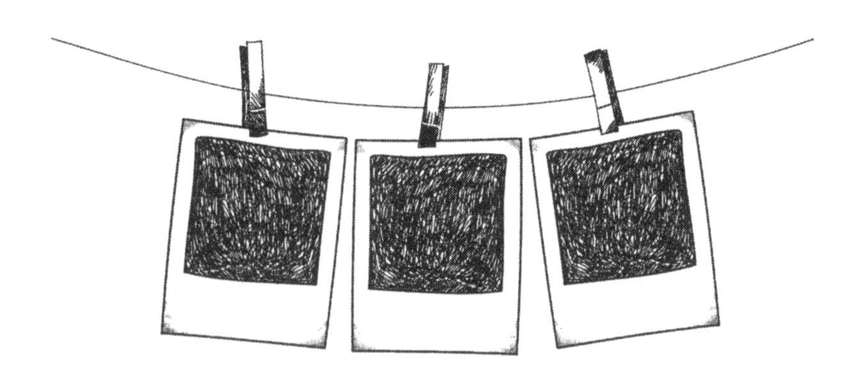

CHAPTER TWELVE

rhett

KINSLEY'S QUIET ON the drive to Jake's place. I try to scoot her closer to the middle of the truck, and she finally takes her seatbelt off, and buckles into the middle seat instead. "You okay?"

She leans her head against my shoulder and nuzzles against me. I feel her nodding her head, but she's still not saying anything. "What's wrong, Sunny?"

"Nothing. I'm good. Just glad to be with you again."

I like her answer, but something tells me there's more to it than missing me. Then again when we pull into the grassy field next to Jake's barn, and the party is already in full swing, I can see why she might be a little nervous about coming here.

I've been to every single football party for the last three years, but this one already has more people at it than I've ever seen. Between the size of the property, and the number of people walking around, it looks more like spring break gone country.

Kinsley's staring through the windshield with wide eyes. I can guarantee she's never been to a field party before—maybe not even a high school party.

"Rhett, I think the entire school is here. I wasn't expecting so many people."

I kiss the top of her head, the need to reassure her before she changes her mind about being here, my only concern. Kinsley's not used to all this. For me, a crowd of a couple hundred is the norm, but for her, it's just a lot of eyes prodding into her personal space. "Jake's place always draws a big crowd, but this might be the biggest party he's ever had."

"If you say so," she says, as she continues to pull on the sleeves of the shirt she's wearing under my jersey. I love that she put a layer under my jersey instead of over it when she went to the game. She's as proud to wear my number as I am to have it on her.

I know just the thing to settle her nerves. At least it always settles mine. "Come on, Sunny. Let's have a little fun."

She lets me wrap my arms around her, shivering as soon as I touch her. It's a little cooler than when the game ended, but from the way she's trembling, you'd think this was a cold winter night. "I've got you," I tell her, as I help her climb out of my truck and set her on the ground in front of me.

Kinsley gives me a sweet smile, the one that's reserved specifically for me. I pull her into my side, tucking my hand in the back pocket of her jeans. Each step she takes, I feel the curve of her moving up and down. She doesn't seem to mind, and I can't help myself. When I'm around her, I have to touch her.

I feel her tense the closer we get to the crowd of people. "Rhett," she whispers. "People are staring."

I peer down at her, our height difference making her seem

extra small tonight. "That's because you're so pretty."

The blush that spreads from her cheeks all the way down her neck only adds to her appeal. She's not strutting around the party like she owns the place, or acting like people should feel privileged to be in her presence. No, my girl might be a little timid at times, but she's as welcoming as they come once you crack her protective shell. They'll all see what I see soon enough. Even if I don't want to share.

"Rhett, it's about time. Thought you bailed."

I glance at my watch. "The game's only been over for like forty minutes, Jake."

"Then you're thirty minutes late. I'll spare you the ten for a shower because your ass stank. And where's your cup?"

I roll my eyes, not even bothering to argue with him. He's already had a couple, I can tell. When Jake drinks, he's even more illogical than he usually is—and it's hilarious to watch.

Becca's at his side, sipping from a Solo cup, too. I wouldn't have pegged her for a beer drinker, then again, I already picture her as the doctor she plans on becoming. And to me, most doctors are a little uptight. At least the ones I've worked with every time I've gotten injured playing football.

I nudge Kinsley. "Do you want a drink?"

She shakes her head, "I don't think I should."

I pull my hand out of her pocket, already mourning the loss. Instead, I hold her hand, rubbing my thumb across the soft skin of her wrist. "I don't mean alcohol. There's soda and water."

"I'm okay, but if you want something, I don't mind. Not that you need my permission or anything."

She's cute when she's second guessing herself, but I wish she wouldn't do it. If she doesn't want me to drink, I want to know that. I want to know her opinions, her thoughts—everything. "I'm fine without it," I tell her.

Grayson stands up from his spot around the fire with a piece of hay sticking out of his mouth. He's a spoiled rich kid with a

Mercedes and a trust fund. He's anything but a farmer. Despite looking like an idiot, he walks closer to us with complete confidence, shuffling a football back and forth between his hands like he didn't get enough of it during the game. "You always get the pretty ones, Rhett. What's your secret?"

"Not a clue, Gray, but this one's special."

I worry I embarrassed Kinsley, but when I look at her, her eyes shine. She surprises me when she stands on her tip-toes, pulling my face toward hers as her back arches to meet me. In front of everyone, she plants a scorching kiss on my lips that I deepen the first chance I get.

Our first kiss was over before it really started, but ever since our second kiss, she can't seem to get enough. Then again, neither can I. I could kiss her all night and never get tired of it.

"Get a room!" Jake yells, as he hoists his cup in the air. He's definitely on his way to drunk. Becca reaches for his hand, setting the cup on the ground in front of him before he spills it all over her. Normally, if someone took Jake's cup from him, he'd probably have something to say. Since it's Becca, he only smiles, taking the opportunity to pull her closer to him.

I wouldn't have coupled them up, but the more I think about it, Becca's the kind of girl to tame a wild soul like Jake. He's a free spirit, often loud, and always obnoxious, but she's buying what he's selling, despite him being a total nut job.

Kinsley laughs at him when he leans forward to kiss Becca and falls off the bale of hay he's sitting on. It gives me an idea—something we both could use a little bit of. Time alone and some peace and quiet. "Will you take a walk with me, Sunny?"

"Sure."

We walk hand in hand the way we came, until we hit the rest of the crowd gathered around the keg. Grayson's dad owns one of the largest beer distributors in the area. He snags free beer for almost every party. Normally, I'd have a cup in my hand, but tonight, all I need is Kinsley.

Once we weave our way though the crowd, the light from the cars lining the field slowly fades. She holds my hand a little tighter, no doubt trying to figure out why I'm walking her into a field of darkness.

"Rhett, where are we going? It's pitch black over here."

"Don't let go of my hand. I know my way around." I push open the door to the barn, slipping us inside completely unnoticed.

"Are we allowed to be in here?" she questions.

"I am, but I don't know about you," I joke. "You might get thrown off the property."

"That's reassuring. What are we doing in here, anyway?"

"I'm kidding, Kinsley. I want to show you something."

I lead her across the hay covered floors, and she yelps a few times when the straw pokes through her jeans, but I keep a tight hold on her, not stopping until we're in front of the last stall in the barn. I know what I'm looking at, and I can tell she doesn't have a clue.

Letting go of her hand, she latches onto my shirt, still unsure of what we're doing in here. I pull out my cell phone, using the flashlight app to light up the space. Shining it over the wooden stall door, I hear the moment she recognizes what's in front of her.

Instantly, she stands a little taller, reaching her hand out. "It's so cute, Rhett. Is it a boy or a girl?"

I shine the light to the banner hanging above her stall. "It's a girl. Her name's Dawn to Dark."

She stares at the foal in front of us, watching as she comes closer to where we're standing. "Dawn to Dark," she repeats. "That's really pretty."

"She's like the sunshine—sunrise to sunset," I tell her.

And then it hits her. She figures it out all on her own. "Just like me," she whispers, as I run my fingertips up and down her back. "It's perfect. Who named her?"

This next part has the potential to freak her out, but I tell her anyway. "I named her."

Her head whips toward me as soon as the words leave my mouth. "You named her? Jake's parents let you do that?"

"They don't own her. I do."

She blinks a couple times, seeming shocked that I'd have a horse. Then again, I don't exactly go around talking about it. My close friends know we have a stable on the outskirts of town, but I've never taken anyone there before. "I can't believe you have a horse."

"Other than Jake, you're the only one who knows about her. My dad trains horses part-time, actually. She was sort of a gift."

"Why's she here if she's yours?"

"I'm fixing up her stall in my dad's stable. Some of the wood was rotting and needed replaced. She'll be back with the rest of the horses as soon as the work is done."

"That's so cool, Rhett. Do you have any idea how much I love horses? I used to ride when I was little." I open the stall door, letting Kinsley inside to get a better look at her. She reaches out her hand, and Dawn, as I call her for short, sticks her nose right in her palm. "That tickles."

"You can ride her when she's a little bigger. Dad has others we can ride until then if you want to ride with me sometime."

"Really? I would love that. I had to give it up when Mom got sick. I didn't realize how much I missed it until you brought me in here." She leans forward and presses a kiss to Dawn's long snout. Already, they've bonded. "I always thought your dad was in business. I had no idea he worked with horses."

"He is in business."

"No, I pictured him selling real estate or working for a bank—something like that."

I can see how she would think that. He definitely looks the part. "He oversees the business side of the stable. He trains when he can. Horses have always been his passion. Now he's trying to pass it on to me."

"The entire business? Or just her?"

Dawn snorts out her nose, being playful with Kinsley. "I'm pretty sure this is the beginning of it. He told me the next horse was mine, and here she is. She's a thoroughbred. She'll race when she's old enough."

"I want to see her again," she says, as she runs her hand down the side of her mane. "Why'd you pick Dawn to Dark? I get the meaning of her name, but why did you name her after the sunshine, too?"

My guess is, she already has her suspicions, but she's trying to ask an honest question, so I'll give her an honest answer. "I named her after you, Sunny. I wasn't sure if I'd ever get you to date me, especially with Wyatt being your brother, but at least I'd have the horse to remind me of you."

Kinsley steps away from Dawn, staring up at me. I shine my light on her face, and I don't see any trace that she's scared. All I see is my girl, her eyes shining with unshed tears. "Nobody's ever done something like this for me. Thank you, Rhett."

"It's not too much?"

She shakes her head, a small smile playing on her lips. "No. It's not too much."

"You don't know how happy I am to hear you say that. I was nervous to tell you."

"I didn't think Rhett Taylor got nervous," she says, playfully.

"When it comes to you, I'm a little bit of everything. I've never felt this way before, Kinsley. I can't even describe it, but it's like nothing can go wrong. That no matter what happens, I'll still be smiling because I have you to look forward to. That probably makes me sound like a pussy."

She swallows, her hand reaching for mine. "No it doesn't. It makes you real. Every time I'm with you, Rhett, I don't want it to end. I think about you all day long."

I wrap her arms around my neck, forcing her to move closer

to me. "Good. That's how I want it. I want to be on your mind. Then you can't forget me."

We sway from side to side like we're slow dancing, but the only music I hear is my heartbeat thumping wildly. I feel hers beating just as strongly against my chest.

"I'll never forget you—no matter what." She pauses for a moment, her forehead resting against me, just below my chin. Then, she raises her beautiful golden eyes, and my heart literally skips a beat. I feel the second it happens.

"What is it?"

I'm positive she's about to lay something big on me, but she stalls, and then she changes her mind. "Nothing. How long have you had her?"

"Almost two months."

"Two months," she whispers. "Since July?"

"I just freaked you out, didn't I?" I told her I've wanted her for a long time. Maybe now she'll be able to see I wasn't kidding. I did get Dawn to Dark in July. Summer was halfway over, football was about to officially begin, even though we were already working out all summer long, and all I could think about was going back to school and seeing Kinsley again.

"Sunny," I whisper. "Say something."

When she doesn't immediately respond, I pull away from her, leading her out of the stall. I close the door behind us, but Kinsley climbs up onto the rails of the wall separating Dawn's stall from the one beside her. I give her a minute to herself, not saying another word until she's ready to talk. But I don't move away from her—I can't.

Holding onto her waist from behind, so she doesn't fall, I let her watch Dawn. There's so much I want to say to her—so many words I want to hear her say in return, but I just rest my chin on her shoulder and wait. I wait for her to be okay with my choices.

"I want to watch her a little more," she says, with no inkling of how she's feeling.

It makes me nervous that I'm not going to like what she says when she does speak, so I let go of her waist, moving away from her entirely. She glances over her shoulder to see where I'm going, but doesn't get down.

I sit down on a fresh pile of hay, close enough so I can still see her profile from where I'm lying. But as I sit here in the dark, watching her, my eyes grow heavy. Eventually I close them, but even then, all I see is her.

I'm on the verge of passing out completely when the hay next to me rustles, reminding me we have some unfinished business. "Open your eyes, Rhett." Kinsley's voice is small, hesitant almost. All I can hear is her breathing mixed with some nervousness.

I turn my head toward her. Normally, she's pretty easy to read, but right now, I can't tell what she's thinking. Whatever it is, I want her to open up to me. "I should have asked you before I named the horse."

She traces the logo on my shirt with her finger, shaking her head in disagreement. "The horse is perfect. I love her name, but it's not even about the horse—not really, anyway."

"You're not going to run?"

"I'm still here aren't I?" She tucks her hair behind her ear, refusing to hide behind it like I've seen her do before. She's letting me in.

"You are, but I would have gone after you if you weren't. I'd fight for you if I had to, Sunny."

She gives me a shy smile before lying down next to me on top of the hay. I'm comforted by the fact that she needs to be close to me. Her head finds the crook of my arm, and her hand settles on top of my chest. I've never felt more at peace than I do with her wrapped around me. This is what I was waiting for—and damn, it was worth the wait.

"You're my favorite escape, Rhett."

"What do you mean?"

"I get caught up being an adult sometimes, always worrying like a parent would, since I don't have any, but you make me feel like a teenager again. I thought those days were over for me."

"I like who you are, Sunny. You are grown up for your age, but it's not a bad thing. You've adjusted. Nobody can blame you for that."

"Thank you. Your opinion means the most."

"Why?"

"Because I sorta kinda like you."

"Only sorta kinda? I'm going to have to step up my game then." She giggles in my arms, and I pull her on top of me, our bodies completely flush against one another. "Tonight has been crazy stupid."

Her breath tickles my neck when she responds, "Is that good or bad?"

I can't help but laugh. Nothing about tonight has been bad. "It's good. Really good."

She snuggles against me, and I wrap my arms tighter around her. "What was it like being on the field? I want to hear your side of it. I know what I saw was pretty amazing."

"It probably sounds ridiculous, but the game was so much better with you in the stands watching me. The plays were working, just like they did in practice, I scored a shit-ton, and you were wearing my number. It was insane."

"That does sound crazy stupid."

"No, it was crazy stupid because I knew you saw it all. That's what made me feel like a rockstar. Everyone else faded into the background."

"You don't have to impress me, Rhett. Remember, we agreed this isn't about the guy on the field—even though he's *really* hot."

Those two sentences slice through me. She gets it. She sees

both sides of me. "And that's exactly how I want it, but it wasn't the game that made tonight perfect. It was you, Sunny."

"Me?"

I have to make her understand what she means to me. She deserves to hear how needed she is—especially in my world. "Nobody else has a clue I sleep on a bed that looks like a bird nest, that I own a horse I named after a girl I was crushing on, or how much I love photography. Everyone at school thinks they have me figured out—that all I care about is football and being popular."

Before I can say another word, she lifts her head from my chest, her brow furrowed. "They couldn't be more wrong if they tried, Rhett. You'll laugh, but I always felt like there was something you were hiding. As soon I saw you at school, in the darkroom, I was determined to find out what made you tick."

"Really?" I had no idea she even thought about me let alone wanted to dig deeper into my world.

She nods her head. "Really. You were never an asshole or arrogant, but there was a time I wouldn't have considered you approachable. Even on the first day, in the darkroom, a part of me still felt that way. But you treat others with respect no matter who they are—even the nerds and misfits who don't fit into any group at school. They aren't invisible to you. You've made me feel welcome, and I won't forget that."

Listening to her perception of me, blows me away. The way she's noticed little details, or subtle changes I've been working on, even surprises me. "Sunny, we're still getting to know each other, but already, you know more about me than anyone else. My own parents don't even know everything about me. Like everyone else, they only see the athlete most of the time. Whether I play another down of football or not, I don't want that to be what I'm remembered for. Because in the end, it's just a game."

"You're talented, Rhett. You should use football to get you

to where you want to be. Think of the free ride to college—all the experiences you could have simply because you're better than ninety percent of other kids your age. You'd be debt free once you graduate and free to live life however you wanted."

I can't help my smile. She's in parent mode and doesn't even realize it. "That sounds like something my guidance counselor told me."

She moves away, like she's going to get up, but I pull her back to me. "I wasn't insulting you. It's good advice."

Looking determined as ever, she nods her head. "Damn right it is."

Now we're both laughing, and the friction she's creating, almost has my eyes rolling back in my head. *Focus, Rhett.* "I just want you to live it up this year. These are supposed to be the best years of our lives. Ones we're going to look back on when we're older and laugh about. We owe it to our forty-year-old selves to be complete assholes for a few months."

She's quiet for a few seconds, but then says, "Maybe that should be my mission this year. Balls to the walls while I can."

"Balls to the walls. I like the sound of that. Do I get to help you?"

"Yes." She leans down to press a soft kiss to my cheek. "You have a little freckle right there. I like kissing it."

"Yeah?"

"Yeah, but I'll need you to force me to live in the moment—to make sure I'm not acting like a boring parent. Think you can do that?"

This will be fun. There's so much I can show her, teach her, have her experience. "I know I can."

"Good. I'll hold you to it."

I exhale and once again, I'm at peace with the girl in my arms. "You have no idea how refreshing you are, Sunny. I can't do the superficial bullshit anymore. All I want is to be me—whether the rest of the school likes it or not. I'm having fun again. Do you know how long it's been since I've said that?"

"I guess I thought since you were so popular you had everything you wanted. I didn't get it until now."

"I have everything I want now." I squeeze her a little tighter so she knows I'm talking about her. Then, I laugh, thinking of my dad's face when I introduced her to him earlier tonight. "My dad likes you."

She giggles. "I wasn't expecting him to hug me the way he did. If I'm being honest though, your mom made me a little nervous."

My mom has always had my back. She's fought battles for me more times than I can count, even getting me out of a couple messy situations where it was clear I was in the wrong. But her little boy can do no wrong in her eyes. Mistakes and all, she's still my number one fan. "That's because she's overprotective. I'm not sure that will ever change, but she'll love you once you get to know her."

Kinsley doesn't look as convinced as I am about it. "Don't worry. As long as I'm happy, she's usually happy, too."

"Even with my background? I mean, I've never been to a country club—I work at a diner."

This is where she sells herself short. She's so many things besides being a waitress. "Sunny, you work harder than most kids our age. She's not going to fault you for your job. Plus, she's going to flip when she finds out you want to be a designer."

"I enjoy interior design like she does, but I want to design clothing. It's not the same thing."

"Doesn't matter. You both have the same creative itch. As far as I'm concerned, it's a match made in heaven."

"I hope you're right," she responds, skeptically.

"I was right about you. Wasn't I?"

"Rhett, honestly, I don't know what you think. I mean, you told me a lot tonight, and that's helped me get inside your head a little."

I roll on my side, laying her gently next to me. "I think you don't give yourself enough credit. I also think you're the most beautiful girl I've ever seen—inside and out."

She picks at a piece of hay in front of her. "Wow. You've gone out with a lot of girls, are you sure about that?"

I don't like the way she compares herself to my past girlfriends. When I'm with her, and even when I'm not, I don't think about them. I don't picture what it would be like to be with any of them a second time—I just don't. The only girl I see myself with is Kinsley. "There wouldn't have been any other girls if I had you first, Sunny."

"You mean that, don't you?" It's a question, yet needed validation, at the same time.

I scoot closer to her, placing a kiss to her hair line, right at her temple. "You're not like the other ones. I need you to believe me."

"How long, Rhett?" She questions.

I'm not exactly sure what she's asking, but I assume she wants to know how long I've wanted her. How long I've had my eye on her, waiting for her brother to go away to college. "Way too long."

"How long?" She says again, stressing the point.

"I remember when we went on a school trip to the capitol building for government class. She made us sit in alphabetical order on the bus, who even does that? Anyway, I don't know if you remember or not, but we were only a few seats apart, and you were sitting next to Grayson. I was beyond jealous. That might have been the first time I felt possessive of you."

"That was the beginning of our eleventh grade year, Rhett. Why didn't you ever tell me?"

"Besides your brother, I guess I was scared you wouldn't want to waste your time on me. You were smart, really focused, and you didn't get caught up in the drama. There's always drama in my world. It was easier to imagine being with you, than to face rejection."

She giggles, even snorts once. "What? That is the most ridiculous thought process I have ever heard in my life, Rhett."

"How so?"

"I didn't exactly have any other offers coming in. Chances are, I wouldn't have said no to you—not that anyone ever turns you down in the first place."

"You say that, but we're in a different place now than we were then. Just about anything could have made you happy—we were barely sixteen-years-old."

"True, but I'm not that much different than I was then—except for being a year older and a little taller. What about you?"

I leave out the fact that her body is banging—because it is. But I don't want her to think I'm only after one thing. Yet I lean into her anyway, biting her bottom lip. "I just want you, Sunny."

She pushes me off her, and rolls me onto my back. Hovering over me, she straddles my hips. "Why did we waste so much time?"

"It wasn't our time. We weren't ready for this."

"And we are now?"

I nod my head the best I can while laying her down on the ground. She feels amazing on top of me, and I want nothing more than to pull her close—so I do. When her head is resting on my chest, and her body is flush with mine again, I wrap my arms around her, and breathe her in. With complete confidence, I whisper, "We're ready, Sunny. Balls to the walls, remember?"

CHAPTER THIRTEEN

kinsley

I LIFT MY head from the warm chest I'm resting on, looking around in the darkness. Rhett's asleep underneath me, his eyelashes resting peacefully on his cheeks. Digging my phone out of my back pocket, I try not to move too much, but I need to see what time it is.

When the light flicks on, I panic when it's almost three in the morning. We've been in the barn for over four hours. I don't have a curfew, but I've never stayed out this late before. It's one of the reasons I have almost ten missed calls and texts from Carson—even one from my sister at work asking where I am.

I nudge Rhett but he doesn't budge. After his game on top of a long day at school, he's exhausted. "Rhett," I whisper. "Wake up." He doesn't make any attempt to move until I try to climb off him.

"Where you going, Sunny-girl?" his says, his voice groggy from sleep.

"It's so late, we have to leave. It's three in the morning."

He rubs his eyes, yawning a couple times as he wakes up. "It's really three in the morning?"

"Yeah, I have to get home. Can you take me?"

He doesn't seem worried about the time, even chuckling. "Well, I'm not going to leave you here," he jokes. But his expression changes when he glances at his own phone, checking his messages.

"What is it?" I ask, concerned he's in a lot of trouble for being out so late or early depending how you look at it.

"My mom's a little pissed."

The last thing I want is for his family to hate me before they have a chance to get to know me. "I knew this was a bad idea coming here."

I move to stand up, but Rhett pulls me back down on top of him. "We're not leaving until you kiss me."

"Really? We're already in trouble, and you want to make out?"

"What's five more minutes? Plus, I was really comfortable. I'd sleep so much better if you were with me every night."

I laugh at him. There's no way he's comfortable with my hundred and some odd pounds on top of him for the last couple of hours. "You're lying, but I'll kiss you anyway."

He places a hand on each side of my face, cupping the curve of my jaw like I might break if he's not careful. The kiss doesn't start out slow like it usually does. No, this time Rhett's all in, his mouth kissing mine like he's starving for me.

His hands move from my face to my back where he tickles the skin peeking out from under the hem of the jersey I'm wearing. I can't get close enough to him, but as much as I want to explore his body more, I'm not ready for that yet. At least

I don't think I am—especially in the middle of a smelly barn. "Rhett, we need to stop."

He groans like it's painful to break away from me, but he stops when I ask him to, never once hinting that he's disappointed, even if he is a little frustrated we have to get up. "You're right, come on. I'll take you home."

"I'm sorry I had to wake you up."

He brushes the hay off his clothing, some still sticking to him no matter how hard he tries to shake it off. "Na, don't be sorry. I don't really want my girl sleeping in a barn anyway."

I smile, my thoughts going back to his bedroom and our game of Jeopardy. "There's always the nest."

"You're the only girl that's ever been inside my nest." He picks a couple pieces of hay out of my hair, his eyes never straying far from my own. Knowing how much he wants me, only makes me want him that much more. "I'd do anything to have you back in my bed, Sunny."

Maybe that means he wants to cuddle like we were earlier today, or maybe it means much more than that, but it's where I want to be, too. Especially if it's going to make him look at me the way he is right now.

"Come on," he says, taking my hand and guiding me out of the barn. Thankfully, he knows the place like the back of his hand, avoiding the scattered piles of hay and beams.

Once we're outside, we breathe in the fresh air that's dropped a few degrees since we got here. All the cars that were here earlier are gone. "Do you think Becca went home already?"

"Probably, but Jake was too wasted to drive, so hopefully she got a ride from someone else."

I chew on my thumb nail, worrying about her. I didn't have a single message from her asking where I've been or what I was doing. That's not like her at all. I only worry more when Jake staggers around the corner, holding onto the side of Rhett's truck to stay upright.

"I's bout to zend a search party, Rhett," he slurs between burps.

"Right here, man. No need to worry. Where's Becca?"

"Ma bed."

My eyes go wide as soon as he says it. Rhett looks at me, also curious about what's been going on while we were in the barn. "Dude, can I go get her? I'll take her home."

"Dat wuz the plan, but you been gone, brotha. With your lil muffin."

I snort when he calls me muffin. Rhett tries not to laugh, but he fails, too. "I'll help you inside. Take me to Becca." He walks to Jake, steadying him by throwing his arm over his shoulder, the same way you'd help an injured player off the field.

"Don't be putting moves on me. Becca's gonna get jealous."

"It'll be tough," Rhett says, sarcastically, as he pulls his keys out of his pocket with his free hand. "Wait for me in the truck, Sunny. I'll be right back."

I take them from him, but before I get inside, I hear Rhett ask Jake the one question I'd love an answer to. "Did you do anything with her?"

All I hear is a grunt in response. It can be taken either way, and is no help at all. Why did Jake have to drink so much?

Waiting for Rhett seems like an eternity, even though it's only been five minutes. My leg bounces nervously as my mind comes with up with all kinds of possibilities about what Becca could have gotten herself into. She's kissed guys before, but she's never done anything more than that. I'd hate for her to have made a bad decision tonight—one she'll end up regretting.

Thankfully, I only have to wait a few more minutes by myself before Rhett's jogging back to the truck—alone.

"Where's Becca?"

"She was passed out in his bed. I woke her, but she wanted to stay until morning."

"It is morning," I remind him.

He chuckles. "Real morning."

I don't like leaving her here by herself. Granted she was alone all night, but at least I was close by if she needed me. Jake's really drunk, and I'm a little worried about leaving her with him.

Rhett senses my concern when I don't respond. "She had her clothes on, Kinsley. She's okay. Nothing happened."

"I heard you ask Jake, but he's been drinking. He couldn't even talk without slurring his words."

"Even drunk, Jake would never take advantage of her. I promise. He'll take care of her even if he doesn't look like he can take care of himself. It's just how he is. He may come off as a piece of work most of the time, but when it comes to people he cares about, he's super protective. He'd do anything for that girl."

"Sounds a lot like you. Minus the part about being a piece of work."

He nods his head, agreeing with me. "Probably why him and I are best friends."

I twist my fingers in my lap, nervous about the trouble he's going to get in once he finally gets home. "You said your mom was upset. How bad is it?"

"My parents won't be thrilled I didn't call, but I don't think they'll be too mad since they knew I was at Jake's house. At least I hope not. I'm more worried about Coach finding out. If he does, he'll work me extra hard at practice."

"But the whole team was there. Wouldn't they be in trouble, too?"

He glances at the clock. "They weren't out until three-thirty in the morning."

"I'll talk to your parents if you want me to, and make sure they know it was my fault. I don't want them to be mad at you."

Rhett pulls into my driveway, a smile already forming on his face. "You're adorable, you know that? It wasn't either of our faults. We fell asleep. I can take whatever punishment I get."

Maybe we didn't intentionally stay out this late, but considering he's the only one facing consequences when he gets home, it doesn't seem very fair. "Thanks for tonight. I had fun."

"Me too, Sunny. I'll call you tomorrow, okay?"

"Okay." I'm opening the door, when Rhett grabs my arm, pulling me back toward him.

"One more kiss," he whispers, already claiming my lips before I can protest. Not that I would. His kisses breathe life into me. They make me feel like I could float all the way to my bedroom without ever touching my feet to the ground.

When he's had his fill, he pulls away. "Sweet dreams, Sunny."

With a smile on my face, I reach for the door handle. Before I hop out, I look over my shoulder one last time at the guy I'm falling hard for. "Night, Rhett."

Despite how late he already is, he still waits until I'm pushing my front door open before backing out of the driveway and gunning it down the street toward his house. I'm preoccupied, remembering the way his mouth feels when I realize I have a problem of my own waiting for me—Carson.

His head is in his hands, his elbows resting on his thighs. When the floor creaks beneath my feet, his head snaps in my direction. Standing from the couch, he walks toward me. All he's wearing is a pair of black boxer briefs. It's wrong to look at him the way I am, but I can't help it. He's not giving me any other choice with a body that's all hard lines and rough cuts. His training for the police academy is paying off.

"Where have you been?"

"I went to the football party after the game."

"Since when do football parties end at three-thirty in the morning?"

I need a distraction, a place to focus my eyes other than his chest or his abs, so I grab a bottle of water out of the fridge.

The top twists off and I fumble it between my fingers, dropping it on the floor. It rolls toward Carson, ending up next to his foot. We bend down at the same time to pick it up, almost bumping heads in the process. He places it in my hand, our fingers brushing ever so slightly.

"I'm sorry it's so late. I didn't mean to worry you." I try to move around him toward the living room, but he doesn't let me.

"Kinsley, I promised I'd look out for you while I was living here. You know how guilty Kate felt when she started working the night shift. She only went through with it when I told her I'd move in."

He's trying to protect me like Wyatt would, but he doesn't realize it's not the same thing. After his confession about how much he wants me, nothing about him even remotely feels brotherly anymore. "I don't need a babysitter, Carson. I can take care of myself. Plus we're like a year and a half apart. It's weird."

He shakes his head, disappointment written all over his face. "You're changing already."

I get that he's hurt, angry even, but I don't want my being with Rhett to change our friendship. I didn't choose Carson, but that doesn't mean I want him out of my life. "I'm still the same girl I was a week ago."

"You didn't have a boyfriend a week ago. You weren't staying out until all hours of the morning a week ago. Hell, you've never even been to a party before tonight—have you?"

"If you're trying to remind me how insignificant I used to be, I get it. I was a nobody, but I don't want to go back to that place—where I was always unwanted. Today was one of the best days of my life. I'm finally happy again."

He glares at me, before a look of complete defeat replaces the anger. "The best day of your life was the day you told me you didn't want to be with me? Thanks, Kins." He turns around, walking away from me, but that wasn't what I meant. He has to know that.

"Carson, wait." I grab onto his wrist, but he yanks it out of my grasp. "Carson, please."

"Go to bed, Kinsley. It's been a long night. I'm tired."

He closes the door to his room, shutting me out. That should be enough for me to walk away, to be thankful it wasn't worse, but it only makes me feel terrible. He took what I said out of context. Our conversation earlier has been in the back of my mind the entire night. I'll never be able to forget the way he poured his heart out to me. Whether he believes me or not, it meant something to me—even if I'm not his girl.

I wait a couple more minutes, hoping he'll open his door so I can talk to him, but he doesn't. Still, I can't walk away. If I do, he'll think I don't have any regard for his feelings. So, I sit down with my back against his door, and I wait.

The minutes are long, and I almost give up a couple times, but Carson's never been one to give up on me, so I'm not letting him go to bed thinking I don't care or that I've somehow changed. Even if there was some truth to his words, I'd still wait.

A full hour passes, and then it finally happens. The door I'm propped up against moves away from me so fast, I'm flat on my back in the middle of the doorway, looking up with Carson staring down at me.

"What are you doing, Kins?"

"Waiting for you to stop being stubborn."

"How long were you planning on sitting in front of my door?"

"Until you opened it." I would have sat here until tomorrow afternoon if I had to, and he knows it.

He runs his hand over his face, his eyes now much softer than they were when he stormed in his room an hour ago. "Stand up."

"I'm not going anywhere until you talk to me."

"I'll talk to you, but I don't want you on the floor." I'd rather talk in the living room, but I stand up and follow him inside his room. There's no time for me to negotiate if I don't want to lose my opportunity to set the record straight. "Why were you really sitting there?" he asks as he sits down on his bed.

I play with the hair tie around my wrist, flicking it against my skin. "I can't sleep if you're mad at me."

"I'm not mad, Kinsley. I'm concerned. There's a difference."

"I didn't mean what I said. It came out wrong."

"Does it change anything?"

I shake my head. "No. I still feel the same way, but I needed you to know I wasn't trying to rub Rhett in your face or make you feel insignificant."

"Okay, I understand. Can we go to bed now?"

"No."

"Why not?"

"Because we're still not right."

"Do you honestly think we can be? After what I told you today?"

"I don't know, but I need us to be."

"Why? You had the best day of your life, Kins. You don't need me."

I move closer to him, standing almost directly in front of him. "No, Carson. I do need you in my life. It would be weird without you—like I'm missing a really good friend."

"Friend. There's that word again."

I pull my arms out of Rhett's jersey, suddenly feeling like I'm shoving the fact that I'm with Rhett down his throat. I ball it up and toss it into the wash basket in the hallway. Carson watches me, and I don't miss the way his expression changes as I start to shed some clothes. "What are you doing?" he questions.

"Removing him from the equation for a minute." I'm not trying to lead Carson on or give him any false hope. All I want to do is be able to lay my head on my pillow tonight without a guilty conscious. And if I'm being honest, I need Carson to be okay, too. This is as much for me as it is for him. "Will you answer a question for me, honestly?"

"I'll try," he says.

"Am I going to lose you completely if I'm not with you?"

He reaches out and hooks his finger in the front pocket of my jeans, pulling me closer to him. "Part of me wants to say yes, that if you aren't with me, then we have nothing. I can't do that though. There's no way I'd ever be able to cut you out of my life, Kins. I don't want to."

"Then, how do we get back to where we were before things got weird?"

"Weird? I don't know if that's the word I'd use to describe it. Maybe real, but not weird."

"Okay, but it doesn't much matter how we label it. Either way, it's different. How do we fix it?"

"I don't know if we can."

"What do we do?"

Carson looks at me, and with pained eyes, he says, "I get over you."

I thought that's what I wanted all along—until he says the words. Hearing him say it out loud only challenges me. It makes me second guess every decision I've made up until now. I'm not ready to let go of Rhett, but I don't want to hurt Carson either.

"Tell me what you're thinking, Kins."

I shrug my shoulders like I'm not sure, even though it's becoming clearer. "I don't know what's going to happen with me and Rhett, and I can't ask you to wait around until I find out. That's not fair to you. I don't know what to do. How can I make this better?"

"You don't have to do a single thing for me. Just be happy. That's all I want for you, Kin. But I don't want you to end up with a broken heart either."

"Because you think Rhett couldn't possibly stay with a girl like me, right? That it's bound to blow up in my face because it's probably too good to be true."

He tips his head back, huffing out a frustrated breath. "I didn't say that at all. You're putting words in my mouth. I told you I'm happy for you."

"You're right. You didn't say that." I'm the one who's thinking it, and now that I'm being honest with myself, I realize it's what I'm fearful of happening with Rhett and me. That someday I won't be good enough anymore or he'll get bored or suddenly realize he has better options.

"You're scared, I get it."

"Maybe a little, but I want you to be happy too, Carson."

He rubs the back of his neck, like he's in pain. Slowly, he raises his eyes from the floor. "I can't be happy, Kins. Not until you're mine."

I swallow the lump in my throat, hating the sadness in his eyes. "Don't say that. That's not true. You can be happy without me."

"I'll wait for you, Kins—just like I stayed up waiting for you tonight."

"I should have called you back when I got your messages. I'm sorry."

"I was so worried something happened to you."

"I'm okay, and if I wasn't, I'd let you know."

Visibly sighing, his shoulders sag in a mixture of relief and defeat. Still, we're right back where we started. Nothing's really changed despite our conversation, and I wonder how many more of these we're going to end up having.

"I'm not used to this, Kinsley—especially with a person I have to live with."

"Me either, but we can make it work, okay? Promise me you won't move out because of me. Kate needs you, too."

He looks me straight in the eye as he promises, "I won't

leave you."

Maybe I need it more than he does, but I move closer, letting him wrap me up in the security he's given me for as long as I can remember. The two people in my life I've loved the most left me, but Carson's never strayed. He moved here to help me—to be with me. And that means more than he'll ever know. Even if we can't be together.

I don't want to blur the lines between us, but I can't stop either. He's been my friend longer than he's been an admirer—and I can't let that go. I can't let him go. Tonight I just want my Carson back—the one who let me cry on his shoulder when my mom passed away. The one who took me to funny movies when I hated the world, and the one who let me drink a lot of vodka after my dad left, even holding my hair while I threw up violently in the toilet. That's who I want right now. Everything else I want to disappear.

"Why do you smell like a heard of buffalo, Kins?"

I laugh against his chest, blinking away the tears that almost fell. "Rhett has a horse. He showed her to me and then we fell asleep on a pile of hay in the barn, watching her."

"*That's* your story?"

"That's my story," I giggle.

"Please don't do it again, okay?"

I nod my head, understanding where he's coming from. "There hasn't been anyone other than Wyatt and Kate for a while now, but they're my brother and sister. They're supposed to get on my nerves."

"Are you telling me I'm annoying?"

I let go of him, shaking my head at his ridiculous assumption. "No, I'm not. I'm saying, thank you for having my back."

"I'll never stop caring, Kinsley."

And as much as I need that from him, as much as it soothes my soul to hear those words, it still feels terrible because I can't give him *more*.

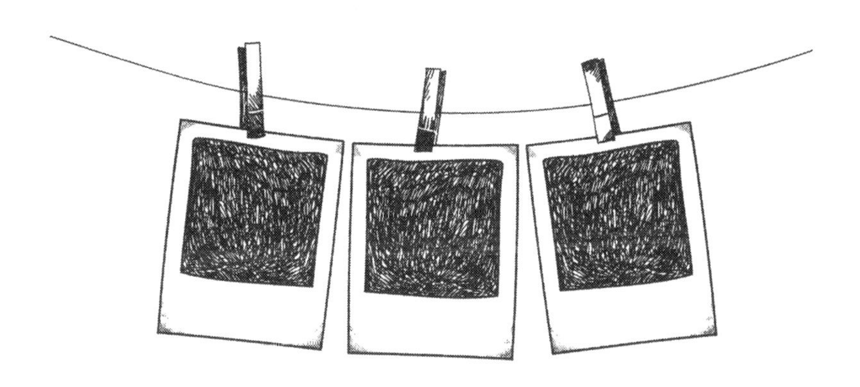

CHAPTER FOURTEEN

kinsley

THE NEXT COUPLE of weeks pass by in a blur. My relationship with Carson has remained strained. Even though we promised to move forward, I still catch him watching me or staring a little too long when he shouldn't be. But I don't say a word or give any kind of indication that it bothers me. I let him do what he needs to do because I'll do anything to avoid another confrontation like our last.

For the most part, he's been easy going. A couple times we even stayed up late watching movies, eating popcorn, and laughing like we used to do when Wyatt was still here. Those are the times I feel the closest to him, and like we really can manage to live together and be friends.

More than anything, I need the stress free Carson as much as possible. Between school, the diner, and Rhett, I'm constantly being pulled in a million different directions. I've been so busy that I've been struggling to keep up with all my assignments while still finding time for everyone. In fact, I've given up sleep just to keep everyone happy. But this morning, when I almost fell asleep standing up in the shower, I went back to bed. After faking a migraine when both Kate and Carson came to check on me, I bought myself a few more hours of sleep. Carson even brought me some Advil before he left for his own day of school.

Kate thinks I'm spreading myself too thin, and that I'm wearing myself out. At least that's what she blamed the migraine on. I don't like lying to either of them, but I don't have room to complain. Both are holding down jobs, maintaining social lives, and paying bills on time—the same as I am.

Still, once I get a couple hours of rest, I get up, and drag my butt to school. I even sign into the office with a note I hand wrote myself and signed Kate's name to. The secretary doesn't question it, and I fall back into my familiar school routine like I didn't just bag the entire morning on purpose. I timed it so well, I even managed to get to school right at lunch time.

"Congratulations, Kinsley," a girl in my first period class says, enthusiastically, as she passes me in the hallway.

"Thanks," I mumble.

"Kinsley West, where have you been all my life," Becca says, as she shoves a couple books into her locker. "You missed one heck of a morning."

"Congratulations, Kinsley," two more girls say, as they pass by on their way to the cafeteria.

Perplexed, I look to Becca for answers. "What's everyone congratulating me for?"

Becca smiles, looking like she's about to jump out of her skin. "Had you not been playing hooky, you'd know you were nominated for Homecoming Queen. You're on the ballot, Kinsley. Can you believe it?"

I lean against my locker, stunned. "No, I can't. How did I

make the court?"

"Who cares how you made it. You made it, that's all that matters. The dance will be even better now. Plus, you get to walk on the field at halftime."

"Do I have to do it?"

She stares at me like I've lost my mind. "I'll pretend you didn't say that. Of course you have to do it. We'll get you a nice business suit for the game, and then you have to find an escort since well, you know. There's so much we have to do. Oh, and your dress for the dance. You picked one out, right?"

"No, not yet." I couldn't go dress shopping the night Becca was going with her mom. On top of the mound of school work I had to finish, I also had to put in a couple hours at the diner.

"Kinsley, the dance is in a couple days. You need to get something as soon as possible. This is a big deal."

"I don't have an escort, Becca. I don't have a father to walk me down the fifty yard line like the other girls. My brother is going to be getting ready for a game the following night, so he won't be allowed to leave campus, and Rhett's on the team, so he's out."

"There's gotta be someone who can do it. Maybe my dad can walk you."

I wave her suggestion off with my hand, dismissing her idea entirely. "No, that's ridiculous." There's only one other person I can think of. Only it's not going to fly with Rhett—even if he is my only other option. "Maybe Carson can help."

Mandi picks that exact time to pass by me, snickering at my predicament. "Just give it up, Kinsley. It wasn't meant to be."

Becca lunges at her with her history book that weighs at least three pounds raised above her head. "I swear if you don't shut that trap of yours, Mandi, I'm going to shut it for you," she threatens.

"Keep talking, little girl," she says, as she walks farther down the hallway.

After I slam my locker door a little too loudly, Becca lowers the book, and takes a deep breath. "I almost beat her. My god, I was so close to whacking her over the head with my book."

"It was pretty badass, Becca," I tease, still laughing at her dazed expression, and how easily she morphed from my sweet, best friend into a lunatic.

"Thank you, but don't worry, Kins, you'll figure it out."

"What will you figure out?" Rhett asks, as he sneaks up behind me, wrapping his arms around me, and kisses my neck. "I missed you in class this morning, Sunny."

I melt into his body, the only place I want to be right now. Everything's easier when it's just the two of us. "Sorry, I hated missing, but I was so tired I couldn't keep my eyes open."

"They would have been open if I was with you," he whispers.

My cheeks heat instantly. The physical side of our relationship has been building over the past couple weeks, ever since our night together in the barn. Each time we're alone, we go a little farther, still never going the entire way. But I feel like it's going to happen soon—and I'm really nervous about it.

Thankfully, Rhett's public displays of affection never seem to bother Becca, even if she does roll her eyes, as she watches the two us. "It's sickening, guys. Just plain sickening. It's a good thing I didn't eat my lunch yet."

Rhett unwraps himself from my body, and takes my hand in his, pulling me along. "Come on. Let's go eat before Becca loses it. I've seen her throw up before. It's not pretty."

She reaches out to punch him, but he dodges her fist before it makes contact with his bicep. "You *made me* throw up dirt, Rhett Taylor!"

He walks backwards in front us, smiling at how easy it is to get Becca worked up. "I thought you said she was over it, Sunny?"

"She's being violent today."

"I almost kicked Mandi's ass with a book," she says proudly.

Rhett shakes his head, mostly because a book being her weapon of choice wouldn't be that strange. Not when she's always reading one.

Thankfully, Becca calms down by the time we get to the cafeteria. Considering I haven't eaten yet today, and it's noon, I grab a little more than usual. But once we sit at our usual table in the corner, the pizza in front of me isn't that appetizing. I'm too worried about dress shopping and my escort for the game on Friday night. I have no idea how I'll figure it out in time.

Rhett notices I'm not my usual self, and he leans closer to me. "What's wrong? I thought you'd be excited about being on the court."

As exciting as it is to be nominated, it's not worth the fight I'll get into with him when I bring up Carson, or the glare I'm getting from Mandi right now. She looks like she's about to make my life more difficult. And she does, as soon as she opens her mouth. "Who's your escort, Kinsley?" she asks, loud enough for the entire table to hear. After she's proud of her work she mumbles to her groupies, "Not that she'll actually win."

I don't sit and cower. No, this time, I speak up right away. I'm tired of her running her mouth like I'm trash. "Not that I owe you an explanation, but it's not about winning, Mandi. I'm happy to be nominated."

She tosses her napkin on her tray. "Oh please, anyone who knows they're going to lose would say that. I mean, everyone wants to win. Though I'd understand if you backed out considering your situation and all."

Rhett slaps his hand on the table, startling me. "Sorry, Sunny," he says, before giving her a warning glare icy enough to freeze the bitch right out of her.

Of course, she doesn't do anything other than roll her eyes at him. "It's getting old, Rhett. I can't believe you're not bored yet."

"Mandi," he says through gritted teeth. "I've listened to you spew your bullshit for weeks. Enough already. I don't even know why you sit here if we make you that miserable."

"Rhett," she says, with her head tilted to the side, her fake eyelashes batting like the little tramp she is. "You know why I sit here. I've always sat with you."

"You and I aren't getting back together, Mandi. Going out with you was a big mistake—the couple times I did it."

Her eyes glaze over as she listens to him tell her there's no chance for the two of them. I know better than most how much the truth hurts. It's probably why I manage to feel a little bit sorry for her despite the way she treats me.

She blinks away her tears, locking up her emotions before anyone else can see her disappointment. "Fine," she says. "But when Kinsley screws you over for her crazy hot, house pet, I won't take you back, Rhett. You had your chance."

As always, she's not satisfied until she has the last word. And Rhett lets her have it—mostly because he's looking at me like I have some explaining to do. It's all too much to handle, and now I wish I wouldn't have come to school at all today. "I'm not feeling very well," I mumble quickly, as I get up from the table, hurrying to the trash can to dump my uneaten lunch.

Once my tray is returned, I lock myself in the handicap bathroom stall outside the cafeteria. I crouch down in the corner, just trying to breathe. Then, I see his sneakers before I hear him. "Sunny, open the door."

Why does he keep coming in here where he doesn't belong? "I'll be out in a minute."

He knocks on the door again. "Please, open it."

I reach up, flipping the metal lock, and the door opens without even having to touch it. Rhett slides in, locking it behind him before squatting down next to me. "What's going on?"

"I'm just stressed out. That's all."

"What was Mandi talking about?"

I shrug my shoulders. "I don't know. I guess she overheard me talking to Becca in the hallway."

He reaches for my hand, bringing it to his lips. "Did something happen at home?"

"No." I never told Rhett about the conversations I had with Carson, the night he told me he wanted me to be with him, but there's been no reason to. Carson's been on his best behavior. I can't tell if he's biding his time, waiting for Rhett and me to break up, or if he's finally accepted a friendship is the only kind of relationship we'll ever have. Either way, by backing off, it's made my life a little easier.

"Then what's going on? Talk to me."

I sigh, wishing it didn't have to be like this. It's a risk even bringing it up, but if I plan to get through the night in one piece, with Mandi nearby, he's the only one I want by my side since Rhett can't be there. "I want to ask Carson to be my escort."

Rhett blinks a couple times, but doesn't respond right away. When he does, his voice sounds like I knocked the wind out of him. "Why would you ask him?"

"Because I don't have anyone else," I whisper.

"What if I don't want you to ask him?" His words are soft, not at all mean or spiteful like I was expecting—only vulnerable.

"Then I won't go."

He stands up, and pinches the bridge of his nose. Now that I've stressed him out, I expect him to reach for the latch and leave, but he doesn't. He waits me out.

"It's just one night. It won't mean anything, Rhett."

"If it doesn't mean anything, then why does it feel like such a big deal?"

"I don't know. I'm not trying to hurt you, but I don't want to look like a fool, either."

"How would you feel if I was escorting Mandi for the whole school and town to see? They'd think we're a couple. Is that what you want people to think about you and Carson?"

"Of course not. Everyone in this school knows I'm with you. They see us together every single day." My chin quivers as I try to spell it out for him. I don't want to cry, but on top of being confused, I'm angry. It's not Rhett I'm angry with though—it's my dad.

"That's not how it's going to look Friday night, Sunny. They'll see my girlfriend with another guy—a guy that she lives with."

"You know what I want?" I try to hold it in the best I can, but my body doesn't let me. Hot tears spill from my eyes, leaving a trail down both my cheeks. It's been awhile since I cried like this—let it all go without caring who sees or hears me.

"Sunny, please don't cry." Rhett kneels down beside me, reaching for me, but I stop him before he can touch me. Right now, I don't want to be comforted. I want to feel the anger inside me because it only hurts more to act like it doesn't exist. I'm tired of pretending I'm a normal teenager with normal teenager problems. What other girl on the court has to deal with this?

I choke out a sob, "I need my dad to come back, Rhett. That's what I want. Then I wouldn't have to worry about finding a replacement for him. I shouldn't need a replacement for a man who's still alive. He's supposed to be here."

"I'll figure something out. I'll talk to Coach and see if I can leave the locker room at halftime to be with you. I want to be with you, Kinsley. Okay?"

I swipe my tears off my cheeks before reaching for some toilet paper to blow my nose. It's not the least bit attractive, but I don't really care. "Don't worry about it," I tell him. "I didn't want to go in the first place. Betty has me on the schedule anyway. It's a really busy night for the diner."

I lie about the last part. Betty insisted I take the weekend off to do normal high school activities. Little does she know, now that I've made the homecoming court, I'm planning on staying home.

"Don't lie to me, Kinsley."

I push Rhett out of the way, but he doesn't budge. "What is your problem?"

"I'm not going to let you do this. You deserve to be on the court, whether the crown ends up on your head or not. I already know you're not working. You have no reason not to show up to the game."

"And how would you know my schedule?"

He turns his head away from me, and I know this next part is going to be interesting. "Because I'm the one who made sure it happened. I went in there the other day and asked Betty to give you the time off. With Fall Fest the following weekend, I figured you'd try to work through homecoming to make up the difference."

I'm shocked—completely and utterly shocked. It's a sweet gesture, but he has no right going behind my back like that. He doesn't understand how much money I'm losing by taking two weekends off in a row. Not to mention I'm spending a lot of the money that needs to be put towards bills on two outfits to wear to some stupid football game and dance.

I was defeated when I left the cafeteria, then sad when I came in the bathroom stall, but now I'm just pissed off. I'm over it. I'm over the idea of being queen of a school that never accepted me until I started dating their star athlete. "I'm going home."

"You just got here."

"And it was a mistake coming in." I push around him, realizing we have an audience as at least ten other girls listen to our conversation while they pretend to fix their hair in front of the mirrors.

"Sunny, wait. Please."

"I can't."

"Stay here, then. Talk to me. You know I can't leave. I'll get benched if I skip."

Right now, I want to be far away from him. I'm mad at him for not accepting Carson when I need him, and I'm mad that I even have to choose Carson in the first place. But the one I'm the most angry with could be almost anywhere in the world right now—my father.

Rhett continues to plead with me the entire way to the lobby, but nothing he could say would ever convince me to stay—not when I feel this low. When I glance back at the school, he's still there watching me leave with his hands against the glass of the door. I don't have a good view of his face, but even from here, I can tell how disappointed he is.

By the time I get home, I'm still trying to calm myself down. Carson's getting out of his car, and I quickly check to see if my red eyes are still puffy. He catches me looking in the mirror, even though I try to hide it. He taps on the window, nodding his head toward the house—my signal that he wants me to go inside with him.

"Where were you?" he asks, as I get out of my car.

"School. It was a big mistake."

"Still not feeling well?"

I shake my head. "I'm okay. It's been a bad day though—they nominated me for homecoming court. Now I have all these responsibilities and outfits to buy. It's ridiculous."

"Don't most girls go ape shit for that stuff?"

"I'm not most girls, I guess."

We walk up the stairs to the apartment, side by side. He unlocks the door, and pushes it open, allowing me to go inside first. After we dump our stuff in our rooms, we both end up on opposite ends of the couch, like usual.

"Wanna tell me about it?"

"Not much to tell."

He raises his eyebrows, not buying my answer at all. "You

don't cry unless you're upset."

I grab the throw pillow next to me, hugging it close to my body. "Rhett and I argued after Mandi said some stuff at lunch. Long story short, it was one giant disagreement and here I am."

"What did you argue about?"

I chew on my lip, not sure I want to open this can of worms, but it's Carson, and we've had talks like these so many times before—even if he wasn't normally part of the problem. "You mostly. I told him I was considering asking you to be my escort."

"I don't imagine that went over well."

"It didn't," I tell him, still able to hear Rhett's disappointment as he spoke to me in the bathroom stall.

He taps my leg with his foot, forcing me to look at him. When I do, his warm brown eyes swallow me up when he says, "You know I'll do it. If you want me there, all you have to do is ask."

I look away, suddenly interested in the stitching of the pillow I'm holding. "Thanks, I haven't decided what I'm going to do yet. I told Rhett I wasn't going to go if you weren't with me. He didn't like that either."

"Wow, you did have a rough afternoon. Why don't we go to the mall? Retail therapy always helps."

I'm hesitant, but I do need a dress at the very least. "You actually want to go shopping? Isn't that torture for you? Wyatt used to moan and groan when I'd ask him to take me."

He stares at me, rolling his eyes. "Wyatt's high maintenance, but I'm here to help you. You need clothes don't you?"

"Yes, I need a dress for the dance and a business suit for the game. I still don't know why we have to look like a bunch of secretaries at a football game, but it's tradition."

"See, you need shit. So, if you want to go, lets do it."

I smile, thankful he volunteered himself. Chances are, I wouldn't have ever gone on my own. "Okay, but when you've had enough, just say the words, and we can leave."

"I promise I'll survive."

THE MALL IS pretty empty considering it's only one o'clock in the afternoon on a school day. We even get a parking spot close to the main entrance. "Where do you want to go first?" Carson asks, as he walks around the back end of his car.

"I have no idea. First place we come to, I guess."

We cross the parking lot, and walk with purpose down the corridor inside the mall. Carson laughs when the first store is in front of us. "I'm not sure this is going to cut it."

"Okay, let me rephrase that. First store that sells dresses." We're standing in front of Hot Topic of all places. The exact opposite of what I'm looking for.

After walking for a couple more minutes, we're inside Macy's, heading toward the juniors' department. I browse the racks, and once I have three choices in my hands, we find the nearest dressing room.

There's a chair next to the entrance, and Carson plops into it. "Go for it," he says. "Toss'em out to me if you don't like them."

"How are you so good at this? It almost seems like you like shopping."

He smiles. "I like shopping with you, Kins. There's a difference. Plus, you forget I have three older sisters. I've been through this show more than once."

"I'll hurry," I tell him, as I slip inside the first dressing room. I wish I had enough time to make something of my own, but with work and school, plus my assignments, I'll never get it done in time.

I unzip the first dress, a bright blue taffeta with a halter style neck. Stepping into it, I pull it up and over my hips, but when I pull the zipper up, it's a little too snug.

A full-length, black satin dress is next. The fabric is cool against my skin, even giving me goosebumps as it trails down my legs to the floor. Right away I know it's not the one. This too, goes back on the hanger.

They say the third times the charm, and I think it might be when I slide into a white dress with three-quarter length sleeves, a cut-out back, and silver, sequin scrollwork. The hem hits mid-thigh, and though it's shorter than I imagined myself wearing, it's my favorite.

"Are you planning on showing me any of the dresses?" Carson asks, as he sticks his head around the corner so I can hear him.

I open my door, running my hands down the front of the dress, making sure the sequins are lying flat against the material of the dress. "The first two didn't work, but I think I like this one."

"Shit," Carson says, catching my attention.

When I look at him, his eyes are fixated on my legs, and they slowly work their way up the rest of my body. He says nothing, just continues to stare at me with a nearly blank expression. "It's too short, isn't it? I can try on another one. Just let me get changed."

He shakes his head, words failing him. "No," he mumbles.

"Tell me the truth. I want your honest opinion."

Finally, he says, "You look amazing, Kinsley. That's the one."

"Really?"

He holds out his hand, and I walk toward him. "You want the truth?"

I nod my head. "Always."

"Okay, the truth." He pauses for a moment, and I have no idea where his mind is. Wherever it is, it looks pretty serious. "Rhett's a lucky guy. I hope he knows it."

I take my hand out of his, letting it drop to my side. "I hope so too, Carson."

Like he's trying to pull himself out of a fog, he blinks a couple times. I catch my reflection in the mirror once more before walking back into my dressing room. Closing the door, I lean against it, needing a second to shake off whatever just happened out there.

I take my time getting changed. I even fiddle with my phone for a couple minutes, but reception is spotty inside the store, and my wi-fi doesn't even work. When I can't stall any longer, I leave my safety net.

"Carson?" He's no longer sitting in his chair. In fact, I don't see him anywhere. *Where'd he go?*

"Over here."

I follow his voice, and find him with a pair of shoes in his hand. "What are you doing?"

"This is always the next stop, right?"

I look at what he's holding and realize they'd match my dress. "I was going to borrow a pair of Kate's."

"Na," he says. "Pick out ones you want. They're on me."

"No, Carson. I can't let you do that. You bringing me here was enough."

He pins me with his stare. "Tough. I'm buying."

I don't bother arguing, considering he doesn't look like he's going to budge. I browse the rest of the shoes, but end up coming back to the ones he showed me first. They're perfect—and now it's really obvious he's done this before.

We go to one more store, The Loft, before I leave with an outfit so sophisticated, I'll probably wear it to a job interview someday.

"We make a good team, Kinsley. I'm just sorry I won't get to see you in any of this."

"You won't be here this weekend?"

"I was planning on leaving Friday afternoon for Penn State to watch Wyatt play on Saturday, but if you need me, I'll wait and go on Saturday."

"Oh. That'll be fun." I try to hide my disappointment that he's not going to be around, but he sees it, even if he assumes it's because I'm not going to get to see my brother.

"Maybe one weekend you don't have plans, we can go up together and catch a game."

"Really? I'd love that." It's been Wyatt's dream to play for Penn State since we were little. Being able to see that for myself, would be amazing. Especially since I know how much it bothers him that his parents aren't there to see his dream come true.

"You got it, we'll figure out which game when we get home, and then make it happen."

"You're the best, Carson. Seriously."

"I'd do anything for my best friend." He accentuates the friend part of his statement, reminding me the friend zone is the last place he wants to be; let alone stay.

Rhett's not going to like it if I go away with Carson for even an hour. Which is why I panic a little when we pull into my driveway, and he's sitting on the stairs leading to my apartment—waiting for me.

CHAPTER FIFTEEN

rhett

I EXPECTED TO find Kinsley asleep when I got to her apartment. What I didn't expect, was to find her car sitting in the driveway while she's nowhere to be found. She hasn't answered any of my texts since she left school, and my calls went straight to voicemail.

It's not like her to ignore me.

All I can picture in my head are her tears, and the way she fought to keep it together, even though she was out of breath, and practically hiccupping. When she told me all she wanted was for her dad to come home, I hurt for her. I can't even begin to imagine what it would be like to be in high school without parents. Mine may drive me crazy sometimes, my mom over-protective, and my dad always expecting the best from me, but to not have them—it's unimaginable.

Most days, she hides her pain well, but today, it came tumbling out of her—and it killed me. Though I don't feel quite as torn up when Carson's car pulls in next to Kinsley's and she's in the passenger seat, laughing at whatever he's saying to her.

Suddenly, I'm more possessive than I ever thought possible, cracking my knuckles and grinding my fist into my palm. She's *my* girl, and he's testing my patience. I've tried my best to overlook their roommate status, even told myself I was overreacting or making something out of nothing, but this is proof that Carson has an agenda of his own that has nothing to do with honoring my relationship with Kinsley.

Better yet, they're so wrapped up in their conversation, neither of them spot me until they're practically on top of me. Kinsley doesn't notice until she almost falls into my lap. "Rhett, you scared me. What are you doing here?"

"I was worried about you," I say, with my eyes directly on Carson's. He gets the hint, and moves past me, carrying a bunch of bags in his hand.

"I'll be inside, Kinsley."

"Okay," she responds quickly before sitting on the step below me, her body angled toward mine. "You're mad, aren't you?" she asks, nervously.

I think about how I want to answer her before I say something I'll regret. The more I think about it, it's not her I'm really mad at—it's Carson. Considering they live together, he has so many opportunities to take advantage of her situation, and it bothers the piss out of me. Plain and simple. "I'm trying to keep my cool."

"I had to leave school, Rhett. I'm sorry. I just couldn't do it today."

"I get that. We all need a break sometimes, but you ran from me to him, Sunny."

She reaches for me, and all I want to do is hold onto her, but I can't pretend her being with him doesn't bother me. If I don't speak up now, I risk losing the only girl who's ever meant something to me because I didn't fight hard enough to keep her when I had her.

When I don't accept her into my open arms, she sits back down on the step, completely defeated. "Don't do this, Rhett. I didn't run to him."

"I can't help the way it looks, Sunny. Watching you run away from me today—again, hurt like hell. I wanted to be the one to put a smile back on your face. I wanted to be the one you needed."

"You are all those things. It was his idea to go to the mall, not mine. I was content going back to bed and waiting until school was over to talk to you, but I needed clothes. Clothes for a weekend I don't even want to deal with."

"Then why go?"

"Because I have to. Look, Rhett. All Carson did was drive me to the mall. It's the kind of thing my brother would do for me if he wasn't away at school."

Hearing her compare Carson to Wyatt, helps some. It still doesn't take away all the time they spent together, but I can't stay mad at her. It's my job to build her up, not tear her down. So, I swallow my pride and get over my jealousy so we can move on. "Okay."

"Okay?" she questions. "You're not mad anymore?"

I only have one question for her. The way she answers will determine if I'm mad or not. "Did anything happen? I mean *anything*, Kinsley—no matter how big or small."

Without pausing or thinking about her response, she gives me a resounding, "No."

"Okay, then I'm not mad at you. I trust you."

She stands up, and climbs into my lap, wrapping her arms around my neck. "Thank you for believing me."

And I do believe her. There's no proof for me not to. I only hope it stays that way. "Did you get a dress?"

Finally, she smiles. "Yes! And a suit for the game. Shoes, too."

"Do you feel better about the court now?"

"Yes and no. I have clothes to wear, but the escort is still a problem."

I pull a piece of her hair out of her eye, debating if I want to bring up Carson again. "Did you ask anyone?"

She shakes her head. "I told Carson about it, but I didn't ask him. You said you'd help me figure it out, so I thought I'd wait and see."

That's what I wanted to hear. "We'll figure it out."

She glances at the time on her cell phone. "Aren't you late for practice?"

"They think I'm still at physical therapy." I finished my final session last week, but I didn't tell Coach yet. As far as he knows, I'm still going a couple times a week to work on the back pain I can't seem to shake.

"Do you have to go back, or can you stay for a little? I can make you something to eat if you're hungry."

I trace the outline of her lips with the tip of my finger, remembering how sweet they taste. "As much as I want to stay, I can't. If I don't show up, I won't hear the end of it."

"Will you call me later?"

"Do you even need to ask?" I can't sleep if I don't hear her voice. I've gotten so used to talking late at night, it would be weird if it didn't happen. "Now, go inside before I toss you in my truck."

She giggles like it might not be such a bad thing to have happen, and before she leaves the warmth of my arms, she leans in for one more kiss. "You're killing me, Sunny."

"Sorry, you should probably leave before we get carried away."

I stand up and set her back on her feet. "Leaving you is always the worst part of my day. Talk to you soon, gorgeous."

She smiles adorably before turning and walking inside her apartment. I glance at the window in the kitchen before I go, and spot Carson staring back at me. He smirks, and it takes all I have to keep walking toward my truck. I even debate going back for Kinsley, but I have to trust her—I just told her I have faith in her. Though it's not her I'm worried about. It's Carson.

He'll get what he has coming—that much I'm sure of.

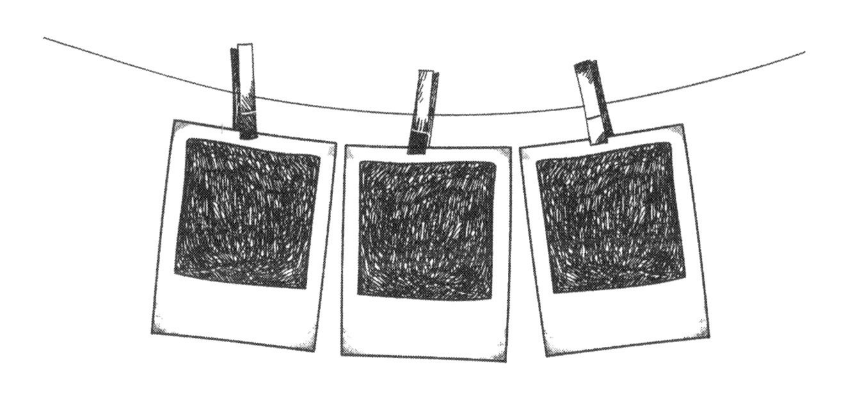

CHAPTER SIXTEEN

kinsley

BY THE TIME the end of the week rolls around, I'm so nervous about homecoming, I'd rather hide in my room and never come back out. I've asked Rhett a million times if he's allowed to be my escort, but each time I ask, he simply says he has it covered and not to worry. Well, guess what? I am worrying. Especially since the game starts in two hours, and I'm still without a clue as to what's going on.

My hair's curled, my skirt and blazer are on, and a pair of Kate's boots are on my feet. I look the part, but the most important part of this equation is still missing.

"Kinsley," Kate calls from the hallway. She's going into work late just so she can take some pictures of my special night. I'm bummed she couldn't sit in the stands tonight, but her job is more important than some silly high school football game.

"Coming." Of course I fidget with my skirt, and itch at my tights. This is as good as it's going to get. When I round the corner of the living room, my night completely changes.

"Wyatt? You can't be here. You have a game tomorrow—a big one."

There's a collective chuckle from Kate, Wyatt, and Carson before Wyatt walks over to me. "I'll still be at my game, Kinny. Don't worry about me. Tonight is all about my little sister."

"I don't understand. What are you doing here?"

"I called him," Rhett says, surprising me for the second time in as many minutes.

I turn my head toward him, completely blown away he'd do something like that for me. "Are you serious?"

"Rhett called me a couple days ago." He pauses, laughing a little before continuing. "I honestly thought I was going to have to knock some heads around, but he told me about the homecoming court. I wasn't about to let my little sister walk down the fifty yard line without me."

"Did you tell Carson to take me shopping?"

"That was all him," Wyatt says.

"You mean all of you were in on this in one way or another, and nobody got hurt? Nobody threw any punches?"

"Not a single one," Rhett adds, proudly.

My mascara's going to run, but I'll have to fix it, because the tears that are falling from my eyes aren't going to stop anytime soon. The closest thing I'll ever have to a complete family stands before me, and they've just given me the best surprise I could ever ask for. "Thank you," I whisper, around a sob. "I've missed you so much, Wyatt."

Wyatt opens his arms and I practically fall into them. I've missed my brother and the security he's always given me. I didn't realize how much I depended on him until he wasn't here.

"Don't cry, Kinny."

Rhett clears his throat, and I pull my head off Wyatt's chest to look at him. "I'm sorry," he says. "But, I have to get going."

I swipe my tears off my cheeks, nodding my head. "Yes, go. You can't be late." As I stare into his green orbs, the magnitude of what he did for me—how much courage it took to call my older brother hits me. More tears follow the ones I've already gotten rid of. "Thank you, Rhett. I didn't' expect any of this to happen. I can't believe you risked bodily harm for me."

He cups my cheek in his hand. "I'd risk it all for you, Sunny."

Without even thinking, the words tumble out of me like they've been waiting for this moment to be spoken. "I love you."

He sucks in a breath as my words slam into him. I panic when I realize I can't take them back, but Rhett doesn't seem like it's a mistake. He simply tips my chin up with his finger so I have no choice but to look him in the eye. He doesn't move at first, but slowly, he leans closer to place one soft kiss to my lips. "I was made to love you, Kinsley West. We were always meant to be."

Another tear falls from my eyes, and I don't even care we have an audience. "You look beautiful. I'll see you after the game."

"See ya," I whisper.

All the eyes in the room follow Rhett as he turns around and walks out of the apartment. Once he's gone, they all focus on me. I wait for my brother to yell, to tell me there's no way I could be in love with Rhett Taylor, but the words never come. His expression only softens when he sees my tears continuing to fall.

Kate stands with her hand over her heart with tears welling up in her eyes. She manages to take one last picture of me standing next to Wyatt before she tosses her phone in her purse, and hurries out the front door without saying a single word. She doesn't have to though. I already know she's proud of me and how far we've all come.

Wyatt rubs my back when I stare at the front door a little too long after both Rhett and Kate are gone. "We have a few minutes before we have to leave. Can we talk for a minute, Kins?"

"Sure."

We walk to the couch, and when we're both comfortable, he begins. "That was intense."

"It just came out, I didn't plan it."

"I know you didn't. I could tell it was as much of a surprise to you as it was for the rest of us—it's the only reason I didn't interrupt your moment."

"You're okay with it?"

"I guess I have to be. You can't help who you love."

He couldn't be more right about that, but he's not specifically taking about me, he's also talking about himself. "You need to talk to Becca."

"Am I that obvious?" He pops open the button on his suit jacket, not enjoying being dressed up any more than I am.

"She mentioned you've been talking."

"It's really not a big deal."

"To me it is. I care about you both, and you two have been tip-toeing around a relationship for what seems like forever." He neither agrees or disagrees with me. He just stares at the coffee table. "I take it you haven't met any other girls on campus?"

"I've met plenty—kind of hard not to in the dorms, but I'm not dating anyone. I barely have time to breathe outside of football."

"But you find time to talk to Becca."

"There's just something about that girl. I can't for the life of me figure it out, but I can't stop thinking about her. And it's screwing with my head."

"Maybe she reminds you of home. What do you guys talk

about?"

"School, our classes—she's concerned about my math grade. I don't have the heart to tell her I'm actually really good at math."

"I think she's known all along, but she enjoyed tutoring you too much to say anything."

"Maybe. Has she been talking to any guys at school?"

I swallow, wondering how I can talk myself out of this. If I tell Wyatt the truth, Becca will kill me. But if I keep it from my brother, I'll be the worst sister—especially after what he's done for me by coming home. I owe him the truth at the very least. "She's sort of with Jake."

Like he's seen a ghost, his face pales. "Why is she with that douchebag? She could do ten times better than him."

I don't want to get into the middle of this mess, but at the same time, I'm happy to see him pissed off. Maybe this is what he needs to finally speak up and go after Becca. Now that he has competition, there's a chance he'll lose her completely. "It's been a couple weeks. They're not serious or anything, but they hang out at the football parties and talk at school."

"Is she screwing him?"

My eyes nearly pop out of my head. "Becca? No way. She stayed with him a couple parties ago after he got too drunk to drive her home, but nothing happened. Even Rhett made sure."

He stands from the couch, fists opening and closing like he's on the verge of punching a hole through the wall. "She slept in his bed—with him?"

"For a little, maybe."

"Jesus Christ." Yanking his phone from his pocket, he paces back and forth, typing text after text.

There's no time for me to warn Becca. I already know she's the one he's texting. All I can do is drag him to this football game and hope he's able to work it out with her by the time he goes back to school. "We have to go, Wyatt."

He stuffs his phone back in his pocket, but not before huffing at the screen. "Right, yeah. Come on, Kinny."

I try making conversation the entire way to the field, but Wyatt's distracted. He drives on auto-pilot to the field he's played on for years. Only this time, he goes back as a starter for the Penn State Nittany Lions.

As soon as we're through the gates, it's like an announcement was made that he's arrived. All eyes are on him, and kids rush to him with questions about football as they ask for autographs. My brother is even more of a big deal in this town than he was a year ago.

He's polite to each and every kid, even making small talk with a few parents. I couldn't be more proud of him. "I'll be in the stands, take your time," I tell him before walking to find the reserved section I'll be sitting in.

I'm spreading my blanket over the cold metal bleacher when I hear my best friend before I see her. "Kinsley West, you look amazing!" Becca jogs up the few stairs, hugging me tightly. "Even if you don't win, I'm so proud of you, but I swear, if Mandi wins, I'll shove that crown down her throat. I can't listen to her brag for the rest of the year."

I laugh, mostly because she's serious, but I also need to have a little talk with her about my brother. "You're not mad at me?" I ask cautiously.

"Oh, I'm pissed, but I'm not going to ruin this night for you. I'll deal with Wyatt if he messages me tonight. I'm sure he's busy with football."

"About that," I start to say, but she stops me.

"No, first you're telling me about Rhett. Don't skip any details."

I decide to talk as fast as I can so I have a chance to tell her about Wyatt before he gets here and surprises her all on his own. "It was actually a little bit of a disaster, Becca. First I get a case of verbal diarrhea and tell Rhett I love him, and then I told

Wyatt about Jake."

"What! Did he say it back?" she asks, curiously, completing ignoring my comment about my brother. "I can't believe this."

That makes two of us. "Once I said it, it was perfect—like a movie. He told me he loves me, too, and I really think he meant it. It feels different now. It's like we're on a new level or something. I can't really describe it."

She's staring at me, hanging on my every word. Becca's always been the real romantic out of the two of us. I always thought it would be her falling in love first. But, before I can talk about Wyatt, and inform her he's here, he climbs up the stairs and stands right next to her. "Hey, Becca."

She whips around so fast, she almost falls over. "Wyatt? Ohmigod!" Her face lights up like she's just been reunited with her other half. I've never seen her look at Jake that way—not even once.

My brother's noticeably mad, but he lets her hug him, all while biting his tongue. It's not going to last long though, I can tell. "Nice jersey," he says coolly.

She pulls away from him, her smile falling. "I'm glad you're here," is all she says. Ignoring the comment entirely

"Are you?"

Becca glances at me, but I pretend to be oblivious. "Of course I am. It's been awhile since I've seen you."

Wyatt points to Jake's jersey. "Couldn't have missed me too much."

She glances at the number scrawled across her chest. "It's not what you think, Wyatt."

He sits down backward on the bleacher in front of us, his head bowed at first. When he raises his eyes, they land directly on Becca's. "You couldn't possibly know what I'm thinking. If you did, you wouldn't be walking around in that thing." It's a spiteful response—one I wish he wouldn't give her, but he can't help himself.

It only gets worse when the team jogs onto the field for their pregame warm-up with Jake front and center. He watches as Becca returns Jake's wave, and any control he was holding onto, disappears. "Why are you wasting your time on him?"

She crosses her arms over her chest, protectively, looking down at the ground. "It just happened."

"Yeah? So, it's okay if I just happen with some girl in my dorm then?"

Her eyes land on his and her sadness is gone. In its place is jealousy. "How do I know that hasn't already happened? I mean, look at you. You've never had a hard time getting attention from girls."

He tosses his hands in the air. "You're right, Becca. I could have any number of girls, no questions asked. Yet somehow the one girl I've had my eye on wants nothing to do with me. How do you explain that one?"

"You really want to do this right now? Here in the stadium?"

"That's just it, Bec. There's never a right time with you. You're always pushing me away, and you know what, maybe I should take the hint. Maybe I should give up on you and go have some fun. That's what you want, isn't it?"

She turns her head away from him, shaking her head. "That's not what I want. Jake and I aren't serious. He's fun to hang out with, that's all."

"Do you know how many fun girls there are, Becca? Does that mean I get to waste time with all of them while I wait for you?"

"No, Wyatt. It doesn't. But what am I supposed to do? Sit around and miss out on every senior year experience because you're two hours away and can't do any of them with me?"

His eyes narrow, like he might finally understand where she's coming from. Becca being with Jake has absolutely nothing to do with Wyatt—even I know that. But all my brother sees is someone else with his girl. He's never going to be okay with it which is why this isn't the best place to be having this conversation. The stands are getting fuller, and they're only drawing negative attention. As much as I don't want to get in the middle, I stand up and put an end to it. "Wyatt, we have to go for pictures."

He pulls his gaze away from Becca, reluctantly standing up to join me. "Come on, I'll help you down."

His hand reaches out for mine, but I wait a second, looking between the two of them. I hate seeing them at each other's throats when all they'd have to do is take a chance. If it doesn't work out, at least they can say they tried. "You guys need to finish this conversation before Wyatt goes back to school, okay? I don't want the two people I love the most arguing. You're both stubborn fools who need to get over yourselves and admit you want to be together."

"I've done that, Kinsley. She doesn't seem to care," Wyatt argues.

"Look at her, Wyatt. Take a long, hard look. Becca wouldn't be on the verge of tears if she didn't care about you." He glances in her direction, but she lowers her head, trying her best to avoid making eye contact while she's hurting. "It's senior year, and she doesn't want to spend it missing you. Maybe it's not the best choice, but it's one she's going to have to live with unless she comes to her senses and admits she's in love with you."

Becca gasps, her hand covering her mouth. "I can't believe you said that, Kinsley." Becca says, completely shocked. Even so, she doesn't deny a word I said. All she does is flip her hair over her shoulder and stomp toward the end zone to sit with the rest of the student body.

Wyatt chuckles at her reaction. "Why do I like her more when she's feisty?" He watches her the entire way to her seat before she's sucked up in the crowd.

THE FIRST TWO quarters drag a little, but only because I'm ready to be done with the halftime festivities. When it's time for us to take our place on the visiting side of the field, we form a line in alphabetical order, leaving me dead last.

I hook my arm though Wyatt's, and he gives my hand an extra squeeze. "They saved the best for last, Kinny." I smile, thankful I have the best brother in the world. One who would throw away his Friday night to come back home to rescue his little sister. He can be intense, insanely stubborn, and even a little cocky at times, but when it comes to his family, he'd move mountains for the ones he loves.

The announcer in the press box begins the introductions, and inch by inch, the line grows shorter as each couple makes their way toward the home side of the field. I'm not expecting to win, and I don't. This entire experience has been about giving credit where credit's due, and tonight that credit went to the right girl.

Once we're seated in the stands, and the third quarter begins, I lean my head against Wyatt's shoulder, finally able to breathe again. Part of me is a little sad my parents weren't here to watch their little girl, but there's no use letting it get to me because in the morning, my situation will still be the same. My mom couldn't help her fate, and maybe someday my dad will realize how much he missed out on and come home.

Maybe.

"Don't think about it too much, Kinny. I know it's not easy. When I took the field at Beaver Stadium for the first time, I almost lost my mind. All those afternoons Dad spent with me in the back yard, teaching me the fundamentals, and he wasn't even there to see my hard work pay off—his hard work."

"Mom's watching, Wyatt. She's really proud of you."

He squeezes my hand. "I hope so. I'm trying to be the man of the family, Kins. I really am. The last thing I want is for us to fall apart, too. You and Kate are all I have."

"We're doing well, Wyatt. I promise. I have Rhett and we both have Carson."

"I tried like hell to keep all those guys away from you, but I knew there'd be at least one who would get to you. I even had a feeling it would be Rhett."

"You're really okay with it?"

"I have to be. You and him are the kind of people that would fight to be together no matter what. It's just how you are."

"Just like you and Becca."

"I don't know about that. She's a stubborn girl, but until I have a reason to give up on her, I won't. Maybe she'll come around. Maybe she won't. But it won't be for lack of trying, that's for damn sure."

This time it's me squeezing his hand for support. "She'll come around."

The final buzzer sounds, and the stands erupt in applause for another blowout victory. It's become expected at Central—that's how good the team is year after year—even with key players like Wyatt out of the picture.

"Do you mind if I find Rhett before we leave?"

Wyatt shakes his head. "I'll go say hi to some of the guys while you talk to him. If we get split up, meet me back here. I don't want you walking all the way to the car by yourself."

"Okay, but if you run into Becca, go easy on her."

"We'll see," is all he says, as his eyes shift toward the end zone. He knows exactly where she is despite being half a field apart.

It breaks my heart to see my brother so down, but I hold onto the hope they'll figure it out. Becca thinks she's doing them a favor by not pushing a long distance relationship, but she's only hurting both of them. Some things you just have to fight for no matter how many obstacles you're facing.

"Sunny!" I turn my head to see my hot boyfriend standing next to the railing, motioning me to come onto the field with him. I snatch up my blanket, and run to him, throwing my arms around his neck. "I missed you," he whispers in my ear. His voice is low enough to give me goosebumps.

"I missed you, too. Is your back okay?" He took a hard shot, to his already sore back that left him on the ground for a few seconds too long. He jogged it off, but every single spectator in the stands could tell by the way he ran that he was hurting.

"I'm fine. It looked worse than it was. How'd halftime go?"

"The crown went to the most deserving," I say with complete confidence, now that Mandi will never get her grubby little hands on the crown.

"Molly?" Rhett asks.

"Yes! Tonight was a lot for her, with her autism and all, but she wore her headphones in the stands to block out some of the noise, and then at halftime, she held onto her dad for dear life, but, she did it. It was an honor to lose to her."

"You're pretty amazing, you know that?"

His words make me blush "Thank you for tonight—for bringing my brother home."

"You don't have to thank me. I wanted you to be happy."

"I'm deliriously happy, Rhett."

"Good. Now, how about we get out of here so I can kiss my girl without an audience."

I want nothing more than to change out of these uncomfortable clothes and spend the rest of my night in Rhett's arms, but I also want to spend some more time with my brother before he has to leave. "Will you come home with me? I was thinking about inviting Becca over, too. Those two need to finish talking, and while they do, we can hang out."

"What about Carson?"

"He's going to Penn State tomorrow, so either he already

left, or he'll probably stay in his room if the rest of us are coupled up."

"All right, I'll shower and meet you there. Wait for Wyatt though, I don't want you walking by yourself."

"You two are so alike sometimes."

"We both care a shit-ton about you, that's why." He drops my hand, and jogs toward the locker room, leaving me with a huge smile on my face.

If I knew this is what it would feel like to fall in love, I would have done it so much sooner. Then again, it wouldn't have been right unless it was Rhett. It's all the more reason why I have to get my brother and Becca on the same page. I want this for them—I always have.

While Wyatt finishes his conversation with the head coach, I type out a text to Becca.

Kinsley: Meet us at the house.

Becca: What about Jake? He expects me at the football party.

Kinsley: I don't know. Tell him you have cramps. He won't question that.

Becca: Does Wyatt want me there?

Kinsley: I want you there and you two need to talk. He knows you're coming.

Wyatt sneaks up on me as I'm typing out my last text, no doubt, reading over my shoulder. "Kinny, why are you trying to play matchmaker? Let it go."

He walks past me toward the parking lot, but I hurry to catch up with him. "It's not about playing matchmaker. My best friend isn't as happy as she could be, and my brother deserves to have everything he wants."

"I have enough."

"Oh, come on. Go ahead and tell me you don't like her. If you can do that, I'll stop getting in the middle."

"I like her, Kin. We've already established that."

"Exactly. So, stop interfering with *my* interfering."

He pulls me toward the parking lot, shaking his head. "That makes no sense, and she's not going to ditch Jake to come hang out with me."

"Wrong again brother of mine. She's coming over. I already invited her."

"Kins, I don't want Jake showing up causing trouble. Jake saw me on the field, he knows I'm here, and he'll know where Becca's going. He won't like her picking me over him tonight."

I didn't even consider that. "I can always invite Jake to come along. I'll tell Rhett to keep Jake occupied while you talk. I'll even send you to the store for food, and then Becca will go with you. That'll give you enough time to talk, right?"

Wyatt opens the car door, ushering me inside. "Just get in the car. This is turning into a production."

Maybe so, but this is one production that demands a happy ending, and I'm determined to make it happen for my brother and my best friend.

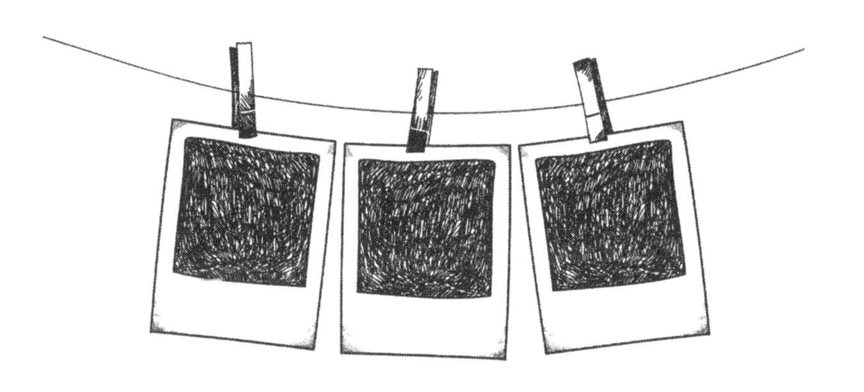

CHAPTER SEVENTEEN

rhett

"DUDE, BECCA DITCHED me for your girlfriend," Jake tells me, as we pack up our bags to head home for the night.

"Sorry, her brother's in town until tomorrow, she wants to stay in tonight."

He tosses his shirt over his head, yanking it down with a little more effort than necessary. "Wait, you're going to?"

"Kinsley asked me to come."

"You're so pussy whipped it's ridiculous."

"No, it's called being in a relationship." He can call me any name he wants because like it or not, I'm going to take the chance to hang out with Wyatt and Kinsley. I see the rest of these guys enough at as it is.

"Since the party will be lame without Becca, I'll just come with you. At least I can see her at Kinsley's."

Jake's my best friend, and I don't want him to be pissed about me choosing a girl over him, but there's no polite way to tell him he's not invited. So, I do the only thing I can—I try to make the night sound as boring as possible so he'll want to go to the football party instead. Kinsley will kill me if I show up with Jake, effectively messing up Wyatt's chance to talk to Becca. "It's not a party or anything. We'll probably watch one of her girlie movies she loves and then I'll go home."

"So I'm not invited?"

"I didn't say that, but it's just me and Kinsley."

He throws his bag over his shoulder before tossing his cleats into the bottom of his locker. "And Wyatt and Becca. Now it makes sense."

"Carson lives there, too, you know. It's not a couple's thing."

He kicks his locker closed with his foot, slamming it hard enough that it knocks over the bottles I have on the top shelf in my own locker. "That's bullshit and you know it, Rhett. Maybe I will show up—make things a little more interesting."

"Please, don't ruin this for Kinsley. She hasn't seen her brother in weeks."

"I'll behave, but if Wyatt touches Becca and you don't tell me, that's bullshit, too. Although I think I already know where your loyalties lie."

He turns and walks toward the exit, but he needs to understand I'm not the one who came up with the plans. Sure, I agree Becca and Wyatt need to have a conversation—it's been a long-time coming. It doesn't mean I want her to give up on Jake though. Bottom line, someone's going to get hurt, and I have no idea who it's going to be yet.

I catch up to Jake before he's in his truck. I'll be honest with him, and hopefully he'll do his part if he wants to have a real relationship with Becca. Because the way I see it, he's only with her so he can have a little fun. "Look, give Becca tonight to sort things out. Talk to her tomorrow and tell her how you feel. If you really want to be with her the way you say you do, it won't be hard for you to convince her."

"Since when did you become Dr. Phil? You talk like a man in love."

"Maybe I care about my best friend."

"Well, before you get all warm and fuzzy, I need to decide what I'm doing."

I open my door, but before I get inside, I encourage him not to be the asshole he's capable of being. "Go to the party, Jake. Don't screw it up before you know the facts."

He nods his head, seeming to understand where I'm coming from—that playing by the rules, even if he doesn't like them, might be the best option for him right now. Especially if he has any shot at hanging onto Becca.

But when I drive through two stop lights, and Jake's still on my tail, I realize I should probably send Kinsley a warning text that it's about to go down. Just as I'm about to send it, Jake finally comes to his senses and turns onto the last street before Kinsley's apartment.

With the drama out of the mix, I knock on Kinsley's front door with a sigh of relief. Wyatt answers, looking as frustrated as Jake did a couple minutes ago. When he lets me in, and I walk toward the living room, I see why. Becca's sitting on the sectional sofa waiting for him.

I turn toward the kitchen, not wanting to interrupt their conversation. Kinsley's standing in front of the island pouring soda into some glasses. Her hair's all piled on top of her head, and she's wearing bunny slippers on her feet. She looks adorable.

I sneak up behind her, pressing my front to her back. At first she jumps, even spilling a little of the soda she's pouring, but once she's realizes it's me, she leans against me while she finishes. "You scared me, I didn't hear you come in."

"I couldn't get here fast enough," I tell her, as I breathe in the sweet smell of her shampoo. "It looks a little intense out there though."

"Yeah, they have a lot to figure out. Help me carry these drinks in, and then we can wait in my room. The pizza's already ordered."

I pick up two of the glasses and follow behind her. She sets two down on the coffee table, and jerks her head toward the hallway, so I follow. "Is Wyatt okay with this?"

She waves off my concern. "He has bigger problems to worry about."

"Don't lock the door," Wyatt yells from the living room.

We both laugh as Kinsley pushes the door almost the entire way shut, but leaving a tiny crack to keep her brother happy. "I figured we'd give them a little space until the food comes."

After setting our drinks on her desk, I walk over to her until the backs of her knees hit the edge of her mattress. She has no choice but to lay down when I keep inching forward, moving over top of her, until she's flat on her back. She reaches up, wrapping her arms around my neck, pulling me down toward her. "I've wanted to kiss you all night, Sunny."

Like all our kisses, the first leads to many more, and the more we kiss, the more I want to take things farther. I slide my hand underneath her shirt, and her back bows off the bed. She reaches for the quilt on her bed, pulling it overtop of us. "Just in case they come in here," she says, against my mouth.

"There's so much I want to try with you, Kinsley." She stares at me with her gorgeous brown eyes, and all I want to do is show her how much I love her with my body—to show her what she does to me from one simple look.

"Now?"

"No, not with your brother a couple feet away. I just got on his good side, I can't screw it up already."

She giggles, knowing I'm right. Still, she cuddles as close as she can. "When?"

Knowing she wants this too only makes waiting that much harder. It's pure torture. "Maybe next weekend. We'll be in our own tent for two nights. I'm sure we can come up with something." The thought alone makes my heart race. Spending the night with Kinsley in my arms, without any interruptions or worrying about getting caught, makes me crave her even more.

"I'm nervous, Rhett."

"There's nothing to be nervous about. It's just me and you, Sunny." Before I can try to convince her how perfect our weekend away will be, there's a crash in the living room that makes the both of us jump off the bed.

"What was that?" she asks, latching onto my arm.

"No idea, but I'm going to look." I slowly inch the door open, and all I see so far is Becca in the corner with her hands covering her face. But the closer I get to her, I hear the grunting and grappling of bodies.

It takes me a second to realize who's fighting Wyatt, but as they spin around, I get a clear look at Jake—and it appears he's had a couple beers before coming here. I warned him not to do this. That coming here and starting trouble wouldn't do him any favors.

Before I have a chance to break it up, Kinsley rushes in between her brother and Jake. I grab her around her waist, hauling her away from them before she gets hurt. "Stay out of it, Sunny."

"Stop them, Rhett. Please."

I take a second to try to calm her down, but she won't even look at me. Her eyes are zeroed in on the fight. Determined as ever, she manages to wiggle out of my grasp, and puts herself in between Wyatt and Jake again. "Kinsley!"

A punch from Wyatt, intended for Jake, just misses her jaw, but Jake's elbow connects with her eye as she dodges the punch. Her hands fly to her face and she falls to the ground, her body curled up in pain. Seeing my girl on the floor, stops time.

With superhuman strength I didn't even know I was capable of, I grab my best friend by the back of his neck and throw him on the couch. Wyatt's still mid swing when I grab his arm and spin him around, pining it behind him. "Enough," I seethe.

Jake rolls off the couch, and then attempts to stagger toward the wall, trying his best to get to Becca before Wyatt can try to stop him again. Wyatt finally sees his sister laying on the floor in a protective heap, and forgets about Jake entirely.

Kinsley's crying, her hands still covering her eye as I bend down to help her. Wyatt tries to get close, but I hold my arm out, giving her some room to sit up with a little help from me.

"Kinny, are you okay?" Wyatt asks, softly. I can tell the adrenaline's still pumping through his body, but he does his best to catch his breath and let go of his anger. "Look at me, Kin," he begs.

"Rhett," she whispers, ignoring her brother entirely, as her body shakes with every tear she sheds.

"I'm right here, Sunny." I scoop her up and carry her to her bedroom where I place her gently on the bed. Everyone follows, except Becca. Suddenly, she's disappeared. "Can you open your eye?"

She drops her hand, her eye lashes slowly opening despite the bruises already forming. "Yes, but it hurts and it won't stop watering."

"Your vision's okay? Nothing's blurry?"

She shakes her head. "It's okay, just feels like I got poked really bad."

"Do you want me to take you to the medical aid down the street?"

"No, I'll put some ice on it. I'm not explaining this to anyone."

Wyatt stands behind me, watching our entire conversation. "I'm so sorry, Kinny," he says over and over. He's calmed down, but he's still shifting from side to side, anxiously.

Next thing I know, Jake's standing next to me holding out an ice pack for Kinsley. Wyatt makes no move to punch him again, or to say a single word. Whatever they were arguing about has been forgotten—at least for the time being. "I'm sorry, Kinsley," he says.

"I suggest you leave, Jake. I told you not to come here in the first place. If you would have listened to me for once in your life, she never would have gotten hurt."

"It was an accident," Kinsley says in his defense. Why she feels the need to stick up for Jake, I have no idea. As far as I'm concerned, he's not welcome here anymore. He's lucky I'm too worried about my girlfriend or I'd be the one punching him in the face.

"I'm sorry, Kinsley," he says one more time before turning and walking out of the room. Shortly after, I hear the front door open and close. Good, let him go.

"Sunny, can you put this on your eye for me, please?" She turns toward me, opening both eyes ever so slightly. I'm careful when I rest the ice against the swollen bruise, but she flinches anyway. "Sorry, I'm trying to be gentle."

Finally, she relaxes again. Now that the ice is on her eye, and I know she's okay, I look to Wyatt for an explanation. "What happened?"

Back in defensive mode, he crosses his arms over his chest, and shakes his head in disgust. "That douchebag came to *my* house trying to pick a fight with me. Becca and I were finally making some progress, and he barged inside and ruined it."

I thought I warned him into staying away, but I should have known better. When Jake drinks, anything's possible—especially when it comes to something he wants. "He was pissed about Becca coming here when we left the locker room. I didn't think he'd actually go through with a fight though."

"All this over some girl."

"She's not just some girl, Wyatt," Kinsley says, with her

head resting on her pillow. "You have to find her. Make sure she's okay."

"I'm more worried if you're okay. She could be anywhere by now."

"I'm sure she didn't go far," I tell him, hoping to lift his spirits a little.

Defeated, Wyatt shrugs his shoulders. "I guess I have my answer if she left with Jake."

Kinsley sits up, the ice covering most of her face. "Find her, Wyatt. She wouldn't have left with Jake, so she's here somewhere. She may be confused, but I know my best friend better than anyone. She wants to be with you."

Like his sister's words were enough to remove any doubt he was having, he pushes off the wall he was leaning against. "I'll find her," he says, convincingly, before leaving the room.

Now that we're alone again, I slide into bed next to Kinsley. She rests her head on my chest and the coldness from the ice seeps through my thin shirt.

"I have a black eye, don't I?"

"Yeah, it's a pretty nice shiner."

"I can't go to the dance tomorrow night looking like a freak, Rhett."

"I think you should show it off, it's pretty badass." She smacks me and presses the ice pack against my face. "Shit, that's freezing."

"It's such a great story. My boyfriend's best friend beat me up while he was fighting with my brother. It will be front page news at school in no time."

"What were you thinking getting between two guys twice your size?"

"That I didn't want either of them to get hurt. And I hate seeing them fight over Becca. The girl needs to make a decision though because she can't play both sides anymore."

"They'll figure it out. Until then, how about we stay out

of it. I can't take you getting hurt again. Once was enough for me."

"Jake and Becca are our best friends, though. Wyatt's my brother—it's a little hard not to care."

I get what she's saying. It's tough when you care about the people involved, but at the same time, it's not our battle. Until Becca's honest with herself, nothing's going to change. Which is why I'm thankful I have a girl who knows what she wants. It's easy with her—I never have to doubt her feelings or get confused about my own. When I see her, I just know. "Not everyone has it figured out the way we do."

"I like what we have."

"Me too, Sunny."

"You're not even a little freaked out about what I said earlier?"

I think back to the moment she told me she loved me. It was genuine although completely unexpected—even for her. "I've never told anyone I loved them before."

"Me either, except for my family."

"You don't want to take it back?" I give her a chance to think it over. To be one hundred percent sure she meant to say what she did, even if there's not a chance I'll ever forget the moment she told me she loved me for the first time.

"I meant it. I love you, Rhett. Completely."

Again, it's like a sucker punch to the gut. "Jesus, Sunny. You have no idea how much that means to me." I run my fingers over her soft skin, pulling her as close as I can. "I love you so much."

Her stomach growls in response, making us both laugh. With all the craziness, we never got a chance to eat the pizza she ordered. "Sorry," she says, as she holds her stomach. "That's not very romantic."

"Don't be sorry you're hungry. Go get some pizza. I'm going to call home quick and then I'll be out."

She climbs over me, not waiting until I get up. "Ugh, watch your knees, babe."

"Sorry," she giggles. "Come get some pizza when you're done and tell you parents I said hi. If you're telling them I'm with you."

"Of course I'm telling them I'm with you. Where else would I be?"

"I don't know. Probably at the party with the rest of your team. Are you going to let me up?"

She's still straddling me with her ice pack in her hand. "If I have to."

"You have to, but we can come back to bed."

"Promise?"

She smiles, sweetly, puffy eye and all. "Promise."

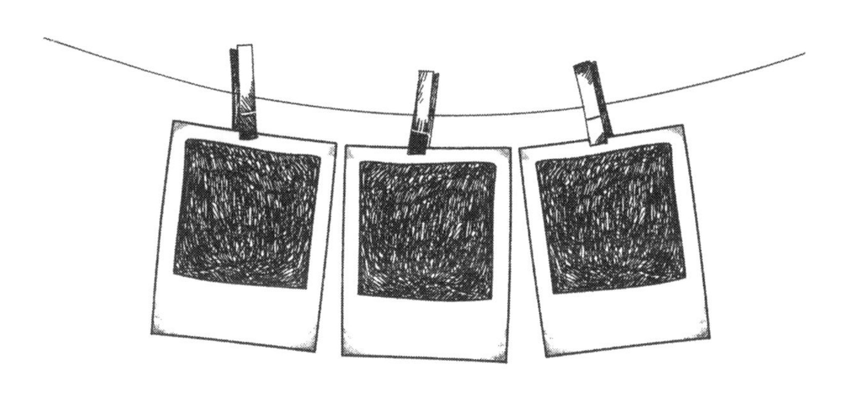

CHAPTER EIGHTEEN

kinsley

I'M FINALLY ABOUT to eat some dinner when the front door opens and Carson walks inside. He sets his keys on the table next to the door, and takes a look around the living room. Nobody bothered to clean up the spilled drinks or pick up the magazines that flew off the coffee table during the fight.

Taking one look at it, he stares at me awkwardly while I'm in the middle of adjusting the ice on my eye. "What the hell happened in here?"

All I want to do is eat my pizza, but Carson isn't going to let this go until he hears the whole story. It's just the way he is. "There was a fight."

"I got that much from the living room, but what happened to your face?"

I set my ice pack on the counter, letting him see the damage that's been done. "Probably looks worse than it is."

Carson stalks over to where I'm standing, bending to inspect my eye. "It's definitely something, Kinsley. How did it happen?"

I move away from the counter, taking my usual stool at the island. "It was an accident. Nobody's fault but my own."

"Who did it?" he asks, again.

"Just drop it, Carson. It's over and done with. I'm starving and it's been a long night."

He stares at me, silently scowling until he hears Rhett's voice coming from my room. Before I can stop him, he takes off, obviously connecting the wrong dots. None of this has anything to do with Rhett, and he's about to place blame on the wrong person.

Here we go again.

I run after him, pleading with him to stop so I can explain, but Carson's already in Rhett's face, asking him to explain my bruises. Rhett doesn't feed into his anger at first, but as soon as Carson swings at his face, Rhett tosses his cell phone on the bed. "Back up," he warns, but Carson doesn't listen. Instead, he lunges toward Rhett, trying to knock him to the floor. But this time, Rhett's ready for his advance and fights back.

"Stop it! Carson, it wasn't Rhett's fault," I plead.

"Don't make excuses for him, Kins. He screwed up the second he put his hands on you."

That's all it takes for Rhett to see red. A look of pure rage erupts on his face the moment he realizes Carson thinks he hit me. The second brawl of the night breaks out. It wasn't enough for Jake and Wyatt to go after each other over Becca, now I have Rhett and Carson fighting over me. Only this time, I don't try to get in between them—I run for my brother instead.

"Wyatt," I yell down the hall. "Wyatt!"

His bedroom door flies open, and he runs toward me in a panic, wondering why I'm screaming for him. "What's going on? Are you okay?"

I point toward my room. "Stop them, please!"

Punches fly all around us, but Wyatt jumps in to break up the fight. He yanks Carson by the back of his shirt, practically throwing him against the closet door. Rhett backs off on his own, and doesn't need to be stopped. This was all Carson's doing. He's the one with an agenda—not Rhett.

Rhett wipes some blood off the corner of his mouth, his chest rising and falling rapidly as he tries to catch his breath. I grab a tissue from the box on my desk, handing it to him. "Are you okay?"

"I'm fine. What's his problem?"

"My problem?" Carson questions, like a total smartass. "You're the one banging around your girlfriend," he spits back.

It's like a game of tennis, my head bouncing from side to side as they volley insults back and forth. Carson has this all wrong, but I'm afraid to say anything until he calms down.

Thankfully, my brother steps up, setting the record straight. "Carson, chill man. I got in a fight with Jake, she caught an elbow trying to break us up. It wasn't Rhett's fault."

Carson gapes at him like he's lost his mind. For a minute it looks like he's about to charge my brother to give him the same attention he just showed Rhett, but Wyatt shakes his head, letting him know it would be the wrong move to make.

I step forward now that everyone's under control. Reaching for Carson's hand, I ask, "Can I talk to you in your room for a minute?"

His eyes finally soften when he hears my voice. With a small nod of his head, he says, "Sure," but he doesn't leave the room peacefully. Even though Wyatt already made a point of saying Rhett wasn't responsible, it doesn't stop Carson from nudging his shoulder as he walks by him—only pissing Rhett off more.

"That wasn't necessary," I whisper to him. When I look over my shoulder, hurt momentarily flashes through Rhett's eyes as he watches me leave the room with Carson. The last thing I want is for him to be upset with me, but I need to have this conversation whether he's okay with it or not.

Carson sits on the bed beside me, cracking his knuckles and flexing his fingers. "What's going on, Kins?"

"Please don't ever do that again. Tonight's been one giant mess since we got home from the game."

"Fine," he responds, stubbornly.

"Carson, if I was in trouble, if Rhett ever hurt me, you're the one I would run to."

"What about Wyatt?"

"My brother would always support me, but he's living his own life at school. You took his place because he felt like you'd handle the job of protector. That's what you were doing tonight when you fought Rhett—protecting me. Even though you had the facts wrong."

"You're not mad I punched your boyfriend?"

"Yes, but you did it with the right intentions. I can't get mad at you for trying to keep me safe."

"You're mad, but you're not. Makes complete sense."

We may have a weird connection that has been building for years, all on its own, but I know the moment I say the words, Carson would do anything for me. He proven tonight what he's capable of and I didn't even have to ask. But then again, if anyone ever hurt him, I'd do the same. I'd stand up for him, no questions asked. "I'm pretty sure you know what I mean."

"I get it. I *am* here for a reason. And I'd do anything for you."

"I know and I'm grateful you gave up living in an apartment of your own to help Kate and I with the bills, but you don't have to be superman all the time. I want you to be happy, and lately, I get the impression you're not."

"I'm happy."

"Are you lying?"

"I'm good, I promise. I'd be better with you, but I'm respecting your decision—even if I don't understand what you see in him that you don't see with me."

I think about his words for a minute. There's no easy way to describe the difference between them. Besides the obvious age difference, the fact that Rhett and I are in the same school, and that we love each other, there's more to it than that. I care about Carson, but he's just not Rhett. Still, I try to come up with a way to make Carson understand. "Sometimes Rhett treats me like I'm breakable. Like if he's not careful, I'll slip through his fingers or crumble."

"That's what you want?"

"It's what I need. I've never had that kind of connection with anyone—that together we're stronger than if we were apart. I've felt so alone for so long, but I finally have a guy in my life that wants to stick around—that isn't leaving. I need that, Carson."

"And you don't think I'd treat you the same way? If not better?"

I turn to face him, wishing he wouldn't doubt how amazing he is. "Carson, you'd treat me like a princess. That I'm sure of."

"I get it, Kins. You don't have to say another word."

I reach for his hand, squeezing it. "Yes, I do because it doesn't mean I care about you less. You're important to me whether I'm with Rhett or not."

He doesn't respond, only staring at my hand resting on top of his. His fingers twitch ever so slightly, like he wants to wrap his fingers around mine, but he doesn't. He stays completely still. I take it as my cue to leave—to give him some space.

As I stand up he says, "I hope it works out. You deserve it."

"You'll find your person, Carson. I know you will."

His warm brown eyes pierce through me as he says, "I thought I did."

I should tell him I'm not the one for him. That there's so many more out there for him, but before I realize what's happening, he leans closer. I turn my head at the last second and his mouth connects with my cheek. "Carson, this can't happen."

I move away from the bed, guilt flooding through my body, even though I managed to stop him before he took things too far. Still, before I'm gone, I hear one last plea. "Just remember, if it doesn't work out, you know where to find me."

"I'll remember."

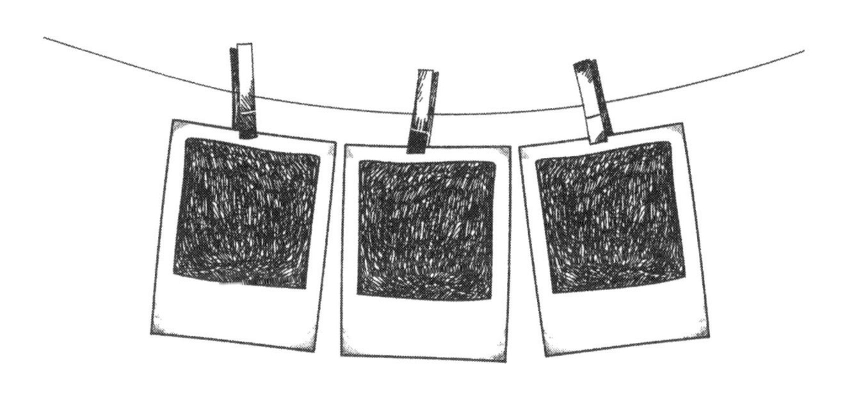

CHAPTER NINETEEN

rhett

I STAYED WITH Kinsley until one in the morning before climbing out of her bed, and driving home. I told my parents twelve at the latest, but I couldn't leave her. She was still in so much pain from the fight, and all I wanted to do was watch over her while she slept in my arms. But after getting a warning text from my dad that my mom was about to come drag me home, I knew it was time to go. I'm eighteen. Kinsley and I are both adults by law, but while I'm living under their roof, I have to play by their rules.

Knowing it's going to be another late night, I slept half the day away before asking my mom to iron my dress shirt for the homecoming dance. Yeah, so much for being a grown adult. Turns out I still need my mom unless I want to do it myself and risk setting the house on fire.

"Mom, do you have my shirt? I have to leave."

She hurries up the stairs, handing me a crisp, white button down that's ironed to perfection. "Do you want me to help you?"

I laugh at her, she's never going to stop treating me like I'm five. "I can dress myself, you know."

"I know honey, but this is my last year with you. Soon you'll be graduating, and moving away, and you'll have a family of your own. You could end up anywhere in the world—I'll lose my baby forever."

"Whoa, slow down, Mom. I'm going to homecoming, not getting married."

"It all happens to fast, Rhett. Slow down a little, please. And I don't want you staying out all night again."

"Mom, it's senior year. I'm just trying to enjoy it."

"You're spending too much time with this Kinsley girl. What about your friends? They'll all be going in different directions soon. Trust me, you'll want your friends when you're all alone in a new place."

"I do hang out with my friends, but I love Kinsley. She's going to be with me whether I'm with friends or not."

"You don't know what love is yet. What you're feeling is all puppy love—the kind that comes and goes and ends up a silly thing of the past."

"That's not how it feels at all. It's real."

"It may seem like that now, but once you're older, you'll see this was just something to help pass the time. That's all she is, sweetie—a distraction."

"Well, I don't see it that way. I'm not sure I ever will."

"Just promise me you'll be smart. Don't let her bring you down. She's not like us, Rhett. She comes from a different place."

I finish buttoning my shirt, and adjust my tie, all while doing my best not to yell at my own mother. How can she be so close-minded? I've never seen her be anything but nice to my friends, but when it comes to Kinsley, she wants her gone. "She's a good person. You'd see that if you gave her a chance." I grab my jacket and sling it over my shoulder, ending our conversation.

"I love you, honey. I do. I'm just worried," she yells down to the foyer from atop the landing. I'm already halfway out the door. Nothing she can say will convince me she's right. I love Kinsley—and I don't see that changing anytime soon.

And that love only grows when I get to her apartment to pick her up, and she's waiting for me in the living room. The dress. Wow. All I can do is stand and stare at the most gorgeous girl I've ever seen in my life. I can't blink for fear she's going to disappear because there's no way I could be lucky enough to have her as my own.

"Rhett?"

I hear my name. It sounds like perfection coming from her painted red lips, but still, all I can do is stare. Her hair's curled just the way I like it with a sparkly feather tucked behind her ear. The things I want to do with that feather.

But I don't stay fixated on it for long. I can't. Not when the heels she's wearing are calling for attention. They make her a few inches taller, and the closer I get to her, I realize I won't have to bend down quite as far to kiss her tonight. All put together, she looks like an angel in white, with more sparkles covering her body, and legs for days.

I motion with my finger for her to spin around so I can get the full effect. She fidgets nervously, obviously unsure if I like what I'm seeing. She'll know when I'm finished looking.

Little by little I admire every inch of her, and hell if it isn't absolute perfection. "Sunny, you look—you're so beautiful. God, I'm so damn lucky."

"You like it? Really?"

"I love it, and I love you. But we need to leave." We need

to leave before I push her into her bedroom and never let her leave.

"I'm ready," she whispers in her most innocent voice while I'm busy thinking all kinds of dirty thoughts.

I take her hand, and link my fingers with hers. With more pride than I've ever had, I walk out of the house with Kinsley on my arm, and once I get my girl safely in my truck, I'm ready to get this night started.

I glance at her as I back out of the driveway. "How's your eye?"

"It's not as puffy. I tried covering up the bruise with make-up. Can you still see it?"

"Barely, and only because I know it's there. I still can't believe you got hit."

"Have you talked to Jake?"

"Nope." I almost called him, but each time I tried, I got more pissed off. Even a text would have been a string of useless curses. He had no right coming to Kinsley's last night.

She sighs, and I know I'm in for an earful—that I won't like. "You can't be mad at him forever. It's over and done with. He's your best friend."

"He hit you in the face, Kinsley. My best friend showed up at my girlfriend's house, even after I told him to stay away, and hurt you. That's not something I'm going to get over or take lightly."

"But I'm fine. I don't want you two being pissed at each other because of me."

This isn't an argument I'm going to win, so until we get to the dance, I keep my mouth closed before I say something I'll end up regretting. She takes my silence as anger, and crosses her arms over her chest. "This is ridiculous," she mumbles.

Maybe it is, but it doesn't change the way I feel.

Almost everyone's already inside the gym by the time we get to the high school. It's my fault we're running a little late.

Between the conversation with my mom, and then ogling Kinsley a little too long in the living room, we could have been here twenty minutes ago.

"Do you think Becca still came with Jake?" I ask her, unsure if she's spoken with Becca since she ran last night. Wyatt told us he found her a couple blocks away from the apartment, swinging on a swing at the playground. She shouldn't have been out so late by herself, but at least he found her before anything else happened.

"I'm not sure what she decided. She was with Wyatt until early this morning. He left at some ungodly hour to go back to school—said he wanted to get some sleep before the game tonight." She glances at the time on her cell phone. "The game starts in ten minutes."

"Sorry you're missing it."

"What? Are you serious right now? I'm pretty excited to go to my first dance with a date if you haven't noticed."

"Another first."

She smiles shyly, her cheeks turning the slightest bit of pink, as we walk hand in hand through the gym doors. Heads turn toward us, and Kinsley grips my hand a little tighter. She hates when people stare at her, but looking like she does tonight, there's no way they can't. She's the prettiest girl in the entire room.

"Dance with me?" I ask her even though she has no choice. I've been waiting for this all day.

"Sure."

We find a spot on the floor, and I pull her close. One Direction's, "Eighteen," plays in the background. People continue to stare, as I kiss her lips while slowly swaying our bodies from side to side, but I couldn't care less. All I see is my Sunny.

Just as the song ends, we almost bump right into Becca and Jake. "Come on, Kinsley." I have nothing to say to Jake. Not yet anyway.

But she tugs on my arm, pulling me back to where we were standing a moment ago. "Rhett, please. Talk to Jake." Her eyes are pained and I can tell it's eating her up inside to have come between the two of us. She doesn't get it though. I'd put her first no matter who touched her.

"Rhett, come on man. This is stupid."

And once again, I'm in his face. "Stupid? You think showing up at my girlfriend's apartment completely wasted and picking fights is stupid?"

"No, I think you being this pissed about it is stupid. I didn't try to hit her. I'd never lay a hand on a girl and you know that."

"He's right, Rhett. He's not a bad person just because he made one mistake."

I whip my head toward the girl I love more than anything. Even she's on Jake's side. "That one mistake could have knocked you out, Kinsley. He shouldn't have even been there!"

"But he was. It's in the past."

"Pfft, maybe for you."

Kinsley pulls me aside, and grabs my face between her hands. "Listen to me. He's been your best friend for years. Don't throw away a friendship because of me. He needs his best friend right now."

I glance at Jake and for the first time I notice he looks pretty miserable. Part of me wants to stay mad, but when I see how much it means to Kinsley to talk to him, I know I have to. There's no way I'll ever forgive him for hurting her, but I can at least try to have a conversation. "I can't pretend I'm not pissed, but I'll try."

"Thank you. I'll take Becca. Find out what's going on."

Once the girls are gone, I have no choice but to work things out with Jake. "Lets go sit down."

"Dude, this is probably the shittiest homecoming ever."

"Why?"

"Because I fucked up. I can't lose my best friend and my

girlfriend in the same weekend. That's serious loser status."

I follow Kinsley with my eyes until I see where they're going. They stop on the other side of the room near the bleachers. Becca's talking a mile a minute like she normally does, and Kinsley's listening to her every word. "I'm still your friend, Jake. But I swear to god if you ever touch her again I will kick your ass—accident or no accident. And lay off the alcohol."

"Done. I don't care if I ever touch it again. Not after last night." Everything happens for a reason and maybe Kinsley getting hurt is enough for Jake to realize there's more to life than getting drunk every free chance he has. He's getting to the point that if he doesn't slow down now, he'll surely kill himself by the time he goes to college.

"Are you and Becca still together?"

"Hell if I know. She's barely talking to me and when she does, it's not like it used to be. Whatever Wyatt put into her head last night worked. I feel like she's already with him and we're not even officially broken up."

"Have some confidence, then. Maybe she doesn't want to break up. You're all uptight about losing her, but you still have her. Make her want to stay." Jake's finally looking a little more optimistic, but now Kinsley has the same look he had a couple minutes ago.

"What's wrong, Sunny?"

"Do you mind if we go back to my apartment?"

"Are you sure? We haven't even been here for an hour."

"I know, but I think Becca needs us right now."

Jake overhears her, and raises an eyebrow. "What's wrong with her?"

Kinsley chews on her fingernail, her eyes looking toward mine for help. I can't help her though—I have no idea what's going on. Regardless, I trust her judgement. If she thinks we need to leave, then we probably do. "We can leave."

Jake's on our heels, not giving up on getting information

out of Kinsley. "Will someone tell me what's going on?"

Becca's standing next to my truck once we get to the parking lot. Tears are streaming down her cheeks, and there's a trail of black shit all over her face. This can't be good.

Jake takes one look at her and a bunch of unspoken words are tossed back and forth before he shakes his head and kicks my tire. "I fucking knew it. I knew you were lying."

His reaction only makes Becca cry harder. "D-don't Jake," she pleads. "I'm s-sorry."

"So am I. I'm sorry I ever thought you gave a shit about me. I would never have cheated on you, Becca. Never."

He turns to walk away and Becca runs after him, grabbing his arm. She holds onto him as she cries into his suit jacket. "Jake, please. I'm so sorry. This wasn't supposed to h-happen."

"It is what it is," he says before peeling her hands off his arm and walking away. Becca falls to the ground, her sobs coming out in short bursts in between her silent tears.

Kinsley and I help her off the ground before I pick her up and sit her inside my truck. Kinsley climbs in next to her and shuts the door.

Becca raises her head from her hands, "I'm sorry I ruined your night."

"You didn't ruin anything," I tell her. I don't even need to know the rest of the story to understand that she hooked up with Wyatt last night. Now she's trying to survive the guilt. It's the worst kind of karma.

Becca's not the kind of girl to randomly hook up with guys which makes what she did sting that much more. Jake knows she would only give herself to someone she needed in her life. And she needs Wyatt—not Jake.

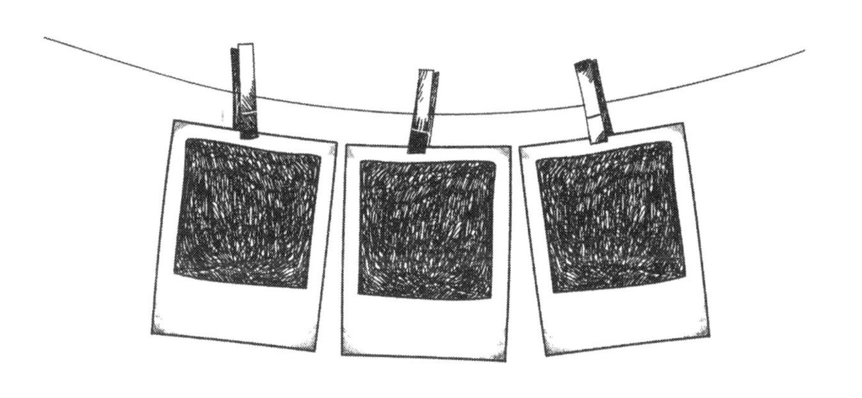

CHAPTER TWENTY

kinsley

WE ALL SURVIVED homecoming week despite all the drama—though some better than others. Oddly enough, after all the fighting and serious talks were over, it all brought us closer together. Now, a week later, it's finally time to have a little fun at Fall Fest.

Rhett and I wanted as much time together as possible, so as soon as the football game ended, we hopped in his truck and drove the almost two hours to the camp ground. My cheeks are wind burned from sitting at the football game, my feet hurt, and I could sleep for an entire day, but I couldn't be more excited for this weekend away.

Rhett has everything we need for the next two days scattered around us on the ground. He's putting the finishing touches on our bright red tent while I finish pumping some air into the air mattress.

"What do you think? Not bad for putting it together in the dark, right?"

I walk toward the tent, leaning down to peek inside. "It's bigger than I thought It would be." Not that we need a lot of room. I plan on staying as close to Rhett as I can, all night long.

"The guy who sold it to me said it's like the Cadillac of the tent world." Rhett says, as he chucks a hammer into the back of his truck. I admit I watched him the entire time he drove all four stakes into the ground—his arm muscles straining against the thin fabric of his Under Armour.

It's a good thing he's done this before because I don't have the first clue about camping. In fact, I can't help but laugh when I think about how this tent would look if he wasn't here.

"What's so funny, Sunny?"

"That rhymed."

When I shiver, he runs his hands up and down my arms. "Are you cold?"

"A little, but we have sleeping bags to stay warm."

"I plan on keeping you warm, but grab your pillow and a blanket out of the truck. I'll get this mattress inside."

I get goosebumps thinking about lying next to Rhett all night long. I've never shared a bed with a guy before let alone a boyfriend. But I have a feeling tonight will be a night filled with more firsts—and there's nobody I'd rather share them with than Rhett.

He's waiting next to the tent, messing with the zippers. "Got everything?"

I nod my head. "Is it okay if I change?"

Rhett blinks a couple times, swallows, and then finally gets it together. "Yeah, of course. I didn't even think about that. Climb inside and let me know when you're done."

I clutch my clothes and my pillow against my chest, trying to get the nerve to tell him he doesn't have to wait out here.

"You can come inside with me. If you want."

"I'll be in. I need a minute."

"Are you okay?"

"I'm more than okay, Sunny. I'm about to lie next to you all night long. I can't think of anything better."

"But you don't want to come inside?"

"I should probably wait out here," he says, as he tries to discretely adjust himself.

Biting my lip, I try not to laugh. "Okay. I'll only be a minute."

Climbing inside the tent, I change out of my jeans and sweatshirt into a pair of yoga pants and a long sleeve T-shirt. I notice Rhett's silhouette pacing back and forth outside the tent. I've never seen him nervous before, but he definitely is.

When I'm finished, I peek my head outside. "You can come in now." I notice he's changed, too. In true Rhett style, he even manages to make sweats and a basic, black pullover look hot.

I lie back on the air mattress, and Rhett flops down beside me. Only he does it a little too hard, and I flip off the side, landing face down on the ground.

"Shit!" he says, as he scrambles over to my side. "Are you okay?"

Laughing I tell him, "I'm fine, but if you didn't want to sleep with me, all you had to do was say so."

My laughter dies in my throat when he says, "Kinsley, all I want to do is hold you—whether it goes further or not. I have to have you next to me."

His words land straight on my heart, and I'm positive he can feel how much I want him right now—how much I've been looking forward to spending the night with him. "I didn't mean—" I start to say, nervously.

"Come'ere, Sunny." He holds out his hand, pulling me on top of him. "There's no rush. We have all weekend together."

I rest my head against his chest, and he rubs soothing circles on my back. It's enough to ease my nerves, but it doesn't last long. Not when my body's touching every inch of his. There are so many things I want to say to him—to tell him I want. But instead, I chicken out and settle for something else. Something boring. "It's really cozy in here. Can we build a fire tomorrow?"

"Sure. Anything you want."

When I gather enough courage, I lift my head and say it before I miss my chance. "If I can have anything, then I want you to kiss me."

"I love kissing you. What else does my girl want?"

The second part takes a little longer to get out, and I'm not sure I can say the actual words. Rhett feeds off my insecurities, and tries to ease my nerves. "What is it? What else do you want?"

I force myself to stay right where I am with my head held high. If this is what I want, I should be able to tell my boyfriend. "I want everything, Rhett—all of you."

"Yeah? Are you sure?"

Smiling shyly, I tell him, "I'm sure."

Rhett closes his eyes, and exhales. When he opens them, I lick my lips, and bite down, waiting for him to make the first move. But I'm the one who started this conversation, so I sit up far enough to straddle his waist, and pull my shirt over my head.

He swallows, his eyes falling to my chest. I reach behind my back and unclasp my bra. We've gone this far before, but it still feels like the first time for the simple fact that this is only the beginning.

"Shit, Sunny." He grabs my waist, and rolls me onto my back. Hovering over top of me, he reaches behind his head and pulls his shirt over his head.

Before I can ask him what he wants next, his mouth is on me. It feels incredible, but when I can't take anymore, I reach down and slide my pants over my hips. He helps me pull them off the entire way until I'm completely naked. It's dark inside the tent, and it helps me feel less self-conscious, but with the way he's looking at my body, there's no doubt he likes what he sees.

"Tell me to stop, Kinsley."

"I don't want you to."

He lays down next to me and kisses my lips. "Your first time shouldn't be in a tent in the middle of nowhere."

"Why not?"

"Because it should be special. I should have flowers or something."

I chuckle because flowers have nothing to do with having sex. "I don't need anything, Rhett. And this is special—because I'm with you."

He pulls his sweats over his hips, and I can't help but stare. But when he reaches above his head and into his backpack, I close my eyes. This is really happening.

I hear the tear of the foil packet, and I lie completely still until he's over top of me again. My heart's beating so fast I feel it pulsing in my ears. I've waited for this moment, and now that it's here, I'm terrified about what's about to happen.

"I'll go slow. If I hurt you, tell me to stop."

I nod my head and bite the inside of my cheek. Slowly, he pushes inside me. At first it's okay, but as he inches in, a burning pain erupts, and I clench my muscles.

"Are you okay?"

"I'm okay," I lie. It isn't the worst pain I've ever felt, but it's not the most comfortable either. But I wanted this, and I'm not about to stop now.

He pushes a little more, and once he's completely inside me, I'm afraid to move, so I don't. Tears prick my eyes, and when he starts to pull out, the pain returns. I bite down harder, and they finally fall, soaking the pillow under my head.

"Look at me, Kinsley."

I move my eyes, from the reflector patch on the side of the

tent where I was focusing, to Rhett.

"Don't cry, baby."

"I'm okay. It doesn't hurt as much anymore."

"Do you want me to stop?"

I shake my head. "No, keep going. I want you to feel good."

"I love you so much, Sunny." He pushes in and out of me, his pace quickening, but still gentle enough that he doesn't hurt me.

"I love you, too," I whisper, as a few more stray tears fall.

Being with Rhett is nothing like I'd imagined it would be, yet it's still one of the best moments of my life. Whether being with him changes us or not, I'll never regret this night. Not with the way he's looking at me right now. Like I'm his entire world.

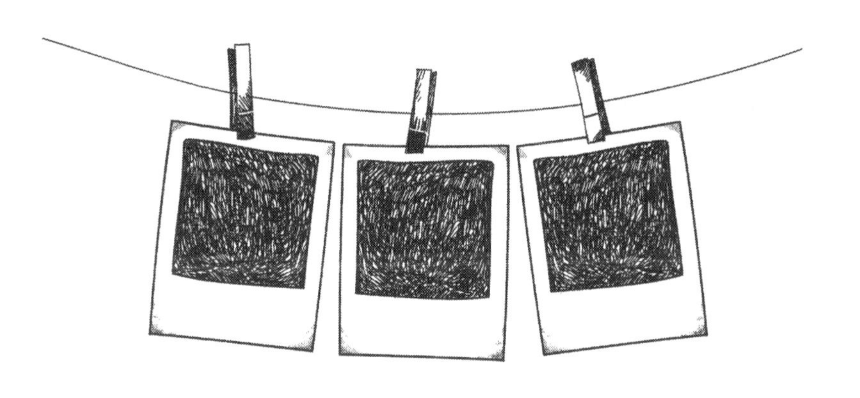

CHAPTER TWENTY-ONE

rhett

KINSLEY'S TUCKED INTO my side with her arm thrown across my chest. I can see droplets from the cold morning air still resting on top of the tent, but inside, we're nice and warm. Part of that has to do with the fact that we've been wrapped up in a sleeping bag big enough for two.

I pictured what it would be like being with Kinsley so many times, and I knew once it happened, it would be even better than I imagined—and it was. We'd grown closer, especially after last week, and I finally feel like this is more than just a high school fling. That this girl is going to be with me forever.

"Sunny," I whisper, as I wrap a strand of her hair around my finger. She moans a little, but doesn't wake up. It does nothing to help my situation under the sleeping bag. "Kinsley," I whisper a little louder.

Her eyes open, and she lifts her head off my chest. "Is it morning already?"

"It's morning." I pause for a second, wondering if she's okay, but not wanting to make it awkward for her. "How do you feel?"

"I'm okay." She climbs on top of me and clings to me like she can't get close enough. I feel the exact same way—that no matter how tightly I hold her, there's still room for more.

She kisses my chest, and I smile against her hair. I don't want to bombard her as soon as she's awake, especially if she's not a morning person, but the surprise I have for her is burning a hole in the front pocket of my bag. "I have something for you."

"I don't need anything else. I have you and Fall Fest."

I reach my arm out, and luckily my fingertips graze the handle on the bag. I slide it closer, unzipping the pocket. "I'm allowed to spoil my girl." I lean a little farther to reach inside.

"I can get off you, you know."

"That's a terrible idea."

She giggles, and I reach into the front pocket, pulling out two tickets to the Penn State game today. I promised her Fall Fest, but when I found out it was a home game, and we're only fifteen minutes away from the field, I knew I had to get Wyatt to pull some strings for us. There's no way I want her to miss one of his last home games of the season.

"I'm going to give you something, but you have to do it. Okay?"

She nods her head, a little bit of nervousness showing through her curiosity. "Okay."

I show her one of the tickets, and it takes her a second to read it, but once she realizes it's for the game today, I'm rewarded with the biggest smile she's ever given me. "Are you serious?"

"As a heart attack."

"I can't believe this! I get to see Wyatt play. Rhett, how did you do this?"

"I called in a favor—your brother's pretty cool, Sunny."

"You called him again?" She sees me nod my head and her eyes grow wide. "I can't believe you two get along. Everything I've wanted is happening."

"Becca's going to be there. He sent a ticket for her, too." She rolls off of me, squealing with excitement. I love seeing her so happy. I'd do anything to keep that look on her face, permanently. I don't know what I did to deserve this girl, but now that I have her, I'm not letting her go.

She sits up and the sleeping bag falls away from her body. For a moment, she forgets she's completely naked. I notice a few marks I left behind when I couldn't stop kissing her last night all the way into early this morning.

When she notices me staring, she shifts her focus from the ticket to her body. And like she's ashamed of it, she grabs the blanket and pulls it up to cover herself. "Don't hide from me, Sunny."

"I'm not used to waking up naked."

I grab her and wrap her in a hug, digging my fingers into her sides. She laughs so hard, she's out of breath within seconds. "That's the best sound."

I remember back to the first day of school when she wandered inside the building with her head down. I had been waiting an entire summer to see her face again, and there she was, her eyes focused on the floor like she'd rather be invisible. The girl I'm holding now is already so different than the Kinsley West that showed up that day. I would have fallen for either version, regardless, but this is the girl I knew existed underneath the protective outer shell.

"When do we have to leave?"

"Soon, it's an early game. We slept in."

"Someone kept me up all night," she jokingly complains.

She doesn't know I was up long after she finally fell asleep. I watched her until my own eyes couldn't stay open, and then

I fell asleep happier than I have in a really long time. It's still surreal to me that I got the girl—and I'm not at war with her brother. "I plan on keeping you up again tonight. You've been warned."

Her cheeks instantly turn pink and the color moves all the way down her neck to the top of her chest. She's picturing being with me again, and as long as she wants me, that's exactly what I have planned. Only tonight, it will be an entirely different experience for her. Tonight, it's about her.

My sweet Sunny-girl.

I'VE BEEN TO Penn State games before, but Kinsley hasn't been since she was little. The way her face lights up as soon as we make our way to our seats, I know this is one place full of happy memories for her.

"It seems so much bigger," she says with excitement in her voice. "I guess it probably is. They've done a lot to the stadium since I saw it last. It still smells the same though."

"What?" I ask her, as I laugh.

"You've never noticed? Even at your games, there's just something about the way a game smells. The mixture of concession stand food, the people, the fall air—all of it. It sounds ridiculous, but it always reminds me of when I was little. When I'd go to the games and watch everyone around me. It was a happy place, one that didn't have sickness or disappointment. The stadium has always been one of the happier memories for me, actually."

"That's not ridiculous at all, it's cute."

We climb the stairs to our seats, and Becca's already sitting in her spot, next to Carson of all people. I guess Wyatt managed to get tickets for everyone. Kinsley sits next to Becca after acknowledging Carson. He smiles at her, asks how she's doing, and then focuses on the field again.

Becca gasps, and I glance at Kinsley who looks like she wants to disappear. "I told you it would happen," Becca whispers, and I realize our night together is no longer a secret.

I give Kinsley's hand a squeeze, letting her know I'm not mad that she told. I never expected her to keep it from her best friend, even though I don't think she was planning on telling Becca right here, right now. But that girl has a way of getting just about anything out of a person when she wants to know bad enough.

Carson on the other hand, overhears the news, and doesn't look nearly as excited for his friend as Becca does. In fact, I'm pretty sure if looks could kill, I'd be dead right now. I make a point to kiss the top of Kinsley's head, and whisper how much I love her in her ear. All while he's staring at me.

Before I can tell him to keep his mouth shut, his focus is directed toward the cute blonde who jumps into his lap. "I finally found you. I'm all the way over there." She points to the student section that's decked out in white for today's white out.

"Who's your friend?" Becca asks him.

I glance at Kinsley to see her reaction. She's looking at the two of them, but I don't see the jealousy I saw when I was watching Carson stare at us. It's a relief.

"This is Stacy. I met her last week when I came to see Wyatt play."

"I'm Wyatt's biggest fan," she says, proudly.

Kinsley sticks her hand out for Stacy to shake. "Nice to meet you, but I'm probably his biggest fan. This one next to me is a close second."

I chuckle at my Sunny-girl who is making sure she sets the record straight.

Carson jumps in before it gets anymore awkward. "Stacy, this is Wyatt's sister, Kinsley, and her best friend, Becca. Guy on the end is Kinsley's boyfriend, Rhett."

Stacy's eyes find mine, and I don't miss the wink she gives me. Thankfully, Carson doesn't notice, but I can't say the same for the girls. "I didn't know Wyatt had a sister," she adds. That comment's not going to score her any points with this crowd. That's for sure.

Becca smiles back, but it's completely fake. "You probably didn't know he was seeing anyone either, but now you do." Kinsley snorts, and covers her mouth when she can't keep her laughter contained.

Stacy's head cocks to the side. "Oh, no I didn't."

This is going well. Wyatt could have warned me what I was in for.

The Blue Band takes the field, and it makes having a conversation difficult, so we watch the show on the field instead. Stacy tries to yell over the music, and Kinsley rolls her eyes at her. "I have to go back to my seat, but I'll meet you back at the dorm after the game. You remember which room's mine, right?"

I almost gag, but Carson nods his head, and returns the kiss she gives him. "Bye, pooky," she says, with a wave of her fingers.

Once she's gone, Becca breaks out into a fit of hysterics. "Pooky? You've known her for a week and she already has a pet name for you? And a stupid one."

Carson shrugs his shoulders, not seeming to care. "It's not that bad. We're not serious. Just hanging out."

"You mean screwing," she clarifies.

He shifts in his seat, neither agreeing nor disagreeing with her. "I didn't say that."

"Well, I'm sure you are, but whatever. She seems special," Becca says with hesitation, biting her lip to control her laughter. If she's planning on being with Wyatt officially, there's a good chance she'll be seeing a lot more of Stacy in the near future. I almost feel bad for her—almost.

Kinsley's stayed quiet during the whole exchange. I'm glad

Carson's trying to move on, but if he's trying to find someone like Kinsley, he'll have to look a whole lot harder. Then again, maybe Stacy's simply a distraction. Lord knows I've had a couple of those when I was trying to get over the fact that I couldn't be with Sunny.

"I have to pee."

I laugh at my girl. The game didn't even start yet. "Do you want me to come with you?"

"No, I'm good. I'll be right back."

"Wait," Becca says, "I'm coming with you."

I'll never understand why girls have to travel in packs, but I stand up and move into the aisle anyway, letting the girls out of the row of seats.

They're gone for almost fifteen minutes, and I'm checking my watch every five seconds. Sitting here with Carson is more than a little awkward. Finally, Becca's jogging up the stairs, only Kinsley's not with her.

"Rhett," she says, completely out of breath.

I stand up, gripping her arms in my hands. "What happened? Where is she?"

"She was fine and then she starting having a panic attack."

"Take me to her," is all I say. She turns around, and goes down the same way she came up. We wind through rows of people, and push through crowds near the concession stands. "Where is she, Becca?"

And then I see her. My Sunny's crouched in the corner, just outside the bathroom with her head resting on her arms. I run to her, automatically pulling her shaking body into my arms. "I've got you, you're okay."

"I'm sorry. I'm ruining the game."

"No, you're not. What happened?"

She sniffles and wipes her tears away with the back of her hand. Her whole body is still shaking. "I thought I saw him. I was so sure it was him—that he came back to see Wyatt play."

"Your dad?"

"Yes," she chokes out. "But he isn't coming back."

I hold her in my arms, rocking back and forth against the cold concrete wall. The roar of the crowd filters through the cracks as the team takes the field. I thought bringing her here was a good idea—that she'd get to see her brother play and be happy. I never expected this to happen.

"Come on, let's go back to the campground."

"No! I can't leave. I want to see Wyatt."

"Sunny, you're shaking."

"I just need a minute. It will stop." She works on her breathing, and eventually she stops clutching her chest. "I'm not so dizzy anymore."

"You're sure? Do you want me to get you a drink?"

"No," she says before pausing. "I promise I'm not crazy."

"Look at me, Sunny." I wait for her to turn her head, not wanting her to ever feel an ounce of shame for the way she feels. When she does, I continue, "You're the strongest girl I know. Don't ever apologize for having a weak moment. You're human, and I love you."

"I love you, too."

We sit in silence for a few more minutes, and then she says, "When we get back, I want it to be like last night. I want to be in the tent with you where everything's easy."

"Okay." I'd promise her the world if it made her happy.

"I love you, Rhett."

I lean forward and press a kiss to her lips. "Always."

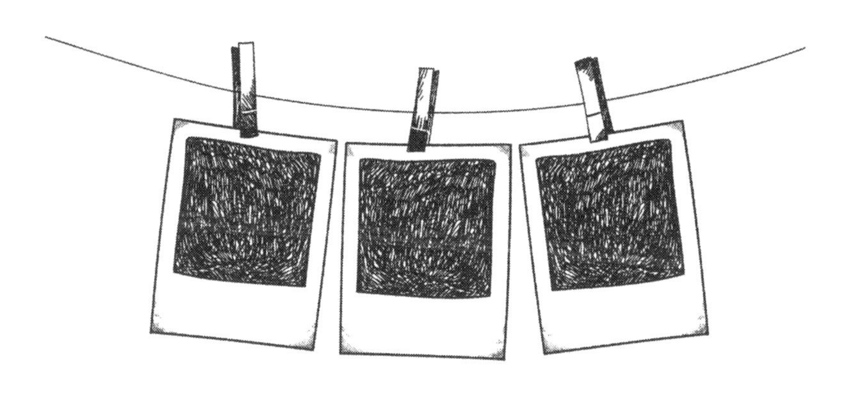

CHAPTER TWENTY-TWO

kinsley

FREAKING OUT AT the football game wasn't in the plans. Yet there I was, hunched over and about to pass out all because I swore I saw my father. Maybe I thought I saw him because I was hoping he would be there for Wyatt. That just for today, he would pick his kids over his grief. We've been hurting, too. We're the ones who lost our parents, but we're the ones expected to move on like the past couple years of our lives weren't complete shit.

I shouldn't say that, the time I've been with Rhett, has been amazing. Which is why I'm determined to spend the last few hours of Fall Fest with the people I consider my family now—pretending like the past doesn't exist. I may never move on from it, but it doesn't have to suffocate me to the point I lose control of my body anymore.

After the game, we came back here and took a nap. Once Wyatt showed up with Becca, we met them at their site and then walked around Fall Fest. We caught a couple good bands, played some games, and ate enough sugar to keep us up all night. By the end of the night, I was so tired, all I wanted was my boyfriend and my pillow. But Rhett made sure I was taken care of before I fell asleep, just like he promised.

We have a little more time to spend together today before we all have to go our separate ways again. It'll be weird not sleeping next to Rhett, and I'll even miss our cozy little tent.

"Whatcha thinking about, Sunny?"

We're still naked from last night, but even that's gotten a little easier for me. I'm trying not to be so self-conscious. "Last night."

"Last night was fun," he says, with a knowing grin. I finally understand what all the fuss is about.

"And how much I'll miss our tent."

He thinks for a second, and then lightning strikes. "We can camp in the barn sometime. I'm moving Dawn over to her new stall soon."

"That would be fun."

Rhett leans in to kiss me, and we're so wrapped up in each other, we don't notice the zipper of our tent opening. "Whoa," we hear before pulling apart.

I pull the blanket over myself, and crouch down under the sleeping bag. "Who was that?" I whisper.

"I'm not sure, hold on."

He pulls his sweats on, and grabs his shirt, but I already know who it is—and I'm mortified. "Don't go out there, Rhett."

"Why not?"

"You're going to end up with a black eye if you do. It was Becca and Wyatt, I hear them arguing. What do we do?"

"We can't stay in here forever. Eventually, we have to face them."

He's right, we can't sit in here all day. Plus, I really have to go to the bathroom. "We get out, and pretend like nothing ever happened. If we don't mention it, they won't either."

"Sunny, you're adorable, but I don't see that being the way this plays out."

"Shit," I mumble, as I chew on my fingernails. "Okay, let's just go."

Once I'm dressed, Rhett unzips the tent, and we file out—a dark cloud of shame hanging low over our heads. Within seconds, my plan to ignore the obvious is shot to shit. Wyatt grabs my arm, and hauls me over toward the trees.

"Be careful with her," Rhett warns, as Wyatt drags me off, a little too roughly.

"What are you thinking, Kinsley?"

"I didn't do anything wrong. How is this any different than what you do? What you've *done*," I stress.

"Because I'm in college. I'm an adult who can make decisions with my head and not my heart. What you have isn't going to last. It's perfect right now, but when it ends, you'll regret it, Kinny. I don't want you to get your heart broken."

There's no use arguing with him about this. He's never going to be on the same page with me. Not when he's busy being a protective older brother. So, I use the only line of defense I can think of. "Is Becca a mistake?"

"What? No."

"Is she old enough to know what she wants?"

"Of course she is."

"Is what you have with her real?"

"It sure as hell feels that way."

"Exactly. I'm no different than Becca. Only my guy is the same age as me."

Wyatt mulls it over for a few seconds, and kicks at a rock on the ground when he realizes I have a point—that his little sister isn't so little anymore.

"I love him, Wyatt, and I don't regret a single second of the times we've been together."

He doesn't say anything back to me. He just shoves his hands in his pockets and walks away. I don't want to lose my brother over a guy, and I don't think I have. Still, he knows the one way to hurt me the most is to leave.

Rhett's by my side once he's gone, rubbing my back in support. "Sunny, why don't we go shower and get changed. He'll come back when he's ready."

I nod my head, because he will. He needs time, and maybe I do, too.

I'VE SHOWERED, EATEN both breakfast and lunch, and still, there's no word from Wyatt. Becca's texted me, so I know they're still walking around the fairgrounds, but she isn't saying much either. I don't understand what's gotten into the two of them, but the fact that they don't want to be around us, hurts.

"Do you want to hang out a little longer?"

I glance at the time on my phone. "No, we have to get back. Is everything packed up?"

"Yeah, but you don't have to rush. If you want to wait, that's okay."

Part of me wants to sit here all night until Wyatt comes back, but we have school tomorrow and at least a two hour drive ahead of us. "He's not coming back. We can leave."

I feel a familiar hand on my shoulder, and when I turn around, I see the remorseful eyes of my brother. "I'm sorry, Kinny."

Rhett walks over to his truck and stands with Becca, the both of them giving us a little space to figure things out. "What took you so long?"

He smiles, but it doesn't reach his eyes the way it usually

does. "What you said, the way you compared yourself to Becca, got me thinking."

"How so?"

"I guess I always knew I liked her. I mean she's been on my mind for over a year now, but when you said what you did, I realized just how much she means to me. And if you feel for Rhett half of what I feel for Becca, then who am I to stand in your way. I want you to be happy. We're both young as shit, but sometimes when you know, you just know. Right?"

"When did you get so wise?"

"I've had a lot of help from my little sister," he teases. "Becca and I are official."

"Really! It's about time. She told me you hooked up at homecoming, by the way."

"It was more than that—always has been. We both knew it, but I think me being away might have been what helped us." He's quiet for a second, before he says, "Do you remember what Mom used to tell us before she passed?"

How could I forget. I can hear her voice, feel her hand on mine, and see her face like it was yesterday. "I'll be seeing you when I fly away," I whisper, remembering how many times she told us she'd always be there, always see us no matter how far away heaven was.

"Yeah," he says. "Well, I thought about that, and no matter how far I am from Becca, I always feel her with me—just like Mom said. She's in all my thoughts, and I feel like maybe it's for a reason. Like maybe Mom sent Rhett and Becca to us so we wouldn't be alone anymore."

"I thought that, too. If she did, she picked two perfect choices."

"I know she did. Fuck, I miss her, Kinny. I'm so mad at Dad, but I think I'm starting to understand a little bit of his pain. I thought it would get easier as time passed, but I still miss her as much now as I did back then—if not more."

"I miss them both. Becca probably told you, but I thought I saw Dad at the game. And then I had a panic attack."

"Do you get them a lot?"

"I used to, but not much anymore. Not since I've been with Rhett, but I don't even know what I'd do if he came back, Wyatt. Part of me needs him to, yet I don't want him to. I guess that's my anger talking."

"We have each other. Always remember that."

"I will. I love you, Wyatt." My big brother wraps me in his arms, and while I may not have the two people who are supposed to love and protect me most, I have the best big brother a girl could dream of.

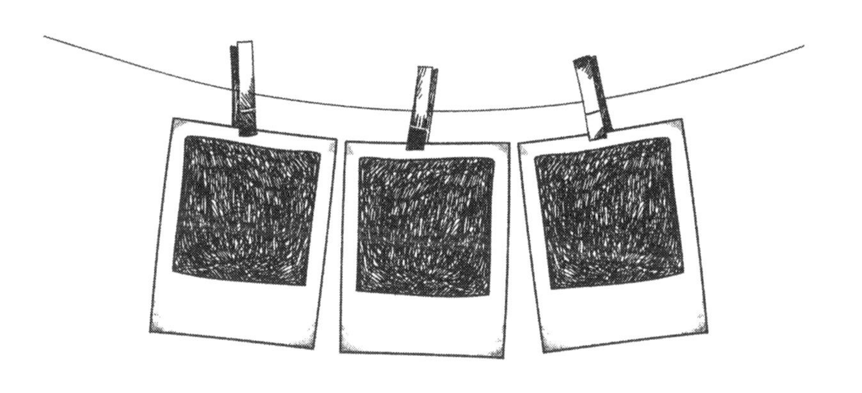

CHAPTER TWENTY-THREE

kinsley

"KINSLEY," WAKE UP.

I open my eyes, and Carson's staring back at me. Not even realizing I slept right through my alarm, I glance at my clock, shocked to see I slept twelve hours straight. "Shit, thanks for waking me."

"You're pretty late for school. Are you sick?"

I sit up, wiping the sleep from my eyes. "No, just tired."

"You've been working too much. Why don't you take some time off, I've barely seen you since Fall Fest and that was a month ago."

Carson's right. We haven't had any of our usual couch conversations. We haven't hung out at all really. With the holiday's right around the corner, I've been working extra shifts at the diner to be able to afford presents. When I'm not at work, I'm usually with Rhett. I don't even know what's going on in my own sister's life anymore. If she's awake, I'm at school. When she's at work, I'm home.

I slide out from under my warm blankets, shivering as soon as my feet hit the floor. "You've been back and forth to see Stacy a lot. You haven't been home much either." I don't say it because I'm jealous, I say it because I don't want him trying to make me feel guilty for spending my free time with Rhett instead of him.

"I go to the campus to see Wyatt, Kins."

"Oh come on, you see her, too."

"It's hard not to. She's practically his neighbor, but it's not a big deal."

Stacy bothers me, but it doesn't bother me that they're seeing each other—even if he swears it's just casual fun and nothing official. "You can do way better than her, you know." He stares at me, and I grab my towel off the back of my desk chair, holding it tightly against my chest.

"I know I can, but *she* hasn't come to her senses yet. There's breakfast on the table when you're finished." He turns and walks out of my room, leaving my head spinning.

I shuffle into the bathroom, praying my headache and cramps are for a reason, but I'm not that lucky—I'm still late. My mind wants to panic, but I try to block out the possibility of being pregnant and focus on getting out of this house.

By the time I get to school, I already missed first period. I wait for Rhett outside our photography class, and when he sees me, he smiles, instantly making me forget about my possible problem. "You need to stop being late. That class isn't as fun without you."

He kisses me, and I wrap my arms around his waist, soaking up his warmth. "I'd still be sleeping if Carson hadn't woken me up."

Rubbing my back he says, "I hate that he got to see you

before me, but I'm glad you're here."

"I guess I'll see you at lunch." I make no attempt to move or to unwrap my arms from Rhett's body.

He chuckles and kisses the top of my head. "Are you planning on letting go of me, Sunny?"

"No. I'm good."

He peels me off his body anyway, and turns around so I'm staring at his back. "Hop on."

"You can't be serious. We'll get in trouble."

"Says the girl who's holding a tardy slip. Just get on me."

I hop up and wrap my legs around him. He takes off, running down the hallway, weaving in and out of bodies that are all staring at us like we've lost our minds. If I wasn't awake before, I am now. "Rhett, slow down!"

He doesn't. Not until we're in front of the locker room where he places me back on my feet again. "I gotta run, but I love you."

Shaking my head, I laugh as he runs back the way we came, high fiving Jake on his way. "I love you, too," I murmur to myself.

I change into my gym uniform and wait for Becca on the bench next to our gym lockers, but when the bell rings, and she's still not there, I reluctantly go into the gym without her. The only reason I survive this class is because she's in it. She wasn't joking when she said Wyatt was the athlete of the family.

We're running our boring warm-up laps around the perimeter of the gym when I start to feel like I'm going to throw up. Running isn't my thing, especially when I've only been awake for forty-five minutes.

"Okay everyone, grab a stick. We're going to play some indoor hockey," Mrs. Haines, the gym teacher on a permanent caffeine high, announces.

I pull a stick out of the box and stand back, letting the other girls move ahead of me. Some are actually excited to knock a hard plastic ball around the gym. Me, not so much. It only gets worse once we move into positions and Mandi ends up lined up across from me.

The whistle blows and she charges at me like we're playing a game of football instead of hockey. "What is your problem?"

"I'm just playing defense."

"Your team has the ball, back up."

She listens and puts some space in between the two of us, but she takes a pass from her teammate, and then, like it's in slow motion, she winds up and swings her stick with all of her might, sending the ball flying directly at me.

I fall to the floor, and my stick hits the ground as hard as I do. Immediately, I know something's wrong. I try to peel my body off the floor, but it hurts too much. "I'm going to throw up," I say to whoever's close enough to hear it. Before the trash can gets to me, I heave all over the floor in front of everyone.

Mrs. Haines blows her whistle, backing everyone up. "Mandi, you're out of the game. Sierra, tell the nurse we need her. Hurry up."

Sierra, like a deer in headlights, runs through the doors, and into the hallway. She's back in a couple minutes with Nurse Cathy by her side. She gives me a once over before she moves me into the wheelchair she brought with her. Everyone's staring, which I hate, but I let her wheel me to her office, too weak to go on my own two feet. I'm trying too hard not to throw up again to really care who sees me.

She opens the small room all the sick kids rest in until their parents pick them up, and wheels me next to a cot. "Lie down for me, Kinsley."

I listen to her, as she runs through a series of questions. I answer them all honestly, even the one about how I was feeling before I came to school. She listens to every word I say, and I think nothing of it. That is, until her next question. "When was your last menstrual period?"

I sit up, not wanting to discuss this with her. "I'm fine."

"We need to discuss this if there's a possibility you could be pregnant. Is this something we need to consider?"

"I'm not talking about any of this at school. You're not my doctor." She can't force me to do anything. "Can I get my stuff from the locker room? I want to go home."

She nods her head. "Will you take this for me at home, and let me know the results."

I take the pregnancy test out of her hand, and stare at it. I'm not walking around school holding a test. Like she can read minds, she hands me a paper bag. "You're not going to tell anybody anything, are you?"

"I can't by law, but if you are pregnant, Kinsley, you need to get to the doctor. Go home and take the test. You'll want to open it, and—."

I hold up my hand before she can go any farther. Even talking about it makes me want to throw up again. "I'll read the directions and take the test."

She lets me leave, but I have to stop in the bathroom to throw up again. It's only when my face is close to a disgusting public toilet that I realize the nurse is right, I need to see my doctor because I'm almost positive this test is going to be positive.

I haven't had a panic attack since the football game, but right now, one's threatening to grip me by the throat, making it almost impossible to catch my breath. Why is this happening to me? Rhett's always been careful—at least I think he has.

As I peel myself off the bathroom floor, all I can think about is how disappointed my mom would be. Kate's going to kill me. Wyatt's going to hate me. But Rhett—he'll leave me, and that's what scares me the most right now.

AN HOUR LATER, I'm sitting in the doctor's office with a tiny plastic cup in my hand. The test I took at home was positive—just like I knew it would be. I'm not ready to be a mother. This was all an accident—a really big accident that's going to cause a ton of trouble if this second test ends up positive, too.

And it does.

Now I'm listening to Dr. Royer's go on and on about my options while I'm still trying to process the fact that I'm pregnant. I can't be more than a couple weeks along, but the second he mentions termination, I already know it's not an option. We learned about what happens in health class, and there's no way I want to go through any of that. "I don't want an abortion."

Nurse Kimberly nods her head, and Dr. Royer, continues to type on the laptop she carries around with her from room to room. "What are you typing?" I ask her, when curiosity gets the best of me.

"Everything we're discussing. It makes dictating easier for me."

"Who looks at it?" I'm already trying to figure out if it's going to get back to Kate, who was my legal-guardian, up until my eighteenth birthday this past summer.

"It all goes into your medical records account."

"Oh, okay."

Another woman walks into my room, pulling a cart with a machine on it. She gives me a hesitant smile, like I'm a fool for getting knocked up at such a young age—like I purposely tried to make a baby with my boyfriend.

"My name's Tammy, I'm going to do your ultrasound for you."

"Why do I need an ultrasound?"

Dr. Royer looks up from her computer long enough to answer my question. "It's protocol, especially for someone who was hit in the stomach."

All this time I've been freaking out, I never once considered that when the ball pounded into my stomach, it could have hurt the baby. I'm too scared to find out the answer, so I don't even bothering asking if they think the baby's injured. I'll know soon enough.

Nurse Kimberly helps me lie on the table, and holds my hand once I'm in position. She's only known me less than an hour, and still, it's comforting having her by my side. I'm glad I'm not going through this alone.

"You can watch the screen, and once I have the probe in place, you'll notice some movement."

The screen's black and white, and suddenly, it sounds like I'm in the middle of the ocean. One summer at the beach, I held a giant seashell to my ear in a souvenir shop. It's the same kind of whooshing sound I heard then. "What is that?"

Kimberly smiles, looking down at me. "That's your baby's heartbeat. One of the best sounds in the entire world." She points to the blob on the screen that's wiggling around. It looks like a gummy bear—a hyper one. "And that right there is your baby."

I sit up a little bit, propping myself on my elbows while keeping the rest of my body exactly how it was. Staring at the screen, it doesn't seem like I'm looking at something inside my own body—that I have a tiny person inside me. "Do you know what it is?"

Tammy shakes her head. "No, it's too early. We'll be able to tell around twenty weeks. You're measuring between five and six weeks today."

I do the math in my head. Fall Fest was six weeks ago. That means Rhett and I made a baby one of our first times together. "You're not going to tell anyone about this are you? I can tell them?"

"This baby is your responsibility now, Kinsley. We respect your privacy as our patient, and we'll send you home with everything you need to begin a healthy pregnancy."

I rest my head against the exam table, wondering how I'm ever going to break the news to my sister. I never meant for this to happen, but now that it has, I'm afraid I'm going to lose everyone I love.

I should tell Rhett first, but I don't know how. What if he breaks up with me?

As soon as the test is finished, I take my papers, and practically run out of the office into the cold November air. It all hits me at once, the baby, losing my friends and family, how disappointed my parents would be—and all I can do is sit on the bench and cry.

The playground across the street is filled with kids, and suddenly elementary school doesn't seem that long ago. I feel closer to a bunch of kids than the adults I was just with. I'm practically a kid having a kid—it only makes me cry harder.

I cry for every dream I'm going to have to give up, every person I'm about to disappoint, and a baby who never asked to be brought into the world. A baby I don't want to have, yet somehow already care about—even if it has the power to destroy me.

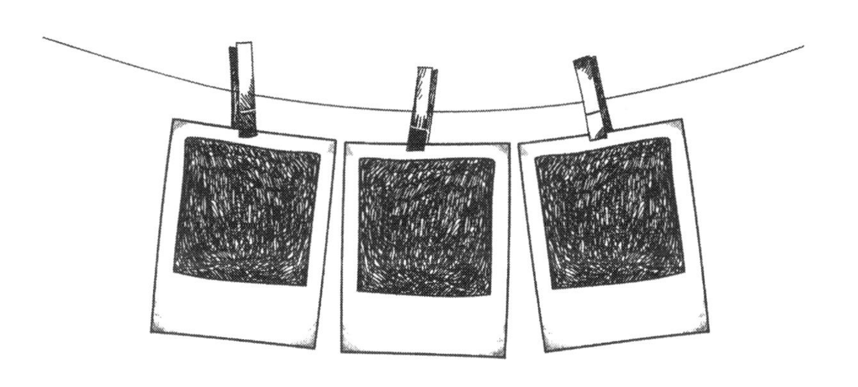

CHAPTER TWENTY-FOUR

rhett

"WHERE'S KINSLEY?" JAKE asks when we sit down to lunch.

"I don't know. She disappeared after gym."

Mandi, who still insists on sitting at the end of our table, glances at me, and then ducks her head. She's been acting weird since she sat down.

Grayson slams his tray on the table, sitting next to Mandi. "What the hell happened in gym this morning, slugger?"

For the first time ever, Mandi's almost speechless. "It was an accident," she whispers.

"That's not what I heard. Rumor has it you made the slap shot of the century and knocked Kinsley on her ass."

I throw my sandwich down on my tray. "What?"

"Yeah, man. It's all over the school. Your girl threw up on the free throw line. How do you not know this?"

I spent last period in the wood shop, grinding the shit out of wood. I pull out my cell phone and dial her number, but it goes straight to voicemail. A text goes unanswered, and now I'm freaking the hell out. "Did she go home, Mandi?"

"I think so. She was throwing up."

I run my hands through my hair, "Jesus, what did you do to her?"

"Nothing! It was an accident."

Accident or not, it still happened. And I know better than to believe she didn't do it on purpose. Everything with that girl does is calculated and planned—to her advantage. Regardless of what she had planned, I try messaging Kinsley a couple more times, but there's still no answer.

I have no choice but to sit and wait.

Each period that passes, the clock moves a little slower. By the time the final bell rings, I skip my locker entirely, not even caring if I have the books I need to do my homework. Now that football is over, I can actually leave school on time which means I'm in her driveway in six minutes flat.

I run up the stairs to her apartment, and knock. Nobody answers, but her car's parked right next to mine. I turn the knob and push the door open. "Kinsley?"

The house is quiet. Her bedroom door is cracked, so I push it open, trying my best not to scare her. She's in her bed with her blankets covering her, but I can hear her crying. "Sunny, what's wrong?"

She sits up, no doubt shocked to see me standing in the middle of her bedroom. "You didn't expect me to stay away, did you?"

She shakes her head, and lays back down. "I was going to call you back in a few minutes."

"How long have you been home?"

"About twenty minutes."

"Where'd you go after gym class?"

"The doctor's office."

"Grayson told me what happened at lunch. What did the doctor say? Are you okay?"

She doesn't answer me, so I take my shoes and coat off, and kneel on the floor beside her bed. Reaching out, I hold her cheek in my hand, running my thumb back and forth across her skin. "I missed you," I tell her, hoping she says something. Right now, she's scaring me a little.

"I missed you too," she says, nervously.

"What's wrong, Sunny?"

She bites her lip, tears forming in her eyes again. "Rhett, I don't know how to tell you this."

"You can tell me anything. Just talk to me. I'll make whatever's bothering you go away."

She closes her eyes just as the first tear falls. "You can't make it better this time."

"Why not?"

"Because—because I'm pregnant, Rhett."

Her words literally knock me on my ass. I hit the carpet and fall flat on my back, staring at the ceiling. She cries harder, and I realize my reaction wasn't the best, but she just told me I'm going to have a kid. A fucking kid. "You're sure?" I ask from my spot on the floor.

"I took a test."

"Could it be wrong?"

"No, I had an ultrasound after the test."

I get off the floor. Still a little dazed. "You saw it?"

"I heard the heartbeat, too."

No wonder she's crying. She's had a long ass day. "What did it look like?" It's a stupid thing to say, it's a damn baby, but I don't know what else to say to her. I'm probably supposed to have all kinds of questions.

"Like a dancing gummy bear."

"Seriously?" She slides her hand under her pillow, and pulls out a little black and white picture. "Is that?" I can't even say it out loud. *Our baby.*

"I don't know what it is yet, but they'll tell me when she's bigger."

I stare at the picture in my hands, amazed that we created something—a little gummy person. She's right, it looks exactly like a bear. "You said, she. Do you think it's a girl?"

"Did I? I guess I always pictured myself having a little girl someday. Not now, though."

"What do you mean, not now? It's already done, Sunny."

"I know that," she snaps.

"Sorry, I just."

"I'm scared out of my mind, and I know it's going to ruin our lives, but I can't," she sobs.

"Shhh, it's okay, Kinsley. It's not going to ruin our lives—I won't let that happen. We'll figure it out." I don't have a single clue how we're going to figure it out, but I tell her anyway, because I'm the one who did this to her. I just want to protect her. "Until I figure out what to do, we can keep it between the two of us."

"I have to tell Kate. I can't go through this without her."

"Just for now, just until I figure out what we're going to do, I want you to keep this a secret. Can you do that for me? I need you to promise me, Sunny." If my parents find out, we won't stand a chance. They'll rip Kinsley and the baby away from me.

"What's to figure out? In seven and a half months, I'm having a baby."

"We have college next year. We're graduating in seven months. There's a lot to consider."

She sits up on the edge of her bed, protectively wrapping her arms around our baby, her chin quivering. "So, a couple weeks after we graduate, I'll have a baby. I might not even make it to graduation, Rhett."

"*We'll* have a baby." Still on my knees, I move between her legs. I wrap my arms around her back, while her hands instinctively comb through my hair. I kiss her still flat stomach picturing what it will look like a couple months from now. Never in a million years did I imagine this would happen, I mean, we're having sex, but we've been pretty careful.

"I'm scared, Rhett," she whispers.

I pull my head away from her stomach, looking into her teary eyes. "Sunny, I don't know what we're going to do yet, but I'm going to do everything I can to keep us together—no matter what." She's quiet, but I need her to believe in us. "Tell me you trust me, Sunny."

"I trust you."

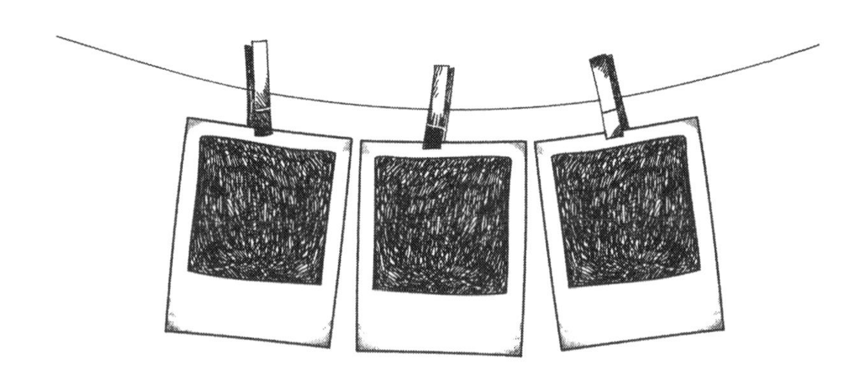

CHAPTER TWENTY-FIVE

kinsley

IT'S BEEN A week since I found out I'm pregnant. Each night, I stay up beyond the point of exhaustion, trying to wrap my head around the idea of becoming a mom. An actual mom with a baby of my own. No matter how many times I run different scenarios through my mind, I can't make any situation work. Rhett and I don't have a place to live, or enough money to survive without the both of us working full-time jobs, yet we don't have diplomas to get decent jobs in the first place.

My interview with Parsons is coming up, which only depresses me more. There's no way I can still go to New York. It was going to be a struggle to support myself in the City. Adding a baby to the mix would be next to impossible. Still, I don't have the nerve to call and cancel the appointment—not yet anyway.

"Are you okay? You've been quiet today." Rhett asks, as we

leave school for the day.

"Just thinking, sorry." I haven't told him I haven't cancelled yet. I guess a part of me is still hoping I can make it work—even if I already know there's no way I could split up my family. Not having one of my own is all the more reason that this baby should have both parents.

"You don't have to be sorry, Sunny. I get it."

"I hate being a problem."

Rhett stops walking in the middle of the sidewalk, turning me to face him. "You're not a problem. I don't want you thinking like that."

"Everything's different though. You're not the same, I'm not the same. All I do is throw up and cry. I kind of can't stand myself."

We start walking again, and when we get to my car, Rhett opens my door and tosses my bag in the passenger seat. He even helps me get inside like I'm nine months pregnant instead of two.

He kneels down beside me, reaching for my hand as soon as my seatbelt clicks into place. "Are you okay to drive? I can take you home." He slides his fingers underneath the seatbelt, making sure it's not too tight on my stomach.

"I'm fine—still feel nauseous, but it doesn't really go away. At least there's plenty of crackers and a never ending supply of ginger ale at the diner."

Rhett sighs, and runs his hand through his hair. It's what he does when he doesn't like what I'm saying. Trust me, I'd rather go home and sleep, but I have to make as much money as I can before this baby comes. Especially considering I might be on my own, sooner rather than later, if Kate decides she's ready to move to Philadelphia. Her own relationship has been strained and I see how much she misses her boyfriend. I hate that she's stuck because of me.

"I'll stop in and see you. At least if I'm sitting at one of your tables, it's one less person for you to wait on."

I reach out and run my thumb along Rhett's cheek, wondering how I got so lucky to get this guy, and so unlucky to get pregnant. In the back of my mind I always knew getting pregnant was a possibility, yet I never imagined it would happen to me. It's stupid to be so naïve, but I thought I had been through enough already. There was no way I'd have to deal with a baby on top of everything else. Or so I thought. "I appreciate what you're trying to do, but I need the money—this baby is going to be expensive."

So much for going balls to the walls this year. I'm back in parent mode—right where I started. Maybe this is the person I was meant to be all along instead of trying to be someone I'm not. The real Kinsley West is responsible, hard-working, and determined. I need to find her again.

"Don't worry about money, okay? I'm going over to the club. There are a couple positions there I think I can get. If I can't, I'll toss around my dad's name until someone caves."

"Did you forget you're *the* Rhett Taylor? They'll want you working for them."

"Do *you* want me?" He asks, quickly.

I stare at him a second, trying to figure out where he's going with this, but I don't have a clue. "Of course I do."

"That's all that matters to me, Sunny. We're going to get judged once everyone finds out, but I like the idea of just you, me and the baby. I want to stay like this for as long as we can."

"I do, too, but I feel like everyone's been staring at my stomach all day. Do I look different?"

"No, you look perfect. They don't know anything. It just seems like they're watching you because we're protecting our secret."

"I need to tell my sister the truth, Rhett. I can't wait much longer. If she finds out from anyone but me, it will only make it worse for us."

Rhett looks over his shoulder, making sure nobody can hear our conversation. That's all we need, for someone like Mandi to hear about it. It would be all over school faster than I can blink. "We shouldn't be talking about this here."

"I know. I have to get going anyway."

Rhett leans in for one more kiss before closing my door and resting his palm against the glass of my window. I match my palm up with his before reversing out of the parking space, and heading home.

The drive's short, but by the time I get there, I already feel sick again. Hurrying up the stairs, I sigh in relief when I don't have to stop to unlock the front door. I'm not sure I could have made it to the bathroom had I stopped.

My backpack falls to the cool tile floor, as I heave into the toilet. My ribs ache, and my headache returns instantly. I've never been so sick in my life. Even the flu has never been this bad. At least that comes in with a vengeance and goes away. This has the potential to linger for seven more months.

When there's nothing left inside me, I flush the toilet, and use the sink for support as I try to stand up. I brush my teeth again, and splash cool water on my face. I'm exhausted.

I reach for the door but it opens on its own. Carson sticks his head inside. "Are you okay?"

"Yeah, I must have eaten something bad at lunch. Haven't felt right all afternoon." I expect him to buy my lie, but I'm still so nervous, I can't even look him in the eye. This is what my life's turned into—one lie after another.

I move to leave the bathroom, but he blocks the doorway, not letting me through. He stares at me, his eyes raking over every inch of my body. "Tell me the truth, Kins."

Instantly, I panic. *He knows. But how?* "I don't know what you're talking about, but I'm going to be late for work if you don't move."

"Then you're going to be late because I'm not moving."

"Carson, please. Betty is expecting me."

"Tell me," he pleads. "Just say the words."

I push on his chest, begging him to move, but he only grabs my wrists and holds them so I can't get away. "Stop it. Leave me alone!"

"Kinsley, I know. I found the box when I was taking out the trash."

"I don't know what you're talking about."

"Don't lie to me, Kins."

Tears prick my eyes, and no matter how hard I try to keep them inside of me, I can't. "Let go of me."

"It's true. Isn't it? You're really pregnant."

"Yes," I whisper. As soon as he comprehends what I'm saying, he lets go of my wrist, and drops his head in defeat. He rests his head against the doorframe, and it's clear how disappointed he is in me. But what he feels is nothing compared to the way I feel about myself.

"How could you let him touch you? Did you really think it would last? That he's going to blow off college to stay home and take care of you?"

Each word out of his mouth stings more than the last. I want to scream at him, but I can't. Not when there's a good chance everything he's saying is the truth. Rhett loves me, but he might love his future more. "Please, stop."

He doesn't. He only drills his point home harder, wrecking me completely. "Does Kate know? Wyatt's going to lose his fucking mind. You realize this, right?"

"You can't tell anyone, Carson. Please. Not yet."

"I've waited an entire week for you to tell me about this. I've heard you throwing up, but I was praying like hell it was a virus and not because of a damn baby. You're in so much trouble, but you don't seem like you care."

"I get it. I'm worried every single second of every single day. It's all I think about."

"How could you let this happen, Kins? How?"

"It was an accident. I didn't ask for this to happen, Carson. I didn't!"

"You messed up the second you let him touch you. You've been more worried about keeping Rhett Taylor happy than staying true to yourself. But let me tell you one thing, the thrill is over. He doesn't want a kid or a needy girlfriend. He wants to go away to school and do whatever the hell he wants with whoever he thinks looks good that night."

That's not how Rhett operates. I know better, but hearing it from a guy who's already in college scares me. "Shut up! You have no idea what you're talking about. You don't know what we have."

"I know enough to know he's going to run like hell the first chance he gets. He's not going to take care of you the way I would have."

And here we go again, more jealously. I thought we moved on from this, but apparently, we've been running in circles. "This isn't about you, Carson."

"You're right, because everything always revolves around you. Everyone makes sacrifices for you while you do whatever you want. For someone with next to nothing you have a real sense of entitlement, Kins."

I can't believe he's turning on me like this. He's always been my friend—the guy I would turn to when I was down or needed someone to cheer me up. More than anyone, he knows how much pain I've dealt with. I didn't ask to lose my parents. I didn't ask to have my life ripped away from me, and I most definitely didn't ask to be pregnant. "You moved in here on your own. Kate stayed here to take care of me because she wanted to. Not once have I asked for a single favor or thing from either of you. I can take care of myself."

"You keep telling yourself that, Princess. I'm done. I'm done giving a shit about protecting you." Carson storms off to his room, and throws his suitcase on the bed. He grabs handfuls of clothes out of his drawers and shoves them inside in a heap. Each item he tosses in, he throws a little harder. "I came here for you!" he shouts.

I slither around the corner of the hallway, watching in horror as he destroys his room, shattering picture frames, and upending anything that's not attached to a wall or the floor. He's allowed to be mad, but he can't move out. We can't afford to stay here without him. "Please, don't leave," I beg. "We need you."

"Maybe that's the problem with this arrangement. You need me, but I don't need you, Kinsley. I could be living in some bachelor pad bringing girls home any night of the week—like a typical twenty-year-old guy."

That's not Carson. He's never been a player and he's never used girls to fill empty space in his life. "You don't mean that." He stares at me before reaching for the book on his desk and chucking it with all his might. I scream, ducking my head before it hits the wall next to me. "Are you crazy?"

For a minute he looks remorseful, like he realizes he's out of control and needs to rein it in, but it doesn't last long. Once he sees I'm okay, the anger replaces any trace of remorse he may have had. The Carson I cared about has already moved out, and I'm not about to stay here and listen to this one rip me to shreds again.

I turn around and run to the bathroom, grabbing my bag off the floor and tossing it on my shoulder.

He's struggling to catch his breath after his temper tantrum when he asks, "Where are you going?"

I don't respond, I just keep moving. I'm in my car and pulling out of the driveway by the time I see him standing on the stairs outside the apartment, watching as I drive away.

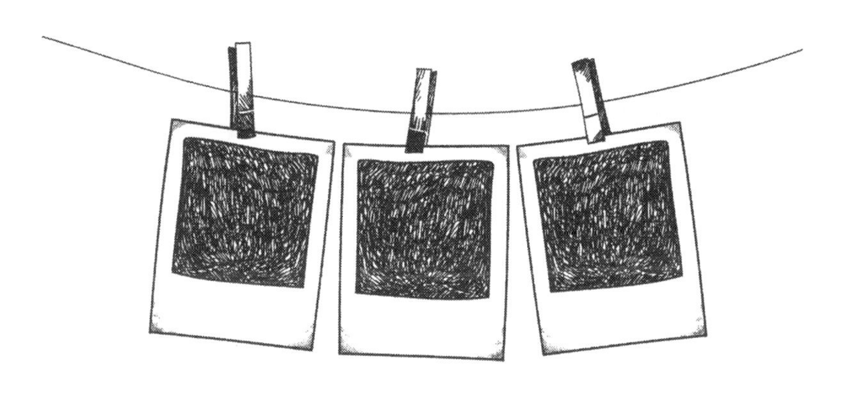

CHAPTER TWENTY-SIX

rhett

I'VE BEEN STARING at the same page in my trigonometry book for the last half hour. I'm trying to finish up my homework, so I can get to the diner to see Kinsley, but it's not happening. Usually I'm pretty good at math, but my mind's too wrapped up in the real world to care about the insignificant problems in front of me.

I'm about to give up when my phone buzzes with a text. I reach into my pocket, and pull out my phone, surprised to see the message is from Kinsley. She's usually doesn't message me unless she's on her break.

Kinsley: Are your parents home?

Rhett: Not yet. Why?

Kinsley: Can I come over?

Rhett: Are you okay? Do you need me to pick you up at the diner?

I knew I shouldn't have let her to go work. Not that I can stop her from doing what she wants to do, but she looked so pale and tired when I said good-bye to her at school. As adamant as she was about going to work, it doesn't make sense why she wouldn't be there now.

Kinsley: I'm in your driveway.

Seriously? Surprised she's already here, I open the front door just as she's getting out of her car. Right away, it's clear she's not okay. I wait until she's standing on the porch before I ask, "What happened?"

She practically falls into my arms, and I pick her up, her legs automatically hooking around my waist. "Shhh. It's okay." Her shoulders shake as she cries into my shoulder. I have no idea why my girl is falling apart in my arms, and I'm almost too afraid to ask.

I hold her until I climb the stairs and lay her in the center of my bed. Pulling off her shoes, I slide her under the covers and climb in next to her. "Tell me what's wrong, Sunny."

Her chin quivers and tears roll down her cheeks. She can barely catch her breath to speak. "H-he knows, Rhett. Carson knows I'm pregnant."

I swallow, trying to process what she's telling me. He's the last person I would trust with our secret. Mostly because he's always wanted her to himself. And there's no reason for him to protect her, especially if he's still jealous she picked me over him. "Is he talking?"

"He's really, really mad. I should have been more careful, but after I took the test, all I thought about was getting to the doctor to see if it was right. He's known for a week, Rhett. An entire week."

If he's kept it a secret for a week, maybe there's a chance he's not going to say anything. Or maybe he's going to use this as leverage to get back at me for stealing his girl—even though she never even knew he wanted her until she got with me. "Did he say anything else?"

"He said some really horrible things about the both of us. After he threw a book at me, I ran out and came here."

"He hit you?" The thought of him hurting her makes me seethe. A rage like I've never felt rips through my body.

She shakes her head. "He hit the wall beside me."

"That motherfucker." I get out of bed, searching for my sneakers. "If he thinks he can control you with this, he has another thing coming. There's no way he's going to play games with *my* family."

She wipes her tears with her fingers, swiping under each eye, quickly. "No, don't go over there. It will only make it worse. He needs some time, that's all."

"You're defending him?" It shouldn't surprise me. The two of them have had some weird bond the entire time we've been together. It's not easy for her to let people go, but Carson doesn't deserve to stay in her life. Not after today.

"What he did was wrong, but he's not like that. He wouldn't hurt me—not on purpose."

"You're the most forgiving person I've ever met, Sunny." I sit down on the edge of the bed, wondering what we're going to do if he talks. I was sure we had more time to figure it out, but now it looks like we've run out before we've figured a single thing out one way or another.

"I'm more scared of Wyatt finding out. If Carson tells him, we're done for."

There's no way that's going to happen. "I told you, I'd risk it all for you, Sunny. I meant it. It's you, me, and our baby now.

I'm not going away to school next year. I can go to class here, like Carson does, and take care of you both. He's done taking care of my girl."

Her eyes widen in surprise. I wasn't planning on dropping it on her this way. I was actually hoping to take her out to dinner and talk it through rationally, but desperate times call for desperate measure, and right now, all I care about is letting her know I'm hers. I'm not leaving her no matter what happens when the world finds out.

"You can't do that. You'll always regret it. I don't want you to hate me someday because I ruined your dream."

"What about your dreams? You want to go to Parsons just as bad as I wanted to play football. Why should you be expected to give it all up, and I get to move on like nothing ever happened?"

"You'll regret it."

"I'd regret it if I went. Not if I stayed, Sunny. You're all I care about."

I feel her phone vibrate against my leg. She rolls over and slides it out of her pocket. "It's Carson."

I reach for the phone, but she doesn't let me have it. "Don't make it worse than it already is. Please. I have to go back to that house."

"I've never hated that you live with him more than I do now."

"He was packing when I left. There's a chance he's already gone."

"What's he texting you?"

"He's just apologizing."

After she types out a response to Carson, that I don't bother to read, I kiss her forehead and run my fingers over her stomach. All this stress can't be good for them. We need some time away—just the two us like when we went to Fall Fest. I felt closer to her than ever that weekend, and I miss it. "My uncle has a cabin in the Poconos. We can stay there over break. Just me and you."

Between Thanksgiving break coming up and winter break shortly after, we'll need a place to go if we want to be together. Especially if everyone we know finds out. This could be the perfect solution.

"What do you mean? Like run away?"

"Think of it as taking a break—not running. I have a key, and nobody will bother us there. We can be us again. Without all this drama."

She links her fingers with mine, bringing them to her lips. "I'll go anywhere with you."

Before I have a chance to tell her about the rest of my plans once we get there, my bedroom door whips open so hard I'm almost positive there's a hole in the wall from the door knob.

My mom barges in, and takes one look at me and Kinsley in my bed, and narrows her eyes. "I trusted you, Rhett Mitchell Taylor."

Whenever she busts out my full name, it's never good. Today I know the reason is because of the baby. She knows.

She points her red fingernail at Kinsley. "You, out of my house! Now!"

Kinsley lets go of my hand, and scrambles to the side of the bed. "Mom! What are you doing? You can't kick her out."

"I most certainly can. This trash is not welcome in my home. Now when she's sleeping around town like the little tramp she is."

Is she kidding me right now? I'm the first guy who's ever held her hand. The first guy Kinsley's ever kissed, and her first date to a dance. I'm the *only* guy she's ever shared her body with, and without a doubt we belong to each other in every way that matters. "You're wrong, Mom. I'm the only guy she's ever touched."

Mom scoffs, rolling her eyes at me. "You really expect me to believe that? Jake's mom filed Kinsley's medical records at the office this afternoon, and then made sure to give me a call. You can imagine what a shock it was to find out at *work* in front of all my co-workers that my son's girlfriend is pregnant. Do you have any idea how embarrassing that was for me? How hard it will be for me to show my face around this town now?"

In typical fashion, she's more worried about her own rep than the one of the girl she's trying to ruin by making false accusations. "Your face? What about hers? Thanks to you people think she's a slut."

"I don't sleep around," Kinsley murmurs over and over, as she slides her feet into her shoes.

"You're knocked up and now you're trying to ruin my son's life. My Rhett wouldn't let that happen. I've let him live in his fantasy world with you for weeks now, but you've taken it too far. You will not blame this pregnancy on *my* son."

I grab Kinsley before she can leave, standing behind her with my hands on her shoulders. "Mom, I love this girl. She's carrying *my* baby." I spell it out for her, really slow, hoping she can accept it as the truth. I've lied about stupid shit in my life, but I would never lie about creating a life with another person.

"How are you going to raise a child, Rhett? You have college next year. You're going to play football while she'll be in some run down trailer park with a baby on her hip."

"Wherever she is, is where I'll be," I tell her with complete confidence. I already told Kinsley that was the plan.

"I don't care if she lives in a damn box behind the grocery store. She's screwed up her future, but I won't let her touch yours, Rhett."

My girl completely breaks down in my arms, but she doesn't let me comfort her this time. She pushes around my mom, running toward the front door.

I've always loved my mom, despite her over-bearing protectiveness, but today she's gone too far. I can honestly say I hate her. I hate the way she acts superior, and the way she puts down a girl with the kindest heart. The kind of girl she would be lucky to have in her family.

"She's running away because she knows I'm right, Rhett. You only run when you're guilty."

She doesn't have to believe this is my baby, but she can't keep me from Kinsley. "Shut up!" I yell at her. "Just stop talking because you have no idea what you're even talking about."

My mother recoils like I slapped her. "Do you see what you've done to my sweet son, Kinsley? You've turned him against his own mother."

"No she didn't, and like it or not, we're having a baby."

"Will you stop saying that! This is not your child. She's living in that house with another boy. How do you know it's not *his* baby?"

I glance at Kinsley, and she looks back at me like she's dying more inside as each second passes. She has one hand protectively covering her stomach and the other dangling at her side. Even destroyed, she's the most beautiful girl I've ever seen. "Because she loves me, Mom. She wouldn't cheat on me."

Kinsley raises her tear-stained face, her eyes desperate for me to believe every word I just said. "I didn't, Rhett. You know I wouldn't."

"I know. Don't even question it."

Mom watches us, and for a minute, I almost think she's going to give us a little support. But the tiny bit of compassion I saw, disappears. "We'll deal with this later, Rhett. When your father gets home."

She turns her attention back to my shaking girlfriend. In an eerily calm voice, she says, "You have two minutes to get out of this house before I call the cops, Kinsley."

Kinsley flinches, and immediately scrambles for her bag. Her hands shake so wildly, she drops it on the floor twice before I pick it up for her.

I knew it was a possibility that the second someone found

out, something like this could happen. Though I never imagined it would be this bad, this fast. "Sunny, don't leave."

"You heard her, I have to. We can't do this anymore."

"Don't say that. You're not the girl my mom made you out to be. She's wrong and you know it." I reach out for Kinsley, but she takes a step back, shocking me. She's never told me not to touch her.

"Why do you love me, Rhett? She's the only mother you'll ever get. You can't throw it away for me."

Her words are the equivalent to a slap across the face. "I love *you*, Sunny. I don't care about what she says or does."

"I wish we could go back to Fall Fest. I would do it all different."

"You don't mean that. That night was ours. It's still ours. And it was perfect."

"It doesn't matter what it was. I have to go."

"It does matter. You and the baby are *all* that matters to me. My mom's mad, but she's not going to get between us. I love you too much to give up now."

Another tear slides down her cheek, and when she reaches up to wrap her arms around my neck, it's unlike every other embrace she's given me. This one's empty. It doesn't have the usual warmth of her body pressed against mine. She's stiff—like she's giving me an official good-bye.

"Don't give up. Don't leave."

"I'll always love you, Rhett," she whispers, before opening the front door, and never once looking back. I'm losing her with each step she takes, and there's not a damn thing I can do about it. Not when my mother's back at her side, making sure she leaves the property.

I stand in the doorway, listening to every word my hateful mother spews. "You'll tell whoever asks that this child is not Rhett's. I don't care what story you make up, or who you say it belongs to, but you will not tarnish this family's name or my son's reputation. Have I made myself clear?"

Kinsley nods her head. "Yes."

She hands Kinsley a white envelope before she gets inside her car, telling her, "You keep your end of the deal and I'll make sure you have enough money to take care of your child. But you'll stay away from my son if you know what's best for you. I won't give you a dime if you break your promise."

Right before my eyes, I watch as my own mother destroys what's left of Kinsley. I was willing to stand up and do the right thing—to take care of my responsibilities. All my mother wants to do is pay off my mistakes. Only Kinsley will never be a mistake.

I want Kinsley to get as mad as I feel—to stand up to her and tell her she could never love anyone else the way she loves me. To throw the envelope in her face and run back to me. I'd pack my shit and leave today if it meant we were together. Only she doesn't do that. She simply nods her head, accepting the deal offered to her without a single question asked.

She isn't going to fight for me.

For us.

Or for our family.

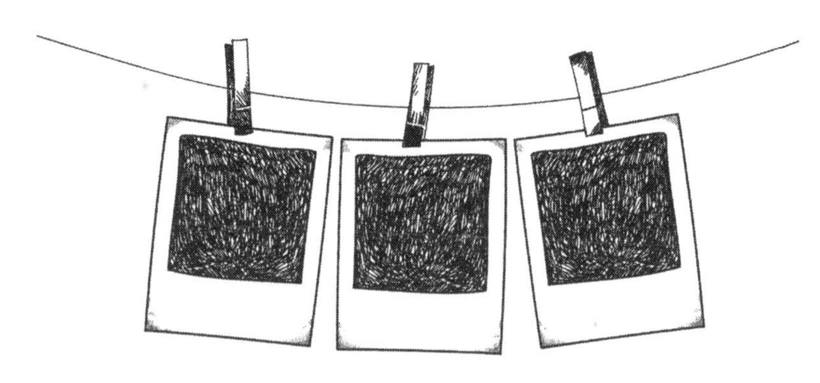

CHAPTER TWENTY-SEVEN

kinsley

MY TEARS ARE falling almost as hard as the rain pounding against the road. Between the two, I can barely see to drive home. My head is pounding, my ears are pulsing, and my chest is so tight I can barely breathe.

Walking away was the right choice, but the envelope I tossed on the dashboard is staring back at me like I'm a total fool. Mrs. Taylor may think she paid me off, but there's no way I would ever take her money. The only reason the envelope is in my possession was to convince Rhett that I'm done. That I want him to pick his family over me. He should work on repairing his relationship with his mother and let me go.

Still, all I want is to turn my car around and run back into his arms where I'm safe. The thought of being without him kills me inside, but in my heart, I can't deprive him of the one thing

I want back more than anything—my mom. He doesn't realize how lucky he is to have both his parents, even if his mom has been a total bitch to me.

Rolling down my window, the cool air whips my hair around, and raindrops land on my arms. I hold the envelope in my hand, ready to toss it into the nearest puddle, but I can't. It's dirty money—money I'll never have a use for, but there has to be someone who can benefit from it. Someone who will use it for good instead of evil.

I stuff the money into my bag, and when I pull into my driveway, I'm relieved Carson's car isn't there. But when I open the door, and let the rain pound down on me, it hits me that I've lost both Rhett and Carson in the same day. All I have left is Wyatt, and I can't go to him with any of my problems.

I'm right back where I started—completely alone.

I take my time walking up the stairs, in no rush to get inside an empty house. The key turns in the lock, and the door creaks open. All the lights are off, except the one above the kitchen sink.

My bag falls to the door, and my soaked shirt sticks to my skin. When I try to peel it away from my body, I notice the faint bump underneath. It looks like I ate too much, and if you didn't know I was pregnant, you wouldn't think twice about it. Only I know what it really means.

I glance inside Carson's room to see if he's gone for good. It's not bare like I was expecting it to be, but the suitcase he was tossing around is gone.

He really left.

It's not supposed to hurt this much, but it does. Tonight I need his shoulder to cry on. I need my friend. The same friend I once thought I wanted to marry. I had it all figured out. We'd fall in love, throw a huge wedding with lots of flowers, and he'd take me on a surprise honeymoon to Paris—just like in the movies we watched.

Since I met Rhett, I realized Carson wasn't the one I was supposed to end up with, despite the feelings I used to have for him. It doesn't matter though. Like everyone else in my life—I lost him, too.

I open the lid to my jewelry box and pick out the yellow twisty tie ring I gave him when we were little kids. The same one he gave back to me a couple months ago when he told me he wanted to be with me—the night I chose Rhett instead.

I slide it on my finger, wondering how different my life would be right now if I would have picked Carson—if I would have listened to my ten-year-old self instead of this eighteen-year-old girl I hardly recognize anymore.

Regret creeps up my throat, threatening to eat me alive. I lost Rhett, and I'm already having trouble imaging a tomorrow without him in it. I lost Carson, too. If I could go back and do it all over, I'd still choose Rhett, but I would have been more careful. I would have thought about the future more, and less about what everyone expected from me.

Now I'm left to figure my life out on my own and a day without support from Carson and love from Rhett isn't one I can imagine. Not when the world is about to find out what we've been hiding.

All I want to do is crawl into a hole and pretend this isn't my life—that it's all a dramatic nightmare I'll wake up from as soon as I snap my fingers. But no matter how many times I click my heels and pray for something to change, it doesn't. I'm still Kinsley West, the failure.

My body shivers I'm so cold. When I look in my closet for dry clothes, all my favorite pieces remind me of time spent with Rhett. I sink down to the floor, staring at the small pile of shoes in front of me. Even those have miles on them—miles I shared with the only guy I've ever truly loved.

I want my boyfriend back so bad it hurts.

And I need my friend to tell me it will be okay.

"Kins."

I'm positive I hear Carson's voice, but I'm not asleep. Like I'm in a dream, my arms are pulled out of my shirt before it's lifted over my head. Warm cotton sucks me up, eventually falling to the top of my thighs.

I hear his voice again. "What did he do to you?"

Nothing. I'm the one who ruined everything. The urge to convince him Rhett's not responsible is so strong, I finally open my swollen eyes. Carson's kneeling in front of me, pulling off my shoes and socks. "It's really you," I whisper.

"It's me."

"You were so mad. Why did you come back?"

He inches my leggings down my legs and when they're off, he tosses them into the wash basket next to the door. Before he asks any more questions, he lifts me off the floor, and carries me to my bed. He sits down next to me and I ask him again. "Why?"

"Because I care about you. I can't believe you're pregnant, Kins. I really can't, but I don't hate you. I never could."

I pull on his hand, silently asking him to get in bed with me. Right now, I need his comfort. I need the reminder of all the times he's held me and promised me I'd be okay because he was right every single time.

He's hesitant when he says, "I can't. You're not mine."

He's right. My heart belongs to Rhett. He's who I'm craving, but can't have.

"Don't cry, Kins."

"We're over. His mom found out I'm pregnant. She kicked me out."

"Rhett let you leave?"

"He wanted me to stay, but I couldn't. He needs his Mom more than he needs me. He just doesn't know it yet."

Carson lays down next to me, pulling me close. We've been in this position so many times. The night my mom died was the first time he protected me in his arms. Ever since, it's been where I go for comfort. At least until Rhett came along.

Like he did before, he reads my mind. He knows what I need without having to ask. "You're not alone anymore. I'll take care of you. Tell me what you need."

Carson has always accepted me just as I am—with every single flaw, mistake, and imperfection. He's never wanted me to be anything other than who I am, and I'm grateful. "I just need you to hold me."

"I've got you."

I DON'T WAKE up until noon the next day. Carson's still in bed next to me, sleeping. Even though I'm not with Rhett anymore, I still feel like I'm cheating by being in bed with someone else. There's not much time to dwell on it though, because as soon as I sit up, I'm reminded of the fact that I'm pregnant.

I rush to the bathroom, and fall to my knees just in time. My stomach contracts painfully, and my throat is still raw from the last time I got sick. Carson's right behind me, pulling my hair away from my face, and holding it so it doesn't get thrown up on.

When I start to feel the nausea pass, I sit back on my heels, trying to catch my breath. Even though I woke up less than five minutes ago, I'm already tired again. "I can't do this anymore."

"Yes, you can. You're going to be a great mother." Carson helps me off the floor, and puts toothpaste on my toothbrush for me. "Open."

I open my mouth and he sticks it inside, running it back and forth over my teeth. I smile at him, wondering what he's doing. "I can handle it."

He hands me the toothbrush, but he doesn't leave. He sits on the edge of the tub, waiting until I finish. When I do, he pulls me onto his lap. The air from the vent hits my legs, and I realize all I'm wearing is one of his T-shirts. I forgot he changed me last night when I was too far gone to do it myself.

"Feel better?"

I nod my head. "For now."

"You sort of missed most of school. Is there anything you wanted to do today?"

"There's only one more day of school before break. I didn't really feel like answering a bunch of questions anyway."

"I guess they're going to know about the baby, now."

"I'm sure it's spread like a wild fire."

Neither of us say anything for a couple minutes, we just sit in the bathroom of all places, absorbing the drama of the previous day.

"I'm really sorry, Kins," Carson says, breaking the silence. "I would never hurt you. When I threw that book, I wasn't aiming for anything other than the wall."

"You scared me."

"I shouldn't have done it. When I saw the fear in your eyes, that you were actually afraid of me, I knew I had to leave."

"Why did you come back?"

"Because I didn't want you to be alone. And if I'm being honest, I needed to be with you again. You think I'm here because your brother asked me. The truth is, I volunteered because I was hoping it would make you want to be with me. But by the time I got here, you already had your sights set on someone else."

"I'll always care about you."

"But you still want Rhett, right?"

"I don't know what I want anymore. I thought we had it figured out—I never expected his mom to react the way she did. I don't know what I was thinking. I mean, what parent would be cool with their kid having a baby?"

"You've been blinded by love."

"Maybe."

"I get it, Kins. When you love someone, you'll do just about anything for them. The past seven days, I walked around this place trying to figure out how to ask you about the baby. Nothing sounded right, and the days kept getting away from me before I could come up with something. Confronting you was stupid. It's not how I wanted to approach it at all."

"You're forgiven."

He leans forward and kisses my cheek. I close my eyes, and all on its own my head turns toward him. Without thinking about what I'm doing or about the consequences, I lean in and find his lips. I've wondered for years what it would be like to kiss Carson. Now I'm finding out.

His hands tangle in my hair, and he turns me around in his lap so I'm straddling his waist. His mouth feels good on mine. His fingers tug on my hair just enough that it prickles my scalp, but doesn't hurt. Everything about our first kiss is good, but it doesn't give me butterflies the way kissing Rhett does.

It's nice, but it's not *him*.

Carson, on the other hand, is staring back at me like I'm his world. I so badly want to feel the same way, so I can put the past behind me and move on like it never existed. He reminds me though when he runs his hand over my stomach. "I'll take care of you. I'll love you both so much."

Here's this amazingly sweet guy willing to sacrifice even more for my happiness. He's telling me he'll take us both, because we're a package deal now. I should be rejoicing—thanking my lucky stars I'm not going to end up alone, but it only makes me want to fix things with Rhett that much more. I can't imagine anyone else raising this baby with me.

"I have to go to the diner to talk to Betty about blowing off my shift last night. Will you take me?"

"Of course I will. I'll make you some toast before we go. You need to eat."

"You're sure I'm not keeping you from something important?"

"*You're* the most important part of my day." He leans in to kiss me again, and like a fool, I let him. When he pulls away, his smile widens. "My holiday break started today. I'm all yours."

He stands in front of me, waiting for me to say something, but I can't think of a single thing. So, I simply thank him, and step into the shower with my shirt still on. Once I hear the door close, I finally release the breath I've been holding. I need to fix this before it goes any farther. I'm just not sure how I'm going to do that. I can't keep leading Carson on.

By the time I get out of the shower, my fingers are wrinkly from standing under the hot spray so long. Carson has toast and a glass of orange juice sitting on my dresser. My mouth's still so dry, I drink most of it before I ever take a bite of my breakfast.

Once I'm finished, it takes me a little longer than usual to get ready. I have to sit down a couple times to make sure my breakfast isn't going to come back up. But after I'm dressed and my hair is dry, I walk into a living room for an unexpected surprise.

Wyatt, Kate, and Carson are all sitting on the couch, staring at me. "What's going on?"

Carson stands up, reaching out for my hand. He pulls me closer and sits me on the end of the couch, closest to him. "I had to call them, Kins. Your family should be here for you. You don't have to do this by yourself."

"Why did you do that? I was going to tell them."

"You didn't tell me until I forced it out of you. I was worried you would do the same thing with them. I thought I should do something to make it easier for you."

I hate that Carson took it upon himself to decide what was the right move for me. This isn't his baby—it's mine. I should be able to decide when and where I tell people—if I tell them at all. "You shouldn't have done this."

Kate scoots to the edge of the ottoman, directly in front of me. "I live here and I know I'm not around much—my schedule is pretty much opposite yours, but I'm sorry. I'm so sorry I wasn't here when you needed me."

"It's fine. I took a test and went to the doctor."

"And the doctor said the baby was okay? You're okay?"

"Yes."

The next words out of her mouth surprise me. "I'm proud of you, Kinsley."

I raise my head, wondering how in the world she could possibly think that. "How can you be proud? I messed up."

"But you did something about it. You got yourself care. That's the best thing you could have done for your baby."

"Rhett's the one who's been taking care of me—at least until last night. He's not too happy with me after what I did."

Kate reaches for my hand and squeezes it. "Something tells me he's not giving up on you just yet."

I shake my head. "He's not."

Carson shifts next to me, no doubt uncomfortable with Rhett being the topic of conversation. I glance at Wyatt to gauge his reaction, but he's not even looking at me. His head is tipped back and he's looking at the ceiling. It makes me feel guilty that he had to drive home to deal with my problems when he clearly would rather be just about anywhere else.

When the doorbell rings, he hops off the couch so fast he almost trips over his sneakers sitting next to him on the floor. "Hey, baby," he says. "Come sit with me."

Becca walks in the room with Wyatt, and she gives me a forced smile. Knowing her, she's pissed I didn't run to her with my news. Wyatt pulls her onto his lap and kisses her lips in front of all of us. I get it, they missed each other. Still, Wyatt doesn't get any happier now that Becca's here. He still isn't saying a single word to me.

"Hey,Becca." I try to break the tension by acknowledging

my best friend.

She doesn't take the bait though like she normally would. All I get is a simple, "Hi, Kins," before she nudges Wyatt in the stomach. "Stop," she whispers.

He rolls his eyes, but finally acknowledges me. "You fucked up." Is all he says.

My brother's opinion means the world to me, and right now, he looks ashamed that I'm his sister—like it's hard for him to even speak to me. He breaks my heart all over again.

Kate senses I'm about to fall apart, and takes another turn, transitioning into guardian mode. "We're all spending Thanksgiving together at Carson's cabin. He's graciously offered it to us, so we can get back to being a family. We've all been going in opposite directions and clearly we've lost you along the way. What's done is done, but I want this baby to be something we can all learn from. I also want it to be a blessing."

"I can't go away. I have to work."

"You'll go talk to Betty and clear your schedule. If she fires you, then so be it. I'll cover your share of the bills. We'll figure the rest out later."

"Okay, but if I'm going to be treated like a problem the entire time, I'd rather stay here." My comment's directed toward Wyatt, but I'm not sure he even hears me. Becca's nuzzling against his chest, and he's holding her like she's his prized possession. Everything about it rubs me the wrong way. Not because I'm jealous of what they have, but because my own brother can't bother to show me an ounce of the love he's giving her.

"You're not a problem, Kinsley." Kate stresses. "I just think we need to stop being too busy for each other."

There's no use arguing about it. I have one more day before we're shipping off to some cabin in the woods to be a family. Though a real family wouldn't have approached me like this—like I'm some druggie off the street who wouldn't have sat down to have a normal conversation with each of them, one-on-one.

"I have to get to the diner."

Carson jumps from the couch, chasing after me like a little puppy dog. "Wait, Kins. I'll drive you."

"I got it," I tell him, as I walk away. Last night the idea of being completely alone brought me to my knees. Now, all I want to do is find someplace I can be by myself. It's crazy how things can change in less than twenty-four hours.

Carson follows me outside even though I told him I was fine on my own. "You're mad I called them, aren't you?"

I stop, only halfway down the stairs. "Wyatt won't even look at me. Becca said two words. Kate's treating me like some case at work. I don't need this stress, Carson. You meant well, but please stop interfering."

"I'm sorry."

"It's fine. I'm going to need support and help, but Rhett and I have a lot to figure out as it is. And those decisions will be made by the two of us—not anyone else."

"Okay, I get it. Will you still let me drive you? I'll take you wherever you want to go."

"Yeah, thanks." Maybe by the time we get to the diner, I'll have figured out how to let Carson go without ruining our friendship. Though something tells me it won't matter how gently I go about it. He's going to be gone for good.

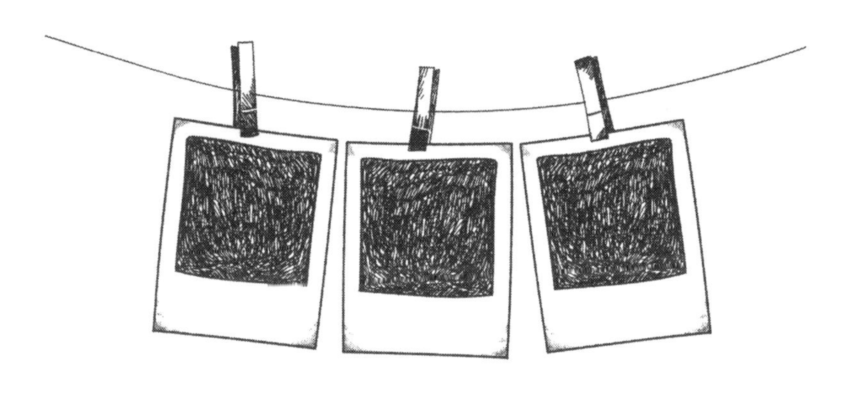

CHAPTER TWENTY-EIGHT

rhett

KINSLEY DIDN'T COME to school today. It was only a half day anyway, but she probably thought news of our baby would be spread all over school by now—and it is. I've fielded curious questions all day long, but it was the ones about us breaking up that pissed me off the most. I didn't break up with my girl. As far as I'm concerned, she's still mine. Whatever my mom tried to do to our relationship isn't going to stick.

I spent most of last night and today thinking up the perfect plan. Finally, while I was running in gym class, it dawned on me there might be a solution. I'm not supposed to get any of my trust fund money until I turn twenty-one. My grandfather put aside a large portion of his estate for me so that when I was responsible enough, I'd have access to the money.

As long as I can convince my dad that I need some of the

money early, and my mom doesn't find out about it, I'll be able to support my family while we both go to college. Preferably far enough away from here that I won't be accused of tarnishing the family name any more than we already have.

When I open my locker, there's a crumbled envelope taped to the inside. I pull it off the metal door, and when I open it up, I realize it's the hush money Kinsley was paid to keep the baby's paternity a secret.

"Thank fuck," I whisper, unable to hide the smile on my face. I'm so proud of my girl and I take it as a sign that she's not ready to give up on us like she said she was. That she's not going to bow down to anyone even if the money would have made her life a whole lot easier.

I shove the envelope in my pocket and take off running toward my truck. When I push through the front doors to the school, I spot Kinsley getting into Carson's Jeep. Considering how upset she was when she came to my house last night, even saying Carson almost hit her with a book, I'm more than a little surprised she's already made up with him. Especially before she spoke a single word to me.

I follow them all the way to the diner, watching as he helps her out, just like I would have done. I hate that he's trying to take my place, but what I can't stand even more is the way *she's* looking at *him*. Like she might actually have feelings for the guy.

He must feel it too because he leans in and kisses her on the forehead like I've done so many times. I have to close my eyes it hurts so bad. I've been willing to look past their friendship because they have a long history, and I would never ask her to give that up, but the guy I'm watching, loves Kinsley. Problem is, she's already mine.

It takes everything I have to hold myself back—to give them a little space. I manage to wait until he's back in his Jeep before I haul ass across the parking lot to catch up to her. When I'm close enough, I reach for her arm, slowing her down.

She jumps, yanking it out of my hand. Once she realizes it's me, she clutches her stomach. I glance at her hand, wondering if she's in pain. "Are you okay?"

Her eyes travel over every inch of my face like she's memorizing me all over again. Finally, she blinks out of her trance. "I'm fine. What are you doing here?"

"I need to talk to you. Do you have to work?"

"No, I'm off, but I missed my shift last night. There's actually a lot I need to discuss with Betty."

As far as I'm concerned, her business is still my business, so I ask, "Like what?"

"I'm taking a little time off."

Finally. I've been telling her to do less for weeks. "Good. You should rest more."

"Did you follow me here?" she asks, looking around the parking lot for my truck.

"I got the envelope, and I saw you leaving school, so I followed you. I've actually done a lot of thinking, and I came up with this plan. It might not work, but there's a good chance it could. I wanted to figure it out with you over break."

At first she looks intrigued, like she really wants to hear what I have to say, but the hope that quickly appeared fades away when she glances at Carson's Jeep. "I'm going away for break. With Kate and Wyatt."

"Is Carson going?"

She nods her head. "He'll be there for most of it. It's his cabin."

I don't want Carson anywhere near my girl and my baby. "I still want you to stay with me. We can go to my uncle's place like we talked about. My parents are doing the country club thing—Mom's not even cooking this year."

She chews on her lip, like she really wants to say, yes. Still, something's holding her back. "Rhett, I can't. Nothing's changed, and they're making me go with them."

"But you gave me the money back."

"I don't need money to keep my mouth shut. I won't spread any vicious rumors. Your mom doesn't have to worry about me interfering, but I can't deny where my baby comes from. I just can't."

"I don't want you to. I'm proud that you're my baby's mom—I'm proud that you're my girlfriend. I've told you that since day one."

"I know. You never cared what anyone at school thought about us being together. Thank you for that."

"I mean every word. I miss you, Sunny. You still love me, too—I know you do."

"I never said I didn't love you, Rhett, but I'm helping you. I may not agree with your mom's approach, but she said a lot of things that were true. You have so much to look forward to. You would be settling if you stayed here with me. Nobody should have to settle for the rest of their life."

"Just like you're settling for Carson. I saw the way he looks at you. You've only ever looked at *me* that way. It's *me* you want, Kinsley. He's never been your first choice."

"It doesn't matter what I want anymore. The baby and I will be fine. Please, fix things with your mom—before it's too late. You don't know how lucky you are to have her."

She turns toward the stairs, but I don't want to leave here without her. "If you think I'm letting you raise our baby with Carson, you're crazy."

She stares at the steps in front of her, her shoulders drooping in defeat. I wait for her to tell me that isn't what she's going to do, but she never turns around. She reaches for the banister and walks into the diner like I didn't just beg her to come back to me.

If I had a better relationship with my mom, maybe I'd listen to her. I'd go home and convince her that I'm going to marry Kinsley someday. But my mom already has me going away to college where I'll meet some bitchy girl with a trust fund as big as my own. We'll fall in love and have two kids, a dog, and a white picket fence around our perfect home.

And that sounds like complete and total hell.

I'm tired of being pressured to be someone I don't want to be. My future won't be spent at country clubs or fancy parties with horse owners. I like having Dawn to Dark, but even she's not how I envision my future.

All I see is Kinsley and our baby.

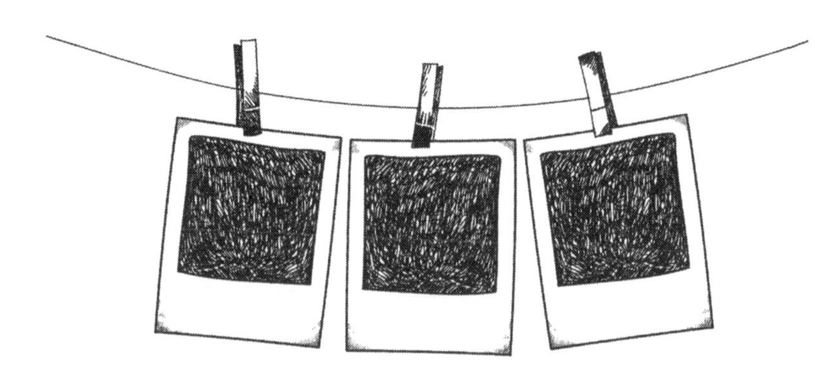

CHAPTER TWENTY-NINE

kinsley

THE DRIVE TO the cabin has me completely nauseous. We waited until Carson and Becca had finished their Thanksgiving meals with their families before we loaded up two cars with everything we'll need for our own Thanksgiving at the cabin.

Carson leads the way, weaving his way through the last couple miles of the trip. I grip the arm rest, praying I don't get sick all over his Jeep. "Are we almost there?"

"Yeah, it's just up around the bend."

It's already dark outside, and I can't see two feet in front of us let alone around the bend. I don't know why, but morning and night seem to be when I feel the worst. The couple hours in the middle of the day are the only thing that make this pregnancy manageable so far.

"We're here, Kins." I open my eyes, clawing the door for the handle. "That bad, huh?"

"The worst."

Once all the bags are inside, Carson points to the bedroom and tells us all to pick one. Of course Becca follows Wyatt, as they'll be sharing a room. Kate gets the master, and even though there's two rooms left, Carson follows me into mine.

"Can I stay with you tonight?" he asks, with his bag slung over his shoulder.

"That's not a good idea. Wyatt will flip out." I have no problem using my brother as an excuse. Truth is, Rhett would flip out, and I don't want to hurt him anymore than I already have. I'll have to tell him about the kiss we shared at some point—and I'm already dreading it.

Carson sighs, obviously unable to disagree with me. Unless he has a death wish, it's time for him to go to his own room. "Do you need anything before I go to bed?"

"No."

"Why are you so quiet? You barely said two words on the drive here."

"I'm just tired. It's been a long day." He saw me talking to Rhett outside the diner yesterday–he has to know my head's still mixed up in that conversation. Rhett's been on my mind ever since I walked away.

God, I miss him. Knowing I could have been at his uncle's cabin instead, makes this trip that much harder.

"You're sure you're okay?"

"I'm good."

He steps closer to me, and my body tenses before he even touches me. "Sweet dreams, Kins," he says, as he hugs me tightly.

"Night," I whisper against his chest, my arms still hanging lifelessly by my sides. Each time Carson touches me, I feel less and less in return. I shouldn't have ever led him on the night I asked him to hold me. He took my need for comfort as more than it was—and I was feeling so low, I never bothered to correct him.

He gives me one last glance before pulling the door closed behind him. I sigh with relief, before climbing into my bed. The blanket's a little scratchy, and the pillow a little lumpy, but I'm thankful for the peace and quiet. Tomorrow will be another full day of family time, and if I want to survive it, I'll need some sleep.

Closing my eyes, I think about Fall Fest, and how perfect it was. What it felt like when Rhett touched me, and how much I wanted him. But most importantly, how protected he made me feel—like he would never let anything hurt me.

Recreating our night is the only way I can fall asleep.

AROUND THREE IN the morning, I wake up to go to the bathroom. I use the light from my phone to light up the hallway and notice it's blinking with a message. I slide my finger across the screen and my stomach does a little somersault when I see Rhett left me a message. Only it's not one, it's three—and he's worried.

Rhett: Are you at the cabin?

Rhett: Let me know you're okay.

Rhett: Talk to me.

I feel bad I never thought to text him, letting him know we got here safely. There's no way he's still awake, but I type out a message anyway. At least he'll see it when he wakes up.

Kinsley: I'm okay. Sorry. I fell asleep.

I set the phone on the counter, but it vibrates with a return message right away.

Rhett: I've been freaking out.

Quickly, I use the bathroom, before hurrying into my room and dialing his number. It barely rings one full time before he picks up. "Sunny?"

"Hey, um, I guess I wanted to call you so you knew I was okay."

"You have no idea how good it is to hear your voice. My head's been like a horror movie, coming up with all kinds of shit of what could have happened to you."

"The ride made me sick, so once we got here, I went right to bed. I just woke up to pee."

He laughs, and I realize I could have left that last part out. "You should go back to sleep. It's still pretty early."

"And you should go to bed."

"Yeah, now that you're safe I can."

"Rhett," I pause for a second, wanting to ask him something, but not sure I have the right considering we're not what we used to be.

"What is it?"

"Nothing, I've been having trouble falling asleep lately."

"Close your eyes," he says, in a soft, comforting voice. "I'll stay on the line until you're asleep."

"Are you sure?"

"I'm positive. My girls need some sleep."

More flutters hit me from head to toe. "Night, Rhett."

"Night, my Sunny-girl."

I have no idea how long he stayed on the line, but the call is no longer connected when I wake up a couple hours later. I even check my call log to make sure it wasn't all a dream, and I'm relieved when I see his text and his name.

My stomach growls so strongly it's painful, so I slide out of my itchy bed in search of some breakfast. Carson's the only one awake, and he's standing in front of the toaster with a butter knife in his hand.

He doesn't even have to turn around to know it's me behind him. "Morning. Sleep okay?"

"Um, yeah. I woke up once, but I got back to sleep."

He sets a plate of toast in front of me, and a glass of juice. "I heard you get up."

"Oh, did I wake you up?"

He shakes his head. "No, but I couldn't seem to get back to sleep. Been working on the puzzle ever since."

I glance at the other end of the sprawling antique table, and he has puzzle pieces all over the place. The frame is loosely built with a few pieces to connect it all together, still missing.

"Do you want to go out for a little while? Maybe take the four wheelers for a drive?"

"I don't know how to drive one of those things."

"You can ride on mine. I won't go fast."

It actually sounds kind of fun, and I don't want him to think I'm not grateful for the offer. He's always trying to make me happy, and I should probably make the most of this little getaway since I'm here. "Sure, sounds like fun."

He smiles and sets some scrambled eggs on the table. "Eat up," he says.

I narrow my eyes, and he laughs. "When were you planning on telling me you knew how to cook something other than toast? All this time I've been making food for you so you wouldn't starve."

He shrugs his shoulders. "Maybe I liked you taking care of me."

"Maybe," I whisper. I concentrate on my food, hoping the awkwardness between the two us will disappear. I would do almost anything to get our friendship back to the way it was before he kissed me. Ever since, it's been weird, and I don't have the heart to tell him I can't be with him. Even if I have to.

"Meet me out back when you're finished. There's someplace I want to show you. Wear something warm."

After I finish my breakfast, I take a quick shower and throw my hair into a lazy ponytail. I dress in a warm sweater, my coat, and jeans. These are the last pair I can actually get on and still breathe. They were my period jeans, as Becca called them—the ones you buy a size or two bigger for days you're super bloated. Now, they've become my everyday staple.

"Who's all coming?" I ask Carson, as he pulls his four wheeler out of the shed. He hands me a helmet, and I put it on, clipping it under my chin.

"It's just me and you. Wyatt's taking Becca to some wine tasting thing. Kate was going to tag along with them. I figured since you couldn't drink, I'd find something for us to do."

"Becca's not even twenty-one. How can she go?"

"It's a little vineyard. Wyatt plays football with the owner's son. So, he invited them to stop by."

I guess when they wanted to spend more time together as a family, it didn't include me. They could have at least invited me. I would have been okay watching.

"Are you mad?"

"It's whatever . . ."

Carson stands in front of me, holding my face in his hands. "It's not whatever. If you're upset, say so."

"I'm pissed my own brother still hasn't spoken to me. And I'm pissed I was forced to come all the way here, and they don't even want to spend time with me. So, yeah. I guess I'm just pissed."

He leans forward and kisses the tip of my nose. "You're pretty damn cute when you're pissed, Kins."

Right now would be the perfect opportunity to tell him I'm not comfortable with him kissing me, not when I'm pregnant with someone else's baby, but again, I chicken out. It's not in my DNA to hurt feelings. "Can we go now?"

"Sure, come on. I'm taking you about a mile from here. There's this really cool bluff that leads to a waterfall. It's not huge or anything, but it's pretty cool. I think you'll like it."

I stare at the four wheeler, wondering where he wants me to sit. "What do I do?"

He chuckles, hopping on first. "Grab onto my shoulders, and pretend you're getting on a horse."

"Sounds easy enough." Once I'm on, Carson reaches behind me, and wraps my arms around his stomach. "Hold on tight, and don't let go. Even if we're not going very fast, okay?"

"Okay." I don't tell him, but I'm actually pretty scared about being on the back of this thing, but he would never put me in danger, so I trust him to get us where we're going in one piece.

He keeps his promise, and doesn't go very fast. As he points out places he's been hunting since he was a kid, we see two deer near his tree stand. He shows me where he shot his first deer, and a couple minutes later, he pulls up next to a rocky cliff. After he helps me off the four wheeler, I peel my helmet off my head.

"We can walk around the back side. There's a little trail over there."

"Thank goodness, I thought we were going to expect me to scale this thing."

"We'll save the real adventures for after you have the baby."

The way he hints at the possibility of a long-term relationship, only makes me feel guiltier for spending time with him. Rhett's the one I should be with today—at his uncle's cabin. I didn't even get to wish him a Happy Thanksgiving yesterday, but falling asleep with him only a phone call away, makes me smile. Even through the rough parts, he's willing to help me.

I follow Carson and he reaches for my hand, helping me slide between some trees. The leaves on the ground are a couple inches thick, and mixed with the rain we've been getting, it's slippery. But he gets us to where he wants to go, safely.

"We can sit here." He points to a large rock with a flat surface that looks like it's been placed here on purpose.

"It's really pretty out here."

He looks around at the trees and all their changing leaves. "It's one of my favorite places to be. Ever since I was a kid."

"It's really special."

"We're you ever going to tell me?" he questions, out of the blue.

I assume he's talking about the pregnancy, so I answer him honestly. "I probably wouldn't have told you yet. Rhett was set on keeping it between us until we figured out what to do."

He nods his head. "Good to know, but I meant about last night."

"Last night?"

"I came to check on you when I heard you get up. I heard you talking to someone, and there's only one person you would talk to that late."

"I didn't realize you were awake."

He stares off into the distance as he says, "I came into your room, and you were asleep. I saw your phone resting on your face, and pulled it off. When I did, I saw he was still on the line."

"Did you hang up?"

"Yeah."

"Did you say anything?"

"Yeah."

"Why would you do that? You have no right coming into my room and messing with my stuff. What did you say to him?"

"That we were going to sleep—and that I'd make sure you were taken care of from now on."

I gasp, covering my mouth with my hand. "Please, tell me you're lying."

"Why does it matter? You broke up with him. You said you couldn't be with him."

"I'm having his baby. His child!"

"I told you I'll take care of you. You don't need him anymore, Kins."

I rip my phone out of my pocket, trying to dial Rhett's number, but there's no reception. I hold the phone in the air, spinning in a circle to get it to work—but there's still nothing. "I have to call him."

I hurry back the way we came, slipping a couple times, but managing to make it back to the top on my own. I check my phone again, but there's no service. "Take me back. Now."

"Kinsley, you're making this a bigger deal than it is. It was late."

I spin around to face him. "No, Carson! You're rubbing it in his face. Nothing about what you did is okay."

"Just, calm down. Talk to me, Kins. I love you so much."

"Carson, no."

"Baby, this is our chance. We can finally be together."

I look him straight in the eye, and never second guessing it, I tell him the truth. "I love Rhett. He's the one I want to be with."

Carson runs his hands over his face, growling with frustration. He throws his hands up in the air, and starts walking in the opposite direction. Where to, I have no idea.

"Carson, if you don't take me back, I'll do it myself!" My threat doesn't faze him. He just shakes his head and keeps walking.

I straddle the ATV like I did the first time, and turn the key in the ignition. I haven't actually driven one on my own, but it can't be that much different than the motorcycle my dad used to have. I get it started, only it's a lot more powerful than I anticipate. I lurch forward a couple times before I get it going.

"Kinsley! No!"

I hear Carson, but I don't stop. He didn't stop for me. I press the pedal all the way down and gun it back to the cabin. The last thing I remember is hearing Carson's voice in my ear, telling me to hold on.

I never figured out what I was supposed to be holding onto before the daylight was replaced with darkness.

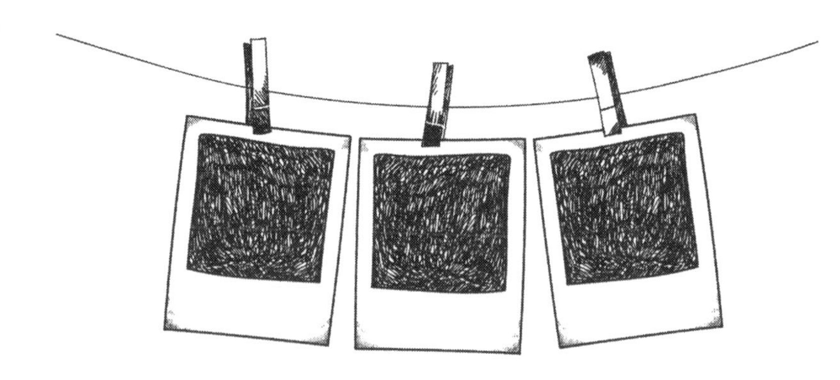

CHAPTER THIRTY

rhett

MOM'S GOING ON and on about the pumpkin pie at the club, and how it's the best it's been in years. She's been trying, since she woke up, to get me to go to the social this afternoon. I already told her I wasn't interested in putting on a suit to eat pie with stuck up people.

Her response? "Then wear a sweater."

She's never going to understand that just because she's living this life, I don't have to do the same. It was fun when I was a kid, going to huge houses, and parties at the kids' club, but now, it's just one big stage for the wealthiest in town to show off.

"You'll be missing out on a fun time."

"That's okay," I tell her. Luckily, my phone rings, saving me from this never-ending conversation.

"Becca?"

She's breathing heavy into the phone like she's been running or something. "Are you at the gym?"

"No, Rhett. I'm just getting to the hospital."

As soon as she says the words, I start to sweat. I sit down on the couch, preparing myself for what's coming next. "What happened?"

Before she can explain, she breaks down, sobbing into the phone. "She had an accident on the four wheeler, Rhett. She wrecked and she hit her head. Carson carried her back to the cabin and then we called 911.

"Fuck! I'm on my way." I hang up my phone, running to my room, grabbing the first pair of pants and shirt I can find.

"Rhett, honey. What is it?"

"Kinsley's been in an accident. I think it's bad, Mom."

She covers her mouth. "The baby."

"I have to get to her."

"You can't drive like this. Let me take you. Your father's in the garage. We'll all go."

My hands are shaking so bad I can barely hang onto my keys. I hand them to her, like she's going to take my truck instead of her Mercedes. She doesn't say anything though, only tucking them into her purse.

I message Becca back as soon as I'm sitting in the car, praying she has good news for me.

Rhett: Is she okay?

Becca: I don't know. They won't let us see her yet.

I throw my phone on the seat beside me, tipping my head back against the head rest. I spend the next hour and a half reciting every prayer I can think of. I've prayed more on the car ride to the hospital than I've ever prayed in my life. But I make sure to say each prayer twice—once for Kinsley and once for my baby.

Dad pulls up to the ER and lets me out of the car before going to find a place to park. Once I'm inside, I search for Becca, and I find her cuddled on Wyatt's lap. "Where is she?"

Kate stands up, walking toward me. "I just left her room. They were prepping her for stitches."

"Stitches?"

"She hit her head and she has a gash above her eye."

Becca stands up and hugs me, tears still falling from her eyes. "Go see her, Rhett. She needs you."

Kate takes my hand, and walks me toward Kinsley. "She can only have one visitor at a time. They're doing some labs and some tests, but they said it's okay to sit with her through it all."

"She's alone?"

She swallows before shaking her head. "Carson's with her."

I take a deep breath before I walk in her room. Carson's sitting in the chair next to her, holding her hand. Her eyes are closed, but they flutter open as soon as I'm near her. "Rhett," she whispers.

Carson's head swings around and I grab him by the back of his preppy sweater, physically removing him from the chair he's sitting in. It's *my* chair. Next to *my* girl. "Get the fuck out of here."

"I don't have to do a damn thing you tell me to do." He's about to come at me when Kinsley starts to cry.

"Carson, I need to talk to Rhett. Alone."

"Sure. I'll be in the hallway if you need me." He glares at me before leaving the room with his head hanging. I can't stand him.

Once I dry Kinsley's tears, I hold both of her hands, warming them up. She's so cold she's practically shivering. "I was so scared. I thought I lost you."

"The baby, Rhett."

"What do you mean?" I knew it was a possibility, but I didn't let myself go there on the ride here. I told myself that if she was okay, the baby would be okay, too.

"I'm bleeding. I-I could lose the baby." She sobs harder and harder as she says each word. Saying it makes it real, and I know it's not easy for her to do. Not when the mere thought of losing either one of them was enough to bring me to my knees.

I pull back her blankets, careful not to sit on any of her wires, or mess with the IV in her hand. "It's in God's hands now, Sunny. But you're going to be okay."

"My baby," she says. "I need my baby to be okay."

"Our baby is strong, Sunny. Just like you."

Before I can give her anymore words of encouragement, the doctor strolls in with a clipboard in hand. Only he doesn't look like we're feeling. In fact, he smiles when he sees the two of us together in her bed. "You must be Rhett."

"I am." I hold out my hand, and he shakes it.

"I'd say luck was on your side today. The baby is doing well, the labs all came back perfect, and your x-rays were clear. No broken bones. Other than the soreness, and the stitches on your forehead, you're doing very well considering."

"What about the blood?" she asks him.

"It may or may not have been caused by the accident. Your placenta is low lying, and this could simply be the beginning signs of placenta previa. It's a fancy word meaning part of your placenta is blocking the cervix. It gradually moves upward during pregnancy, but if yours stays low, it might be cause for concern. You could possibly need a C-section during delivery. We'll know more with time."

"She's not from this area. Will her doctor get all this?"

"Absolutely. We'll do another pelvic exam in a couple hours and we'll continue to monitor the baby. If all goes well, we'll discharge you tomorrow and you can follow-up with your physician."

I need a little more clarification after he rattled all that off so fast. "The baby is okay though, right?"

"Yes, perfectly fine."

We both sigh with relief. "See, Sunny. The baby is strong."

The doctor jots down a few of her vitals before leaving the room. As soon as we're alone, Kinsley reaches for me and I hold her tighter than I ever have before. I rest my hand on her stomach, gently stroking her skin.

"I love you, Rhett."

"You have no idea how much I love you, Kinsley West." She sniffles again, and I reach for a tissue on the tray near her bed.

"Thank you," she says, as she takes it from my hand. "I'm so sorry Carson lied to you last night. He told me what he said to you, and I was so upset. I took the four wheeler so I could get back to the cabin to call you. I was so scared you would think I didn't want you."

She wrecked and almost lost our baby because of Carson. "I get that you care about him, but I don't want Carson anywhere near you or the baby anymore."

"Okay."

That was too easy, so I say it a second time in case she thinks I'm not serious. "I mean it. Even if you have to move."

"Rhett, I kissed him," she says in a rush.

As if this day couldn't get any worse, another bomb's dropped on me. The thought of her lips coming anywhere near his, makes me want to break things. A lot of things—everything. "Did you sleep with him?"

She lifts her head off my chest, shaking her head. "No, I could never do that. I don't even know why I kissed him. I regretted it before it was even over. My head was so mixed up about losing you."

"You didn't lose me, Sunny. You left."

"I know. I regret that, too."

"All you have to do is come back."

"You're not mad at me?"

I'm so mad at her for leaving me in the first place, but after what she's been through, I'm more thankful to have her than anything. "Sunny, it would be a whole lot easier to marry you someday, if you were my girl."

She giggles, and it's the sweetest sound I've heard in a really long time. I lean in to kiss her, wanting and needing to remove Carson from her memory. All I want her to think about is my kisses—my lips claiming hers.

I hear someone clear their throat, and I know we're not alone anymore. But I don't expect it to be my mother.

"Mrs. Taylor, I wanted to—"

Mom holds up her hand, shushing Kinsley. "No, let me first. I spoke to the doctor for myself. He couldn't give me specifics, but he said the baby is okay."

"Yes."

"Until today, Rhett has always been *my* baby. I've coddled him more than I should. I put up with more than I needed to, but I love him more than anything in this world. Sometimes, I lose sight of the important things. For that, I'm sorry. I'm sorry I threw you out of my home. I'm sorry I called you names a mother should never speak of. I'm ashamed of the way I've behaved and I can only ask for your forgiveness."

Kinsley's eyes are watery when she looks at me, but she doesn't need me to save her this time. This time, she can handle my mom all on her own. "Mrs. Taylor, I love your son, and I love this baby."

"I know you do, sweet girl. The thought of losing either one of you would destroy my son. I didn't realize until this afternoon how much it would destroy me, too. Life is precious and we're only given one chance to get it right. I've messed up so many times, but I'd like a chance to love this baby. I'd like a chance to love *you*."

"That's all I've ever wanted."

"That's all *we've* ever wanted," I add.

My mother walks to Kinsley's bedside, and leans down to hug her. It's the most amazing feeling in the world to have two of the most important people in my life getting along. Today was pretty awful, and could have ended up tragic, but every new beginning comes from a beginning's end.

Today was the end of the feud.

Today was the first day of our happily-ever-after because I don't plan on losing my girl ever again. Not when I have it all.

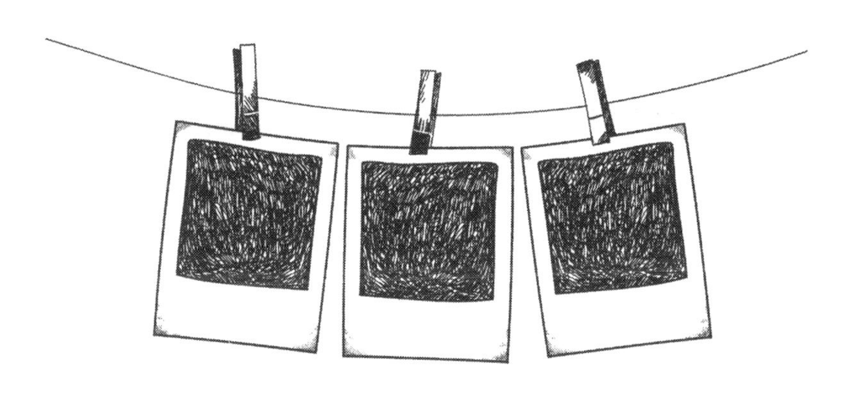

CHAPTER THIRTY-ONE

kinsley

two weeks later. . .

I WAKE UP with a sense of urgency. The need to see Rhett so strong I can hardly stand it. Even if it's going to be hard to listen to the whispering, I'm excited to go back to school to see both him and Becca.

After the rest of Thanksgiving break was spent in the hospital and on bed rest, I've been going a little crazy being cooped up inside my bedroom. Now that I'm allowed to be on my feet, I rush around, making sure I leave on time so I'm not late for photography class.

Wyatt's back at school and while Carson's still living here, we haven't been on speaking terms. Still, he leaves me toast on the counter each morning. It's either his way of apologizing for what he did, or because he's desperate to stay connected to me in one way or another. Rhett wants him gone, and I can't blame him for the way he feels, but Kate and I can't bring ourselves to kick him to the curb until he makes arrangements. Even then, I'm not sure how hard he's trying to find something else.

But I forget all about Carson as soon as I'm at school—even if I am running a little bit late.

"I wasn't sure you were coming," Rhett says, as he clears his papers off my spot at the table.

"I was planning on meeting you at your locker."

He raises his eyebrows. "Yeah? What stopped you?"

"I got sick."

Before he has a chance to respond, Mr. Jasper starts class by announcing we have the entire period to work on our final portfolio. With as many classes as I've missed, I'm farther behind than most everyone else in the class. I was planning on doing my project as a gift for Rhett. Since I found out we're having a baby, my plan's changed a little bit. I'm shifting the focus from us as a couple, to me and the baby. I'm hoping to give him one of the pictures as an early Christmas gift.

As soon as we're set free for the period, I stand up from my stool, hoping to snag one of the tripods before they're all taken. Rhett reaches for my waist when I walk by him, stopping me. He looks directly in my eyes, and I swear my heart rate is beating double time from one simple look. "You got sick? Are you okay?"

"I'm better now." His thumbs rub back and forth over my hip bones, and all I want is for him to pull me closer to kiss me. I can't stop staring at his lips, and he knows it.

"Hey," he says with a laugh. "Focus."

"Sorry."

"Tell me if you need something—anything. I'll get it for you."

"I need a tripod."

He stands up, grabbing one off the higher hooks most of us can't reach. "Where are you taking it?" Rhett asks, curiously.

"Um, I'm not sure yet. I have to think about it some more." I already know the only place I can take the kind of picture I'm looking for is someplace private. I cleared it with the nurse already, and she gave me permission to use one of the curtained rooms in her office.

"I guess I'll see you when you're done then."

At first it's a little weird posing in front of the camera when I'm so used to being behind it. Once I try a couple different poses, and get the hang of the timer on the camera, I get into my usual rhythm.

Even though I haven't seen it yet, I already know the third shot is going to be my favorite. I'm so excited about it, I want to hurry back to the room to develop it, so I can give it to Rhett by the end of the day. He deserves something special after taking such good care of me.

It's complete dejavu once I get back to the classroom. Being the first two done, Rhett and I are alone in the darkroom like we were the very first day of school.

"How'd it go?" he asks, when I lean into him for a hug.

"Perfect."

I'm trying to tie my apron when Rhett sneaks up behind me, taking the strings out of my hands. "I got it," he whispers, against my neck, as he wraps the strings around my back and to the front of my stomach where he ties them in a bow.

His fingers linger over my growing bump, and like he always does, he rubs his fingers back and forth on my belly. "I think it's a little bigger today."

"That's because she's always hungry."

I grab some photo paper off the shelf, and while I could work beside Rhett like we've done so many times, I need a little space—mostly to keep my surprise hidden.

He glances out of the corner of his eye, no doubt wondering why I moved to a different table.

"Do I smell or something?"

"Nope, you're wearing my favorite cologne, but you can't see what I'm working on yet."

"Hmm," is all he says, when he shrugs his shoulders and continues working on his own project. He doesn't say anything else until he's cleaning up his space. He's so much faster at this than I am. "Do you need anything before I go?"

Looking up from my tray, I blow a piece of hair out of my eye. "You're so good at this."

"Nah, but I'll wait for you if you want."

"No, it's okay. Go ahead. I'll be done in a couple minutes."

He nods his head, but is still hesitant to leave. "Are you going to sit with me at lunch?"

I'm actually dreading lunch. I need to eat, and if I don't, I'll probably throw up, but the thought of everyone watching me do it makes me want to run the other way. Everyone's going to be wondering how much the pregnant girl's going to eat.

"You're nervous about it, aren't you?" Rhett asks, reading me like a book.

"A little."

"Meet me at the table. I'll bring your food out with mine."

I dig into my pocket for some money, but he stops me. "I've got it, Sunny."

"Thank you." He has no idea how much I missed hearing him call me that when we weren't talking. I haven't felt much like sunshine these past few weeks, but when I'm with him, it's all a little easier. The idea of becoming a mother in a couple months doesn't consume me the way it did when I thought I lost him. I would do it by myself if I had to, but with Rhett by my side, the entire experience isn't as scary. He makes me feel like the most beautiful girl in the world—even when I know I'm gaining weight by the day, and my body's doing things I never knew were possible.

RHETT'S WAITING FOR me at the lunch table when I get there, just as he promised. I slide behind a couple chairs, making my way down the row. I suck in my stomach, but Mandi takes it as the perfect opportunity to sling an insult at me. "Look out, the heifer's coming through."

Her stuck up groupies all giggle, but Rhett's already flexing his fists, waiting to pounce. If she says one more thing, I know he's going to lose his mind.

He pulls out my chair for me, and I sit down next to him. "Relax," he whispers, as he sets my sandwich, banana, and crackers in front of me. "I got you apple juice and milk, too."

"Aww, they're playing house already. How cute."

Without thinking, I know he didn't because he would never hit a girl, he picks up one of his mandarin oranges and chucks it at Mandi's head. Luckily, it only grazes her shoulder, but she grabs it off the table, and chucks it back at him.

He catches it before it has a chance to hit either of us, but she holds her shoulder in pain, like she was just hit with a brick, and not a tiny piece of fruit. The cafeteria proctor walks over to talk to us, shaking her head at the childish behavior she witnessed. "Is everyone okay?" she asks.

Mandi puts on one of her more impressive displays, trying to earn sympathy from those around her. "Rhett should get detention. Did you see what he did?"

She nods her head. "I did. I could also give you a detention for bullying and throwing produce. It's your call though."

"I'm fine," she mumbles. "It doesn't hurt that much."

"I don't want to see or hear another negative thing from this table or you'll all go to detention. Understood?"

"Yes," we all reply like robots.

Rhett rests his hand on my thigh while we finish eating. He makes sure I'm full before he lets me leave the table. If he's this protective with me, I can only imagine what it will be like once our baby is born.

"I have to get to the auditorium, but I'll walk you to your next class." The entire end of the day is reserved for the winter talent show. Rhett's performing with a couple of his friends. It should be a complete disaster.

"Break a leg."

He smiles, a mischievous gleam in his eye. I can only imagine what they have planned. Rumor has it, they're doing a dance routine to a medley of One Direction and Taylor Swift songs. If that alone isn't enough to pique curiosity, I don't know what is.

Funny this is, some of the participants actually take their performances seriously—because they have actual talent. But it's the over-the-top, outrageous acts the student body goes wild for—and Rhett knows it.

I meet up with Becca after Rhett goes backstage to get ready. "Lets sit up front. I can't see back here," she says, as she yanks on my arm until we end up in the sixth row on the right side of the stage.

"Since when do you care so much about the talent show?"

"Since Rhett and Jake are performing," she says, with excitement.

"It is going to be pretty epic isn't it?" I snort, imagining the dance moves they're going to come up with.

"Grayson, Brady, and Kyler are all in it, too. And we already know Grayson has zero rhythm."

She's right, the kid can't dance for shit. Even the organizer must know how outrageous their performance is considering they're scheduled to take the stage dead last. It makes sitting through all the other acts that much harder.

Once they do finally take the stage, the roar from the packed auditorium is the loudest it's been the entire show. Even the teachers seem excited for what's about to happen.

They begin with a couple snippets from One Direction songs, even managing to get lights from the drama department, a fog machine, and costumes. The entire audience is going completely crazy, hanging on every lyric blaring from the speakers, but they manage to kick it up a notch. Just when I was sure it couldn't get any better than it already was, Jake runs onto the stage dressed like Taylor Swift in a silver sequin leotard that's blinding when the light reflects off it. "Shake it Off" takes on a whole new meaning with Jake dancing front and center.

Becca snorts, doubling over in laughter. "Can you believe I kissed that thing?"

"Strangely, I can." They're not together anymore, and I don't get to talk to Jake the way I used to when they were seeing each other, but I've forgiven him for hitting me. Even Rhett's worked on repairing their friendship. Love makes you do stupid things, and Jake did his fair share of them while he was fighting for Becca.

"Ohmigod, if he shakes it any harder, that costume is going to rip in half. Are you seeing this?" She elbows me in the side she's so worked up, and then gasps, realizing she just hit my stomach. "Are you okay? I'm so sorry."

"I'm fine, but you're telling Rhett." She blanches, sliding down lower in her seat. "I'm kidding. It's not a big deal. You didn't hit me that hard."

As soon as the last note is sung, the auditorium is on their feet, whistling and clapping. Jake curtsey's in his sequins, and another round of laughter pours from the crowd. It was everything I expected and then some.

After a final bow, they file off the stage—well everyone except for Rhett. He walks over to the microphone stand like he's about to announce the next performance. And he does.

"We're the final act, but I have one more performance for you. This next act will be a solo gig. I'm not the best singer, at all, but there are two pretty amazing girls in the audience I'd like to sing a special song to. She knows who she is, but Sunny, I love you."

Ever since I called our baby a girl, he's believed we're having one.

"Holy shit," Becca mumbles, in complete surprise.

The school chorus teacher takes her place behind the piano and although Rhett looks more uncomfortable than I've ever seen him, my heart melts into a puddle of mush when the he starts singing "You Are My Sunshine" to me and the baby.

I can feel hundreds of eyes boring into the side of my head as he sings, but I could honestly care less. The guy I'm completely, head-over-heels in love with, is singing his first nursery rhyme to our baby. Whether it's a little girl or a little boy, it doesn't really matter. It will be loved all the same.

Tears stream down my face, and by the time the very last syllable is sung, I'm crying so hard I can barely hold it together. He doesn't take a bow like he did with the guys performance, he blows me a kiss, and walks off the stage like he didn't just completely pull the most romantic move I've ever seen.

"Did you know about that?" I ask Becca, as I dry my eyes with my sleeve.

She shakes her head. "He told me to make sure you sat down here, but he didn't say why. I figured he wanted you to have a front row seat for his ridiculous performance."

The school principal leaves us with a few parting words and instructions for dismissal. We're free to go for the day. I need to get up, but my body's still shaking.

"Are you coming, Kins?" Becca asks, as she files into a long line of students all trying to leave the auditorium through the same four doors.

"I need a bathroom."

Naturally, she assumes I have to throw up. Lord knows she's been with me enough times while I did. "There's a trash can over there."

"I can't pee in a trash can, Becca."

"Oh! Crap. The hallways are all jammed up. How can we get you out of here?"

She's right, the hallways aren't moving, but I have to pee so bad I can't wait any longer. "I'll call you later," is all I say, before I climb the stairs to the stage, and scoot out the crew exit. I'm pretty sure I pass Rhett in the darkened corner, but I can't stop.

When I walk into the closest bathroom, all eyes are on me again. Girls whisper back and forth like I can't hear them. Only this time, they don't seem to be gossiping the way they usually are. In fact, they're actually a little jealous Rhett wasn't singing to them.

I want to thank Rhett for the song, but when I weave back through the hallways, I can't find him anywhere. He's not at my locker, or his. I try the lobby one more time before giving up and walking to my car.

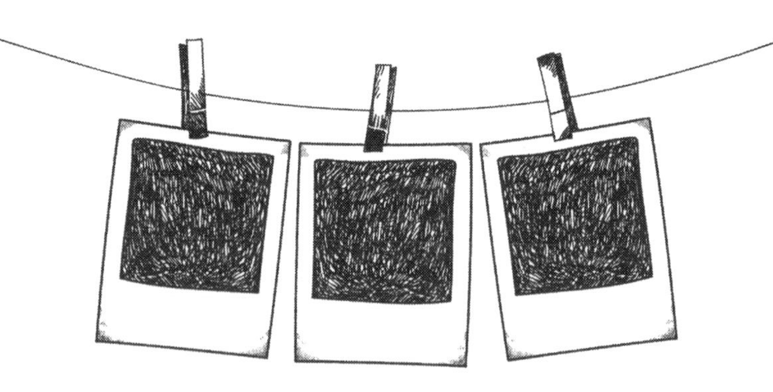

CHAPTER THIRTY-TWO

rhett

I'VE LOOKED FOR Kinsley all over the school. She's not at her locker or mine, and the lobby's almost empty already. I saw her crying when I was singing to her, but I thought she liked it. I knew how much she hates the attention, but I wanted to do something special for her and the baby—something unexpected.

Maybe it was a little too unexpected.

Once I'm in my truck, I dial her number. It rings twice before she picks up, and she's still sniffling. "Where are you?" I ask her, before she even has a chance to say hello.

"I'm in the lot at the park."

"What are you doing at the park?"

"I don't know. I didn't feel like going home, I guess."

"Will you meet me at my house?"

"You're sure?"

She's only been to my house once since her bed rest ended. My parents weren't home, so she didn't have any awkward run-ins. Mom's been asking about Kinsley every single day—like she really cares how the mother of my child is doing. "I promise you, it's fine."

She sighs, giving in like I knew she would. "Okay. I'll meet you there."

Mom's car is in the driveway when I get home, and I'm already a little worried about getting Kinsley inside. She pulls in beside me a few minutes later, eyeing Mom's car the same way I did.

I hop out of my truck, anxious to make sure she's not mad at me. "I couldn't find you."

Before she says a single word, she jumps into my arms, wrapping her body around mine. "What's this for?"

"It was perfect, Rhett. All of it," she tells me, hugging me even harder.

"I love you Sunny-girl."

The front door opens, and Mom sticks her head out. One hand's stuck inside a pot holder and the other's waving a spatula in the air. "Will you two get in here, it's freezing. Kinsley's going to get sick."

"You hear that? She couldn't care less if I get pneumonia as long as you're okay."

She giggles, sliding down the front of my body, making me groan. "Sorry," she says.

"I'll forgive you because you're cute in that coat. You look like a little marshmallow."

"I'm so fat," she says, as she tries to flatten her puffy, down coat.

"You're pregnant. There's a difference."

We walk hand-in-hand into the living room. Mom hurries us into the kitchen and sits us at the table. She places a tray of freshly baked chocolate chip cookies on the table before handing Kinsley a bag with tissue paper sticking out of the top. This is unlike her.

"Eat up. I'm making chicken for dinner. You like chicken, right, Kinsley?"

She nods her head, clearly wondering what's gotten into my mom. "Yes," she finally says.

"Good. Open the bag! I was shopping on my lunch break."

Kinsley sticks her hand in and pulls the tissue paper out. She peeks inside and her eyes are wide when she pulls out a light blue box. "Tiffany's?"

I glance at mom, and she's watching with her hands clasped together. I can't believe she did all this for her.

Kinsley gasps when she pulls the lid off the top of the box. Her eyes shift to my mom and then back to the gift. Her tears start to fall, and she swipes at them, like she's embarrassed for crying in front of us. "It's so pretty. This is really for me?"

Mom stands behind her and helps her take it out of the box. She places the necklace on her neck and fastens it for her. "It's for you and my grandbaby."

Now that it's hanging around her neck, I see it's a silver heart pendant with a tiny key dangling next to it.

Kinsley fingers it on her chest, and smiles. "Thank you so much, Mrs. Taylor."

"I'm glad you like it. Once that baby is born, it'll be like you're walking around with your heart outside of your body—there's really no other way to explain it. The key represents the future, and all the doors you still have to unlock. This baby might seem like the end to all the dreams you've made for yourself, but it doesn't have to be that way. There's still so much more to come, I promise."

Kinsley hangs her head, focusing on the cookie in front of her. "I'm not going to Parsons."

"Rhett told me. I have some friends working at The Art

Institute. It's only about twenty minutes from here. They have a wonderful interior design and fashion marketing program. I showed them some of your work, and they'd love to have you."

Her eyes are wide when she hears the news. "You did?" Mom mentioned it once, but I didn't think she was serious about it. I figured it was just her trying to push us in opposite directions.

Mom nods her head. "Kinsley, you might have to scale back your original plan a little bit, but you're so talented. I'd love to have you work for me. When you're a designer, the job can be very flexible. You'd be able to be with the baby a lot and still use the talent you've been blessed with."

"A job? Really?"

"Take some time to think about it. Rhett made some decisions of his own, and once you talk about them, I'm positive we can work out an arrangement."

She looks to me, and already I can tell she's worried about my choices more than her own. Since day one, it was always about me giving up what I wanted. But she doesn't realize my priorities have shifted now that I'm going to be a dad. What I wanted a few months ago, isn't what I want now.

I take her hand, helping her out of the chair. "Lets go upstairs and talk."

She grabs her bag before walking up the stairs in front of me. I keep my hands on her waist the entire time, wanting her to know this is a good conversation, even if I'm not sure how she's going to take it.

Once we're in my room, she stands in the center, staring at the wall above my desk. I forgot I hung it up. "Do you like it?" I ask her.

"It's beautiful, but it's huge."

I stand behind her, my chin resting on the top of her head. "She is beautiful, isn't she?"

I blew up the picture I used for my photography project at

the beginning of the year—the inspiration picture of Kinsley. Mom framed it for me, and now it's the focal point of my room.

Kinsley turns around in my arms, a perplexed look on her face. "What's going on? I feel like I walked into the Twilight Zone."

"We had a lot of time to talk while you were in the hospital and then stuck in bed. It shouldn't have, but I think once my parents saw we could lose the baby, they realized how much it would hurt if we actually did."

"I was so scared."

"We all were—even her. Every night since, she's talked to me about the future. She's finally hearing me. They want me to do what makes me happy—and what's best for the both of us. I'm not going to take the scholarship to play football next year. I'm staying here and going to school locally."

"You can't do that! This is a once in a lifetime experience, Rhett. You'll regret it."

I shake my head, expecting this kind of reaction from her. She's always selfless. Always thinking of me and what I want, but she's my top priority now—not a stupid football game. "You and this baby are once in a lifetime, Sunny. I'd regret leaving you."

"But your scholarship."

"What about yours? You didn't ask for any of this to happen. I did this to *you*."

She walks over to the window, staring out at the pool in the backyard. "I've given up dreams before. Why should we both throw it all away? I'll be a good mother and I'll tell the baby all about you. She'll always know where she came from."

The way she's talking, it sounds like she's leaving me. For a minute I panic. "I don't want to miss out on her. I love you so much. We can be a family—together."

When she turns around, there's a new resolve in her eyes. "What do *you* want? Not your parents, not me, just you."

"You. Our baby."

She blows out a breath, obviously trying to wrap her head around all this. And then it hits her—I finally get through to her. Her tears start slow, but within seconds, she's sobbing into her hands. "You're really giving up your dreams for us?"

I wrap my arms around her, rocking us back and forth like we're dancing without music. She's soaking my shirt with her tears, but I let her get them all out. I rub her back, needing her close. "I love you, Kinsley West—I think I always have. But I have a new dream now. I want to stay here and raise our baby together."

She pulls away from me for a second, walking over to her bag, and reaching inside for an envelope. She hands it to me with her trembling hand. "Open it."

I slide my finger under the lip of the envelope, and pull out a black and white photograph of her—with her hands covering her bare baby bump in the shape of a heart. "You took this today?" This is what she was trying so hard to hide in class this morning, and now I know why.

"Do you like it?"

I look up from the picture, where my eyes are entranced. My whole world captured in a single picture. It all started with the one hanging on my wall, and now it's ending with the one in my hand. Pieced together, they form our story. "It's perfect."

I stare into her beautiful brown eyes, pleading one last time. "Let me take care of my family, Sunny."

"I want that so bad, but I'm scared you'll regret it someday."

I hold up the picture, showing her where *my* heart is. "I can't regret this—I just can't."

"You're sure? You want us forever?"

"Baby, we did this together. This is ours."

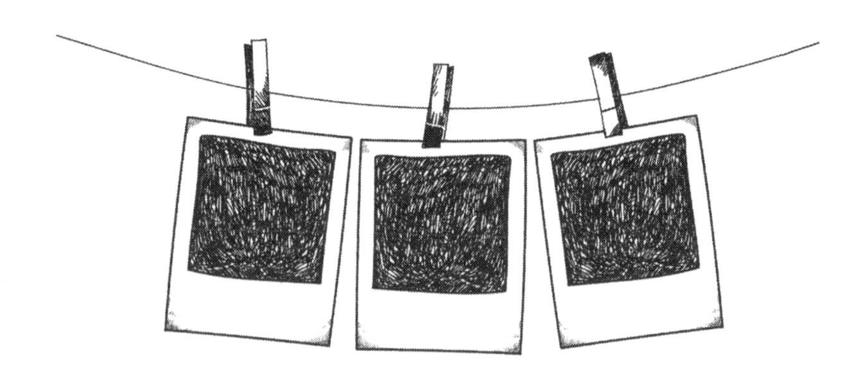

EPILOGUE

rhett

the fourth of july

"IF I GET any bigger, you're going to have to roll me down this hill to get me home."

To say Kinsley's tired of being pregnant, would be an understatement. She's so excited for the baby to come, but these last few weeks have been tough. Between the ninety degree weather, her ankles swelling, and her blood pressure getting a little on the high side, she hasn't been able to do much of anything.

Bringing her to the fireworks show in the park was supposed to make her happy, but as I lay our blanket on the ground, the one she made during one of her late night sewing sessions in the spare bedroom, she stretches her back and groans. I wish I could make it better for her—but I can't.

I've been doing everything I can to take care of her now that she's living with me. She actually moved into my parent's house as soon as school ended. Now that we're high school graduates, and about to be first time parents, they felt it was a good time to make the switch. Once we're settled, and a little less dependent on my parents, we plan to move into a place of our own.

Now that Kate's found a new job in Philadelphia, she's finally moving in with her fiancé. They got engaged on New Year's Eve and have been making wedding plans ever since. Kinsley's going to miss having her sister around, but the two and half hour drive isn't going to keep them apart for long. We'll be able to make some trips once the baby gets a little older.

As for Wyatt and Becca, they're still together. Becca's over at the house a lot, helping Kinsley and my mom prepare the perfect nursery for the baby. I'm pretty sure they bought out most of Pottery Barn and Babies R Us this summer. I never realized little people need so much stuff.

We finally got around to packing the hospital bag last night, and even that turned into two bags instead of one. I didn't even get any clothes of my own put in either of the bags.

"Rhett, help me sit."

From the back, you'd never know Kinsley was even pregnant, but once she turns around, it looks like she ate a basketball. And maybe she did because my girl can eat. The same girl who used to push her lettuce around on her plate at lunch would probably eat the plate itself if she was hungry enough.

I reach up, grabbing her around the waist, and setting her on my lap. "I'm too heavy. I'm going to make your legs fall asleep again."

"Just relax. I'm fine."

"I'm so hot."

"I know, Sunny. You're smokin'."

She smacks me with the back of her hand. "Behave for five minutes, please."

"I'll try, but we still have ten minutes until the fireworks start. And it's pretty dark back here."

She shakes her head. "I'm not doing anything here, Rhett. People are everywhere."

"You can kiss me."

She turns her body sideways, and I shift her in my lap. Her

belly rubs against my chest and I feel the baby kick as I'm kissing her. Total mood killer.

I pull away, and she frowns. "What's wrong?"

"I can't make out with you when she's watching."

"Who? Becca's not even paying attention to us."

"The baby."

"The baby? Rhett, I still have two weeks until my due date. I can't go that long without kissing you."

I hold her close, kissing her temple and resting my hand on her stomach. The baby kicks me a few times, and I push back, waiting for her to do it again. "She's really angry."

"She's probably hot, too. It's like a thousand degrees out here."

"What are we going to do if it's not a girl? I'm so used to saying, 'she.'"

Kinsley shrugs her shoulders. "Start saying, 'he'"?

I laugh at her puzzled expression. "Okay, Captain Obvious."

Before she has a chance to smack me again, the first fireworks light up the sky. Just as the first loud boom rumbles overheard, we both jump at the same time, looking down at the blanket. "Rhett, what did you do?"

"Nothing. Did you just pee on my leg?"

And then it hits us. Her water broke. I help her scramble to her feet, and she looks like she's about to cry. "I'm all wet. Everyone's going to think I peed my pants."

"It's okay. It's dark out. Here." I fold the blanket in half and wrap it around her waist. "Hold onto the ends so it doesn't fall down."

She does as I tell her, and I smack Wyatt on the back of the head. "Dude, come up for air. We're going to the hospital. Can you swing by my house and get the bag?"

"The bag?" And then it registers. "Shit, Kinny are you okay?"

Kinsley's still walking, not bothering to wait for me or talk to her brother. "Her water broke. Oh, and grab me a change of clothes while you're at it."

"Yeah, okay. Holy shit. I'm going to be an uncle."

Before I get a step closer to Kinsley, Wyatt's hand reaches out and grabs my arm. "Take care of my sister. She's pretty important to me."

"Me too, Wyatt."

I have to run to catch up to my girl. For someone nine months pregnant, she can still haul ass. "Sunny, slow down."

"I'm afraid it's going to start to hurt, so I want to keep moving."

"Does it hurt yet?"

"Not really. I feel like I have cramps."

By the time we get to the hospital, she's in a little more pain. They get us into a room pretty fast, but once she takes a look at all the monitors and the baby warmer, I can tell she's getting scared. We took the baby classes, we read all the baby books, and we even toured the maternity wing. Still, nothing could have prepared us for this moment.

"Rhett, I don't have my music."

"I'll text your brother. He's already stopping at the house." I fire off a text to Wyatt, hoping he can remember everything. I'll do anything to make her worry less. All she should be focused on is the baby.

"I have to pee."

I help her into our private bathroom, and while she does her business, I make sure to text everyone and tell them where we are.

"Rhett!"

I turn around, almost knocking into the IV pole they haven't used yet. "What's wrong, Sunny?"

She starts to cry, and when I bend down in front of her, I see some blood on her legs. Her chin quivers as she says, "I don't know."

I let go of her hand, and run into the hallway. "We need help in here!"

The heads of a couple nurses whip in our direction, and one look at my panicked expression, and they come running. "What's wrong?"

"She's bleeding on the toilet."

I end up catching the attention of one of the doctors, and even though he's not Kinsley's doctor, he comes in the room anyway. She has three people all stuffed in her bathroom, checking out what's going on. All I can do is pace while they talk to her and ask her questions. I don't even know what half of it means.

After they help her change into a gown, they get her into bed, and I swear, it's three minutes tops before they're wheeling her to the operating room. I follow behind her bed, my heart racing so fast I'm about to throw up. If we make it this far and lose our baby, I don't think we'll ever be the same.

They push her bed through the doors and the nurse holds me up. "You can go in as soon as she's prepped," she tells me.

"I don't want her to be all alone. She can't be alone."

"She won't be." The nurse hands me scrubs, like the ones on all the hospital shows Kate watches on TV, and I slide them on. I even put the lunch lady cap on my head. Once everything's in place, I look like I'm the one about to go deliver this baby.

What seems like an eternity later, I'm finally allowed to go to Kinsley. The operating room is freezing, and her teeth are chattering when I get to her. "It's okay, Sunny. I'm here."

"I'm scared, Rhett."

I sit in my chair next to her head, and brush my finger across her cheek. And then it hits me, I could lose both of them if something goes wrong. For all I know, something already did go wrong. But I have to pretend like none of this is fazing me. If I panic, she'll panic.

"Don't be scared. We're about to meet our baby."

She smiles and a tear slides down her cheek, soaking the

paper under her head. Her eyes close, and she grimaces like she's in pain. All I can do is kiss her cheek. It's the only part of her I'm allowed to touch.

"You're so strong, Kinsley. I'm so proud of you," I whisper in her ear, over and over until the cries of a baby fill the room.

The doctor passes the baby to a team of nurses who huddle around the warmer. I don't even know what they're doing, but I'm too scared to take my eyes off Kinsley to check.

"Go see, Rhett. Go look."

I'm hesitant, but I stand up and peek inside the warmer. And for the first time, I see my little girl. She's just as beautiful as Kinsley. Her tiny hands pump back and forth and her feet kick as they poke at her. She's angry but she's amazing.

Once she's cleared, they wrap her up like a little baby burrito. They give her to me like I'm supposed to know what I'm doing with this tiny little person. She's even smaller than I imagined she'd be. "Hi, princess. I'm your Daddy."

She squirms and struggles to open her eyes, but they have so much goop on them she blinks over and over until she finds me. And the first time our eyes meet, I know I'm completely in love. "Your Mommy wants to meet you."

I walk her to Kinsley, who's been watching us the entire time. She cries harder when she sees us getting closer. I sit back down and bring the baby as close to her as I can get. Kinsley kisses her cheek and they lock eyes the same way we did.

"Your mom was so right, Rhett. I love her so much."

"We got our little girl, Sunny. We got her."

"STOP HOGGING THE baby," Becca says, as she leans over Wyatt's shoulder and smiles at Katey.

We named her Katheryn Marie Taylor—after both of our mothers and in honor of Kate. I'm pretty sure both Kate and my mom cried for two days once we told them. We made our baby a Taylor, and soon, we hope to make Kinsley a Taylor, too. But no matter what last name Katey has, she's a little piece of everyone.

"Wyatt, seriously! Let me hold the baby."

Kinsley laughs from the kitchen where she's helping my mom with some lunch. Wyatt has to go back to school later today, and Kinsley wants to have a little party before he gets busy with football camp.

Even though he's been staying with Carson this summer, he's been over at our house more than he's been at his own. He can't seem to get enough of Katey. I can't say I blame him though, we make cute kids.

"You'll be able to see her for like a month before you go to school. This is my last day."

Becca nods her head and walks up the stairs toward our bedroom—pissed off.

"Rhett, can you come take your daughter. I have to go apologize for being a pain in the butt."

I laugh at him because those two do more fighting and making up than any couple I've ever known. They're either hot or cold, but when they make up, you don't see them for days. He told me to use his imagination on that one, but Becca's practically my sister, so I don't necessarily want to do that either.

"Hand me my little nugget."

Wyatt kisses Katey's wrinkly little forehead before handing her back to me. She coos at me, and nuzzles against my chest. All those books we read warned us about holding her too much, saying it would spoil her. Well guess what, that's exactly what I plan to do with my little girl—spoil the shit out of her.

I only get one chance to get this right and I'm not about to mess it up. Not when the two most beautiful girls in the world are counting on me.

This may not have been the path I envisioned for myself

when the year started, but I wouldn't have it any other way. Not when I have a girlfriend staring at me like I hang the moon each night and a baby who gives me sweet kisses.

Before I met Kinsley, my life was full of loose ends. This past year, each one found its place—fitting exactly where it belonged. And now, I have it all.

My life's no longer *In Pieces*.

Thank you for purchasing In Pieces. Please consider leaving an honest review.

about the author

GIA RILEY IS from the small, but mighty state of Delaware. She's a lover of all things romance—a firm believer that everyone deserves a happily ever after.

When she's not writing, you can find her roaming the aisles of Kirkland's, up to her elbows in Play-doh, or trying to hunt down spoilers for Big Brother. She loves reality TV almost as much as she loves a good chick flick. Her newest addiction is a Starbucks iced mocha—they keep her up late, doing terrible things to her characters.

You can connect with Gia on Facebook, Twitter, and Instagram. She also has a reader group, Gia Riley's Books, on Facebook. Stop by anytime, she loves hearing from readers!

Here's where you can find her:

www.giariley.weebly.com

giarileybooks@gmail.com

Facebook, Twitter and Spotify

other work by gia riley

THE BEGIN AGAIN DUET

Lighter

Weightless

acknowledgements

ONCE I FINISHED Weightless, I was so excited to jump into this novel. It was sitting in my head for a while, begging to be set free. The journey started with a single word on my laptop, and morphed into what it is today. Of course, I can't take all the credit. Publishing a book isn't simple, and it takes a strong, supportive team to get it done. I appreciate each and every one of you who encouraged me along the way. Thank you for taking a chance on a girl from the country with a dream to write. Without you, none of this is possible.

To the creative forces behind In Pieces—Sommer Stein of Perfect Pear Creative Covers, thank you for understanding the concept for this novel. You didn't give up until I had exactly what I wanted, and even then, you took it a step farther to add the personal touches that topped it off. Your work continues to amaze me, and I'm so thankful to have you on my team.

Christine Borgford of Perfectly Publishable, thank you for understanding when I needed to bump my date back. You're always so accommodating and want the best for the project. You continue to light up the inside of my books, making them stand out in their own unique way. Your attention to detail makes my life so much easier.

Sassy Savvy PR & Marketing—Linda, you're my PR goddess. From the moment we first spoke, your excitement was infectious. Your organization, timely responses, virtual high fives, and willingness to get the job done make my life easier. Thank you for embracing a new client—and thank you for sharing this journey with me.

To my readers–In Pieces is a little different than what I've previously written. Still, your excitement for my words blew me away. Your continued support means more to me than you could ever imagine. Thank you for wanting more. You challenge me every day to be more and more creative. I hope I've done you proud.

To every blogger who has supported me—thank you for taking the time to promote my work. A simple post or shout out makes my entire day. I've gotten to meet some of you at signings, and each one of you stop at my table with so much enthusiasm for books. It's that spirit that pushes me to write more. Always remember, no matter how big or small you are, your voice matters! Thank you for all you do.

To my Bitchesnachos—Paypal loves you. Thank you for being totally inappropriate at all the wrong times. Even the right ones, too. You teach me new things every single day—though some are more useful than others. Thank you for encouraging me when I'm down, for making fun of me when I deserve it, and for encouraging me to find my inner dirty bird. P4D—hold on tight.

My betas—Tina, Kelly, and Ashley.

Tina, thank you for sneaking pages at work without getting fired. Your love for Rhett and curiousness about Carson had me laughing on a daily basis. I can always count on you to keep it real and I love you for it. You don't always give yourself enough credit for the things you accomplish, but please know that you deserve all the good things that come to you.

Kelly, thank you for being so excited about this book. Every single day you pushed me to get it right. Each time I sent you something new, you jumped on it and fired back with messages. I can't thank you enough for taking time out of your busy day to help me. We have a lot more to look forward to.

Ashley, you've been by my side since day one. The fact that you've stuck around to help me on this journey means the world to me. Thank you for helping out with my group and for always bringing the fun. I look forward to finally meeting you in person.

To my parents—thank you for always believing in me. Ever since I was little, coming up with crazy ideas, you've never once told me my dream was too big. Whether I was sucking it up in the outfield or succeeding on the infield, you've always been my biggest cheerleaders. You gave me the belief in myself.

And finally, my husband and son. Our journey is different than most, but it's ours. Our pieces will always form the most beautiful picture.

Made in the USA
Lexington, KY
16 May 2017